T0349161

"Very charming and delightful. If you like Louise Penny's novels, this is right up your street." —CBC Ontario Morning

"Think a young Katharine Hepburn—beautiful, smart and beyond capable. Winslow is an example of the kind of woman who emerged after the war, a confident female who had worked in factories building tanks and guns, a woman who hadn't yet been suffocated by the 1950s perfect housewife ideal." —*Vancouver Sun*

"I absolutely love the modern sensibility of these novels, of their feminism, sense of justice, their anti-racism, their progressiveness, which somehow never seems out of place in a tiny BC hamlet in 1948." —Kerry Clare, author of *Waiting for a Star to Fall* and editor of 49th Shelf

"Iona Whishaw's writing is worthy of taking its place alongside the works of Agatha Christie and Dorothy L Sayers... deftly crafted and briskly paced." —Fiona Valpy, author of *The Dressmaker's Gift*

"What a delight!... crafted with such charming finesse that readers will fall in love as I did." —Genevieve Graham, #1 *USA Today* bestselling author of *Bluebird*

"An engaging, superbly crafted page turner of a mystery." —Alan Hlad, international and *USA Today* bestselling author of *The Long Flight Home*

"Stellar... " —Eliza Knight, *USA Today* bestselling author of *Starring Adele Astaire*

THE COST OF A HOSTAGE

THE LANE WINSLOW MYSTERY SERIES

IONA WHISHAW

THE COST OF A HOSTAGE

A LANE WINSLOW MYSTERY

TOUCHWOOD

TouchWood Editions
touchwoodeditions.com

This book is a work of fiction. Names, characters, places, and incidents are either products of the author's imagination or are used fictitiously. Any resemblance to actual events or locales or persons, living or dead, is entirely coincidental.

Edited by Claire Philipson
Cover illustration by Margaret Hanson

CATALOGUING DATA AVAILABLE FROM LIBRARY AND ARCHIVES CANADA
ISBN 9781771514545 (softcover)
ISBN 9781771514552 (electronic)
ISBN 9781771514569 (audiobook)

TouchWood Editions acknowledges that the land on which we live and work is within the traditional territories of the Lkwungen (Esquimalt and Songhees), Malahat, Pacheedaht, Scia'new, T'Sou-ke, and W̱SÁNEĆ (Pauquachin, Tsartlip, Tsawout, and Tseycum) peoples.

We acknowledge the financial support of the Government of Canada through the Canada Book Fund and the Canada Council for the Arts, and of the Province of British Columbia through the British Columbia Arts Council and the Book Publishing Tax Credit.

This book was produced using FSC®-certified, acid-free papers, processed chlorine free, and printed with soya-based inks.

PRINTED IN CANADA

29 28 27 26 25   1 2 3 4 5

For Diego, my dad's geological partner, who once saved me.

PROLOGUE

September 1942

SHE PUSHED OPEN THE DOOR of the farmhouse, and the two men at the table turned to look at her. It was dark, except for the flickering of the oil lamp casting an eerie light on their faces. It was cold outside for early September. She knew she should have brought more clothes. She wasn't going back, no matter what happened. She'd thrown her lot in with him, and this was it. Still panting from the run to get there, she stood for a moment catching her breath and then closed the door behind her. This was supposed to be a Special Operations Executive safe house. How had they known? They must even now be waiting for one of the agents to come with a radio. Charlie, maybe? She didn't know. But she knew who he would be meeting here. And she couldn't care anymore, she just couldn't.

In a moment she picked out Ean where he sat at the head of the table, smoking. She didn't know the other man but saw three glasses. There was someone else there as well.

She was about to apologize, but he stood up, tossing his cigarette on the earthen floor, and approached her.

"Why are you here now?" he whispered. His anger shocked her. He had said he loved her, had sworn it. But now he gripped her arm hard and pushed her into the little room opposite the kitchen. The light from the lamp made no dent in the darkness of this room. His breath smelled of garlic and drink.

"I came . . . I came with the money. I want to give you the money and come away with you." She knew it sounded desperate and was not at all what they had planned.

"Why?" His voice was icy, and even in this obscurity she could see his eyebrows pulled together. She was pierced by his coldness. She felt suddenly as if she didn't know him at all. "No one told you to come here," he hissed. "You have a job. Leave the money, go back. You do what he says." He lifted his chin toward the other room.

She put her hand on his chest, resting it delicately on the rough wool of his sweater, the buttons on the shoulder only half done up. "I want to be with you. I know you'll understand. I'll come with you, fight with you . . . I'm very good with a rifle . . . I just can't betray . . ."

"*Merde*!" he said, giving up on whispering. He pushed her away and turned as if he would walk off and leave her there, but he came close to her again. "Then you will tell us when the next drop is, who comes after the man with the radio, *then* you can show us your shooting skills."

"I . . . I can't. You see, that's the point. I can't. Anyway, you already know about Charlie." She prayed it would be Charlie. "If you don't want me, I'll go back, and I'll ask to be reassigned so you don't have to see me. Here, I'll leave this money like you said." She put her hand in her jacket pocket and pulled out an envelope. "Everything he gave me is there. I don't want it." She pushed the money toward Ean, anxious to be rid of it. He only stared at her, shaking his head. Even in the darkness she could feel his dark eyes piercing her.

"My God, woman, what world do you live in, eh? Are you out of your mind?" He jabbed violently at his own head with a large finger.

She began to be afraid, really afraid. She was here alone, rogue, without any sort of cover. She felt suddenly a great hollow sense of her own madness. *Had* they known about Charlie? Or had she . . . ? The utter despair of the betrayal washed over her. Ean's, her own. She'd thought he loved her, that she was coming to be with him, to make his cause hers, his life hers.

"Well?" He had her wrist now and was yanking her upward, as if she were a toddler misbehaving. "There is no point, madam"—he ground this word out with violent sarcasm—"unless you can tell us what we need."

She shook her head. "I can't. I just can't." She could feel tears burning her eyes. "If you were me, you wouldn't either."

"Ean, what's going on?" It wasn't the man she'd seen in the other room when she'd come. This one was English. With a gasp she realized who it was. Why was *he* here? She could hear a chair being dragged, but now the Englishman and the other one were speaking Breton, and she couldn't understand.

Ean answered him through the door, and she could hear the man sit down. "Don't you English call a stupid woman a

3

cow? You're a real cow." Ean took her upper arm and flung her away from him, making for the door. She fell against something hard. Her neck snapped back and she hit her head on the floor. She felt herself slam hard and then she lay still, smelling the acrid odour of the pounded earth floor, covered in ash and spilled food and God knew what else. In that moment of complete darkness, she heard the door locking behind him, and she knew then how wrong it all was, and how very bad it would become.

CHAPTER ONE

August 5, 1948

Lane Winslow closed her Proust and frowned out at the lake. It was a beautiful early August day, and she wasn't entirely sure she was putting it to good use. August 5. What did that remind her of? Something from so long ago it was just a date hanging loose in her memory. And then it came to her. Alma's birthday. She felt her heart lurch. This was her second assault on this book. But it was her very own *temps perdu* she was drawn to suddenly. She'd been reading Proust in the bedsit she shared in London with Alma during the war, she remembered, until that awful day. She closed her eyes and could see herself lying on the bed with the book. That scrap of a pillow with the poky feathers rolled up under her neck. Had she been reading or pretending to read to block out poor Alma's chatter?

She put the book firmly on the little iron table that served as the outdoor eating place at the home in King's Cove, British Columbia, she shared with her husband,

and stood up. She'd chosen this slightly mildew-smelling volume in French out of a sense of virtue. It didn't do to let one's few skills languish. Her skills, after all, included French, German, and Russian. They ought, she realized, glancing down at the lawn below the veranda, to include cutting the grass. Proust would be no help here.

With a sigh she put a slip of paper into the book to mark her page and pushed the volume back into her shelf for another time. It was after nine, and the dew had dried off the lawn under the already hot morning sun. With determination, she pushed the war behind her yet again, an exercise that seemed to get slightly easier with time and practice. This beautiful day in a beautiful place certainly helped. She slipped on her shoes and padded out to the garage to get the mower. She smiled at how smug she would be about her industry when her husband, Frederick Darling, got back from Nelson in the evening.

The lawn that lay between the house and the barn was quite shaded by the evergreens and therefore not only patchy, as lawns go, the years of fir needles choking the grass, but still damp. She pulled the machine down the slope past the weeping willow and the pond she'd been building and began to push it down toward the bushy edge of the green. Kenny Armstrong had come over a couple of weeks before with some sort of tool and sharpened the blades, so they sang through the grass now, sending up a shower of fragrant green tips. She was so busy trying to decide if she should mow back and forth in rows, or go around and around in diminishing circles, that she didn't hear the telephone.

"REMINDS ME OF *The Rime of the Ancient Mariner* around here," O'Brien said from his usual seat on the stool at the reception desk of the Nelson Police Station. "Nothin' moving. Not even a lost dog or a stolen car." Of course, this was exactly the way he liked things. He could get on with his crossword puzzles without even having to look surreptitious. "You must have memorized the contents of that whole thing by now."

Constable Terrell, seated at his desk in the corner, did not care much for idleness and was reading his police officer's manual. He looked up. "It's very interesting. There's a section here that says that admissions by the accused are evidence against him, as is his behaviour. For example, if he is silent when he's accused of a crime that an innocent person would at once deny, that might suggest evidence of his wrongdoing." He put the book on his desk. "I don't know about that. There must be any number of reasons someone might not speak. They might be afraid, or wanting to protect someone else, or frozen by the shock of being arrested. I think you'd have to be very careful with this approach."

O'Brien shook his head. "Better men than I must have put that together. The way things are going, we won't be needing anything out of that book." He turned back to his crossword.

Inspector Darling, the head of the whole outfit, was in his office thinking about being home in King's Cove and perhaps lying on the wharf in the sun with a picnic basket nearby, Lane in her red swimsuit. His plan to tidy up the contents of his filing cabinet was momentarily suspended. After all, there was not much in the thing. All finished cases were moved to the basement cabinets. He smiled happily at the thought that Sergeant Ames was at this very moment in that basement room with instructions to tidy up.

Ames was not smiling. He was sneezing. Knowing it was going to be his ill fate to clean up the place, he'd borrowed a feather duster from his mother and was now sweeping it inexpertly over the surfaces, sending up clouds of dust. "How the hell does it get like this?" he muttered. He'd been in the place less than a year before, looking for some old paperwork. He'd dusted it then, and it already had another thick layer. Pondering the science of dust, he sneezed again.

Into this pleasant summer lethargy, the door of the station was thrust open by a frantic young woman whose long dark hair had not been brushed that day and was bunched in a tangled mass at the back of her neck with a rubber band. "I need help!" she cried. "Someone, please!"

Both O'Brien and Terrell were on their feet in an instant.

"Now then, madam, take a deep breath. That's it. Constable, can you get the lady a glass of water?" O'Brien said. "Now then, what's happened?"

"My little boy, he's gone! I put him to bed last night and he wasn't there this morning." She choked back tears and her hands trembled. Terrell came with the glass of water, and she reached for it with two hands to try to keep it steady, and then put it down on the counter with a thud, without drinking.

"Perhaps he's gone to visit a little friend?" O'Brien suggested, taking up a notebook. "What's his name, madam, and his age?"

8

"He's called Rocky Junior. He's only five! Where would he go off to on his own? I called Bonny, she has a boy the same age, but he hasn't been there."

"And what is your name?" O'Brien continued.

She groaned as if having to give her name was the least of her worries. "Radcliffe. Linda. Please, we have to find him!"

By this time Darling had plunged down the stairs, three at a time, and Ames had come up from the basement, duster in hand.

"I'm Inspector Darling," he said, pulling a chair out. "It's important to get as much information as possible so we can focus our search. Where do you live?"

"Just up on Silica and Stanley." Mrs. Radcliffe swept a hand across her eyes to wipe away her tears.

Darling thought about whether a child of that age might find his way to the water. "Has he wandered off before?"

"No, never! I don't understand it."

"Have you been down to the beach lately?"

"Yes, we were all there yesterday. We took a picnic."

"Can you describe him, please."

"He's blond, about this tall. Blue eyes. He has a slight scar on his forehead where he fell and cut his head when he was three. He's in his pyjamas, I guess. They weren't in his room."

Darling gestured to Terrell. "Get down to the waterfront instanter and look there. Ames and I will start at the house."

"Sir." Terrell took his cap and opened the door in one move, and was gone, running down the hill toward the water, his heart in his mouth.

Ames drove Darling and Mrs. Radcliffe up the hill at a speed that belied the torpor of this August morning.

"Ames, house to house, please. Corner store, that sort of thing," Darling said. "Mrs. Radcliffe, can you show me his bedroom?"

Inside the house, a small wood-frame home like most on the street, Rocky's mother led Darling down the hall to the end bedroom. "I tucked him in last night after we said our prayers and read a book. He has always been a good sleeper. He was out like a light before the story was finished."

"This window is open. Do you keep the window open at night?"

"Oh, yes, especially on these warm nights. We have nothing to—" She paused. "I was going to say 'to fear,' but now I don't know. Could someone have taken him?"

Darling was at the window. Eight feet to the ground? An older child might attempt it, but a five-year-old? "What about the front and back doors? Do you lock them?"

"Yes, yes, of course. Those I lock. I live alone. I know it's very safe here, but I don't know. Since his father left, it just makes me feel more secure."

"When you came out this morning, were they locked?" Darling's mind was already racing ahead to the father.

She put her hand up to her face and frowned. "Oh, I didn't think, I just ran out. Yes. No, no. Wait. I think the front door was unlocked. Did he just open it and go out?"

"Let's go have a look in a minute. Just tell me about what you see here. Do you see his clothes missing? Shoes? Did he have a pair of slippers?"

"His slippers are gone." She looked around. The bed had been slept in, and the covers were pushed toward the foot of the bed. She pulled them straight and then cried, "Oh! His rabbit is gone. He has a stuffed rabbit. It's brown with a little red jacket." She pulled open the closet door. There was a small chest of drawers inside. She pulled open the three drawers one after another. "All his clothes are here." She turned and looked back around the room. "He has a bathrobe somewh—" She stooped with a sob and pulled a terry-towel belt out from behind a small toy box. "The robe isn't here!"

Darling took the belt. "Anything else?"

She sniffed, looking around the room once more, and then shook her head.

"You say your husband left?"

"Yes. I mean, we're still married. I'm Catholic, or I'd have divorced him long ago. He's in the Yukon with some tart." Her bitterness was palpable.

"How long has he been gone?"

"Almost two years now. He sends a bit of money. Not enough. I have to badger him for it. He acts like he doesn't even have a child."

"So Rocky Junior has always lived with you?"

"I would never, ever give him up." She looked angrily at Darling, as if he'd suggested she might. "Anyway, he left, and he said a child should be with his mother, so I can credit him with that much sense, anyway."

"Can you give me your husband's full name and address?"

In answer she went into the kitchen and took an opened envelope out of a mail holder on the wall and pointed at the return address. "Here. It's all on there. As you see, he's called Rocky as well. I thought that was cute at the time. Now I feel sorry for Junior. But at least he's nothing like his father."

Darling went to the front door. It had a simple Yale lock on the inside, which was pulled back and latched in place. "It was unlocked like this when you came out this morning?"

"Yes." She took a sharp breath. "You *are* saying you think someone kidnapped him?"

Darling looked noncommittal. "It's one possibility. In these cases, it is sometimes the absent parent. In a way, that can be good news since the child is likely to be safe."

She screwed up her face. "All the way from Whitehorse? Why? He never wanted him to start with."

"Parents can change, begin to miss the child. Had there been any discussion lately about a visit?"

"No. He's never shown any interest. I mean, he tried to get me to bring him up there a year ago. I told him a flat no. The poor kid was only three when his father left, but he was devastated. He used to waddle around and around the house looking for him. I couldn't stand for him to go through that again."

"Do you have a separation agreement?"

She hesitated and then looked slightly defiant. "I did go to court to get an order for Rocky Junior to stay with me."

There was a quiet knock on the door, and Mrs. Radcliffe jumped, startled. Ames pushed the door open, removing his hat. "It does not seem that he went to any of the neighbours. No one has seen him. I talked to the man at the corner shop. He was in early to shelve some new stock, and he saw nothing except a delivery truck heading down the street at about six thirty."

"Was there a business name on the truck?"Darling asked.

"Oh, I did check that. He said it was a new one to him. 'Grace Produce.'"

Darling turned back to Mrs. Radcliffe. "I am going to alert the RCMP and contact Whitehorse. I've sent one of my men down to the waterfront, just in case. It would be best if you stayed here in case there is word. If you have a phone number for your husband, he ought to know about this, as the boy's father. Do you have any relations nearby, the child's grandparents?"

"Rocky's folks are dead, but my parents live in Creston."

"Have you told them?"

Mrs. Radcliffe looked away and then shook her head. "We don't talk. They want nothing to do with me or little Rocky."

Darling found that hard to believe. Even in some of the worst cases of estrangement he'd experienced, parents usually came around if there was a grandchild. "They don't see him, or ask about him?"

She glared at him. "If you must know, they don't even know about him. I haven't spoken to them since I was eighteen, when I left home."

A far cry from wanting nothing to do with their grandson. Darling kept his expression neutral. "And their names?"

"You don't need their bloody names. I don't want them interfering."

13

LANE PUSHED THE mower back into the barn with a satisfying clang and then went through the house to the porch to gaze at the lawn. The air was redolent with the smell of new-mown grass. She was contemplating her next task but saw that it was nearly eleven, when the Armstrongs, who ran the little post office nearby, were likely to pause in their labours and have a cup of tea. She hadn't gone for the mail yet, so, happily wondering what sort of biscuit or cake Eleanor might have on hand for the mid-morning tea, she started for the door.

No sooner was she outside than the phone rang. She paused. Two longs and a short. Hers. Perhaps it would be Angela, her American friend up the hill, offering a glass of very sweet lemonade or iced tea, her preferred beverages in the heat of the summer.

"KC 431, Lane Winslow speaking."

"Oh, Lane, thank heavens you're home! It's Isabel, you know, Bob's fiancée?" The speaker's voice was wispy, as if she had trouble catching her breath.

Surprised, Lane said, "Yes, of course, Isabel. How lovely to hear from you. I hope you are calling with good news of an upcoming wedding?"

"Oh, I wish I was!" Her voice caught. "I just tried to reach Frederick at the police station, but he's out on some sort of emergency. It's just that Bob's gone missing. Roger asked me to call. He's beside himself."

A bolt of alarm ran through Lane. Bob was Darling's younger brother, and Roger, their father. "Missing? How do you mean?"

"He was in this place in Mexico somewhere. Some sort of American mine. He was supposed to be there for three weeks as a consulting geologist. I don't know the details. He'd been phoning me or Roger every three days or so, but then we stopped hearing from him about a week ago. We called his office, and they contacted the mine manager to try and track him down. The manager reported that they had only just discovered he was missing. Bob and his crew were supposed to be gone for a week but didn't report back. I don't know what to do!"

"Oh, I am sorry, Isabel. How terrifying. Did they say if the police were involved?"

"His boss told me the manager was contacting the police. But I don't know. It's so far away. Anything could be happening!"

"Okay, look. Is there any sort of embassy in Mexico City? See what you can find out. And there might be a Mexican consulate in Vancouver I can call. I'll try to get Frederick. If I don't reach him, I'll drive into town."

"All right. Consulate. Good idea. I'll tell his father. Please, have Frederick call him as soon as he can."

Lane hung up and immediately put a call through to the Nelson Police Station.

"Mrs. Darling. How do? I'm afraid we're all at sixes and sevens here just at the moment," O'Brien said. "Child gone missing."

"Oh, how dreadful! I'm afraid it's a bit of a day for it. I've just had a call that the inspector's brother has gone missing in Mexico. I know no details, I'm afraid, but Frederick's father is most anxious that he telephone."

O'Brien was silent for a moment. "We're just organizing a search at this end for the wee kiddie. RCMP, that sort of thing. I'm not sure how long he'll be, but I'll tell him right away. What a day this is turning out to be!"

"A missing child. Nothing more dreadful than that," Lane agreed. "The poor parents must be beside themselves."

"Just the one. Father off away. Left them for another woman." She could hear his disapproval.

"Could it be he?" Lane asked.

"We have Constable Terrell tracking him down."

"I should leave you to get on with it. In the meantime, I'll telephone my father-in-law in Vancouver and see what details I can get, so the inspector can spend his energies on the child."

O'Brien hung up the phone, wondering why everyone couldn't be as clear-thinking and sensible as Mrs. Darling.

CHAPTER TWO

"**MR. DARLING. ROGER. IT'S LANE.** How are you doing? You must be quite frantic."

"Lane, thank you." He sounded tired. "I can't understand it. He was fine. It's an American mining outfit. From what he said, they all live in a big walled enclosure . . . I can't remember what it's called . . . has-something. Of course, he goes out to the countryside and does whatever geologists do. This time they were taking samples, somewhere they could only get to on horseback. There was Bob, his colleague, and a guide, and none of them has come back. The mine manager, a fellow called Fine, Thomas, I think, says they've got people out looking. He tells me not to worry, but he doesn't sound any too confident himself."

"Of course," Lane said. "Impossible not to worry! Frederick will call you soon, I'm sure, but in the meantime, would you mind if I take down as many details as you have? The location of the mine, the telephone number, and so on. I've written the name of the manager, Thomas

Fine. Do you know the name of the mine, or the town nearby?" She held the impossibly old-fashioned earpiece against her ear with her left hand, anchored the paper on the wall with her left elbow, and held her pencil at the ready with her right hand. Honestly, she thought, they ought to come into the middle of the twentieth century and get a proper rotary telephone on a table like normal people.

"Here it is." There was the rustle of paper on the other end of the line. "The number is FR 998, and you have to go through quite a production to get put through. The last operator I talked to didn't have a word of English. The mine is called R and T Ventures, and it's in a town called . . . I don't know. I can't pronounce it . . . but it's spelled F-R-E-S-N-I-L-L-O. I understand from Bob that's more or less in the middle of the country. It's in a state called Zacatecas, or however you say it. I tried to call just before you rang, and I couldn't get through at all."

"All right. Try not to worry too much. I know Isabel is seeing about an embassy. They'll be able to help, I'm sure."

"Yes. I think she's doing that now. Thank you so much, Lane. I'm sorry I'm being . . ." He couldn't finish.

"You're being exactly what anyone would be, Roger. Just have a cup of tea and wait; I'm sure Frederick will be ringing you soon. I know it's impossible, but do try not to worry too much."

What a ridiculous thing to say, she thought as she replaced the earpiece on its hook. Right up there with "It will be all right." Perhaps she was too hard on these bromides. Maybe they really did help people be calmer.

She had thought of going to the post office, but it was no time for a cup of tea and whatever marvellous thing Eleanor might have just pulled out of her oven. She'd have to stay put and wait to see how she could be of help.

Fresnillo. She'd never heard of the place, but what she didn't know about Mexico was encyclopedic. She went to her bookshelf and pulled out her beloved atlas and opened up the index to see if Fresnillo was even listed. It was. A tiny dot. There it was, in Zacatecas, a state slap in the middle of the country. The distances index told her it was almost 2,600 miles away from Vancouver.

Feeling powerless, she decided she'd make her own cup of tea. She didn't see how she could realistically offer any help. She didn't speak Spanish, so she couldn't leap into the breach as she had been able to with her Russian and German from time to time. And she knew almost nothing about the hazards present in Mexico. But then, she reflected, as she turned the electric burner on under the kettle, that was life, really. One doesn't know the hazards of anything until one is right in them. Like that awful day in France. She put a spoonful of tea in the teapot and then stopped, her hands on the table, feeling overwhelmed by the sudden memory of that day. Of course, it was damn Proust that had put her in mind of it. No, not just Proust. Alma's birthday. With a shake of her head at the workings of the unconscious, she picked up the spoon and reached for a cup. It was six years ago already.

It had been shortly after an extended training session with radio communication. She could scarcely recall how they had got back to England. She had not been able to

19

take in the magnitude of her first brush with the real brutality of death, and she remembered that it filled her mind completely and she'd been unable to pack it away. It had been the utter careless anonymity of watching helplessly while someone she knew was shot right in front of her and left, a heap on the ground, just another casualty of war. Of course, she'd "hardened up" with time, with the advice of her handler. But she'd never really "hardened" to the idea of someone taking another person's life. Perhaps it was why she was so involved in some of her husband's cases. The real monstrousness of that business in France, though, had been the betrayal.

France, September 1942

"SOMETHING'S WRONG. Get down!" he hissed.

Lane dropped onto her haunches behind the bushes, nearly toppling backward down the slope behind them. The dry remains of the dusty garden before the safe house looked tired and empty. She could hear nothing. She started to turn to him, and a movement caught her eye. The door of the farmhouse was pushed open and Charles, gazing at his watch, came out, looking in their direction.

"No, it's all right," she whispered. "It's just Charles." She started to get up, preparing to wave, to call out, "It's all right. We're here!"

He gripped her arm and pulled hard, then urgently pointed toward the barn visible at the farther side of the house. What had he seen? And then she saw it too. The barrel of a rifle held at waist height visible behind the door.

They had discovered the safe house! Suddenly a man came out, and in a movement that slowed to a dream, he raised his rifle and fired. Charlie's chest exploded outward, and he pitched forward, staring at Lane and Antoine, as if he could see them, as if he would say something to them. He hit the ground and there was a dreadful moment of silence.

She felt a wave of shock, like a piercing light rolling through her, taking with it her capacity to breathe, to think. A woman called out in a high-pitched scream from somewhere. A second shot came from the barn.

As they watched, the first man called out to a second who came out of the barn, looking back for a moment at something inside, and then they both hurried into the house. Was there another watcher in the woods past the barn? Frozen to the spot, she tried to see, but again she felt her arm being pulled urgently.

"We have been betrayed!" he whispered right into her ear, his hot breath on her cheek.

She still couldn't catch her breath properly. She could not shake the look of Charlie's eyes, the terrible fragility of his life blown apart before them. She'd only just come on the job when they'd opened the service to women, but she saw now that she could never have been prepared for what this sort of work would mean for them all. "But, who . . . ?"

"Don't ask me! Maybe you, eh?" He was looking at her as if she were the enemy they were fighting.

The two men came out of the house, talking loudly now, as if they had nothing to fear, one of them holding a small suitcase, and the other some sort of antenna and wires. What were they speaking? It was not German, and not French. "No, no . . . I mean, who are they?" she finally managed. She tried to ignore the speed at which her heart still pounded, at the desperate urge to run away.

"Nationalists," he spit. "And they have our radio." He looked at his own revolver. "I would shoot them like the dogs they are, but there is someone else there, waiting."

She stared out at the two men retreating toward the forest, and that's when she heard, in English, plain as plain, "Got it?"

But why were they leaving? Lane thought. The safe house had been discovered. These men must have known that she and Antoine would be meeting Charles there. They must have. But the men who shot him were leaving, disappearing into the forest with the radio. They should have stayed, waited for them, killed them as well. And who was the woman who screamed?

LANE SAT IN the smooth wooden chair provided by the field officer, Deniel Harrison, a short wiry man, his red hair combed straight back from his face and an expression that suggested he did not trust her. They both had their hands folded, hers in her lap, his over a sheaf of papers on the desk. A small lamp threw an unsatisfactory swath of light across part of the desk, leaving everything else, including the officer's face, in shadow. It was late, and Lane was exhausted. She told the story, omitting no detail, as she had been taught. She and Charles had been the only ones to parachute into Brittany. They went separately, Charles first. She was met six hours later by Antoine. Alma was meant to come, but she'd said she had to go see her ailing mother. She thought of Alma's body, tied to the chair still. Perhaps if she'd survived Brittany, Alma would have remembered whatever it was this man seemed to be searching for that was missing in Lane's narrative.

Even if Alma hadn't died, Lane would not have had the satisfaction of being able to tell her about their mission when she got home to the bedsit they shared in Hammersmith. Secrets. Everything, all the time, secret, even from the people one worked with.

"Why was Alma there, sir? I don't understand. Shouldn't she have been with us if you wanted her over there?"

Harrison shrugged. "Not our doing."

"What are you saying? She went on her own?" Lane frowned, trying to imagine what on earth would have persuaded Alma to go on her own. No. Of course she wouldn't have. Would she?

He said nothing.

Knowing he never would, Lane asked, "Will you be able to get their bodies back, sir? For their families?"

"I bloody doubt it. The Jerries will have seen to that."

"Not Jerries, sir, I told you. Local people. They spoke Breton."

"Yes, yes, that's what I meant," he answered irritably. "I doubt they'll get what they want from their German friends: independence from France. And you're lucky to be alive, for starters." He sounded resentful about it.

They sat in silence for some minutes, and then Harrison got up and walked around the desk and leaned close to where she sat.

"What about that Antoine fellow? Where does he live again? What do we know about him, after all, for all he's working for us?"

"I know less than you, I'm sure, but he got me out to safety. If he was in on it, he could have dispatched us both. He was angry because we had been betrayed. I could tell he was looking at me. I doubt he will trust me ever again."

"Yes, well," was all the field officer said.

WHAT HAD HE meant? Lane asked herself. Suddenly aware of the violent bubbling of the water, she took the kettle and poured the water into the pot. As she organized her cup and some milk, she thought, It could have been "Yes, well, they don't trust anyone" or "Yes, well, it could have been you, couldn't it?" It still made her angry after all this time that Harrison could have suspected her, when—Her reflections were interrupted by the jolting sound of the phone jangling in the hall. Two longs and a short. It was Darling, sounding slightly breathless.

"Lane, it's me. I've just rung my father. Neither of them can get through to the British embassy. No Canadian presence, so they act for us. Can you try? He's pretending not to be worried, but I can hear he is, and I confess, I'm worried myself. He said he gave you all the details he knows."

"Yes, I have them. Of course, I'll try. How are you? What news of the missing child?"

"You know how it is. That awful sense of powerlessness. We've got Mounties on it, and Terrell has rung Whitehorse— that's where the father works—and they'll call us back when they've found him. We've been out scouring Nelson, to no avail. One worrisome thing is that there was a van out early in the morning, and we wanted to ask the driver if he'd seen anything, only the business advertised on the van doesn't exist. It has now become a vehicle of interest. So, there we are. It seems as if he might have been snatched right out of his own room."

"The poor mother!"

"Indeed. We've told her to stay home in case someone calls. Though who would I don't know. There is certainly not enough money there to make a ransom kidnapping worthwhile."

"Has she someone to stay with her?"

"Yes, darling. Rough policemen though we are, we did think of that. Her friend Bonny is over there as we speak. Her priest has gone around as well, to offer what comfort he can and deliver some prayers to the Almighty, who, we can only hope, has the child within eyesight."

"You laugh, but you'll look pretty silly when you die and it turns out there is an Almighty to whom you must be accountable."

"I'm not laughing, and I never said there wasn't. But if He wants to be useful, He could communicate where the child is. It would save us all a lot of grief. Look, I have to go. See what you can dig up from the diplomats."

"Yes, darling. I love you."

"Well. That's something, anyway." Darling sent a disconsolate kiss down the line.

Lane rang off and thought about her assignment. Perhaps getting through to Mexico City was too complicated. Was there a Mexican consulate in Vancouver? Perhaps they could advise her.

HAVING ASKED TO be put through to the Mexican consulate, Mexico's presence in Vancouver, Lane waited impatiently, leaning on the hallway wall and looking out at the day that was heating up outside her open front door, her cup of tea abandoned. How often in life did circumstances make beautiful days wait? Only, of course, days didn't wait. They carried right on enjoying themselves while humans flapped about, having crises.

"This is the consulate of Mexico. How may I help you?"

"Yes, hello. My name is Lane Winslow Darling. May I speak to someone who might help with the problem of a Canadian missing in Mexico?"

There was a silence at the other end of the line. Lane heard something being put down on a wooden desk. "Oh, I'm sorry. Under what circumstances?"

"He's a geologist. He was last heard from two days ago. The mining outfit he works for reported him missing."

"I see. Please wait."

There was another very long wait, in which she heard voices in the background speaking Spanish. Finally, a man with a deep, smooth voice came on. "This is Martín Alejandro Delgado at your service. I am the consul general. I understand you are calling about a missing man?"

"Yes, thank you for taking my call, Mr. Delgado. My husband's brother is a mining geologist in a town called Fresnillo. He went out two days ago on horseback with an assistant and a guide, and no one has come back. The mine management assures us they are being searched for, but we are unable to reach anyone in Mexico City to report this or get some guidance about how we should proceed."

"I am most grieved to hear this, Mrs. Darling. Canadians—you will need to talk to someone at the British embassy. I do have a colleague there: Captain Herridge. I can try to ring through to discover the state of things. If you will give me all the details."

THEY HAD SCOURED the town and come up with nothing. Terrell's search along the lake had included asking a few early-morning fishermen and dog walkers if they'd seen anything, and he was fairly certain that the child had not wandered down to the water and drowned.

None of the grocery stores in town, nor the new supermarket, had used or received deliveries from Grace Produce.

Darling felt the anxious burden of waiting, and he found himself dwelling not only on the child but on his brother. Having someone go missing, someone who has been there, part of one's life, present only a short time ago and then disappeared, shredded the comfortable solidity of life. It left a terrifying yawning gap into which one could fall with no means of stopping oneself. It was a physical assault, like mourning. One could not tell oneself to be calm, that they would be found, and they would laugh later about how silly it was that they were visiting someone the whole time, or had wandered to the school playground, or had decided to camp for a few nights in a beautiful but remote place. Fear took over and upset every part of one's nervous system.

Of course, he recalled, fear was supposed to sharpen the mind. He was feeling none of this effect at the moment. He jumped at the sound of the telephone and snatched the receiver. "Darling."

"My name is Rockford Radcliffe. One of your men talked to my boss this morning. He told me something about my son going missing. What's going on?"

Radcliffe sounded genuinely worried. His voice was urgent. "Thank you for calling, Mr. Radcliffe. Are you in Whitehorse?"

"Yes. I'm in the foreman's office. What's going on?"

Darling explained the happenings of the morning.

"You think he was taken from his room?" Radcliffe sounded incredulous. "What about that van? Do you have people out looking for the van?"

"Yes, the RCMP are out and have notified any towns that have a detachment." How to ask the next question? "Is there anyone you can think of who might want to hurt either your wife or yourself?"

"No. That's ridiculous! Who would kidnap a kid to get at the parents?"

"What about the boy's grandparents? Perhaps they were upset by the separation?"

Radcliffe snorted derisively. "My parents are gone, and her parents haven't talked to her for years. They don't even know there's a grandson."

"May I ask, Mr. Radcliffe, what the circumstances of your separation were?"

"How is that going to help? You should be out looking for my son!"

"I understand how you feel. But the more information we can get about the family circumstances, the more likely we are to be able to find him. Was your separation a mutual decision, or was there a third party involved?"

"No third party. I did leave, I'll say that. But I left when it became intolerable. Linda completely changed after Rocky was born. She completely cut me out. Wouldn't let me near him, constantly off to her best friend. Belittled me, like suddenly I wasn't good enough for her. It was that friend of hers, Bonny. She was always putting ideas in her head. I couldn't take it anymore. I'll never get a divorce out of her. I'll never get to see my kid. I came north. One day, when he's old enough, he'll wonder about me, and I'll be here."

"You are living with another woman?"

"There you go, you see? She told you that, didn't she? I am not living with another anybody. I'm working hard, trying to put away money for Rocky. And I'm sending her money every month."

"And tell me about Bonny," Darling said. This was the friend she'd asked to come and be with her. This missing child, he was becoming surer, was the result of deeply entangled human troubles.

"Bonny Sunderland. They've been friends since school. Sun rises and sets on her. She never liked me and said so to my face."

"And your wife's parents? What are their names?" Could the grandparents have known after all, and taken him?

"Lila and Keith Bolen. They live out Creston way. No love lost there either. As I said, Linda hasn't spoken with them since she left home. The only reason I know them is

29

that I saw it on her birth certificate. They lived in Penticton when she was born."

"Do you know them? Have you talked to them?"

Radcliffe was silent for a moment. "This can't get back to Linda. She'd kill me. But when Rocky was born, I tracked them down. After they'd retired to Creston. It wasn't easy to find them. I was going to tell them, because I had lost my own parents and I thought how much they would have loved to know they had a grandchild. In the end I didn't. I didn't want to go behind Linda's back. I suppose she had a good reason to cut them out of her life."

Darling fancied he could hear Radcliffe shrugging.

DARLING AND AMES sat in Darling's office, waiting for Terrell, who'd been on the phone. He came in, puffing after taking the stairs three at a time.

"Sir, that was the Mounties. The van was found on the side of the road near Balfour. It looked abandoned, the way it was parked, and showed no signs of having had a child in it."

Ames snorted. "They say."

Darling turned to him in surprise. "Meaning what, exactly?"

Ames coloured. "Sorry, sir. I just wondered if we ought to go out and give the van the once-over. They might have missed something."

"Actually, sir," Terrell interjected, "they told me they got a radio call about gunshots being fired in Harrop, so they didn't have time to do anything but have a quick look."

"Well, given your enormous faith in our mounted colleagues, you can both make the forty-minute drive to Balfour and find out if anyone saw the driver and a child."

CHAPTER THREE

LANE LONGED TO GO ACROSS to the post office, if only to relieve some of her anxiety with the ordinary act of chatting with her neighbours. She especially wanted to know how the Sasakis were doing. Nine-year-old Sara had been found injured and her mother dead by an unexploded bomb near King's Cove earlier in the summer, and now she lived with her grandmother and a great-uncle in a completely refurbished house up the hill past the Bertollis'. She knew Angela Bertolli saw them often, especially because Sara Sasaki Harold was chums with Angela's three boys. Lane sighed. There could be no leaving until she heard back from the consulate, and that could take hours.

She looked around the kitchen to see if anything needed to be tidier than it was, and then wandered into the sitting room and contemplated reshelving her books in some sort of order, but she was waylaid by the atlas again. Opening it up to Mexico, she looked at the location of the state of Zacatecas, and then found the North America page and saw again how very far it was from where she stood at that moment. She imagined Darling having to go there, wondered how one actually got there, and then in the next instant persuaded herself that no such contingency would be likely—Bob would be found, apologetic about causing all the worry and perfectly hale.

Even though she was expecting a call, the loud ring in the hallway made Lane jump. This would be him now, calling to reassure everyone he was fine. It wasn't.

"Mrs. Darling? This is Martín Delgado, at the consulate. I have been able to reach Captain Herridge at the British embassy in Mexico City. He is third secretary there. I have given him all the information, and he will contact the police in Zacatecas and the manager of the mine."

"That is excellent news, Mr. Delgado. I don't know how to thank you. One feels so powerless in these situations. My husband will be relieved to know this."

"You are most welcome. These are distressing circumstances. Herridge said he will telephone tomorrow with anything he has learned. Sometimes tracking everyone down takes time."

"Me?"

"Señora?"

"I'm sorry. I mean, will he telephone me here, or will we be hearing from you?"

"Of course. I have asked him to phone directly to your husband if it is during the working day, otherwise to your home."

"You've been very kind. Thank you so much for all the trouble you've taken."

"I am only too happy to help, Señora Darling. Please don't hesitate to contact the consulate if there is anything more we can do."

LANE RANG OFF, called to give Darling the update, and then finally felt free to go off to the post office. Pulling on her plimsolls, she stepped out and took a big breath of the late morning air, feeling it revive her. The leaves of the little stand of birch trees she had to go through to get to her neighbours rustled softly, and she stopped under them to listen.

In the next moment, the sound was obliterated by the happy cries of Sara, who caught sight of her.

"Miss Lane!" shouted Sara, hurrying toward her, her cane clacking. She couldn't run yet, but even with her cane made good speed. She threw herself into Lane's arms. Mary Sasaki, Sara's grandmother, watched this reunion with her arms crossed, smiling. She had had the care of her granddaughter since Sara's mother had died.

"Look at you!" Lane exclaimed, holding the child away at the shoulders to get a good look at her. "Walking along almost perfectly!"

"I practice every day. Great-uncle Akio is in the garden and I'm going to the beach later with the boys. Now we're going to pick up the mail."

"Well, so am I. And it's a lovely day for the beach. Good morning, Mrs. Sasaki." The two women watched Sara hurrying to meet Alexandra, the Armstrongs' West Highland Terrier. "How is she doing?" Lane asked.

"She is happy, I think, because she loves school and her friends. But when the bustle of the day is over, she

34

becomes quiet and can have trouble going to sleep. I think she still thinks about her mother. She wants me to tell her stories of her mother's childhood so that we can both remember her and feel sad together. My daughter was such a lovely girl, full of spirit just like Sara." Mary looked away to where Sara was completely engrossed with Alexandra. "I regret I missed so much of her life," she added, almost to herself. "How are you?" she asked finally, turning to Lane.

Lane took a big breath. "I'm fine. But my husband's brother, a geologist, has gone missing in Mexico. It's such a business to get hold of anyone to find out what has happened."

"Oh, I am sorry!" Mary exclaimed. "How very worrisome. I think I somehow thought that with the war so long over, that sort of thing would never happen anymore."

Lane thought about the many losses the Sasakis had endured during the war as Japanese Canadians. "Yes. You're right. I think we all thought that. But I suppose life just keeps going. How is the house? Everyone here thinks it's haunted."

Mary Sasaki smiled. "It's lovely, actually. A new coat of paint and new furnishings seem to have dispelled the ghosts. And Akio is very happy with the garden. It's so funny. He was more or less forced to do agricultural work where he was interned, but now you can't get him out of there."

"Because it's his own garden, I suppose. Well, he's fitting right in with everyone here. They're all mad for gardens."

"Mr. Harris has been very kind. He helped Akio clean up the area and took a lot of things that had been discarded in the yard to the dump. In fact, they are going to take the boat into town because Akio wants to buy a second-hand truck."

Lane smiled. No one at King's Cove, in spite of his recent aberrant kindness, could believe that Robin Harris had truly turned over a new leaf and suddenly become helpful and kind. Perhaps he was only helpful and kind to the Sasakis because Sara had won his heart, and his heart now encompassed the whole family. It certainly had not yet encompassed the rest of King's Cove.

WHEN MRS. SASAKI and Sara had disappeared up the hill with a handful of flowers and a sizeable greaseproof paper full of ginger snaps, Eleanor turned to Lane.

"She's doing so well! It is hard to believe the tragedy she endured. Having her grandmother here caring for her has done wonders. Have you time for a cuppa? I think Kenny is just about ready. He's been wrestling with some overgrown gooseberry bushes and could use a break."

"I certainly have. It's been quite a morning, and not in the best way."

"Well then, come along and tell us. It will do you good. I'll gather the tea and you take things out to the porch for me. And call Kenny in."

TERRELL PULLED THE car up behind the van, which was settled at a slightly rakish angle because the rear right tire was resting in a shallow ditch beside the road. It had been driven some two hundred yards down a small road that connected to the main approach to the new ferry landing.

"It looks like a normal produce van," Ames observed. "Except that sign was slapped on by someone with a can of paint." They'd gotten out of the car and stood looking at the small van. "Well, come on then." He opened the driver-side door and surveyed the driver's area. "He's left the keys," he called out to Terrell, who was opening the rear doors of the vehicle.

The rear of the van was dim, so Terrell opened both doors wide and could see that there were a couple of empty wooden crates, but none of the sort of remnants you might expect in a produce van: wilted carrot fronds, bits of blackening lettuce, a withered beet.

"Aha!" he cried, having climbed in and crawled to the back on his hands and knees.

Ames had come around to the rear of the van. "What is it?"

"I've found a child's slipper." He backed out and stood in front of Ames, holding up the article.

Ames took it, frowning. "So, the bastard threw the kid in the back of the van, in the dark, and drove off with him. Kid must have been terrified!"

"I fear so, sir. I'm going to get the flashlight and have a closer look." He went back to the police car and pulled the flashlight out of the glovebox. Quailing, and holding his breath, he looked for any signs the child had been injured. He breathed out in relief. No blood anywhere, at least.

"The question is, why stop here? Where would they go from here?" Ames asked, looking around. "They could have walked onto the ferry, I suppose."

Giving a quick speculative nod, Terrell climbed back into the van and went over the whole thing more slowly.

"I think he put the child against the cab in the back here, behind this box, perhaps to keep him from rolling around on the drive. If the little boy was reluctant to come out, he would have had to crawl in and pull him out. That's probably how he lost the slipper. Ah."

"You've found something else?"

"A half-empty packet of Black Cats." Terrell took a clean hanky out of his pocket, wrapped up the pack of cigarettes, and slid the rest of the way out of the van. "We don't know that it belonged to the kidnapper, of course, but I can see how it might have fallen out of his pocket, crawling back here on his hands and knees to get the child. If the kid put up any resistance, the cigarettes might have fallen out of his breast pocket."

"That's something anyway. Maybe there will be finger-prints on it." Ames turned toward the approach road to the ferry. "I can't think why else you'd stop here except to take the ferry across the lake to Kootenay Bay. Let me get the keys out of the ignition and we can go ask." He fetched the keys, pulling them out with his handkerchief, and put them, carefully wrapped, into his jacket pocket. He took another careful look around the cab but found nothing. They would have to dust the steering wheel for fingerprints as well.

"I DIDN'T SELL a ticket to anybody. The trip's free. We just get them on and get them off on the other side. Our first sailing would have been at seven thirty this morning. I can't say I saw anyone walk on with a child. We don't get that many walk-ons unless it's teens getting dropped off here and picked up on the other side. If they were in a car, I wouldn't likely have seen them at all," the ferry worker in the small hut said.

"Oh, yeah, I forgot about that. I've never been over on this ferry," Ames said.

"Hey!" someone shouted. All three of them turned toward the café fifty yards away at the side of the ferry approach. A man in brown coveralls was standing on the top stair, waving at them. "It took you long enough! I near turned into stone waiting." He looked at his watch and strode toward them. "I called at quarter to eight this morning and it's past ten!" The man was in his forties and had short dark hair with a severe military cut. "I haven't got time to hang around drinking coffee and eating doughnuts like you do. I have work to do!"

"I'm sorry, sir, I don't follow," said Ames.

"You're here about my damn car, aren't you?"

"We're here about a missing child, sir. What about your car?"

"Someone stole it from right under my nose. I was in here having a cup of coffee and when I went out it was gone."

"What kind of car, sir?" Terrell asked. He'd taken his notebook out.

The man looked startled, as if he hadn't expected Terrell to speak, though he had approached them because Terrell was the one in uniform. "Blue Chevy, '46. Bought it to celebrate getting back from Europe in one piece. Four-door. I went all out. I don't appreciate someone stealing it."

Terrell and Ames glanced at each other. The kidnapper might have switched vehicles. So who did the van belong to?

"What's your name, sir?"

"Henry Neil. I live in Harrop. I fix appliances. I had all my damn gear in there. Cost a fortune. Probably across the line by now, the time you guys took to get here!" he complained.

Terrell made a note as Ames took the licence plate number.

Ames said to him in an undertone, "Go call the boss and let him know what we've found. I'm going to find out when the next ferry is. Tell him we're going over to Kootenay Bay to help the Mounties. Get him to let the detachment know we are looking for another stolen car." He made his way back to the ferry worker.

"Hey, where are you going?" barked Neil, watching Ames stride away.

"He's going to check if your car went over on the ferry, sir," Terrell said. "It's possible that our kidnapper took your car."

"HERE WE ARE again, twiddling our thumbs and waiting," Ames said impatiently. "Another forty-five minutes for the damn thing to come back, then it has to unload, and then load up again. We are about as useless as we can be as law enforcement."

Terrell reached into the back seat and took up his print kit. "I'll go get the prints now."

"Good. And we're going to have to find out who the van belongs to. See if there are papers in the glove compartment."

Theirs was the first car in line for the next sailing, and they were now sitting in the car, having purchased a couple of sandwiches at the café. During their conversation with Mr. Neil, the traffic had begun to line up behind them.

"Okay, a man went over on the seven thirty in what now appears to be Mr. Neil's stolen car. No one loading up vehicles sees a child with him. Maybe someone on the ferry did," Ames said. "And no papers in the van. I called O'Brien in the café while you were dusting. He's going to get a tow company to take it to the lot. Maybe someone will call us about it one day. It doesn't look like anyone loves it much though."

"That description the ferry guy gave of the guy in Mr. Neil's stolen car is a pretty standard description of nearly every man who lives around here. Beige jacket and a peaked cap. Probably in his thirties." Terrell shrugged. "I'm not sure about that part. How much could he really see under the cap? But I guess not a man of fifty or sixty, anyway."

"And," Ames said, his impatience welling up again, "he could be just about anywhere now with that little boy. For all we know he's stolen another car, and we're sitting here like bumps on a log!"

"Inspector Darling said he was contacting the RCMP to keep a lookout over on the Kootenay Bay side. And on the plus side, I guess, there was no evidence of blood or anything in the van, so we can hope the child hasn't been harmed. And between the keys, the cigarette packet, and the steering wheel, we're going to find some prints. If we don't catch him now, we will later."

"But will it be too late for the child?"

"No good in thinking that, sir."

"No good at all," Ames agreed, trying to still the anxious churning in his stomach. "I'm just scared the child might

41

not be safe for long." He sighed and drummed his fingers on the window frame. The morning air, now warmed and fragrant with the lake and the trees, stirred slightly. It had the welcoming and open feel of a summer's day. It was in stark contrast to their urgent mission. "I've been hoping it was the result of some crazy thing going on in the family. The father wanting to have his son back, maybe, I don't know . . . unhappy grandparents. I don't like this series of stolen vehicles. It's like some horrible game of paper chase."

"I know what you mean, sir. That makes it seem like we're dealing with a more practiced criminal. But wait, sir," he said after a moment. "Wouldn't someone who was going to do . . . that sort of harm . . ." He swallowed. His experience on the Nelson Police had so far not prepared him for the sort of crime he was imagining. "Wouldn't that sort of kidnapping be more of a snatch? Someone taking advantage of a child being unguarded on the street, or going home from school, or on the beach? Rocky was taken right from his home, out of his room, by someone who knew enough to bring his bathrobe and his favourite toy."

Ames nodded. He didn't want to allow himself to hope, but Terrell's argument was persuasive. "You make a good point. I hate this sort of thing. Give me a good old-fashioned murder any day of the week!"

"I wonder why that Mr. Neil thinks we eat doughnuts?" Terrell mused.

"I wondered that myself. I could use one about now!"

DARLING, HAVING FINISHED notifying the RCMP, now sat feeling almost as helpless as Ames did. He could hear

O'Brien answering the phone downstairs. "Nelson Police Station. Sergeant O'Brien."

Then his own phone rang. He seized the receiver hopefully.

"It's for you, sir. Someone in Mexico."

"Inspector Darling? This is Captain Herridge in the British embassy in Mexico City."

Lane had told him this man might be calling, but he nevertheless felt unprepared for it, and his heart was in his mouth. "Yes, this is he."

"I'm sorry about this spot of trouble you're having." Herridge had a clipped English accent. He sounded like someone used to being in command. "We've contacted the R and T Ventures mining company out in Zacatecas, and they are certainly doing their utmost. They've engaged the local police; now, I don't know how good they are, or how many are available for this sort of thing. They've sent someone out to the site your brother was going to, but there's no sign they ever arrived there."

Darling listened, his anxiety growing. What was uppermost in his mind were the words *no sign they ever arrived*. "What sort of hazards are they likely to encounter? Is the terrain difficult?"

"I haven't been out that way myself, but I understood from Thomas Fine, the mine manager, that the place they were going is mountainous and rough. They went on horseback because there is no road there as yet."

Darling shuddered at the thought of his brother and his companions pitched over the side of a mountain, never to be found. He pulled back from this terrifying vision. "Is it possible they're simply lost?"

"Entirely possible. Listen, I don't know about the local police . . ." He hesitated. "Probably perfectly fine and all that, but there's a lot of poverty in this country and bribery is practically a way of life here. If they've fallen into the wrong hands, well, I mean, the police might not be your best bet."

"Wrong hands? What sort of wrong hands?" Darling asked, frowning. He felt his heart jolt with anxiety.

There was a silence at the other end of the line. It went on long enough that Darling thought the connection might have been lost. Then Herridge spoke. "There are gangs—well, that's a strong word perhaps—groups, *bandidos*, if you will, who will kidnap foreigners in the hopes of a ransom. There is a fair amount of controversy about land distribution and all that sort of thing, and once one's well out in the country, it can be dicey. There's a good deal of hostility to foreign interests operating in the country, of course. They nationalized our interests in the '30s, and it created quite a diplomatic chasm. We've only just reopened the embassy in the last few years."

Bandidos? Even without the benefit of Spanish, he knew what that meant. "I see. What do you suggest? What course of action is best? Will it help if I go there?"

Another silence. "Perhaps . . ." Herridge sounded doubtful. "Perhaps you could lend your expertise to the search. You are a policeman, I understand. If you can get yourself to Mexico City, there is a train service to the town. Or we could provide a car and a driver, who can translate if you don't speak Spanish. You can fly down here. If you'd like to stop in at the embassy, I will, of course, do what I can.

I'm familiar with R and T. They hire people from all over. It's quite international."

All the people that Mexicans trying to nationalize their interests might not like, Darling thought. "Thank you very much, Captain Herridge. I'll let you know what I decide. I appreciate your offer of help."

Putting down the receiver, Darling turned his chair to look out his window at Elephant Mountain, rising magnificently across the narrow strip of lake, bathed in sunlight. He often gazed at the mountain and told himself it brought perspective and sometimes a new view of a problem. But Elephant Mountain had never been presented with a kidnapping, if kidnapping it was, in Mexico or anywhere else, and it was clearly unequal to the task. Stare as he might, Darling got no insights from the activity. He thought about Bob. No matter that they were both adults, Bob would always be his little brother, and his heart ached at the thought that he might be suffering.

CHAPTER FOUR

***

Vancouver, 1932

THE FRONT DOOR OPENED SLOWLY, and Frederick knew to be afraid. He put the hand of cards he held face down in a fan on the kitchen table and waited, staring down at them, and Bob looked at him, puzzled.

"Hey . . ." But then he saw his father standing in the door of the kitchen, his hat still on. He glanced over at Frederick, his eyes full of worry, and then back at his father.

"She's gone," was all their father said. He turned away, back into the dark hallway.

Frederick got up and pulled his chair next to Bob's and put his arm around him. All he could feel in that moment was sorrow for his brother, who was still staring at the place where his father had been, his eyes beginning to fill. He knew that Bob, ebullient, happy Bob, had never fully understood how ill his mother had been. Maybe, he thought, it had been wrong, trying to keep it from him. It had been a conspiracy between him and his mother to protect Bob. And now the world had been knocked out from under the kid.

Bob pushed away from Frederick, getting up abruptly and knocking his chair over, looking at his brother with a wild fury that neither could fully comprehend. Frederick sat helpless while his younger brother stumbled away, angrily brushing tears from his face. He heard him run down the hall, heard their bedroom door slam.

"Bob," he called. But it was too late.

He sat on at the table, thinking about his brother, and then about their mother. She had told him, the last time she'd gone into the hospital, "He doesn't need to know yet, sweetheart. He's such a happy boy. Let's leave him that, can't we?" He remembered sitting numbly by her bed. He wanted to say, "He'll have to know sometime," but he'd sat silently, his hand on hers where it lay on the bed beside her. "Promise me you'll look after him, please. Poor kid. And your dad. He might not be up to much for a while." She'd smiled slightly at this.

Now he didn't see how he could look after anyone. He felt hollow, as though his chest had been carved out. It had begun to get dark, and he finally got up and turned on the kitchen light. The kitchen felt empty in a way he could never have imagined. As if it knew her soul had left. With a huge effort of will, he ran water into the kettle and put it on the stove.

The living room was dark. His father sat at the end of the couch, looking toward the window where the curtains were still open. Frederick moved to the lamp his father sat next to and turned it on, causing his dad to look up at him.

"Dad, I've put the kettle on."

"Yes . . . yes. That's a good idea." But he didn't move, his arm resting on the arm of the old maroon sofa delicately, as if he didn't want to crush it. He watched his eldest son close the curtains and then stand for a long moment with his back to him. "You should see to your brother."

Bob looked up when Frederick came into the room and sat down beside him. Frederick had stood outside the door listening to his brother sobbing, and wondered why he himself couldn't cry.

"It's not fair!" Bob threw his arms around his brother and buried his head in his shoulder.

"No. It's not. It's not fair." He held his brother, rubbing his back until he heard his father knock on the door and push it open.

"Boys, there's tea."

"Come on, Bobby. Let's go be with Dad."

That night Bob wanted the light on.

"Why did Mom have to die?"

"I don't know. She was sick, I guess." Frederick was acutely conscious of not knowing, of having no adequate answer.

"What are we gonna do?"

"Go to school and stuff like we usually do."

"I don't want to go to school. Everyone will know."

"I know, Bobby, but I think she'd want us to go to school. You know how she is about school." He couldn't say *was*.

"Are you going to die?"

"Hey, no! You should try to go to sleep. I'll be right here when you wake up, I promise. I'll look after you, okay?"

Frederick lay awake long into the night until he could hear his brother's even breathing, and in that moment he felt utterly and completely alone.

HE THOUGHT ABOUT his mother's "He's such a happy boy." Bob had continued to be happy, making an almost care-free way through his life. Darling swivelled his chair back around. He would go. He'd have to. His father would be frantic. It was diabolical that this should occur just as he was confronted with a serious case right here at home. With any luck the child would be found swiftly. Ames and Terrell were already on to a vehicle that was likely the kid-napper's transport. And they were going over in pursuit. Between them and the RCMP, the child would probably be found at any moment. These reflections calmed him slightly, and he applied himself to deciding what his next course of action should be.

He asked to be put through to King's Cove 431. He would tell Lane what he had decided, and what he'd learned from Herridge, but there was no answer.

He sat some moments more, in the grip of indecision about telling the men he'd be away yet again. They were quite competent to carry on without him. He groaned. The other person he would have to tell was his boss, Mayor Dalton. He should go down to Brown at the travel agency and put things in motion. Time was of the essence. Damn! Why wasn't Lane at home? He'd have to tell her what he was planning. He mentally practiced, "No, absolutely not! You are not coming with me. Under no circumstances!" several times and then decided he had better get some coffee and a grilled cheese sandwich across the road. He wasn't sure how much of an appetite he had, but waiting in his office for something to happen would drive him mad.

At the café, sanity had been restored because April McAvity had completed her initial policing course in Vancouver and was back at her old job serving up food and good cheer. Though, he thought, in some ways he might miss pitting his wits against Marge, April's temporary replacement. Marge was surely the surliest waitress in the country. Still, he thought how disappointing it must be for April to be back at her old job.

ELEANOR AND KENNY could not have been more worried or sympathetic to the plight of Bob Darling. It was something so far out of their experience that they struggled to know what to say.

"Of course, you have that sort of thing in these countries," Kenny said, taking a stab at being philosophical.

"Do you?" asked his wife. "How do *you* know?"

"Well, I mean, you hear about it. Banana republics sort of thing. Disorder. Anarchy."

"Are you trying to comfort Lane with this nonsense? Only I don't think it's working."

Lane smiled. "It's all right. He couldn't say anything I haven't already thought myself. I know nothing whatever about Mexico, though Brown does have some nice posters in the window of the travel agency. Lovely beaches."

"That's true," Eleanor said. "I saw in one of Angela's movie magazines that Rita Hayworth goes on holidays down there."

"What I'm worried about," Lane confessed, "is that Frederick will have to go down there. If that happens, I will most certainly want to go."

"Do you speak Spanish as well as all the other languages? What is it, French, Russian, German?" Eleanor asked.

"No, sadly not. I'll be of no actual use to him in that regard. Anything could have happened to Bob . . . Frederick shouldn't be alone, that's all."

Kenny reached across the table to pat Lane's hand. "There, now. It may never happen."

Eleanor rolled her eyes. She wasn't going to say, "Or it may," but she was thinking it. Life didn't always unfold just the way one wanted. Her own life had taught her that.

"FINALLY," DARLING SAID. "Where have you been?"

"Having a cuppa with Eleanor and Kenny. A man was supposed to telephone you from Mexico. Has there been a development?"

"This Herridge person called me from Mexico and he's recommending I go down there. He doesn't sound all that confident about the police there. I won't have any standing, of course, but I can't bear to have the whole thing unfolding halfway to kingdom come, with no idea what's happening."

Lane nodded and then said, "I knew you'd want to go. I'd like to go with you. While you're in town, you might as well see what Brown at the travel agent can tell us. I'll talk to Angela about the boys keeping an eye on the garden. Oh, and Sara, too. Her uncle Akio will be very useful in this regard—"

51

"Stop! Lane, stop. You are *not* coming with me, absolutely not!" It didn't sound as strong as he'd imagined it would, but Darling persevered. "I don't know what I'll be going into. It could be dangerous, if what Herridge at the embassy tells me is true."

There was a long silence. For a moment Darling thought anger might have silenced her. "Lane, please. I—"

"I don't want you to have to face whatever is happening alone," Lane said simply. "I know you're worried about the danger, but I have faced danger before. And anyway, we don't know, do we, what we'll be facing."

Darling was flummoxed. "It's just—"

"It's just nothing," she said gently. Had he conceded? "Go to Brown, find out how to get the two of us down there. I can point out in the atlas where it is, if you're interested. And anyway, Rita Hayworth goes there on holiday."

"Get in touch with her. Maybe she can help. Give us the lie of the land."

"There's no time for talking nonsense. Brown's, now! I'll get our suitcases ready. Oh, and can you stop at the bookstore and see if Mrs. Treadwell has a Spanish phrase book of some sort?"

LINDA RADCLIFFE STOOD looking out the window in her son's room. She was clutching the blanket from his bed to her chest, as if in an effort to contain the burgeoning hard mass of fear that had lodged there. She tried to imagine how Rocky had been taken from here. Had it really been through this window? Why had he not cried out? Had they put something over his mouth? Had he been drugged? She felt her utter helplessness and rebelled at it. Why hadn't the police found him by now? Why hadn't they called to tell her what was going on?

At that minute the telephone in the hall rang, and she ran into the hall tucking Rocky's blanket under her right arm. "Hello?"

"What the hell is going on? Why did I have to hear about this from some policeman?" Her husband sounded angrier than he usually was.

"You have him, don't you!" It wasn't a question; it was an accusation that she only just realized had been burning inside her.

"Don't be an idiot! Why would I call you if I had him? I'm up in Whitehorse, and if you don't believe me, you can talk to my boss. He's right here. How could you let this happen? When I left him with you, I assumed you could take care of him. You're—"

"Shut up! Just shut up! You think I'm not frantic? Someone came into this house, in the night, and took him. I don't understand it." She began to cry, gulping great sobs. "It is you, isn't it? You never wanted me to have him. I knew you'd do this one day!"

"How many times do I have to tell you, I don't bloody have him!"

"You could have sent someone . . . you could have . . ."

"Well, I didn't." His voice softened. "Look, Linda. Try to think. Have you talked to any strangers? Has anything unusual happened?"

"Oh, yes, 'cause I talk to strangers every day of the week!" Linda brushed aside a little surge of guilt. Anyway, it couldn't

53

be that; he wasn't a stranger. And he wouldn't have taken him. He'd never even seen him. She'd made sure of that. "No. Nothing! We see the same neighbours every day. He plays with the same children. In this weather, we go to the beach, and we have picnics, and the children play in the water."

"Someone there, then. Someone watching you, someone followed you home maybe." He was beginning to feel his own fear overcoming him. The idea of a stranger taking him . . . "Look. I'm coming down there. I'm sure my boss will give me time off for something like this. It'll take a couple of days. With any luck, he'll be found by then, and it will be good for him to have both his mother and father on hand. Okay?"

Linda Radcliffe nodded. "Yes," she mumbled. "Yes. Please come here. I don't think I can face this on my own."

Penticton, May 1942

"I'M NOT STAYING, Mom. Not in this little one-horse town. I don't want to help Dad in the stupid orchard, and I don't want to get a job in the café." Linda Bolen was wondering why she had to say this all again. She was standing on the porch of their farmhouse, already holding her suitcase. She had her ticket in her hand and wild hope in her heart. She turned and took the two steps down.

"Don't think you can waltz back here when it all goes wrong! Your dad is sick of your tantrums! You go, then. See how you get on on your own!"

Linda turned at that and looked at her mother, standing with her hand holding the screen door wide open, her ample frame wrapped in a faded peach housedress that washed out her features and somehow seemed to highlight the twisted anger on her face. Linda was going to say something, but seeing her like that, all she could think was how much she hated her, and how she would never, ever be anything like her.

She thought about missing Bonny, but then remembered Bonny was angry and not talking to her. Well, she was making a big deal over nothing. The guy was an idiot. Anyway, she couldn't stay. Not now.

On the train she stared out the window, her thoughts divided between the excitement of getting away, of being anywhere else, and a kind of mental recitation of all the reasons she had to hate her mother. These still had the upper hand. Her mother had never approved of her, had never given her an ounce of love. Constantly belittled her. Any sort of care had been left to her bewildered father, who had never seemed to get anything out of her mother either. She'd always wanted to ask him why he'd married her. She never had, but now she thought about it. It came to her in a flood of shame. He'd had to!

At this horrific thought she looked down at her handbag where it lay under her hands on her lap, feeling her face suddenly hot. There was nothing in her to counter this idea, and the story lodged itself in her mind like a worm in an apple. Her mother had been pregnant with her before she married. She must have been! She tried to think of the dates. Her parents' anniversary was in late January, on the 25th. Her birthday was six months later, on July 15. Well, she thought angrily, she was either premature or a bastard!

She remembered her father saying to her once, when she'd stormed out to the barn in a rage about something her mother had said, "You shouldn't be so hard on her. She gave up a lot to come here and look after us." She'd asked him what she'd given up. He'd told her she had been at university studying law, one of the few women students in the faculty.

"You call what she does looking after us?" she'd asked, incredulous. "Why did you even come out here in the middle of nowhere?"

He'd hesitated. "We wanted to start a new life. She never would have been able to be a lawyer, and I was never that interested. It's something my father wanted for me."

"Why couldn't she be a lawyer? She'd make a better lawyer than a mother!"

"She got married, of course," her father had said. "She wouldn't have been able to work."

She'd been right all those years ago. What had she been, eleven? Her mother was a lousy mother. She should never have married. She only did it because of me. No wonder she hates me, she thought.

With this, Linda turned her gaze back out the window, feeling the rocking and clacking of the rails underneath, taking her far away from all of it, to her own new life, but with the same dark stain of guilt as her mother. She lay her arm across her abdomen and tried to sleep.

CHAPTER FIVE

AMES AND TERRELL STOOD ON the ferry deck, leaning on the railing and looking out at the far shore as they glided along. The whirl of wind was warm and soothing despite their errand.

"That's King's Cove over there," Ames said, pointing across the water. "The only way to recognize it is that wharf and that tower with the water gauge. Otherwise, the whole place just disappears into the forest and mountains. This ferry's been going a couple of years, and I've never been on it. The view is great."

"It seems a lot more wild out here than where I come from in Nova Scotia, that's for sure," Terrell said. "How many times have we driven along that road, and it looks completely different from this vantage point."

"Creston is out this way . . . isn't that where the mom's parents—or maybe the dad's, I can't remember—live?" Ames asked.

"Yes." Terrell pulled out his notebook. "Lila and Keith

Bolen. Mrs. Radcliffe's parents. I think we should go and visit them. Maybe the boy's mother telephoned them, in spite of the estrangement. Or they might be involved. It seems too coincidental that they live here, and the stolen car has gone that way."

"Well, I'm still hoping this is some sort of family trouble," Ames said. "It would be wonderful to arrive and find the kid safe and sound with Grandma and Grandpa."

"Except, as you say, they don't know he exists."

Shrugging, Ames said, "I know, I'm just grabbing at straws."

When they rolled off the ferry on the Kootenay Bay side, they pulled into a tiny service station to ask where the RCMP detachment was located. They were told the nearest was in Creston, fifty miles south. Ames asked to use the telephone.

"Yes," the man on duty in Creston said. "We found that blue Chevy abandoned just on the edge of town, and we have a reported car theft right near there. It would appear that will be the modus operandi of your kidnapper. Sergeant Cooper is out in our car." He rustled some paper. "He called in on the car radio about half an hour ago and he's following the suspect south. Where are you now?"

"We just pulled into Kootenay Bay."

"It'll take you a good hour to get here. By then we might have news."

Ames asked him where he could be found and asked him to look up the address of Mrs. Radcliffe's parents.

"HELLO?" THE MAN'S voice was raspy, as though he rarely used it. He looked older than he probably was.

Ames held up his warrant card. "Yes, hello. This is Constable Terrell and I'm Sergeant Ames, of the Nelson Police. Are you Keith Bolen?"

Bolen clutched the door. "Something's happened to Linda!" His voice faltered and he seemed to choke.

"No, no, Mr. Bolen. Your daughter is all right. Can we come in?"

Bolen looked back as if he might be in trouble with someone inside, and then opened the door tentatively, moving only a little so that they had to squeeze by.

"Who is it?" a woman's voice called sharply out of the darkness of the little sitting room.

"It's the police. They say Linda is all right." Bolen nodded his head toward the end of the hall. "Go on through. That's Lila, my wife."

Mrs. Bolen was still in a dressing gown, as if she were an invalid. "What do you want?" She didn't sit or invite them to. She stood in the entrance to the kitchen, holding a cigarette.

"We're here because your daughter's five-year-old son went missing this morning. Have you heard anything at all about this?" Ames asked.

"Son? Linda has a son? What's his name?" Mr. Bolen asked, taking a step forward.

"The little fellow is called Rocky Radcliffe. We're wondering—"

"Rocky. That sounds like the sort of thing she'd name a child. *How* old is he again?" Mrs. Bolen sounded as if she couldn't take it in.

"He's five, Mrs. Bolen. Have you been contacted about this by anyone?"

59

"She hasn't spoken to us for over five years. We know nothing about her life," Mrs. Bolen said, taking a long pull at her cigarette.

"We think he's been kidnapped, and we've traced a stolen car that was making its way here to Creston, we think. That's why—"

"You think we have him? We didn't even know he existed! And we certainly couldn't look after a child. Neither one of us is well," Mrs. Bolen snapped, then began a round of convulsive coughing.

Ames sighed. "Thanks, Mr. and Mrs. Bolen. If you do hear anything, can you call the Nelson Police?"

Mr. Bolen looked down and cleared his throat, then asked softly, "Linda. Is she all right?"

"She is very well, Mr. Bolen, but she's understandably frantic about her little boy."

Mrs. Bolen advanced into the living room, one arm still across her waist, and stubbed out her cigarette in an overflowing ashtray. "She made her bed. She has to lie in it."

As a dismissal, this was as effective as any.

"May I ask what you mean, ma'am?" Ames asked as he was turning to leave.

"Well, I'm assuming she has no husband. A baby out of wedlock. That would be typical of her," Mrs. Bolen nearly spat out.

"Oh, no, Mrs. Bolen. I ought to have clarified. She is married, though she's separated at the moment."

Ames nodded and he and Terrell made their exit.

"WELL," AMES SAID.

"Yes, sir. An unhappy family."

"Let's get back to the detachment and see if there's been any news. I don't know when I've been more depressed by a couple! They hate each other, they hate their daughter, they don't seem to care they have a grandson."

Terrell slid the car into gear and started down the street. "It seems like that, though the dad looked like he might be interested. But maybe they have had a lot of disappointments in life. A grandson no one told them about might be just one more."

"It's not a very good advertisement for marriage!"

Terrell glanced at Ames with a slight smile. "Sir?"

"Don't you start."

They were at the RCMP detachment in a matter of minutes, and they pushed open the door, causing a secretary to put out her cigarette and jump up. "We've been trying to reach you two! Why don't you have a radio in your car?"

"Sorry," said Ames. "They promised us we'd get one soon. What's up?"

"We have the boy! The sergeant lost track of the suspect, and then we got an anonymous call, and we radioed Cooper to go get him. He found him sitting beside the road on a big rock, holding his bunny. They're on their way back here now."

"That's great!" Terrell said, feeling a thrill of relief. "He's all right?"

"Tip-top. He wasn't even crying. Apparently, he likes the police car. We asked him to tell us about the man who took him, but all he said was that he gave him candy and

61

told him to be quiet. The man told him to wait and not to leave the rock. He never came back. No sign of him."

"Can we use your phone to call our boss?" Ames asked.

"Help yourself," the secretary said. She stood up and moved away from the desk, so Ames could sit down, and came to rest next to Terrell. "You work at the Nelson Police?" she asked him.

He smiled. "We do."

"That must be interesting."

"I suppose as interesting as working for the RCMP in Creston," he said, smiling.

She shrugged, pulled a packet of cigarettes out of her dress pocket, and offered him one.

He shook his head, and she took one for herself and lit it. "You don't get a kidnapping every day," she commented, watching Ames talking at her desk.

"No, thank heaven," Terrell said. "What we have to find out is who did this. Did the anonymous caller leave any information?"

"Nope," she said.

They both turned when the door opened and a tall, uniformed man in his thirties came through carrying Rocky, and set him down. "Here we are. All safe and sound. He's pretty hungry, though, aren't you?" he said to the child.

The little boy, his blond hair tousled, and still wearing his pyjamas and bathrobe, nodded. He was in bare feet, and the officer was holding one slipper.

"Hey, we've got your other slipper in the car," Terrell said, going back outside. The boy stood quietly, as if he were waiting to see what was going to happen. Terrell came in and offered him his slipper. He put it on, and the Mountie handed him the other one.

"There now. A whole pair. Are you hungry?" Terrell asked.

"Oh, I can run across the road and get a sandwich from the restaurant. Would you like a sandwich?" The secretary had crouched down to be at Rocky's level. She took his hand. "Come on. We'll go over and see what we can get. We'll leave these guys to take care of things."

Rocky nodded solemnly and held his rabbit tightly.

Ames hung up the phone, and the three of them watched the boy and the secretary leave. Terrell offered his hand to the Mountie. "Constable Jerome Terrell, Nelson Police. Thanks for finding him. His mother will be so relieved. This is Sergeant Ames."

The Mountie nodded and shook Terrell's hand. "Well, I'll be. You must be a rarity. I'm Sergeant Cooper. We were just lucky, if you want the truth. We almost drove right past him, sitting there in his little dressing gown. He looked like an advert for Christmas morning. He's not saying much. Maybe he'll talk to you on the way back. I'm going to have to go back out to have a better look at the kidnapper's car. Blue Chevy, a couple of years old."

Ames nodded and scratched his head. "That's the one that was stolen at the Balfour ferry. It's a pretty weird thing to do, leaving him on the side of the road like that. Dangerous to boot. I wonder if the kidnapper got spooked and decided he couldn't go through with it."

"With any luck, we'll find him, and he can explain himself," Cooper said.

"I wonder if he was doing it for someone else. I think if he was doing it for himself, he'd have kept the child. This suggests it was just too much trouble," Terrell said.

"He was taking an awful risk, leaving the boy like that," Ames said, shaking his head.

AMES FINISHED HIS notes and stretched. He felt depleted, as if he'd been on some long mountain trek. Rocky had been returned to his mother and seemed little the worse for wear. When they'd been sitting in the ferry on the way back to Balfour, the child had said the man told him he was his uncle, and he was going to take him to see his daddy. Ames and Terrell had looked at each other. The father *was* to blame. They would contact Whitehorse and ask that Radcliffe be questioned on the matter.

He threw down his pencil and went downstairs.

"You hungry?" he asked Terrell. "I could eat a horse just about now."

"Yes, sir. I am a little hungry," Terrell answered.

"I bet you are," Ames said with a smile, thinking about April being back at her post in the café. Terrell and April were what Ames thought of as "a definite possibility." "Let's go get a quick bite. Not too much. Mother would kill me if I had no appetite for dinner."

O'Brien shook his head as he watched his two younger colleagues out the door. He reached under the counter and took out his lunch box. Lunch had been dispatched at the proper time, and now he wanted tea. He took out a Thermos and a couple of nice-looking peanut butter cookies.

"I THOUGHT YOU two had gone on a diet," April said by way of greeting. "I didn't see you at lunchtime." She smiled at Terrell and then as an afterthought at Ames.

"We have"—Terrell lowered his voice, glancing around for other diners—"been pursuing a kidnapper."

"Oh, no!" April whispered, ushering them to the corner window seat. If they wanted to talk about the case, it was the place they'd be least likely to be overheard. "A child?" she asked softly when they'd sat.

Terrell nodded. "He's all right. Back with his mother. We haven't had time to eat, though. What's the pie today? Marge would never tell us. It was always a surprise."

April smiled. "She had her little ways. Would you like to be surprised?"

"Her little surly ways," Ames said. "But, now that I think of it, the surprise might be fun."

"Shouldn't you two eat something healthy if you haven't had lunch?" April countered.

"Nope," said Ames. "I'd like surprise pie, and one for my friend. And two coffees. We're celebrating."

"Well, I'm sure glad the kid is all right. I think that's the worst kind of crime! Still, more exciting than what I get in here."

When April had gone, Ames leaned forward. "Any progress?"

"On the case, sir?" Terrell said innocently. "All tied up with a bow, as my gran used to say."

"You know what I mean!"

Terrell sighed. "This kidnapping is going to be easier to figure out than what's going on in *her* head." He tilted

65

his head toward where April was taking pie out from a glass case.

Ames leaned back, making a disgusted sound. "It's plain as the nose on your face what's going on in her head. You just have to make a move."

"As you know, sir, it's not that easy. I wouldn't want her exposed to whatever Nelson might dish up if we were together." He hadn't said that out loud before. He'd thought it plenty of times.

"That Sergeant Cooper called you a rarity," Ames said. "Do you mind that sort of thing?"

Terrell shrugged. "I've had worse. I don't think he meant to be rude. And I guess I am kind of a rarity." He leaned forward, folding his hands on the table, wanting to go back to the case. "You know, earlier I was at the church to see if anyone who runs that little kindergarten knew anything. They have about eight children there, all around Rocky's age. According to them, he is a very nice child. Plays well with all the others and has already learned how to share, which many of the others have not. They've never seen anyone unfamiliar hanging around, and the only person who ever collected him was either his mother or Mrs. Sunderland; that's her friend, Bonny, who also has a child there."

"That's that, then," Ames said. "I'm guessing his father is going to have to own up to this now." He could see April pouring their mugs of coffee. "Listen, can you keep a secret?"

This sudden turn in the conversation startled Terrell, and he too looked nervously at April, who by now had loaded the two mugs and two plates of what, from this distance, looked like peach pie onto a tray.

When April had been and gone, he leaned forward. "Yes, sir, I can."

"Peach. Yum." Ames took a bite and ate it thoughtfully. Then he put his fork down and looked at Terrell. "Look. I'm thinking of . . . you know."

"I don't, sir."

"Getting married." He said the last word in a very low whisper.

At this Terrell straightened up, all smiles. "I'm sorry, sir. That's no secret. Everyone knows. We're all just waiting for our fancy embossed invitation."

"How do you know? I haven't even told my mother!" Ames said, a little outraged.

"Oh, you can make a sizeable bet that she already knows. Anyway, it got out that you bought a ring."

THE RETURN OF Rocky Radcliffe to his mother relieved Darling enormously. He could safely leave Ames to sort out who was behind his abduction. He walked down the hill toward Brown's travel agency still struggling with conflicting emotions. He was profoundly relieved by the return of the child, but that made way for a growing, gnawing anxiety about his own brother. He stood for a moment outside the door of the travel agency, looking down as if he were trying to decide something, and then with resolution he pushed open the door. He would win the day and not take Lane into unknown dangers. It would distract him to be worrying about her when he wanted to put all his energy into finding his brother. Who knew how long it would take and what unknowns he'd be exposed to?

"Ah, Inspector Darling. I've been expecting you. Everything is ready. I've worked out everything for either one or two travellers. Have a seat, I'll walk you through it all. I'm sorry it has to be under these awful circumstances. Normally a trip to Mexico would be very exciting. A lovely place. I vacationed there a couple of years ago with the wife. Acapulco. Very fashionable!"

"My wife called you?"

"Yes, that's right. Together we worked out the quickest way to get there. You'll take the train . . ." Darling sat back as Brown laid out the plans in detail. "And that should get you to Mexico City in three days' time. This place you have to go is actually quite far north of Mexico City, so I initially suggested you get at it from Monterrey, but she explained about the embassy in Mexico City. It's just a question of whether we're planning for one person or two. Either way, we could have you leaving Thursday morning and then flying out of Vancouver on Saturday. I've actually booked you a hotel, the Gran Hotel. It's very historic and beautiful. The wife and I stayed there on our way to Acapulco."

"This isn't a pleasure trip, Mr. Brown. Historic and beautiful are of no use to us."

"Yes, I see that," Mr. Brown said hurriedly, "but Mrs. Darling suggested you'd want to be near the British embassy. From there you will need to hire a car, or perhaps they've arranged something at that end. It's about a ten-hour drive to this town we're going to. Four hundred and fifty or so miles."

We? Oh, are you coming too? Darling thought, but only

nodded. Almost without thinking, he made his decision. "Speed is of the essence. Can you book it for two?"

"I did take the liberty of booking for two; easy enough to cancel one, but Mrs. Darling said you would need to go as soon as possible. We have booked everything, but we have a day if you really need to change anything." Mr. Brown stood up with an expression that suggested changes would be ill-advised. He picked up the folder with all the travel arrangements and handed it to Darling.

Darling had nearly an hour on the drive home to consider his situation. He sat in the car on the ferry out of town, drumming on the steering wheel. On the one hand, he felt he ought to have put his foot down. There were many reasons to. He'd gone through them in his head, and here they were back again; he didn't want to be worried about her safety, he didn't know what circumstances he'd be going into, he ought to be able to tell his wife that she couldn't come. There's not a man jack out there who wouldn't feel it was his right to put his foot down. Full stop.

The chain clanged down and he started down the ramp onto the road. They'd never really come to such an impasse before. There'd never been a time when, with minor scuffles, to be sure, they hadn't been in complete harmony. *Why* ought he be able to tell his wife no? Because he was the "husband"? The argument was weak, and he could tell his brain was falling back on "the head of the household" as a rationale because he couldn't really think of a good argument. Not one she'd accept, anyway.

Did he just want to "win"? Say a firm "no" and have her accept, obey, even? He was aware of a profound discomfort with this. It made him feel small. Why did he want her to stay home? It was obvious. He was afraid. He was afraid for himself, and for her.

But, some other part of his brain interjected, as he was passing the mansion and the beautiful stretch of water it looked out on, he had decided, had said to Brown that they would both be going. And he knew in his heart of hearts he meant it, and was grateful she'd left it up to him. And anyway, she was a trained . . . a trained what? He didn't even know what. But a trained something to be sure, and a veteran, just as he was. She was used to dealing with unfamiliar territory—more than he was, he was certain. In truth, he'd only flown over unfamiliar territory. Lane had had to . . . but here his imagination gave out. He knew only one story about her: that someone had been shot leaving a safe house, and she'd felt responsible.

Being married to Lane was like having a massive volume on a bookshelf in a foreign language one could never read, full of stories and whole lives with which he would never become familiar. He, on the other hand, he thought morosely, was just a well-thumbed paperback, which she had already read completely, including between all the lines.

CHAPTER SIX

"I THOUGHT ABOUT IT ALL THE way home. I'm not sure I'm suited for a role like this after all." Darling and Lane were sitting on the porch with glasses of sherry. He had arrived home to find two suitcases packed, and the table set. They were waiting for the leftover stew to heat up.

"What role is that?"

Darling shrugged. "You know, lord of the manor. Man of the house. I wanted to swashbuckle in here and tell you that you weren't coming with me and that's flat. But I realized my reasons are not sound. I keep thinking, What if something happens to you? I'd never forgive myself." He turned to her and took her hand. "I resent not knowing things about you. For all I know you are a trained jiu-jitsu practitioner who could be no end of use in a crisis."

Lane smiled. "I knew I should have attended that particular training session. I'd have dispatched that man who wanted to kill Sara much more handily." She became serious. "I'm sorry. About the things you don't know, I mean. And I'm not trying to push myself forward here. I too am afraid. I don't want you to go at all, but if you must go, I don't want you to go alone. We can't know what we'll find. It might take two of us to sort. And if anything has . . . happened to him, I don't want you to have to cope alone. And it is a little selfish . . . I'd spend the whole time here feeling powerless and wretched because I might have helped."

"You know, there is this idea out there about the little woman, isn't there? She's the weaker sex, she defers to her husband, she can't buy a car on her own without her husband's or father's permission, she can't handle the banking. And she is most certainly not to be taken into dangerous situations. At work I see that sort of thing all the time in families I have to deal with. But I always wonder what goes on that we don't see. How many women are actually in charge of the whole show? I have no experience of my own to go on, because my mother died when I was so young, but what I do remember is that my father always said, 'Go ask your mother' about just about anything, as if she was the authority. I think I must have developed the idea that the woman is, in fact, in charge."

"'Behind every great man is a good woman' sort of thing," Lane suggested.

"Behind nearly every man, period. Mind you, I've seen too many women abominably treated by their husbands, who fall back on 'I can do what I want with my own wife' when you try to stop it or charge them. Courts back them up. The official police manual says, for example, rape occurs when a man has carnal knowledge of a woman 'not his wife' without consent. The wife who has not consented is left with no protection." Darling interrupted these dire contemplations. "What's that smell?"

"Blast! The stew!" Lane leaped up and seized the pot off the stove and peered into it, shuffling the contents about with a spoon. "I think it's still manageable. Otherwise, there's peanut butter to fall back on."

Darling looked at the stew. "Does it taste burnt, do you think?"

Lane spooned a little out and handed the spoon to Darling. "You decide. You're the head of the household."

"*Très amusant.*" He blew on the morsel of beef and then said, "You've caught it just in time."

"*You* caught it just in time. You were telling me about non-consensual carnal knowledge. I was just thinking how interesting it would be to have a police manual so I knew what you got up to every day. But seriously, I am also without much personal experience of this sort of thing, as I had no mother at all, but knowing my father as I did, I bet he would have pulled rank without hesitation. On the other hand, my grandfather has always been terribly solicitous of my grandmother. Theirs, I think, is a marriage of equals."

"Unless he just assumes he's in charge but doesn't push his weight about, and she goes along with it."

Lane considered this, pot in hand, ready to scoop out the last dregs of edible stew. "Does it matter what he assumes as long as he treats her as an equal? Isn't action the key thing here?"

Darling devoted the next few moments to his dish of stew. "This isn't bad, all things considered, with a nice piece of buttered bread. Is there something for afters?" he asked. "One wants to feel there's a payoff at the end."

"Eleanor gave us a bit of lemon slice," Lane said, pointing at a tin on the shelf.

"And you've been here, alone with it, the whole day? I'm surprised to learn there's any left."

Lane smiled. "Ye of little faith. I was busy with the packing."

"And how would you know what I need packed?"

"In my day, a gentleman never packed his own bags. He wouldn't know how."

"I'm not a gentleman. I know how. I will have to check your work."

"Quite right. I looked up the mean temperature at this time of year in Mexico in the atlas and was guided by that. It can get cool at night where we're going."

"About your grandparents," he continued. "My impression is that they are friends. I wonder if that is important. I'm not sure that old 'man of the house' business really can allow for genuine friendship."

Lane nodded. "I think you're right. Does this mean you're not going to make a fuss about my coming to Mexico with you? I saw you come in with the folder from the travel agency. Mr. Brown was most accommodating."

"Thank you for leaving it to me. In a mad moment I lost my head and I told him to book for two. I don't know why. Much will depend on the lemon slice. Ask me again after that."

"I MUST SAY, it's hard to beat something like that," Terrell said, as they discussed the kidnapping over their pie.

74

"When you think how often we have to be the bearers of bad news, seeing that little boy back in the arms of his mother is the best thing."

Ames nodded. "It's too bad, really, that he couldn't tell us more. The guy who did it can just melt into the woods and never be found. Or he's getting ready to try again with some other poor kid."

"I didn't get the feeling that he really meant to harm the boy," Terrell said.

"You mean besides scaring him half to death?"

"Yes, sir. I see your point. And I agree with you that it will probably be difficult to find him. And he's dangerous. But I'm still wondering if he's something to do with whatever is going on in that family. That comment that he was going to take Rocky to see his father," Terrell said.

"That could have just been a ploy to calm the kid down," suggested Ames.

"That's the most likely, I guess. Sir, any idea when we're going to get a radio phone?"

"Search me. That's between the boss and the mayor."

"FINALLY!" O'BRIEN SAID when they came through the door. "You've had a call from Whitehorse. This guy." He handed Ames a piece of paper. "Sergeant Farley. Could you please call him back. Kiddie all right?"

"Yes, Sergeant. And happy to be back with his mother. Unfortunately, he didn't snap a photo of his kidnapper, so we're working blind here," Ames replied. "All the little fellow could offer was 'Not as tall as you,' pointing at Terrell, black hair, a grown-up. He had a blue shirt on. The boss?"

75

"Ah, well now. He's gone off to the travel agent."

This stopped both men in their tracks.

"He's going away, *again*?" Ames asked.

"Yes, he is. It's not a holiday. His brother's disappeared somewhere in Mexico. I didn't catch the name of the place. Leaving day after tomorrow. We're going to have to cope on our own."

"Is Miss Winslow going with him?" Ames asked.

"I did not inquire as to his domestic arrangements, Sergeant. Now if you'd be good enough to call Sergeant Farley back, I have work to do."

Terrell watched Ames go up the stairs and then turned to O'Brien, shaking his head. "Inspector Darling must be awfully worried about his brother."

"Do you think so, Constable?"

Chastened, Terrell went to his desk and got to work on the notes from the day's trip to rescue Rocky. He took out his foolscap pad and balanced his pencil, ready to write. He had the notes he'd made from the moments when they were still in pursuit of the kidnapper to everything the child had told them. He did not feel satisfied about any of it but had trouble putting his finger on what exactly might be wrong. Knowing that often when he compiled his notes, it helped him think more clearly, Terrell plunged in, using the little black book as a springboard. It was clearly a story in two parts, the hours when they were in anxious pursuit of the kidnapper and his young victim, and the moment everything changed when the boy was found—when it became a case about finding the criminal.

He looked at his notes when he'd reached the bottom of the page and was about to flip it to start another. The point of his dissatisfaction became clearer. The person who abducted Rocky went right into the boy's bedroom. He knew where it was; perhaps he knew the window would be open. He knew about the rabbit. He took the boy out the front door and into his van. Or did he? Did he perhaps tell the child to go out the front door, leaving it to be found unlocked in the morning? During all of this the child had kept quiet. What child would go quietly with a stranger and not kick up some sort of a fuss? Even if offered something nice, he'd surely want to talk to his mother?

Then there was that comment about the boy seeing his father. Either he really was expecting to take the child to his father, or he knew that Rocky's father did not live with him and offered it as an inducement to come along quietly.

"Constable, Ames needs you upstairs," O'Brien said, interrupting his thoughts.

"Yes, sir."

He found Ames contemplating his telephone, as if it might have more to offer. "Sir?"

"Just talked to Whitehorse. They have a pretty mad Rockford Radcliffe—who names a child that, anyway?—in for questioning. He says he had nothing to do with it. Farley seems pretty convinced he's telling the truth, wants to know what we want to do with him."

"What convinced him?"

"Says he sounded genuinely shocked by the idea that he'd hire anyone to kidnap his own child. For one thing, he'd never put his child in that kind of scary situation." Ames sighed and rocked his chair back. "The problem is we have absolutely no evidence."

"Yes, sir. That takes us back to the idea that the kidnapper told the kid that they were going to the father to calm the child down."

"Yeah. I don't see how we can ask them to hang on to him. Not till we've found more to hold him on."

"I agree, sir. Are you worried he'll bolt?"

"Well, if he does, that could suggest he is guilty of paying someone to kidnap his son. We could get them to go through his banking to see if there's any discrepancies there. According to him, he sends most of his pay to his wife. Any expense outside of that might tell us something. Okay. Thanks, Constable."

Terrell smiled and nodded. "Any time, sir." He returned to his desk to finish his notes and get cracking on finishing the fingerprints.

DARLING SPENT HIS last morning at the station reviewing the kidnapping case and anxiously anticipating his meeting with Mayor Dalton just after lunch.

"So the only thing remaining is to find the kidnapper. The boy is safe, and Whitehorse believes the father when he says that he was not involved with it," Darling summed up. "And the Mounties are looking for the kidnapper since he fled from Creston to somewhere."

Ames and Terrell both winced slightly at this summing up.

"No?" Darling asked.

78

"Well, yes, sir. But neither one of us feels that is the end of the story. I feel like we're waiting for the other shoe to drop, kind of thing," Ames said.

"I tell you what," Darling said. "Let's leave the shoe collecting to the Mounties over in Creston. The kidnapper is presumably over there somewhere. Why don't you two get started on some sort of boat and water safety campaign? We've already had a near miss with a capsized motorboat. There's a shoe that's actually dropped. I agree with you that it's unsettling not to know exactly what was behind Rocky's abduction, but you had an objective, get the boy home, and you did that. Until there's another crime actually committed, you might focus on an area where we can be certain trouble is brewing—drinking teenagers trying to commit acts of derring-do on the water."

"Sir," both Terrell and Ames said simultaneously, rising.

"I've got to go see Dalton," Darling said with irritation, as if to explain his shortness.

"Ah," Ames said, pausing at the door.

Darling waved him out. "Run along. If I need your sympathy, I'll ask for it."

SURPRISINGLY, HE NEED not have worried about the mayor being upset. Dalton was all sympathy and concern.

"Beastly!" he declared. "I wouldn't venture down there for all the tea in China. You're always hearing about this sort of thing. It's a good time for it, though. It's always a bit slower here in the summer." He said this with no evident consciousness that it was never a good time to learn one's brother had been kidnapped. "When are you leaving?"

"Tomorrow, sir." Darling was seated in the chair opposite the mayor's desk and was more aware than ever that his chair was slightly lower than the mayor's. He always felt like a boy summoned to the principal here.

"How long d'you expect to be away?"

"That's the thing, sir. I'm not sure. I hope with the help of the local police and authorities we can find him and his party quickly."

Dalton gave a knowing nod. "Good, then. It sounds like the kidnapping here had a happy conclusion."

"Yes. They'll still have to find the kidnapper, but the RCMP are helping there, and I've asked the men to focus on a water safety campaign. We've already had one episode with a drunk boater."

"That's the stuff. And the little woman will keep things steady on the home front."

Darling paused before he spoke. He knew it was best to just leave Dalton with the idea of the little woman stoking the fire while he was gone, but he felt a certain loyalty to his wife's view of things, and one thing she didn't view herself as was "the little woman."

"My wife will be coming with me, sir. It is possible that we may have more success with two of us on hand."

And now the mayor winced. "You surely are not planning on taking a woman into that sort of situation? You're out of your mind! Have to put your foot down, Darling! She'll only get in the way, and you'll spend your time worrying about her instead of finding your brother. That's no place for the weaker sex!" He shook his head energetically. "No, no, no, Darling. I strongly advise against it."

Darling rose. "Thank you, sir. I will be in touch with my men. If anything comes up, Sergeant Ames will be able to keep you abreast."

Dalton rose and reached out his hand. "Good luck, and don't say I didn't warn you."

"No, sir."

He stood back on the street, waiting to cross, feeling, as he always did, relief at being out of His Worship's presence. He'd met the mayor's wife once at a do of some sort. She was short and plump and seemed most deferential, except for that twinkle in her eye that had suggested to Darling that she'd been pulling the wool over the mayor's eyes for years. He remembered wondering at the time why she wasn't the mayor. She'd been witty and trenchant in all her observations about life in Nelson and what made it tick.

CHAPTER SEVEN

———

KENNY HAD DRIVEN THEM INTO town in Darling's car, so Eleanor and Alexandra could come along, and they had stood on the station platform in the early morning sun, waving them off.

"They're so lovely," Lane said, watching until the train had gone around a long bend and Nelson had disappeared into the crest of the cascading mountains that surrounded it.

"They are," Darling agreed. "I must say, they remind me a little of your grandparents."

"Yes!" exclaimed Lane. "You're right. The same affectionate, respectful relationship. Perhaps Eleanor is slightly less bossy than Grandmama, but one doesn't know what goes on behind closed doors. Now. When we get to Vancouver we will go and visit this Martín Delgado. We should arrive at one, and we can take a cab to the consulate. He's expecting us."

"We have sixteen hours to think about this. Shouldn't we leave ourselves something to think about tomorrow?"

"I know," Lane said with a little regret. "I don't want to think about how beautiful it is here right now, and how hard to leave it. Even with the assurance that the children will be watering the garden." She gazed out the window, hearing the muffled rock and clack of the wheels on the rails passing beneath them, and watching the sun pouring out over the passing forests as it breasted the mountain. "Anyway, we must turn our faces to what's coming."

Darling nodded and took her hand. "Whatever that is."

DELGADO PROVED TO be a slight and dapper man in his forties, full of suppressed energy. He was charming, and his staff had prepared quite a lavish lunch for them. "You have had a long journey! I worked in Spain when I was younger, and it is always a shock to be reminded of the distances in North America. In the amount of time it takes me to travel between Mexico City and Monterrey in the north, one could travel the whole length of Spain! It is almost the same distance."

"Thank you, Mr. Delgado. This is so kind. I do feel as if I've been on the train for three days!" Lane said. Delgado held the chair for her, and she subsided happily before the very elegant and welcome lunch.

Darling had become more and more nervous as this meeting approached, as if he feared that Delgado would have found out something terrible, but all Delgado had done was establish communication with his British counterpart and prepare him for the arrival of Darling and his wife.

"But I think I can help, perhaps, pave the way. If you will permit me to give you a few tips. Mexicans, like many

83

people in Europe, for example, appreciate the niceties. Even in a difficult situation, if you wish to secure the help you need, a courteous approach is best. North Americans, I'm afraid, have made themselves unpopular with their tendency to businesslike pushiness. Take time for a proper greeting. It does not help if you criticize the locals within their hearing. In addition to this, I consider it advisable to take some extra money. The police are very badly paid as a rule and will sometimes ask for money for services rendered. Most are not dishonest, to be sure, but they are poorly paid. If you can view these little extra payments to the police as support to their meagre salaries rather than bribes, you may feel better about it." He smiled ruefully. "Of course, it is not strictly legal . . ." He shrugged. "You did not hear this from me."

"We will be at a disadvantage because we don't speak the language," Darling suggested, his heart sinking at the thought of how exactly one "supported the salary" of a policeman in a foreign country.

Delgado nodded. "Many people speak excellent English, Inspector, especially in DF. Sorry, that is a shortcut for 'Mexico City.' In Spanish it is called *Distrito Federal*, the Federal District. But outside the city you may encounter more difficulty. I will recommend you take someone with you to negotiate along the way. It will cost very little. Captain Herridge will be able to recommend someone."

ISABEL SWUNG OPEN the front door of Darling Senior's house before they'd even knocked. "Thank God you're here! We've been so frantic. Roger!" she called. "Frederick and Lane are here!" They heard a shuffling as Darling's father struggled out of his chair.

Darling was shocked. His father was gaunt and appeared to have aged ten years since they'd seen him only a year and a half before. He tried to keep his dismay hidden as he went forward to shake his father's hand. "Dad. We came as soon as we heard." Behind him he could hear Lane and Isabel talking quietly.

"Son." Darling senior nodded and shook his son's hand and then stood uncomfortably for a moment. "We've got your old room ready for you."

"That's fine, thank you." His father's discomfort felt contagious, and Darling filled the nervous space with looking around, and then saying, "I'll just get our bags upstairs, and then I can tell you what they said at the consulate."

Upstairs Darling sat heavily on the bed. "It'll be tight for the two of us on this thing."

"Isabel and I are going to make supper. Or rather, she'll make supper and I'll try to help. I'm bound to learn something." Lane sat next to him and took his hand. "Is it depressing being in your old room?"

He shrugged. "It's depressing seeing Dad in that state. He's never had to confront anything like this."

"But that's not strictly true, is it? I mean, not this, per se, but real difficulty. He was in the Great War. And he had to worry about you and Bob during the last one. And," she added quietly, "he lost his wife. He may have deeper reserves than you think."

Darling smiled sadly. "I see it will be your job on this trip to jimmy me along, trying to cheer me up."

Lane nodded slightly. "I don't think I'd presume to try to cheer anyone up in the face of real trouble. But I think having an eye to anything that is helpful is important. Now then. I heard him clinking bottle and glasses. I'm going to help Isabel, and you and he can have a natter."

"Ha!" Darling pushed himself to his feet, contemplating the unimaginable prospect of his father nattering.

"Thank you for coming," Roger Darling said, when he and Darling had settled with glasses of scotch. Darling was about to speak, when his father continued. "I was disappointed when you chucked over your education and became a policeman."

Taken aback by this sudden dip into the distant past, Darling took a drink, winced, and put his glass down. "You never said. I worried you'd be unhappy. I wanted to do something important, I suppose."

"Yeah, well, I was going to say it seems useful right now." He sighed and drank. "You're taking your wife along." He said this in a noncommittal tone.

Wondering if he disapproved of this as well, Darling said, "She's resourceful. She'll help me see things I might miss."

His father nodded, drank some more, and then sat silent. Finally, as if to himself, he said, "You're lucky in her. Your mother, she was always a lot smarter than me. You'd have been better off if I'd been the one to die, but that wasn't what happened." He shrugged. "I did the best I could, with both of you."

"Dad, you were a good father. The best."

His father nodded slightly, obviously touched. "I just miss your mother, is all. I don't know how I even got her.

Did you know we met at the university? After the Great War. I went back to finish my degree, and she was there, auditing engineering classes. They didn't have too many women there in those days. There was one studying engineering, so I suppose that's why they let her audit. I got through thanks to her. She must have had a soft spot for lame ducks." He heaved a great sigh, put down his glass, and turned to his son. "What are you going to do about Bob?" Then suddenly he leaned over and whispered, "If you don't get him back, I'll become Isabel's next project. She's pretty bossy."

In spite of himself, Darling smiled. Lane was right. He had reserves. "Mr. Delgado has given us the name of someone to see in Mexico City, and that person, Herridge, I think it is, will find someone to accompany us out to the mine Bob was working at. And from there, I don't know. I don't know what more I can do that hasn't already been done. He was out with an American geologist, and the Americans have presumably got people down there as well. I hope it will be clearer once we get on the ground."

"I'm sure you'll be able to do something," his father said unconvincingly.

This remark was as ringing an endorsement as he was likely to get from his father. They sat in silence until, much to Darling's relief, Lane came in to announce dinner.

"Isabel has everything in hand. She started the whole thing hours ago. Come, eat!"

"WHERE DO YOU think you're going?" O'Brien barked at Ames and Terrell.

"It's lunchtime," Ames said, looking at his watch, and then casting a longing glance toward the café.

"Too bad. I have Creston on the phone. They think they have your guy." He lifted his chin toward Terrell's desk and put the call through.

"Sergeant Ames."

"Yeah, hi. This is Sergeant Cooper. We found your party. He was camping in the rough. One of my men spotted smoke and went to take a look. Smoke coming from the woods at this time of year is worrying."

Ames nodded. "How do you know it's the right man?"

"He said so. He isn't really one of life's campers, and he was getting tired of hiding. Told us he was hoping to 'borrow' another car and make his way home. Name's Jim Tanney, twenty-four years of age. Works at the power plant near you there. He said he was paid by someone else to take the kid. Wouldn't give us the name. Maybe you'll have better luck. He has a record for petty things: swindling, drunk and disorderly."

"How does he even have time for work?" Ames said. "All right. Where does he live?"

"Castlegar. You want him brought to you? I have to go across the lake. I can deliver him."

"Yes, thanks. We'll buy you a beer." Ames settled the receiver back into its cradle. "That's that then. We can celebrate with a sandwich. If they set off right now, depending on the sailings, I don't expect to see them till around four. Crime wave over." He made a show of dusting his hands off.

O'Brien shook his head vigorously and reached under the counter for his lunch box. Roast beef sandwich today. One of his favourites. The last of the meat from Sunday's dinner. "I wish you wouldn't, Sergeant," he said. "You'll jinx us."

"Don't tell me you're superstitious, Sergeant O'Brien!"

Terrell, though not superstitious, tended to agree with O'Brien. It did not do to tempt the fates. He opened the door and held it for Ames.

APRIL LOOKED UP from where she was clearing a table and smiled at the two men. Her favourite time of day, when these two came in, though she quite enjoyed seeing their boss as well. "Good to see you. All quiet on the Western Front?" She leaned on the back of the booth and watched Terrell slide into the seat opposite.

"According to Sergeant O'Brien, Sergeant Ames has just jinxed us by saying that our crime wave was over, because the boy's home and the kidnapper has been caught. It's quiet now, but it may not be for long," Terrell said.

"Well, I'm so glad you got that little boy home. Poor mother must have been frantic. What'll it be? If you say 'the usual,' I'll hit you both with these menus. Where's the inspector, by the way?"

"In Mexico, if you can believe it," Ames said. He'd been hoping for the usual but now paused and looked toward the kitchen, trying to imagine what else he'd like. He always had the same lunch. Grilled cheese. It was hard to improve on. Would Tina think that a failing in him?

"Mexico? Does that mean you're in charge again, Sergeant? Why is he in Mexico?"

"I guess so. His brother was working there and has gone missing."

"Is he taking Miss Winslow?"

Terrell nodded. "I think so." Would April want to keep her family name if she ever married?

April nodded with satisfaction. "Good. She'll sort it." She laughed. "I can see you two struggling like trout in a creel. I'll just bring the usual, shall I?"

They both nodded in relief. "Thanks, April," Terrell said, catching her lingering look.

"Oh, for Pete's sake! You two should get on with it!" Ames said, when April had gone to the kitchen.

"You should talk, sir."

"I have got on with it, Constable, as you well know."

"Did you tell your mother you got engaged? Did you even tell Miss Van Eyck?"

"Don't be ridiculous, of course I asked Tina. I mean, I bought the ring. Just before the jeweller was robbed and the place closed." He still didn't like to think of the way the jeweller himself had been robbed of his very life.

Terrell stared at him, astounded. "You mean you haven't given it to her yet?"

Ames looked at his hands, his mouth working. "I was going to, and then with everything that happened the day after I bought it . . . I don't know . . . I think I felt it might be cursed or something. Anyway, I did finally give it to her."

"Now who's superstitious? Those are two things that are not related, Sergeant. I confess, I thought you chickened out. Sir."

Ames felt his face redden. "I did no such thing. I asked her and she said yes. She . . . she didn't seem to expect a ring or anything. She doesn't even wear it. And for your information, I did tell my mother. In fact, you two are singing from the same songbook. She wants me to get on with it too."

"Your mother is a smart woman. I'd listen to her if I were you."

"You think that Tanney guy is going to tell us who he works for?" Ames asked, trying to change the subject, when the sandwiches had arrived.

"He gave himself up pretty easily. He might. I don't think he realizes how serious car theft and kidnapping are. Excuse me, sir." Terrell put down his sandwich and got up. "I'll just get us some more coffee."

"Isn't that April's job?" Ames said to Terrell's back.

Terrell had seen that there was a lull in April's work. They had their lunch and no one new had come in. She was wiping down the counter, and the nearest customer was on the other end.

"Oh, hi!" she said, looking up. She put down the rag.

"I was thinking, there's that new film—" The rest of what he wanted to say was interrupted by a man bursting through the door.

"Sergeant Ames! You better come quick. Something's happened to O'Brien!" Ames bounded out of the booth and Terrell ran to the door. "I was stopping in to ask about something—my neighbour's garbage cans—and I found him slumped over the counter," the man explained as they hurried across the street. "I called the hospital, the doctor is on his way, and they are sending the ambulance down. He was still breathing. I left my wife with him. She has nursing experience."

They arrived just after the ambulance and a doctor was leaning over the sergeant, ordering the attendants to bring the stretcher.

"Might be a heart attack," he said, looking up when Ames and Terrell burst in.

"But he was fine when we left him half an hour ago!" exclaimed Ames.

"That's the nature of a heart attack, Sergeant. They are sudden. Can you get hold of his wife? And stand out of the way."

The stretcher was being hurried in, and Ames and Terrell jumped away. "Yes. What should I say, Doctor . . ." Ames suddenly couldn't remember the name of this young doctor.

"Flight. Just say he's been taken to hospital. Suspected heart attack."

"He's not . . ."

"No, he's not. We've arrived on time."

"If you could get her on the phone, sir, and I'll go collect her," Terrell said, pulling the keys off the hook by the door.

Ames nodded and made for the phone on Terrell's desk.

CHAPTER EIGHT

"**I**T IS VERY *GRAN* INDEED," Lane said when the taxi had deposited them on Cuauhtémoc at the Gran Hotel. A young man in maroon livery and white gloves rushed out and took their bags and led them through a door held open by a sedate older version of himself. The young man stood to attention nearby while they were checking in.

Lane's gaze drifted upward to the astonishing glass vaulted ceiling above them. It was Art Deco at its most magnificent. The elevator was a confection of metal in the centre of a vast lobby, operated by another stately man in livery, who called out the floor softly in English when it opened in the lobby. She'd seen elevators like it from the Belle Époque in Paris.

"Mr. and Mrs. Darling. Welcome to Mexico City. We have a lovely room for you with a balcony overlooking the historic *zócalo*."

Lane turned with interest to the conversation at the front desk. Delgado had been right. Everyone seemed to speak English. Their cab driver had worked in California picking oranges for a number of years and had chattered along all the way into the city about the history of the country and the importance of *el ángel* as a symbol of Mexican independence. He urged them to visit the Palace of Chapultepec. He wondered if they knew his friend Jim Lindsey in San Francisco.

If only, Lane thought sadly, we might do any of those touristic things. Darling concluded the negotiations and the young man hurried forward to take possession of their bags again and steered them into the elevator. Before Darling could say what floor, the young man had said, "*El cuarto,*" to the elevator operator, who in turn smiled at them, nodding.

"It's a beautiful place," Darling said. The young man had thrown open the doors to the balcony, where a tiny table and two chairs were positioned, and then had bowed so low over Darling's tip that Darling wondered if he'd overdone it.

When the bellboy had left, Lane threw herself on the bed and closed her eyes. She felt she could still hear the loud thrumming of the airplane in her ears, but gradually that familiar feeling took her over. What she thought of as the feeling of arrival. As she lay still, Mexico settled around her and she felt her limbs relax into this new place. She could hear Darling go outside to lean on the railing. The noise of people and cars floated up, and she opened her eyes and sat up. Honking was the dominant theme, punctuated by the calls of vendors.

She joined him. An intriguing smell that combined exhaust and smoke from unseen fires as well as unfamiliar food being charred somewhere rose up from below.

"You could muster an entire airborne division in this square. And look at that." Darling pointed to the top of the square where a cathedral of monumental proportions sat, the afternoon sun highlighting its spires and baroque exterior. "I read it is standing right on top of the old temples of the Aztecs. In fact, the whole city is. It's quite a statement of possession."

Lane stood next to him and slipped her arm around his waist. "You know, I feel a bit light-headed."

"I'd love to think that it is my irresistible personality that has you all of a twitter, but I expect it will be the elevation. I suppose one gets used to it."

"I wish being in such an exotic place could just be a holiday. I've been reading about Mexico City and there is plenty to see. But"—she pulled away and looked at her watch—"it is time to get to the embassy."

Having been given instructions, they joined the highway of people on the sidewalk and made for Río Lerma number 71, following a little map drawn by the man at the front desk. They found themselves in a beautiful neighbourhood with quiet streets and large trees.

"This looks like it," Darling said. The embassy was set back from the street and fronted by a classical garden. A gardener in white trousers and a straw hat pointed to the right, and they found some steps leading up to a heavy wooden door.

They were admitted directly into a large chancery and invited to wait by a young man whose English was excellent. The room looked to be furnished for every diplomatic eventuality. A heavy oak table with ten chairs filled the centre of the room and a sitting area with several armchairs gathered around a hearth. The walls were panelled and sported several formal portraits, including one of King George VI in full military kit. Two large windows looked out on a patch of garden, and the sun cast a great rectangle of light across the table.

They had been there for only a few moments when a good-looking young man with dark hair and an expensive double-breasted black suit approached them. "Mr. and Mrs. Darling. How do you do? I'm Randolph Scott, one of the many minor functionaries here." He had a wide smile and a vigorous handshake and, seeing their expressions, added, "I know, like the American actor. Would that my life were that glamorous!" He pulled two chairs away from the table. "Please sit down. Captain Herridge will be right with you."

"This room is the embodiment of subdued and reassuring diplomacy. I wonder if they ever have to light a fire in here?" Lane said when Scott had disappeared.

Darling shrugged. "At seven thousand and some feet I imagine it gets cold here in the winter. I don't know how reassuring they can be under the circumstances."

Just then, the door at the far end of the room opened and a short, very stocky man whose suit appeared a size or two too small for him stood in the door with Scott behind him. Darling and Lane rose. There appeared to be a moment of indecision, and then Scott went around the other man and preceded him into the room.

"Mister . . ." Scott stopped and looked at a slip of paper. "No, I'm sorry. Inspector Darling. This is Captain Herridge, undersecretary here at the embassy."

"How do you do?" Herridge shook hands with Darling and gave a brief nod to Lane and then waved them back into their chairs. "I understand your brother and his colleague have disappeared in the state of Zacatecas somewhere. You must be worried," Herridge said. His thinning pale hair was combed back, and his moustache and thick glasses gave the impression of a near-sighted walrus. His manner was unsettlingly that of someone trying to be sympathetic and failing miserably.

He addressed himself entirely to Darling, leaving Lane free to observe. What she observed at once was the scent of a long-forgotten flower she had loved. She glanced around the room, but it was clear it was purely functional and used only for meetings. No pot of flowers anywhere. She wondered if either man wore a scent, but it was so unmasculine a smell that she dismissed the idea. In that moment she recognized the smell, tuberose, and saw that Herridge wore a small sprig of it in his lapel. He looked to be a man careful of his toilet, but the tuberose surprised her. Perhaps it was a common flower in Mexico.

It did not surprise her in the least that she was not part of the conversation. In the dark blue suit she had brought for the occasion, her handbag held demurely on her lap, anyone might be forgiven for assuming she was but the little woman. And of course, it was Darling's brother, not hers, who had gone missing.

Scott took a packet of Chesterfields from his pocket and offered one to Darling and then to his colleague, and only as an afterthought did he finally look at Lane and hold out the cigarettes. She smiled and shook her head, and with some reluctance he looked away to light his cigarette.

Herridge shook his head. "Beastly business. We'll find someone to go with you who speaks the lingo. González, I think. He'll have a car, if you don't mind the expense. Saves you trying to drive on these godforsaken roads."

Darling readily agreed, and Lane turned away from her momentary contemplation of a portrait of a Great War general whom she struggled to place and looked curiously at Herridge. What was it about him? She had certainly never seen him before. Perhaps it was something in the accent or the timbre of his voice. He reminded her of any number of military men back in Britain. Just as she turned back to attend to something Scott had said, she saw Herridge glance at her. Darling was speaking now.

"Should I exchange my money? I've only got Canadian dollars at the moment," he said.

Scott nodded. "I would. You should change some into American dollars, at a great advantage to you. The Canadian dollar is much stronger than the Yankee dollar, but the US buck is considered valuable here and might come in handy. You can get some pesos for day-to-day purchases, buying gas, and the like. We can recommend a bank, Banco de México. Not sure what you'll get. They've just started letting the peso float."

Now Scott's gaze had drifted to Lane, much to her annoyance. Having accepted the role of the little woman, she was irritated to find herself the focus of anyone's attention.

"The driver, González, speaks English. He will contact you at the hotel tomorrow, and you can set out. In the meantime, I recommend you relax and enjoy what you can of Mexican hospitality. It is justifiably legendary. Wonderful food." Herridge stood to indicate the interview was over. He bowed slightly in Lane's direction and shook hands with Darling. Scott followed suit, but surprisingly offered his hand to Lane as well. She shook his hand and gave him a wan smile.

"I'll show you out," he said.

Instead of going out the entrance at the side of the building they had used when they arrived, Scott took them through another door, through two more offices and a large reception area, and out into a covered patio full of comfortable furniture and made green with rows of plants in large ceramic pots.

"I thought you'd enjoy seeing a bit more of the building. I'll take you out the front through the formal entrance."

They had arrived in a drawing room with an enormous chandelier and thick rugs. There were occasional tables scattered about with silver-framed pictures and crystal ashtrays, portraits on the walls, and, against the inside wall, a long dark oak sideboard with a massive pot of white calla lilies in the centre. It was like the formal sitting room of a manor house.

"It's beautiful," Lane exclaimed. "It must be quite lovely for the ambassador and his family to live here."

Scott smiled. "Alas, the quarters are getting cramped. They are working on designing a new residence, and this will all become offices."

He showed them out the massive double doors onto a patio overlooking the formal garden they'd seen from the street. A set of stairs down either side led to the walk. He shook Lane's hand again and indicated with a touch on

Darling's arm that he should hold back. Lane was down on the path and had turned to say something to her husband, when she saw Scott speaking to him in an undertone at the top of the stairs.

She used the opportunity to step back and look at the building in its entirety. It was lovely, clearly built at the turn of the century on the model of formal buildings of the time. A bit like the bank and city hall in Nelson, built in the same period. The garden and trees softened the look and let it fit in with the rest of the street. Her eye was arrested by a movement of the curtain in a window to her left. A man stood slightly hidden by the drapes, and with surprise she realized it was Herridge. At first she thought he might be looking at them, but then she realized he was looking out at the garden, smoking a cigarette, as if he were taking a welcome break from a hard morning.

Darling trotted down the stairs to join her, and they took the path out to the street. "Very businesslike. I'm sure they all have people to see and things to do. We are but a tiny diplomatic problem, which, in fairness, is not even their problem," Darling said. He steered them back toward the hotel, taking Lane's hand. "Come on, my little woman, let's go explore that cathedral and then get a recommendation for dinner."

She smiled. "Ah, you noticed."

"I certainly noticed. It's not often I get to upstage you. It was quite refreshing. I felt commanding, the master of all I surveyed. In fact, the veritable man of the house, head of the family. Except for that Scott excrescence ogling you."

"I'm sure he wasn't ogling, but I was a little annoyed

because I wanted to fade into the background and just be a fly on the wall."

"You, fading. Ha!"

"And what did he say to you in that little confab as we were going out?" Lane asked sweetly.

"Oh, the usual. Don't take your wife, it could be dangerous. I am beginning to worry about how consistently I've been getting that advice. If I left you behind, you could do all the sightseeing you want." What Darling didn't say was that Scott had warned him that Lane's beauty might attract unwanted attention from what he called "bad actors."

Lane did not dignify this with a response. "That Herridge is an archetype of the British military man. Though a trifle out of shape."

Darling nodded, then had to smile apologetically at a woman in a dark shawl carrying a large round basket full of groceries, who stepped aside to let them pass. "He is a bit of a type. Barky manner, toothbrush moustache, too many sausages at breakfast. I bet you've seen hundreds like him in your day."

"Yes, of course I have," Lane agreed. "We'd better go to the bank first, I suppose. The hotel can tell us where it is."

The sidewalks were busy with purposeful to-ing and fro-ing. Expensively dressed men and women in the latest fashions hurried along the street. Such fashions, Lane thought, as she had seen only in Angela's magazines. It is a capital city, after all, she mused. But in addition, there were many people who appeared to be poorer, or at least less sophisticated, perhaps. Women with dark shawls, either wrapped around them or covering their hair, or rigged to carry a baby. The shawls were like the ones she'd seen for sale in a Mexican shop in Tucson on their honeymoon. Many of the men pushing carts or brooms wore straw hats and loose white trousers.

"Do you know there are almost three million people who live here. In one city. It's staggering. The whole of Canada is probably, what, ten million?" Lane said.

"I'm hungry and beginning to feel a bit tired. You can indulge your passion for data after I've had a meal. Let's go to the hotel, get to the bank, find a nice place to eat, and then do a little sightseeing. And you're right, the rarefied air is a bit debilitating."

"SIR?" SCOTT SAID. He'd been summoned peremptorily to Herridge's office when he'd got back from showing the Darlings out.

"We have a problem."

Scott unconsciously half glanced back at the door, as if the problem had slipped in behind him. "Sir?"

"That woman. You know, I think I know her. From the war. She worked for the SOE."

"Sir?" Special Operations Executive. He almost wanted to look back to where Lane and Darling had gone to ascertain if she remotely looked like the sort of woman who would belong to the SOE.

"Yes," Herridge said, drawing out the word. "Yes." He tapped his mouth with his pen. "Just go away and get the car organized and let me think, will you?" He watched Scott hurry to the door and then said, "I may have an assignment for you."

TERRELL WAS SITTING with Mrs. O'Brien, who maintained a stoic silence as they waited at the hospital.

"Can I get you something, Mrs. O'Brien? Water? Perhaps there's some coffee to be had."

She only shook her head.

"I'm sure he's getting the best possible care." To this she made no response at all.

Finally, after what seemed an interminable period to a young man whose limbs have been confined to a small wooden chair, a tall woman in a white coat came through and nodded at them from across the room. "Hello, you must be Mrs. O'Brien. Constable Terrell."

Terrell and Mrs. O'Brien stood, and she said anxiously, "Will the doctor be coming? I'd like to see him."

The tall woman smiled and held out her hand. "Mrs. O'Brien. I'm Dr. Edison. I have goodish news. Your husband has not had a heart attack as such. It's what we call a cardiac syncope. It's as if his heart flagged suddenly and didn't deliver quite enough blood to his brain. It caused him to faint. He's awake and talking now. He'd like to see you."

Mrs. O'Brien looked past the doctor toward the door. "Has another doctor seen him?"

Dr. Edison nodded patiently. "Come, we'll explain everything when you've seen him." She turned to Terrell with a smile. "We'll send her home in a cab, Constable Terrell, if you'd like to get back to the station. We'll be keeping the sergeant for a few days to do some more tests in case there are other heart problems, and I expect he'll have to rest at home for a few weeks. I'll explain the program to Mrs. O'Brien."

Relieved at being able to leave, Terrell nodded. "Thank you. I'm not sure how we've left things there. Just give us a ring if you want anything."

"Yes, of course. Thank you, Constable Terrell."

"Thank you, Dr. Edison. I'll let the sergeant know."

"IT DOESN'T FEEL the same without him. Kind of empty," Ames commented. He and Terrell were leaning on O'Brien's counter. He was idly holding the half-finished crossword puzzle O'Brien had cut out of the paper. "I could take him this. He could finish it in hospital."

"I'll man the desk if you like, sir."

"That's all right for now, Constable, but if something comes up that needs the two of us, we'll be in a pickle. We can't ask Thompson. He's already on nights. Says he likes it. We should get someone in just till the sergeant's better."

"Well, sir," Terrell said slowly. "There's Miss McAvity. She did take that course this summer, so she knows a good deal about police procedure. It would be better than hiring someone off the street, as it were."

"You sly dog." Ames laughed, aiming a punch at Terrell's arm. "But you're right. You know what this means. Mad Marge back at the café. Can we take that?"

"Well, sir. Miss McAvity may not want to come fill in for just a few weeks. She's just settled back in to her old job."

"Nonsense. Of course she will. Now, I wonder how one goes about this? I suppose I'd better go see the mayor or something. The boss would know, but we can't reach him."

"HE'S A HEART attack waiting to happen," Mayor Dalton snorted. Ames had been ushered into the mayor's presence at once, when the situation was explained. "So, what are you proposing to do? Bloody Darling would be away when this happens. I don't know why I bother with him."

"Yes, sir. We have an idea. Miss McAvity, the fire chief's daughter? She took a course with the Vancouver Police. It's the first step in formal training, and she's back. She knows something about police work, so we thought of asking her to step in, just while Sergeant O'Brien is off."

"What's a girl like that want to do that for? As if she's ever going to be a policeman! It's right in the name, for God's sake! I can't think why McAvity allows it." Dalton fondled his paperweight and screwed his mouth into various positions. "Still. It would be cheaper than hiring a man. It's got that advantage. I suppose I'll have to keep paying O'Brien even while he's off." This wasn't, Ames knew, a serious comment.

"Shall I ask her, sir?"

Dalton heaved a great sigh. "I guess there's nothing for it. If she says yes, get her to come over and fill out the paperwork. She can start tomorrow."

"IT'S ONLY FOR a couple of weeks," Ames said, more to stem the tide of April McAvity's excitement than anything else.

"I know! I know! I'll have to call Marge, though. Oh my God! I'm so excited!" She looked behind her at where Al, the cook, was watching them through the kitchen delivery window, his arms folded across his chest, a cigarette dangling from his lips.

"I don't think it will be that exciting," Ames cautioned. "Judging by O'Brien's output, it's just a lot of sitting around waiting for the phone to ring. He gets through a lot of crossword puzzles."

"I don't care. It's a foot in the door."

"Should you call Marge now? Mayor Dalton wants you over there to fill out papers before closing time." He could see Al behind April, shaking his head and dropping his ashes—gosh, he really hoped into an ashtray and not someone's sandwich.

April clapped her hands and turned to the cook. "You hear that, Al? You get to work with Marge again!"

"Oh, joy," he said. "You want this sandwich or not?"

Remembering the solitary customer by the front window, April nodded energetically and fetched the sandwich. "Okay, see you later, Sergeant Ames, and thank you soooo much!" she said on her way to the front.

"WE'VE HAD A message from the embassy," Darling said, holding up an envelope he'd been given when he'd gone to pick up the key. He looked at his watch. "Shall we try the bar? I think I'm ready for a little drink. And I wonder if we should just have supper here. I'm a little woozy from the altitude, and I feel like I've been on the road for weeks. What is it about modern travel that is so exhausting?"

"Yes to both," Lane said. "I wonder if I can get something so mundane as a gin and tonic."

She could. They were directed to a table on the balcony overlooking the zócalo. A warm light breeze had blown up and they both removed their hats.

Darling opened his envelope. "I'm afraid that cathedral will go unexplored. This is a note from Scott. He'll come for us at eight tomorrow morning. How's your drink?" He raised his own glass of scotch in her direction.

"Scott? Didn't they say a local man would be driving? My drink's lovely, by the way. The lime is not like anything I've seen or tasted. It's a veritable explosion of pure lime flavour. I don't think I'll ever have one of these with lemon again. I wonder if I can bring a bag of these home?"

"We'll have to shelve that important question. I'm afraid we have to concentrate on the problem at hand now, and if it is Scott, at least he speaks English." Darling shot back some scotch. "I hope everything else is going well back at the station. I'm just happy that kidnapping got resolved. Maybe they can have a quiet couple of weeks. I wonder if I should give them just one last call before we plunge into God knows what?"

"Darling, enjoy your drink. We might as well wait to confront troubles when they're upon us. Ames has proven himself many times. He and that smart Constable Terrell will have everything in hand." She swirled the ice in her drink. "I've been thinking about our visit to the embassy, and that plump little undersecretary with the tuberose in his lapel. I wish I could remember who he reminds me of." She sighed and took a sip of her drink. "It's like one time in France. We were pulling into the station at Lyon, spring of '44, I think it was, and there were crowds of people on the platform. They'd fled from the north, and it was a real melee as people were leaving the station, and I suddenly saw someone so like my father I almost called out to him.

Of course, I didn't know at the time that he was already dead, but I certainly knew he wouldn't be in France. The likeness was so uncanny I couldn't take my eyes off him, and then he turned, and it was clear at once it wasn't him. He didn't recognize me, and I could see on closer inspection the nose wasn't quite right. But it really shook me up. I remember my heart was racing and it made me wonder if that old saying is true, that we all have a doppelgänger somewhere on earth."

Darling smiled suddenly and took her hand. "You don't. You are unique and unlike anyone else. Anyone who ever knew you would never mistake you for someone else."

CHAPTER NINE

"**A**LL RIGHT. YES, I SEE.**"** April was standing attentively next to Ames as he showed her what she would be doing. "I answer the phone, make a note here, and send the call to either you or Constable Terrell, by pressing here and holding."

"Yes, that's the stuff," Ames said. He was reassured by her repeating exactly what he'd told her. "Any questions?"

"I don't think so. Oh, is it all right if I take notes from your police handbook? I know we covered most of this at my course, but it was more of an introduction. I'm very excited to see these things in action!"

"Knock yourself out," Ames said. It wasn't the most scintillating job. He wondered how long before she might be driven by boredom to the crosswords. "Oh, and one of us will spell you off so you can go for lunch every day." They hadn't done that for O'Brien because he loved eating the elaborate lunches his wife packed for him.

"Doesn't Sergeant O'Brien always bring his own lunch?"

"Well, yes. But that's him. There's no need, and you might want a break to walk around, go across to the café, I don't know. Go buy a chocolate bar."

"If I go into the café, I'll just feel like I'm on a busman's holiday, thanks very much. I pack a lunch for Dad every day, so I can just pack two. I might want to pop out for a chocolate bar, though." She smiled, her hand resting delicately on the counter as if it were a precious antique.

"Right. Well, I'll let you get on with it." No sooner had Ames turned to go up the stairs and April settled herself on the stool than the phone rang. "Your first call! I'll dash up to my office in case it's for me!"

"Nelson Police Station," April said crisply.

There was a momentary silence, and then a man's voice said, "I thought I'd get one of the fellas. Where's O'Brien?"

"He's away from his desk just at the moment," April said, casting a glance back to where Terrell sat watching at his alcove desk. April realized they hadn't told her what she was to say about the ailing sergeant. "How may I direct your call?"

"Hmm," said the voice. "Well, this is Pete Samuel down at the dock. The *Moyie* just came in half an hour ago, and there's a man trapped in the paddlewheel well. He doesn't look too clever. Direct me to anyone who's gonna deal with that."

"Oh. One moment." April, her heart beating and her hand shaking slightly, performed the pushing of the various buttons and got Ames on the line. "Sir. It's Pete Samuel, at the dock. They found someone trapped by the wheel of the *Moyie*. I'll put you through now." Leaving Ames to deal with Samuel, April hung up and turned to Terrell, who by this time was up and by her side.

"That's a bit strong for your first-ever call. Are you all right?" he asked.

"I just knew it! This job is going to be so exciting!" she said breathlessly, her eyes shining. "Oh, if he's trapped in the wheel, he must be dead. No one would survive that!"

If Terrell was shocked by this girlish excitement in the face of death, he hadn't time to figure it out, because in that moment the front door flew open and Sergeant Cooper burst in. "Constable, where's the sergeant? We've got a problem. Tanney escaped somehow!"

EVEN A CITY with three million people has a beautiful fresh feeling first thing in the morning, Lane thought. The air was cool with an almost endearing underlying note of car exhaust that reminded her of London. The pale sun was just making its way across the zócalo, and she watched the square slowly coming to life. Men and women were sweeping the streets with twig brooms, and a gaggle of schoolchildren in uniforms and leather rucksacks waited at the corner for the streetcars to pass, fidgeting and laughing. Already women were moving along the treed walkways toward the cathedral. Vendors pulled wooden carts into place and began to prepare for the day.

This new day, with all its purposeful and familiar activity, was in such contrast to the urgent quest into the unknown they would be undertaking, but she could not still the lift of happiness she always experienced in the first moments of an early morning, especially in a place she had never been before. Darling, she saw, was lost in his own thoughts, anxiously scanning the road for their car and driver.

"Ah," he said. "Good." He looked at his watch and nodded.

The car, a sombre, black, late-model Chevy, stopped in front of where they stood. Scott, dressed in a brown suit with a jaunty maroon tie, stepped out and gave them a hearty smile.

"Morning! All ready?" He went around the car and opened the trunk.

"Good morning, Mr. Scott. I must say I'm surprised to see it's you. I think I assumed our driver would be Mexican."

"Oh, that's all right," Scott said, taking Lane's bag and smiling broadly at her. He heaved it into the trunk and stepped sideways to allow Darling to throw his in after. "I speak Spanish."

"Darling, you ride in the front," Lane said. "I'll be quite happy in the back." She was content with her fly-on-the-wall status.

"Good to get an early start before the traffic picks up," Scott said, settling into the driver's seat. He reached up and adjusted the mirror.

Lane glanced at him, drawn by the movement of his hand, and saw that he was looking at her. She smiled briefly and turned away, watching the growing activity on the street in front of the hotel. But inside she felt a small tug of alertness. Why had they sent Scott? He wasn't a chauffeur. He was a mid-level functionary at a large embassy. Did they know something about Bob's disappearance that they weren't saying?

Scott pulled into the street and joined the throngs of cars and buses. "We'll go north, out of the city. Have you been here before?"

Both Darling and Lane said, "No" at once, and then Lane said, "It is such a lovely city. So busy. I see a lot of construction, and all these beautiful old buildings."

Scott's eyes, again in the rear-view mirror. "Yes, indeed. I was born here, actually. My father was a professor at the university. Place has a great history. England and America used to be the enemies, but that's all over now. That's Mexico all over. There was a huge kingdom here before the Spanish came. Aztecs. Now they all speak Spanish. Well, mostly. There are a large number of Indigenous languages as well."

Lane smiled. "How interesting. Did you go to school here?"

"Yup. A British school when I was little, then I was sent to Kent to a boarding school as a teenager. Went to Cambridge and then signed up when the war started. I served it here, actually, what with my Spanish being useful. Germans tried to get Mexico to invade the States in '17, so they wanted some eyes on the ground in case of a repeat." Lane nodded. So, possibly he was in intelligence. "But what's Canada like? I have a cousin who went there. He says it is gosh-almighty cold."

"It can be," Darling said. "How long will it take to drive to this place?" he asked, as much to stem the flow of this man's garrulous enthusiasm as to try to prepare himself.

Sighing and lifting his shoulders, Scott said, "It's almost 690 kilometres." He looked at his watch. "It's eight thirty now. With any luck, we'll be there before six. It depends on the highway. It is mostly paved road, but not all. We will stop for gas, and for something to eat."

Lane settled back and looked at the city passing outside the window. A city with three million people seemed at first to be almost unimaginable, but of course London itself, and all the villages it had swallowed on its spread across the country, must be well over that.

"Tell me about your brother, Darling. Has he been here long?"

"I'm not sure. Only a matter of weeks, I think," Darling answered.

"Just his bad luck! I'm afraid this sort of thing isn't unheard of," Scott said with a sigh.

"Well, we don't know exactly what has happened, yet," Darling said, trying to reassure himself that still, after all this time, a simple explanation would be found for his brother's silence. "All we know is that he stopped calling home, and the mining company he works for has not heard from him either. He could simply be lost."

"Let's hope so," Scott said. "Let's hope it is something as simple as that." Lane could hear his skepticism even in the back seat. Being lost wasn't what Scott was imagining, she could tell. But being lost seemed quite bad enough.

At long last the city began to dwindle into scattered low buildings, more and more interspersed with countryside, until they were driving steadily upward out of the great basin where Mexico City sprawled.

"When we reach the top, if you look back that way, you can see the two famous sleeping volcanoes, Popocatépetl and Iztaccíhuatl. It is easier to see when we are out of the city."

"They *are* sleeping?" Lane asked, looking out the back window.

"So far. We have little earthquakes every now and then. The Aztecs believed there was a god who lived inside the mountains."

Maybe, she thought, Bob had been captured by just such a god. Wasn't mining perhaps an affront to the spirits of the earth? She pulled herself together. This sort of thinking was the result of her increasing sleepiness.

They had been out on the highway, on the descent onto the great desert plateau, when Darling, who'd himself been dozing, came to at the feel of the car slowing. Ahead he saw two black cars on the side of the road, and in the middle of the road was a man in a brown military uniform waving them down.

"Please," said Scott under his breath, "let me do the talking." He pulled the car to a halt and rolled down the window.

"*Buenos días, señores.*"

The man who'd stopped them leaned on the car window and said something to Scott, while a second man extricated himself from the group by the cars and looked in at Darling and then walked around to look into the back seat at Lane.

Scott turned to Darling. "They want to see your papers. Do you have your passport and tourist card?"

Darling and Lane fished in pocket and handbag for their passports, and Darling found the two tourist cards they'd bought at the airport in the inside breast pocket of his suit. He collected Lane's passport from her and handed the lot over to Scott. The soldier took them and looked slowly at each document, leaning into the car to scan their faces. He indicated with a cranking motion that Lane should roll down her window.

"To where are you going?" the soldier asked, not relinquishing their documents, and staring directly at Lane.

Darling started to speak, but Scott indicated with a slight raise of his palm off the seat that he should not. He spoke for some moments in Spanish, during which they heard their names, and the word *policía*.

Holding up his hand, palm out, in a "just a minute" gesture, the soldier walked off with the documents and consulted with his colleagues.

"Is this usual?" Darling asked, watching the soldiers congregate around their passports. He wondered if there would be trouble because Lane's passport was still in her maiden name.

Scott shrugged. "Not that usual. I mean, they will stop people in trucks to see what they are carrying, but a private car . . ." He shook his head, then glanced down at his watch. "This is going to set us back some."

"They seem to be looking for someone," Lane said. "I wonder if there has been some sort of escape from a prison, and the authorities have been put on alert?"

"Maybe," Scott said. "I don't know what they expect to find with me and a couple of Canadians. They're just being bastards throwing their weight around, excuse my language."

Darling watched as the discussion continued and then with relief saw that they finally appeared to have satisfied themselves about the papers. The soldier went around to the driver side and handed the papers through the window to Scott. The two men talked for a moment and then Scott nodded and lifted his hand in farewell. "*Sí, muy bien. Muchas gracias.*"

Scott put the car into gear and drove very slowly forward. When the soldiers were well enough behind, he increased his speed, uttering an expletive of some sort in Spanish.

"What did they say?" asked Darling.

"He says that we should be careful because there are bad men on the road. Bandidos. *They* are the bandidos, if you ask me. One time the sister of one of our local employees was riding on a bus to Puebla to see her aunt, and the army stopped the bus, walked up and down with their guns looking at papers, and then demanded that she get off the bus. They said her papers were no good. The soldier climbed off the bus and waited for the girl to get off, but just before she stepped out, the bus driver slammed the door and drove off. He wasn't going to let the soldiers take a young woman off the bus by herself for no reason. Everyone on the bus cheered, but they were all waiting for the shots to be fired."

"How terrifying!" Lane exclaimed, giving vent to her own feelings about being stopped and stared at.

"She was terrified. The bus driver was a real hero."

"Did they ask where we were going?" Lane asked suddenly after some minutes had passed.

Scott shook his head. His eyes in the rear-view mirror again. "No, why?"

"I guess I'm surprised. I suppose they could have stopped us just to have something to do. It must be boring standing about on the road waiting for people to pass by."

The road before them was so straight that the end of it was lost in a watery mirage, as the sun rose higher in the sky. Lane took off her jacket and lay back on the seat, watching the passing of the increasingly dry landscape dotted with shrubs that looked like they'd mastered living without any creature comforts. What she was remembering was the last time she'd been stopped by the authorities.

CHAPTER TEN

AMES HAD INSTRUCTED APRIL TO call Ashford Gillingham, their medical examiner, affectionately—if affection was the word for so tart a colleague—called Gilly. Now he, Cooper, and Terrell stood on the dock looking at the back of the paddlewheel with the skipper, who was in a state of some alarm.

"Oh my God! I think that's him! Tanney. Those are the clothes he was wearing! How did he get in there?" Cooper exclaimed the minute he laid eyes on the corpse, even face down as it was.

"At least it's not one of your passengers, Captain," Ames said to the white-haired man in charge. The man looked resplendent in full captain's uniform, but certainly old enough to have retired. Ames wondered why he still worked.

"Thank heaven for small mercies! We don't take passengers on a daily basis as a rule. We're freight and barges normally nowadays, though we run people up to Kaslo

119

and Lardeau once a week. I don't know how *he* got there. It's nothing we did."

Hearing the captain's alarm, Ames turned to him. "Don't worry. I'm pretty sure this isn't your fault. Did any of your crew spot him in the lake?"

"No. Nobody. I think he must have been just under the surface when we picked him up, if you can call that being picked up." He gestured with a shudder at the body. The man was face down near the right side of the machine, the back part of his body dangling off the beam across the back of the paddle box, the other half inside the paddle box, unnervingly close to where the paddles rotated "He must have got caught on the paddle somehow and got thrown onto the support."

"Did it not affect the working of the wheel?" Terrell inquired.

The captain shook his head once. "It's a big, powerful wheel. We might not have felt a thing. I must say that's a first. Poor bastard."

"Whereabouts do you reckon you picked him up?" asked Cooper. "I swear to God he was with me on the ferry till we were almost at Balfour. We saw you coming behind us on your way here."

"I couldn't say exactly. You can't really see the back of this housing from the decks. We wouldn't have seen anything like this till we docked."

All three turned at a slight commotion behind them, just as Ames was about to ask Cooper when exactly he had last seen his prisoner.

"Can't you people give it a rest?" said Gilly by way of greeting. He wore the expression that was customary on these occasions, a combination of irritation and curiosity. He put his bag down, approached the edge of the dock, and looked over to where Ames pointed. "You've outdone yourself, Sergeant. How do you expect me to get at him?"

Ames held his hand out to Terrell, who handed him his camera bag. "We can take pictures of him there, and then I guess we're going to have to manoeuvre him free. Constable, could you take statements from Sergeant Cooper and the captain and any of his crew that might know something?"

"Sir," Terrell said, readying his notebook and pencil. He'd have liked to stay close to see what form the manoeuvring would take, but he asked Sergeant Cooper if he could join him a little farther up the dock.

A small murmuring crowd had gathered at the top of the dock, unable to properly see what was going on, but knowing something must be up because all the police were there. One man tried to push through and walk down the dock, but Terrell and Cooper, as one, moved toward the crowd.

"I have to ask you to stay back, sir," Terrell said.

"Why should I? Who the hell are you to tell me what to do?"

Someone behind him called out, "Come on, Peters, don't be an ass."

Either this remonstrance from the crowd or the looming presence of an RCMP officer had its effect, because the man backed away, grumbling.

"OH!" AMES SAID, recoiling. They were obliged to stand well behind the boat because the paddle had a decorative screen on both sides, and the paddles themselves could be

121

seen only if they stood some steps away from the aft portion of the boat. He pointed at what he could now see more clearly because he'd been leaning right over, taking pictures. From that angle you could just see the front of Tanney's body hanging inside the wheelbox, and where there ought to be two arms hanging down there was only one. The man's right arm was missing. Ames turned his head away and took a couple of deep breaths to still the rising of his breakfast.

"That won't have been what killed him," Gilly said in a businesslike manner. He turned to Ames. "You're a tropical flower, Sergeant. You should toughen up. Imagine what I see every day of the week." He was leaning over and looking closely down at what was visible of the corpse. "He could have drowned, I suppose, unable to extricate himself from this, or was going down for the third time, as it were, when the paddles picked him up."

"How are we going to get him out?"

"I'm a doctor, not an engineer. You might do *something* to move this thing along."

"I'll wait till the constable has finished with Sergeant Cooper, then between the three of us we can figure it out."

"Among," corrected Gilly. "Fine. I'll get the van boys down here to collect him, and then"—he looked at his watch—"I'll go get myself a nice lunch. Rare roast beef sandwich, I think." Saying this in a hearty manner, as if to emphasize his sang-froid in the face of a gruesomely mangled corpse, he walked back up the dock.

"THAT'S THE THING," Cooper was saying. "I did have him off the leash, as you might say. It's a long ride across the lake and it was hot. I didn't want us to be cooped up in the car, especially because he was pretty ripe with all that camping. We got out and stood at the railing. There was a commotion at the front, and I turned to look because one of the crew dropped those big heavy chains they use, and when I turned back, he wasn't there. I wasn't worried at first; I thought he'd gone off to use the toilet, but when he didn't come back, I got worried. We searched every part of the ferry. It didn't take long to realize he wasn't on the ferry anywhere."

"Do you think he might have jumped off to get away?" Terrell asked.

"I guess he did. Pretty crazy. You've been on that ferry. It's going along at a good clip, churning up water. You could be pulled under in a second. It's surprising because I never got the idea that he wanted to get away. He didn't resist us when we picked him up. He was pretty at ease. Told me it hadn't been worth the effort. He never did tell me who put him up to it."

"Did he seem nervous to you? Like he was afraid of something, or someone?"

"Nope." Sergeant Cooper shook his head. "If anything, relieved it was all over. I don't think he was cut out for a life of crime. He even told me he was coming into some money, and he was going to give up crime, maybe start a business or go make a fresh start somewhere else."

"Did he say how he was coming into money?"

"I couldn't get that out of him."

Ames was waving them over. "We gotta get this guy out of here," he said when they approached. "Gilly's sending the van down."

"Do these blades lock?" Cooper asked the captain.

"There's no need. It takes a powerful push from those drive arms to get them to move. In fact, each arm is driven by separate steam engines." He pointed vaguely toward the rest of the boat. "If we have to do any work we usually just throw a couple of planks up to that support and climb on that way. One of the fellows used to working on the wheel can do it."

"Great," Ames said, vastly relieved that he would not have climb along on a plank over the water in his two-toned brogues to extricate a one-armed man.

"MY WIFE'S PASSPORT is still in her maiden name. I am surprised they didn't become suspicious about that," Darling said. He too was continuing to think about the army road stop.

"Ah, that's no mystery. It's quite common here for husband and wife to have different last names, because they use their mother's family name in the last place. If they aren't used to foreign passports, they would not necessarily have picked that up. Anyway, as you say, they were probably looking for an escaped convict."

Scott had his window open and his elbow resting comfortably on the ledge. His dark hair was ruffled by the warm air blowing in. Very few vehicles were on the road. A bus once, going toward the city, overladen, Lane thought, with luggage loosely and precariously strapped to the top. Mostly, though, donkeys being driven along the side of the road, piled high with wood, or straw, or panniers with who knew what thumping against their sides. Sometimes they passed wooden carts that trundled slowly almost down the middle of the road, drawn by a tired horse or an ox. They seemed to be far from anywhere, and Lane looked across the countryside on both sides of the road to see if there was a village or a ranch the carts might belong to. There was something almost dreamlike in seeing these fellow travellers, apparently unmoored and from another age, not bound to any place, moving slowly across this deserted and shimmering landscape.

About an hour and a half after the stop by the army, Scott slowed, and his passengers saw that they were approaching a gas station with the name Pemex emblazoned on a board above the gas pumps.

"Here. A sign of Mexican independence. Pemex is their answer to Standard Oil." He stopped in front of a pump, and a young man ran out to fill the car.

The travellers got out of the car and stretched. Scott put his hands in his pockets and sauntered to where a bright red Coca-Cola cooler stood just outside the door. "Ah, the national drink of Mexico!" He opened the lid of the cooler and slid a bottle along its rails and pulled it out, glistening and dripping.

"Don't mind if I do," Lane said and gladly accepted the cold bottle. "Do they have other flavours?" She peered into the cooler, holding the cold wet bottle on the back of her neck.

"Fanta is very popular. Orange. Would you like something different?"

"No, this is lovely, thank you!"

Back on the road, slurping Coke through their straws, the party felt very much livelier, and Scott began his history lessons again. "Maybe you have noticed the many Indigenous people here," he began.

Lane sat back contentedly with her drink, the wind battering her hair. Just at that moment she finally felt they'd arrived somewhere very far from where they had been before.

COOPER, HIS MISSION complete, though hardly to his own satisfaction, got into his cruiser and drove off back to his base in Creston, rehearsing how he was to account for the day's mishaps. The extraction of the body, which Ames felt duty bound to stick around for, had been unpleasant and had been accompanied by a number of irritated exhortations and much cursing by the crew of the *Moyie*. But eventually the body had been loaded up and driven to the morgue in the hospital, where Gilly told them they might expect to be able to come and take a look and get a report sometime around four that afternoon.

Ames and Terrell now sat in Ames's office, going over the information the constable had collected.

"The deceased, James Tanney, was standing about ten feet away along the railing, starboard side. Cooper, I mean Sergeant Cooper, was not unduly concerned, since there was nowhere he could go, and he didn't think Tanney would take the risk of jumping overboard, especially since he'd come along willingly and just wanted the whole thing to be over. He said he took his eyes off him because there was a commotion at the front. One of the crew dropped a heavy chain on the metal deck and it made a lot of noise, and he turned to look at that. When he looked back, Tanney was nowhere to be seen. He, the sergeant, thought Tanney had gone off to the WC, but when he didn't come back, he began to go up and down looking for him. By that time, they were entering the narrows toward Balfour, and Cooper affirms he wasn't on the boat. At the dock, they held up the traffic so that he and the crew could check who was in the vehicles. Once the ferry was unloaded, he and the crew did one more thorough search, but his prisoner was clearly gone. He got in his car and rushed here to let us know." Terrell turned the page, ready to report on the interview with the skipper of the paddlewheeler.

"So," Ames said speculatively, "Tanney did take the risk of jumping off, maybe got drawn under the ferry or hit his head or something, and along comes the *Moyie* and scoops him up and brings him here. Poor devil!" He gave a sigh of commiseration for Tanney's untimely end and then turned back to Terrell. "What did he say about Tanney's involvement with the kidnapping?"

"Well, sir, that's the thing. Not very much. Tanney told Cooper that he'd rather just talk to us and explain everything when he got here. He assumed we'd take him into custody. Cooper said several times he didn't seem very worried, because the boy hadn't come to any harm, and he'd let him go, and anyway, when he got out of prison for attempted kidnapping, he was coming into some money. Cooper was going to try to broach the subject of the money on the drive into town from Balfour, with the result that we don't know about that either."

The telephone rang on Ames's desk and he leaned over to pick it up. "Ames here." It was April.

"Sir, you asked me to find out if there is any police record for James Tanney. He was picked up in Castlegar and spent the night in the jail for an affray after a night of drinking back in December."

"In Castlegar?" Ames asked, trying to get used to the idea of April calling him "sir" in that formal way.

"Yes, sir. He lives, er, lived there. With his mother. He worked at the electric power plant. I have his address, and the name of his mother if you want. Myra Tanney. She's in a wheelchair. I guess he looked after her. Oh, she doesn't have a telephone. I asked. You wouldn't want to tell her something like this over the phone, anyway."

He wouldn't want to have to tell her this by any method. "Thanks . . ." He was almost going to say "April" but in keeping with the formality she'd established, he said, "Miss McAvity. Can you type that up?"

"Yes, sir."

Ames put the receiver into its cradle. "Do you think she's going to call you 'sir' as well? It will be very strange for you going around with a girl who calls you 'sir' all the time."

Terrell ignored this and waited.

"The poor bastard has a mother in a wheelchair. We're going to have to go see her after we've met with Gilly. Shall we brave Marge? I'm hungry and it's after one thirty."

Marge evinced no great joy at seeing them come through the door and make for a booth by the window. While April had been away, Marge had been dragged, apparently kicking and screaming, out of retirement and had made every patron she served suffer as a consequence. She seemed to reserve

128

her special malevolence for the police, who she believed ought not to be sitting around in cafés while the streets were not safe for law-abiding citizens. No doubt her antagonism had redoubled because they had taken April off the job and forced her back into the café. "Well?" She stood with her arms akimbo, glaring at them.

"It's nice to see you back, Marge," Ames said, reverting to his attempts to win her over with an endearing smile, which had proven singularly unsuccessful during her previous stint. Seeing she was not disposed to exchange pleasantries, he plowed on. "I'll have the grilled cheese and maybe a coffee?" He realized framing this as a question made him sound tentative and he cursed himself inwardly.

"I'll have the same, then," Terrell said, also trying his smile.

Marge turned on her heel and went back to the window to bark the order at Al, who had been watching the interaction with interest. It amused him, watching the police trying to be nice to Marge. No one else bothered.

He didn't mind her, himself. She smoked, one pastime they had in common, and she wasn't disposed to lecture him about it like April did.

"Maybe you should take Miss McAvity," Terrell said. "I'll stay back with the phones. She's bound to be sympathetic with a mother who's lost her son."

"You're saying I'm not?" Ames said, smiling. "Not a bad idea. We've never had a woman to deploy for this sort of thing before. If Tanney's mother is the only next of kin, she's going to have to identify him. I think April would be just the ticket to have sitting beside her."

"It's a puzzling case, sir. Not a good old-fashioned murder, but interesting nonetheless." Terrell pivoted to what was on his mind. "We'll have to find out if Mrs. Radcliffe knew Tanney, and Mr. Radcliffe as well, though he might not tell us if he did, especially if he was behind the kidnapping . . ." He hesitated.

"The boy did say that Tanney told him he was being taken to see his daddy," Ames pointed out. He leaned well back in his seat as Marge approached with their coffee. He could never quite shake the fear that she might dump it into his lap one day. He smiled. "Thank you!"

"Thank you, Marge." Terrell leaned forward. "That is so, sir, but was it just a way of making sure the child didn't make a fuss?" He leaned back again and poured cream into his coffee.

Ames sighed and watched Al slap the two grilled sandwiches onto the counter. Would Marge try to punish them by leaving them there until they were cold? "Could be. But what if Rockford paid Tanney to take him? He could have had the child brought to him without having to leave work to get him. He sure as heck doesn't get along with his wife, and he knows she'd never give the kid up willingly."

"Yes, that's true enough. He made a big fuss about how he wasn't set up to look after a child, though."

Ames sighed. "To throw us off the scent? But if not him, who? Her parents? They don't seem set up for a child either."

Ames's fears were for nothing. Marge came over and gracelessly plunked the plates down and then walked toward the door to the kitchen, pulling a packet of Player's out of her pocket.

At four o'clock precisely, April put a call through to Ames. It was Gilly with the results of his autopsy.

"Your boy was shot," he said, "right through the head."

CHAPTER ELEVEN

I T WAS NEARING EIGHT IN the evening when they finally
bumped along the cobbled streets of Fresnillo. Lane and
Darling both felt as if they'd been bathed in dust. The
setting sun threw a golden glow across the desert that
immediately made it seem less desolate. Scott drove slowly
up the main street, looking right and left. "I'm not sure
where this place is." He stopped the car and stuck his head
out the window, calling to a passerby, who was pushing a
bicycle along the sidewalk.

A woman walking in the opposite direction with a large
cloth-wrapped bundle stopped to watch. The man with the
bicycle looked curiously at Lane and Darling and waved his
hand in the direction they'd been going, and then indicated
a left turn. The woman said something, and Scott thanked
them both and put the car in gear.

"It's not very far. This wall we're passing is part of it.
We have to honk so they'll open the gates."

Lane turned her attention to the wall. It was then she

saw that they were indeed outside a wall that had very small windows, and high up.

"The gate is around the next street."

"It's a walled-in place," Lane said. "Like Spanish compounds."

"Yes, an *hacienda*. Everything will be inside. All the houses, even a school for the American and foreign children probably." He turned a tight corner and stopped at an enormous dark wooden gate in the wall and honked once. To the left of the gate, a heavy door creaked open, and a very stout old man came out and looked at them.

"*¿Sí?*"

Scott waved and said something and indicated his passengers.

The old man shuffled forward, looked in at them and shrugged, and went back through the door and closed it. In due course the two gate doors were pulled open with a good deal of loud creaking, and they were waved through. Waiting until the gate was closed and bolted, Scott asked him for directions to the manager's house.

Inside the gates, the road went both left and right, and appeared to skirt the whole perimeter of the enormous compound, past houses that were built against the wall. To their right, they could see where the road turned sharply left, still following the wall. On the left was a long building and then more houses. They were, however, directed straight ahead, toward the middle of the hacienda, where beautifully tended lawns and gardens were laid out on either side of a drive. A house loomed up ahead of them, with another large building next to it, the two properties separated by a thick growth of cascading bougainvillea.

"Good. I think this is it. Inspector, can you go knock on the door? Find out where I can put the car."

Darling and Lane got out and stretched. The air was cool and felt refreshing after the long drive. "I feel rumpled and pummelled," Darling said. "You don't seem to have suffered in the least from ten hours of desert driving." As they approached the door, it opened and a man in a white jacket stood before them.

"*¿Inspector y Señora Darling?*"

"*Sí*. Good evening," Darling said, removing his hat.

The man stepped aside and reached for Darling's hat. "Good evening, señor. They are expecting you. Please follow me." He turned and made a sign to Scott, who was waiting by the car for instructions.

Lane felt not unscathed by the journey, but rather dusty, creased, both in clothing and person, a sensation that was heightened by the quiet luxury of the place. She felt they ought to have been let in through the back door. They were led down a wide hall lined with a long, narrow, wooden cabinet with a massive vase of white flowers, calla lilies and tuberose. Lane smelled them with delight. The bouquet appeared doubled by its reflection in the huge mirror framed in dark wood. The man opened a door and announced, "Inspector and Señora Darling," and ushered them through.

They were in an enormous sitting room filled with furniture that would not look out of place in an English country house. A tall, thin man, impeccably dressed, came forward and seized Darling's hand. "Inspector Darling. You're here at last! I'm Thomas Fine and this is my wife, Leonora. Mrs.

134

Darling, please, please, come in. You must be exhausted." Mrs. Fine proved to be nearly as tall and slender as her husband and was dressed in an elegant dark-blue dress, her pale gold hair pulled back into a bun. They were both in their fifties, Lane guessed.

Lane gazed at the fireplace, where a modest fire burned quietly. It was only then that she realized the temperature had indeed gone down. "I'm sure we are not as exhausted as Mr. Scott from the embassy. He drove the whole way."

"Dinner will be ready when you have had a chance to settle in and wash up. Don't worry about anything. Javier will make sure your bags are brought in. Ah, Mr. Scott, I presume." Scott had appeared at the door of the sitting room, shown there by the same man who'd let them in. "Honey, let's get these poor people to their rooms and let them wash up, and then something to drink?"

The door opened and Javier stood respectfully. "The rooms are ready, Señora Fine."

Mrs. Fine stood up. "Thank you, Javier. Mrs. Darling, Mr. Scott. Javier will show you to your rooms. You have your own bathrooms so feel free to spread out your things. Wash the travels away and come down in, say, half an hour for dinner? Inspector, may I have a quick word?"

"THEY LIVE A bit like grandees," Lane commented, looking around their palatial bedroom. She took off her hat and went into the magnificently tiled bathroom to splash cold water on her face. It was going to take some doing to get her windswept hair into some sort of order. "This place is like a palace in Spain. I hadn't realized how much dust

135

we accumulated. I've ruined this towel, and I'm afraid I've smudged up her lovely chintz sofa. I think I'd better change out of this suit and put on the flowered frock."

"O for a mine manager's salary," Darling said, testing the bed. "But I suppose this is all company housing. Maybe they are both just like you and me and shrink back to normal-people size when they return to their modest middle-class house in Philadelphia or wherever they come from."

"They are very hospitable, and seem genuinely concerned about Bob," Lane said, pulling her dress from the suitcase. "Though there is something of the British upper class, what with the servants."

"You can talk. Well, I'd better gird up my loins and prepare to make small talk through dinner, as much as I would like to close my eyes right now." He scrabbled about in his suitcase for a clean shirt and went for a splash in the bathroom.

Moments later he was back, drying his face. "Fine said he and I and Scott are to meet after dinner in his study. He is going to go over what's been done. Tomorrow we'll meet the police, and I guess we'll spend the afternoon getting ready to ride out. Every day that goes by might put Bob in greater danger." Tucking in his shirt, he mused, "What I don't understand is why there's been no ransom demand or anything. Surely if he'd been snatched by some bandit, that is what we'd expect?"

"You're worried he might have had an accident instead."

Darling shook his head. "In truth, I don't know what I should be worried about. This whole thing is far out of my experience in every way. All I know is that I'm tired, worried, and hungry, in no particular order."

Downstairs, feeling more human, Darling, Lane, and Scott found Thomas Fine busying himself with making drinks from what appeared to be a well-stocked bar. He dropped ice cubes into the glasses. "You won't need to worry about these. All our ice is made from boiled water. You have to boil everything here!"

Darling hadn't known he ought to be worried. "It's very good of you to put us up."

"My dear inspector, think nothing of it. We are absolutely sick about your brother and his colleague, Arnie Grant. The Grants live in the hacienda here, and his poor wife is frantic. And there's the guide, Pablo Ramírez. He and his family live in town. We've had people out from the moment they didn't return. The police say they've been looking as well." He stopped, his skepticism about the police evident in his tone. "Listen, we can really get down to brass tacks in the morning. I have organized a meeting with the local police for us tomorrow, and we can firm up our plans."

"Yes," Darling said. "The sooner the better. I look forward to going out there."

Fine nodded. "Good, then. I can provide a man to guide you and some mounts. What about you, Scott?"

Scott, who was sitting deep in an armchair with his legs spread out toward the fire, a scotch in hand, nodded. "I'd like to go along, sir, if you've enough horses."

"Good, then," Fine said. "For now, let's get these down us and then have supper." With drinks in hand, they settled in front of the fire.

Lane could feel the exhaustion stealing over her in waves as she sat. The fire murmured in the grate, adding to her

137

languor. She thought about the country they had driven through and imagined traversing it on horseback. It had seemed so vast, stretching to the horizon in all directions. Would one ever be able to find anyone lost in that great empty wilderness? She turned at the sound of Leonora Fine's voice.

"Tell me about your trip here. What sort of help did you get from the embassy? They telephoned here to say you were coming."

"I wouldn't say we had a lot of direction, but they have provided us with Mr. Scott both as driver and translator. Their remit here must be enormous, and one lost Canadian must be very small on their horizon. I suppose it falls on them because until last year Canadians were considered British subjects. I think they've been quite generous, when all is said and done."

Mrs. Fine said, "And how are you finding Mexico?"

"I've scarcely had time to form an opinion," said Lane. "It is very different from any place else I've been. We've been very worried about Frederick's brother. I only wish I spoke Spanish—I feel I could be of more use. Mr. Scott has been a godsend."

"Of course you're worried. My goodness, of course you are! I was so interested to learn from the embassy that you would be coming with your husband. You don't have children?"

Lane smiled and shook her head. "We've been married less than a year. Have you children?"

Mrs. Fine sighed and lifted her head to look at her husband. "We were never able to. Just as well, I guess. Thomas's work keeps him very occupied, and anyway, there are plenty of children here. The geologists, engineers, and foremen who live here all have children. We have a little school with two very nice teachers. One Mexican and one American."

Dinner was served by Javier, who rolled it out on a trolly from somewhere in the back. Lane looked at her plate and realized she was absolutely famished. They had stopped briefly in León for a sandwich-like affair on a bun, called a *torta*, with a nourishing mix of chicken, black beans, and avocado, and another soft drink, grapefruit that time, but that all seemed to have worn off long ago.

"This is delicious," Lane said. "This rice. I'm not much of a cook myself, but I must learn how this is done."

"My cook, María, is a marvel. I'm sure she will be delighted to show you. She's tried to explain it to me, but of course I've very little time, with the charities, and children, and my responsibilities. We have an annual event for the children of the Mexican miners coming up in a short time, but with Bob . . ."

"And there's been no communication," Darling was saying to Fine. "If he'd been kidnapped, wouldn't there be a ransom note?"

"That's why it's more likely an accident of some sort, though an accident that took all three of them would be unusual. If he was kidnapped, the lack of a ransom demand is most unusual. The damnedest thing is that I'm sure people in the town know things, and they're likely afraid to tell us or the police."

"There's just the dessert to go and then you men can go discuss things and make plans," Mrs. Fine said. "María's

139

made flan, a most typical Mexican dessert. It will remind you of a French custard, and that is because the French, during their very brief sojourn here, managed to make quite a culinary impact."

Lane, divided by the excellence of the flan and her concern about being sidelined with her hostess when she wanted to be in the conference with the men, tried to steer the conversation back to the purpose of their trip. "Is there a group with political motivations that might have been responsible?"

"I'm sure Thomas will go over everything," Mrs. Fine insisted, putting her napkin back into its heavy silver ring, and standing up. "Come, Lane. May I call you Lane? Let's go relax in the sitting room and leave the men to it. Please call me Leonora."

It really was like an English manorial house, Lane thought, feeling a growing sense of rebellion. The women go off to the drawing room and the men sit around with cigars and port discussing the real grown-up business.

But she was to be surprised. The minute they'd made themselves comfortable on the armchairs on either side of the fire, Leonora leaned forward and said, "I'll tell you this right now, I think Thomas is depending too much on the authorities. That is why I was thrilled to learn you both were coming down in person. I think he's being fobbed off with official reassurances. And to answer your astute question, there are any number of political groups with one complaint or another. But there are also out-and-out gangs, and in fact some of the political groups exhibit some very gangland traits. Thomas doesn't speak Spanish, but I made a bit of an effort when we were posted here. He doesn't need to; his main business is with the English-speaking professionals, who include Americans, Canadians, even some Europeans. Below him there is the cascading hierarchy of who deals with whom. But I deal with the servants, you see, and I hear things."

"Oh. I do see," Lane said, with a flood of relief that they were not to be engaged in small talk. "I imagine that what you hear is different from what he hears?"

"Not entirely, but in some respects, yes. He is right that people in the town know things. He's not right that we can never find out what they know. Tell me, does your husband take you seriously?" She tilted her head slightly, with a look of both curiosity and surprising vulnerability.

This question, posed suddenly like this, surprised Lane, and she had to think about how to answer. "He does, yes, I think," she said slowly. "He is the police superintendent in a small town, in a very rural community, but it is an interesting place, with quite a League of Nations sort of mix of people. I've been able to help a couple of times because I speak Russian and German and whatnot. He jokes about my interference, but yes, on the whole, he does."

Leonora turned and gazed at the fire. "You're lucky, then," she said after a moment. "I attended Wesleyan, and when we met—Thomas was a Harvard man—we seemed to share a good deal more than we do now. He used to say he felt so lucky marrying an intelligent girl, but over the years, as he's climbed the ladder of responsibility, he's reverted to type. His father was an awful old misogynist, kept his wife firmly under his thumb. Thomas at least isn't rude about it.

141

In fact, he's very dear, and he lets his responsibilities quite weigh him down. I think he fondly imagines he's keeping me from having to worry. He's come to see women as delicate flowers to be protected from all forms of stress and worry."

"But you do worry," Lane said.

Leonora smiled wryly. "I don't think he has the first concept of what sort of worry three miscarriages creates. Poor thing surrounded me with comforts to help me 'get over' them. But never mind that. It is long in the past. I do worry about what's happened to Bob. The servants, María in particular, have heard things in the town. There is a bandit who has a sort of compound about thirty miles from here, well hidden up in the hills. He's kidnapped Americans before. María thinks they have him. She says he has a small army of at least thirty men, and many more in towns who back him, willingly or unwillingly. He supports his own men by exacting payments from all the local landowners. In New York, where I grew up, we'd call that 'protection' money. And they're armed to the teeth."

"Do you think he is wanting to extort money then? From whom?"

"The mine owners, I'd think. Only no one has heard from this man. I've told Thomas what I've heard, and he said he has the thing well in hand. He thinks Mexicans are unreliable, so he discounts anything I've heard from María."

"You mentioned you're not confident in the police."

"I'm not. I mean, there are many dedicated officers, but they aren't well paid, and bribing is a bit of a way of life here. They could know everything, but I wonder if they're being paid to keep quiet and pretend to keep looking. Don't get me wrong, Thomas has done everything, including sending out some of the security men who look after the property here. But they've come back empty-handed. In fact, they were allowed right into the compound, and the headman—they call him 'El Jefe,' singularly unoriginal I must say—generously let them look around, and they found no trace of Bob. He doesn't deny his involvement with it. In fact, he said he would look into it himself and send word. I'm certain he's just bamboozling everyone. In fact, María said she's heard that he has more than one compound, and a house in Mexico City!" She put her hand on Lane's arm. "But Lane, I think Bob is safe for now. I'm certain I'd have heard if he'd been killed. He is worth more alive than dead."

Lane nodded, surprisingly relieved by this bit of logic. "You agree we should go ourselves."

"Yes, though I don't think anyone expects *you* to go. The embassy told Thomas that your driver is to go with him, and of course we will send one of our men, too, as guide. The compound can only be reached on horseback. Do you ride?"

Lane was surprised. "I do. And I want to go."

"Thomas would never allow such a thing, I warn you. He will actively discourage it. You are going to have to dig in if you insist."

Lane turned at the sound of the men's voices in the hallway. Mrs. Fine said quickly, "While the men are with the police, why don't you go with María when she does the marketing? It's a lovely market." She sat back and smiled as her husband, Scott, and Darling came into the room.

143

"What have you ladies been up to?" Fine said, smiling broadly and making for the liquor cabinet. "A little nightcap? We have a full day tomorrow, the three of us."

"I've just been telling Lane about our charity for the school in town."

"Good. Good. Darling, Scott, a cognac?"

CHAPTER TWELVE

"**S**HOT?" AMES ASKED, DUMBFOUNDED. "HOW do you mean, shot?"

"I mean," said Gilly, "someone lifted a handgun and emptied a bullet into the back of his head. He didn't drown. He was already dead when he reached the water."

"Were you able to get the bullet?"

"I was not able to recover it, no. It exited above his left temple. A little lower down and it would have lodged in his brain."

"I don't understand how we didn't see that when he was taken off the wheel."

"Ah," Gilly said. "That's because whoever did it managed to shoot him where hair would cover the wounds. I would almost say that was deliberate, possibly even professional, though we can't know. The blood you'd normally see was probably sloshed off by his time in the water. There are still traces of burn marks, though."

Ames rubbed his eyes tiredly when he'd hung up the

phone. "You heard."

"Yes, sir. I'm as surprised as you. That almost certainly means that whoever did it was on the ferry with them. Someone knew they would be crossing and got on the same sailing," said Terrell.

"Exactly. And about the only way we could find the killer is if we knew who every single person was on that sailing."

"That would be difficult. They don't sell tickets and have no records of who sails. We'll have to find out everything we can about who this Jim Tanney was and what sort of trouble he might have gotten himself into. I'll compile everything I can while you and April go to talk to his mother, sir."

April was daunted by the task. She'd never had to tell anyone this sort of appalling news before. Her father had had to deliver bad news, she knew, in the course of his duties as the fire chief. She stood up straight and said, "Yes, sir. Of course, sir. Would you like me to drive?"

"You drive?" Ames asked in surprise.

"Of course, sir. It *is* 1948. I drove all over hell's half acre during the war, collecting scrap metal and the like for the war effort."

"Of course. I'm sorry. Can you stop calling me 'sir'?"

"No, sir." She held up the keys.

"Yes, okay. Watch the gearshift. It's fussy."

She nodded. Once in the car, she eased it into the street and made for the road to Castlegar. "Um . . . I guess you've had to deliver the bad news before. How do people react, generally?"

"All kinds of different ways. Mostly people actually can't believe what you're telling them. It's kind of awful when

146

they keep telling you it can't be true. Then we have to take them to see the deceased to identify them." Ames winced as April changed gears to take the hill out of town.

"Sorry, sir," she said. "What would you like me to do when we get there?"

"I guess leave the talking to me, but you might have to get a glass of water, or a hanky, or even make some tea. I think a woman might be a comfort."

"Are you suggesting men can't be comforting? Anyway, I'm not sure how much comfort I'll be. I've never done anything like this."

Ames smiled at the worry in her voice. "You'll be just fine. I've seen how you deal with people. You're always nice no matter what they throw at you."

They rode along in silence for some miles, then Ames, who was himself dwelling on his anxiety about their sad errand, tried to push it to back of mind. "How was the course in Vancouver? Did you actually enjoy it?"

"I really did, though some of the boys I was with were downright hostile. They said girls had no business taking work that should rightly go to men. One man, a vet, got asked to leave the course because he had a really bad temper; he'd had a really bad war, one of the secretaries told me, and he blamed me. Well, not me exactly, but women in general. He just fixed on me because I was there. He saw me as he was being escorted out and really let loose. He said they'd never be able to afford to get rid of him if 'certain women' stayed in their places. The commander told me not to worry about it. He said the guy would never have made it anyway, because he was insubordinate, and he drank.

147

I felt sort of sorry for him, if you want the truth. Where could a guy like that go?"

Ames nodded. He wasn't sure how he himself felt about women on the police force. It seemed to him that it was dangerous, and it just didn't seem like the right sort of job for women. On the other hand, there was Miss Winslow. He had no idea what she'd done before, but she was braver than all get-out and knew how to get herself out of scary corners. Could every woman do that, or was she just an exception? And then there was Tina. She'd actually done a man's job in a dangerous place. You didn't see her cringing at the first sight of danger.

He still had warm thoughts about Tina sloshing around in his breast when they arrived in Castlegar.

"Here's the address, sir. Can you just read it out to me?" April fished in her handbag, pulled out a scrap of paper, and handed it over.

The house proved to be around the corner from a Texaco station. It was small, set back in a messy and unkempt yard. It looked like the lawn had not been mowed for months. Ames knocked on the door and stepped back. April stood behind him. There was no answer, so he rapped louder, calling out, "Mrs. Tanney?"

He stopped and listened. There was an indistinct voice coming from inside, and then the sound of a Yale lock being turned, and the door was pulled open. Sitting in a wheelchair, frowning up at them, was a woman of nearly sixty, Ames guessed. Her hair was white and pulled back in a ponytail, the thin wisps of hair cascading down a thick, padded, and none-too-clean dressing gown. "Yes?"

"Ma'am, are you Mrs. Tanney?" Ames asked.

She nodded. "If you're selling something, I don't want it."

"No, ma'am, Mrs. Tanney. I'm Sergeant Ames from the Nelson Police, and this is Miss McAvity. Can we come in?"

"Why? What's happened?"

April stepped forward. "May we come in, Mrs. Tanney? It's important." She used her kindest voice.

Mrs. Tanney moved the wheelchair back with a show of reluctance but left room for them to come in.

Ames was surprised to see how tidy the little sitting room was. The state of the yard had led him to expect the inside of the house to be as bad or worse, with accumulated garbage and unwashed dishes. Instead, it was tidy and dusted, and what he could see of the kitchen was also orderly.

"Something has happened to Jim," she said simply. "Only time you people ever come here is when he's in trouble. What's he done this time?"

Ames's heart fell and he was about to speak, when April came forward and sat next to Mrs. Tanney and took her hand. "I'm so sorry, Mrs. Tanney, but a body has been found, and we have reason to believe it may be your son, Jim."

Mrs. Tanney looked away but did not take her hand back from April. "Found how?" she said, finally.

If Ames was surprised by April's stepping in, he didn't show it. He said gently, "He was killed, Mrs. Tanney."

She turned her eyes back to April. "I don't know why I'm not surprised. Did he . . . did he suffer?"

"No, ma'am. He would have died instantly."

She finally glared up at Ames. "How do you know that?"

149

"He was shot by someone. He was travelling back with an RCMP sergeant from Creston on the ferry."

"He was arrested?"

Ames took a surreptitious deep breath. "Miss McAvity, could you see about a glass of water for Mrs. Tanney?"

April let go of Mrs. Tanney's hand and stood up, making for the kitchen.

"He was arrested for kidnapping a little boy in Nelson."

"Kidnapping? *Kidnapping*? That's ridiculous! Jimmy would never hurt a child!"

This, thought Ames, must be the denial. He looked up with relief when April came back with the water. "He didn't hurt the child, Mrs. Tanney. In fact, he did the right thing. He turned himself in, leaving the child to be picked up by the Mounties."

"Then why was he shot when he was in the custody of the RCMP?" Mrs. Tanney turned to April and took the water and slurped it, her hand shaking. April held her hand under the glass. "I don't understand," Mrs. Tanney said. "No. That's a lie. I do understand. Just what you'd expect from the Mounties! You hear about that sort of thing all the time."

"We don't understand either, Mrs. Tanney. It's possible someone followed them onto the ferry," April said in a soft voice.

"Can you tell us anything about his friends or what he did with his time? He worked at the power plant, I understand," Ames said.

"Yes, he was making very good money. He told me he'd had a promotion. He wasn't involved in anything shady, if that's what you're trying to say!" Mrs. Tanney's eyes flashed with sudden anger. April took her hand again, and she appeared to calm down. She took her hand back. "I don't know about his friends. We lived in Penticton when he was young. He hasn't kept up with any of his friends from there as far as I know." She glared at Ames. "You're acting like him getting shot is his fault!"

"We just want to find out what happened," Ames said soothingly. He waited a beat. "Mrs. Tanney, would you be up to identifying him, or is there another family member?"

"There's no one else," Mrs. Tanney said.

"We could drive you to Nelson and then bring you back," Ames said.

"How am I supposed to go anywhere in this?" she asked, indicating her wheelchair.

"Oh, that's all right," April said. "We'd be going to the hospital, and they can provide a wheelchair there."

WHILE DRIVING THE reluctant Mrs. Tanney back to Nelson, Ames thought about Jim Tanney. There was something funny about that promotion. According to Sergeant Cooper, Tanney had time to go around kidnapping a child and then hide out in the woods. None of that sounded like a responsible plant foreman. And there was that talk of money again. He'd said he was coming into money, and his mother said he'd had a pay raise.

Mrs. Tanney had only nodded when the sheet was removed from Tanney's corpse down to the shoulder, and then had sat in the wheelchair, looking away, waiting to be wheeled back to the car.

"On the way back to Nelson, we'll stop at the power plant," Ames said quietly to April while an orderly helped the grieving mother back into the car. "Mrs. Tanney," he said through the door once she was settled, "is there someone who can come and spend a bit of time with you? Just to help around the house a bit?"

She looked at him from the shadows in the back of the car but did not respond.

"A neighbour?" asked April.

"Yes," Mrs. Tanney said slowly. "My neighbour. She's pretty nice. She helps me sometimes." She collapsed against the seat back and closed her eyes.

"I HOPE SHE'S going to be all right," April said, looking back at the house as they were driving away. The neighbour had indeed been very kind and told them not to worry. "Her son might have been the only one bringing in money."

They pulled in front of the Corra Linn Dam and power plant on the way to Nelson and, shouting over the noise, asked a man in coveralls where they could find the manager. The man pointed with a wrench and they went into a long, low building full of machinery, where the sound was only slightly dulled.

"Yes? I'm Ed Hartley. How can I help?" the manager asked after Ames had introduced them.

"We're here to inquire about one of your foremen, Jim Tanney," Ames said. April had been instructed to take notes, and she was poised with her pencil and notebook.

"Foreman? Ha! Who told you that? Not only was he not any kind of foreman, we fired him a few weeks ago.

He never came on time, his work was bad, and he came in hungover, when he did come. Why are you after him?"

Ames hesitated, then said, "He's dead. We're trying to find out what happened. Did anyone here have any kind of quarrel with him?"

Hartley shook his head. "Dead? His poor mother. She doesn't deserve that. Well, I'm the only one who was plenty mad at him. And no, he didn't have too many friends on his shift."

"Hmm," Ames said. "His mother said he was coming home with more money."

"Not from here. Wouldn't surprise me though. I always thought he was a bit shady. First time he really missed a spell of work was when he got arrested and spent a couple of nights in jail. He got in a fight with someone over a gambling debt. I'm sorry he's dead, at least for his mother, but he wasn't up to much. You can't help feeling life just caught up with him."

"You wouldn't know where this gambling took place?"

"Nope, and I don't care to. Anything else? I got work to do."

"YOU DID WELL," Ames said. He was back at the wheel, and April sat next to him, looking at her notes. "You seemed to know what to say to that poor woman."

"Thanks. Boy, do you ever find out stuff when you start to look at people. It seems like Tanney was living a whole secret life."

"Only from his mother. The thing is, he was bringing money home. If he kidnapped Rocky for someone, he must have gotten a payment for that, and then he told Cooper he was 'coming into' some more money."

"Maybe he got a down payment to do the kidnapping, and he was going to get the rest after he did it," April said. "But wait, he never delivered the boy to anyone, and he gave himself up. He wouldn't get that second payment, so where would he expect to get more money?"

"Let's assume the person he kidnapped Rocky for lives over Creston way. If you have enough money to pay someone to kidnap a child, you're probably a criminal."

"Not necessarily. Maybe just a desperate father. Or, grandparents who maybe *do* know about the child and want to get him away from his mother."

"But the desperate father is up in Whitehorse." Ames nodded several times. "I think we have to go talk to Rocky's mother again. I wonder if she's told us everything."

CHAPTER THIRTEEN

"**W**E'RE GOING TO NEED YOU, I expect, Mr. Scott," said Thomas Fine, folding his napkin after breakfast. "The chief of police speaks only a little English." He rose, and Darling followed suit. "After that I suggest we meet with one of the fellows who took some people out the minute we realized Bob was actually missing and not just late coming back. We can come up with a plan. Hmm. I wonder if we should keep it under our hats that you're a police inspector. It might put their noses out of joint. It might smack of foreign interference to them."

"There. They're gone," Mrs. Fine said briskly, as the door closed behind the three men. Gone was her slow, elegant, lady-of-the-house manner. "María usually goes off to the market right after breakfast. Would you still like to go with her? I've got to prepare for an event coming up or I'd go too. I'm not sure how much opportunity you'll have to visit a typical Mexican market during your time down here, but I love the market. She'll take you to see the church and the little zócalo as well. And I know she wants to stop by her brother's house in case there is more to be learned."

"Why might the townspeople know more than the police?" But as soon as Lane asked, she remembered how much people in villages in France knew about what was really going on during the Nazi occupation.

"I don't believe the police don't know anything. What you have to understand is that there are families here whose sons, nephews, or even fathers are either members of these groups or are beholden to them in some way. It is practically an open secret, but it's more than their life is worth to speak about it to the police."

"Tell me, why are the police not still out looking for him?"

Leonora shrugged. "They say they're looking but have found nothing. They gave it as their opinion that your brother-in-law met with an accident. The canyon trails are dangerous. If he has met with an accident, it is quite possible that he would not yet have been found. The countryside is very rugged."

THE MORNING WAS warm and, incongruously, felt full of promise, the way sunny mornings can, as Lane and María climbed over the sill of the hacienda door and into the street. They walked along a narrow sidewalk, María carrying a large round wicker basket. A bus ferrying workers drove past, rattling on the cobblestone road.

"*Mineros*," María said, "for the mine. They are late."

Lane, even knowing the gravity of their mission, was entranced with the town, the warm feel of the air on her face, the symphony of smells so different from King's Cove. They were similar, she realized, to the smells of her childhood when Lina would take her to the market in Riga. As they got close to the market, she was hit with a heady mix of flowers, ripe fruit, charred meat, vegetables, burning charcoal, and other smells not so familiar, perhaps the corn tortillas they'd had with dinner. Scrawny dogs roamed among the vendors, sniffing the ground.

"*Aquí estamos*," María said, waving an arm at the rows of vendors, many under cloth awnings to keep off the sun. She smiled at a woman eyeing a pile of onions. "*Órale pues, Gabi, ¿cómo estás?*"

The other woman turned and greeted her, then looked at Lane, lifting her chin in her direction in mute inquiry. Lane smiled and raised her hand in a little wave, and the woman smiled back, nodding. While María was apparently explaining her presence on the marketing trip, Lane watched. The woman, like María, carried a basket and wore a flowered apron over her dress. Her hair was braided, and the braids coiled at the nape of her neck. She looked to be around thirty with beautiful dark eyes. Was this just a chum of María's, or was she someone María hoped to learn something from?

The woman selling onions held up a couple toward Lane, saying, "*Ándale, señorita*, bery good!" Lane smiled and nodded in a noncommittal way. She hadn't thought to bring any pesos with her. She turned her attention back to her companion, who was nodding and shrugging.

Lane turned to take in the sweep of the market. It was roughly divided into vegetables, fruit, meat, and kiosks selling more commercial offerings like tinned goods and sweets, and, much to her delight, a section selling kitchen items. Her eye rested on an unglazed ceramic jug made of burnished clay with a scene of donkeys and cacti painted around its fat middle. It had a long neck and no handle. Flower vase? Or maybe something for water? It would have looked nice sitting in her kitchen, but how was she to fly home with such a thing? There was a large section featuring flowers right nearby. She moved toward the flower sellers, pulled by the scent, turning to signal to María, who, without hesitating, gave her a quick nod and kept on talking.

Massive bundles of calla lilies and marigolds were on offer, and buckets of tuberoses, with their delicate pinky-white blooms emitting the most overpowering scent. They must grow like weeds here, she thought, remembering the enormous bouquet in the vase on the hall table at the Fines' house. The seller, a young girl no more than thirteen, nodded at her and held one out for her to smell. "*Nardo. Dos pesos los diez, no más, señorita.*"

Lane smiled ruefully and was saved by the arrival of María, who pulled some coins out of her purse and bought ten, handing them to Lane to carry. "Is called *nardo. Hermosísimo, ¿no?*"

Lane was sure the correct answer was "*Sí*" and she offered it.

When the basket was full, María inclined her head toward a church, which stood at the base of an open square, at the tail end of the market. They passed food vendors and people selling soft drinks and drinks made from every kind of fruit, and a kiosk with comic books hanging on a string, secured with clothespins. Perhaps she should get one of those. It might help with her Spanish. A little boy with a grimy face pulled at her dress and offered little packets of chewing gum. Lane patted his shoulder and shrugged at her lack of money, but the little boy persisted, tugging on Lane's skirt until María turned on him and told him in no uncertain terms to take himself off.

On the steps of the church, María reached into the pocket of her apron and pulled out a triangular black lace veil, which she handed to Lane, and then fetched out another for herself. She draped it over her hair and gestured for Lane to do the same.

The contrast from the noise and brightness outside to the cool, quiet darkness inside the church hit Lane forcibly. It was at once soothing and blinding. María dipped her hand in a little stone basin of holy water, crossed herself quickly, ending the process with a kiss of her thumb, and handed Lane the basket.

"You wait, please." She walked purposefully between two sets of pews and went into a confessional, pulling the curtain closed behind her.

This gave Lane, whose eyes were becoming used to the obscurity, a chance to look around at the church, which smelled heavily of incense. She could hear María murmuring in the confessional together with the low tones of a male response, though in a moment she became aware that there was murmuring all around her. There was a scattering of people throughout, praying, bent over rosaries, mostly women with dark shawls over their heads. What sorrows were they asking help for? Lane wondered. Perhaps she should light a candle as well, for the success of their mission.

Which saint would be suitable for lost people, or, she gulped, lost causes?

It was almost too much to take in at once. She was amazed by the ornateness of the altar, and the bewildering number of saints, all of whom appeared to have a cast-iron stand of candles burning before them. Her eye was caught by an alcove at the rear of the church full of tiny paintings, and she picked up the basket and flowers and moved across to look more closely. The paintings lined almost every surface of this wall, and there was a pile on the floor. They showed simply rendered scenes of bus crashes, drownings, or people sick in bed, people with limbs severed in accidents, or scenes of someone being shot, and always, hovering above them, a saint, or the Virgin Mary spreading light down from her fingers. She looked closely at the writing, distinguishing the one word she knew, *gracias*. The tableaux were fascinating, and in such numbers that Lane was overcome with a dark foreboding. Life here seemed tenuous and full of deadly hazards.

She knew they must be stories with happy endings, death averted by the intersession of the Virgin or a saint, but she turned away, feeling suddenly oppressed, wanting to go back outside, into the light. With relief, she saw that María was just coming out of the confessional and was waving her toward the door.

"Now, *mi hermano*," María said, crossing herself again, and leading them out into the sun.

They walked along a series of cobbled streets lined with low adobe buildings. Though it was still morning, the streets were mostly empty. The miners and men and women working

160

in fields and market gardens had set out at dawn.

María knocked on a door painted a rich green, and a child of about five opened it, his face lighting up at the sight of María.

"*¡Tía!*" he cried, holding up his arms. Lane took the basket so that the hug could take place.

"*¿Dónde está tu papá?*" María asked.

"*Aquí,*" said a voice from an inner room, and Lane's curiosity about why a working man might be at home during the day was answered. Alfredo, lean, younger than his sister, with slicked-back hair and a warm smile, was in a wheelchair.

They were introduced, and then María went off with her nephew to get soft drinks. Lane sat on a battered couch after being rebuffed in her offer to help and smiled at Alfredo.

"*Accidente,*" her host said, waving his arm to indicate his legs, which were under a blanket. "*En la mina.*"

"I'm very sorry," Lane said, shaking her head.

"Okay," he said. "*La voluntad de Dios. Mi mujer trabaja ahora.*"

Lane nodded. It is the will of God. This much she understood. She turned as María came in.

"He says his wife is working now. *Salón de belleza.*" María fluffed her own hair to demonstrate.

"A beauty parlour," Lane said and nodded at the man, smiling.

María said something to the little boy, who hopped up and ran out past the beaded curtain that divided the rooms, and then came back, holding a comic book.

"He wants you to read. Maybe in the kitchen," María said almost apologetically.

161

"That's fine," Lane said, taking up her soft drink and following the boy. They sat down kitty-corner from each other and he plunked the comic down. Something she knew. Superman. She listened for a moment to the conversation in the sitting room, but it was low and earnest and in Spanish, so she smiled at the boy and looked at the title page. An evil man in a spaceship seemed to be confronting a confused-looking Superman. She began to sound out the words. "*Escucha, Superman . . .*" The boy giggled and she took heart. She might learn something.

THEY MET IN Thomas Fine's office. It had the dark solidity and luxury suitable to the manager of an international mining outfit. He had tried to discourage Lane from joining, but he would have had to cross into actual rudeness to keep her out. Scott had a notebook on his lap.

"The police have done what they can," Fine said. "I'm inclined to agree that perhaps the party met with an accident. The question is, what to do now? It is a needle-in-a-haystack situation out there."

Lane cleared her throat. "If I may. María spoke with some townspeople today. According to what she told us, it may not be an accident."

"Oh, for God's sake, what are they going to know?" Fine said impatiently.

"They know of a man who was found dead," Lane said. "He had been shot. The son of a baker. He worked for a man named Salinas, a bandido. His body was found a few hundred metres from the mine tailings. They think he was coming here."

"People are shot in Mexico every day of the week," Fine said irritably. "What's it got to do with this?" It was difficult to know if he was irritated by the intrusion of what he considered doubtful theories from the townspeople or by Lane being part of the discussion.

"María's brother believes he carried a message for you," Lane persisted. She had debriefed thoroughly with Leonora, who had helped translate what María had learned.

"What sort of message?"

"Apparently, he carried it in his head. He told his father before he died that he'd been asked to deliver it. He'd never been asked to carry any such message before, and he was afraid. He said they had kidnapped some North Americans and wanted money from you." She nodded at Fine.

Fine leaned forward. "We can't accept the word of the servants. How long ago was this supposed to be?"

"Less than two days ago. They say the men are still alive, but they've moved them. They had been in the place your men already searched, but they were moved before your people got there. We're only hearing about it now because the boy was shot, and the family has been completely shattered by it."

Fine leaned back and rested his hand on his chin, frowning, as if he was struggling to accept Lane's information. "If that were true, we'd have to send the army. This is ridiculous that our men should be held captive by these outlaws!"

Scott, who had been watching Lane closely, now spoke up. "I think it's a bad idea, sir. If this man is threatened by the army, it will be a bloodbath. He will shoot his hostages and he and his men will fight, and the army will lose. This has already been discussed in DF."

"What do you mean, 'already discussed'?" Fine barked. It was evident that he was beginning to feel he was not in charge of this disaster.

"The embassy, sir. They discussed what should be done if the men were not merely lost but kidnapped. Of course, they do not want it to be easy for bandits to get money out of kidnapping North Americans, but an armed response would be risky for the hostages. These groups often have ex-army members in them, and that is a risk for the army. If Mr. Darling and his guides are hostages, they have recommended an approach of negotiation."

"Negotiate with criminals? Are you mad?"

Scott shrugged. "It's money they want."

"Give those bastards—excuse me, Mrs. Darling—give them money and what's to stop them setting up a whole industry of kidnapping foreigners?"

"It is the very discussion they had at the embassy, sir. It is a dilemma. But I assume you want your people back alive." Scott paused. "I have some money with me."

Everyone turned to stare at him. Driver and translator, my eye, Lane thought.

"How much?" Darling asked.

"Not quite enough, I expect. We don't yet know what amount they want, but I expect if this gentleman can add to it, we might have enough. This will become a diplomatic mission, of sorts."

"What usually happens in these situations? Is there an intermediary? A neutral meeting place?" Darling asked.

"None of them will come out into the open. We likely must go to them."

"This is ridiculous!" Fine said.

"Where are we to find them?" Darling said urgently, ignoring Fine. "I'll go on my own if I have to."

"You don't know the country, Inspector," Scott said.

"I could send a man with you," Fine said. "A native. Can't send you off on your own. But Scott is right. It's dangerous. And you'd be sitting ducks."

"It is difficult," agreed Scott. "He wants the money. This much we can count on. I don't think he will risk everything by taking more hostages. If we went to the original place Mr. Darling was going to do exploration, he would find us. I suggest Mrs. Darling go along. It will reduce any apparent threat to Salinas."

"Absolutely not!" Darling exclaimed.

"I agree completely," Fine said. "It's no place for a woman. You'd be held up; you'd be looking after her. Excuse me, Mrs. Darling." Again, he turned to Lane. "But you do see. This needs to be done quickly. Get in, pay the money, get the men out. You can't have a woman involved in this sort of business."

Oh, dear, thought Darling, I do wish he hadn't put it quite like that.

THE EARLY MORNING light was just beginning to spread across the low hills surrounding the town. The distant sound of a train whistle was carried on the blessedly cool morning breeze. It would be hot by ten. Hoofs clattered on the cobblestone street outside the gate of the hacienda as

165

the seven horses skittered restively, impatient to get going. A mule laden with supplies stood stoically, his rope in the hands of the guide, who was already mounted. Darling stood next to Lane, holding the reins of a tall chestnut with a roan coat.

"He's called El Diablo," Darling said with a sigh. "It was this or El Demonio over there. Neither choice seems safe. I left the Demon to Scott."

"El Diablo seems very sweet. I'm sure the name is ironic," Lane said.

The stable hand held the reins of a small black mare and waved Lane over.

"*Tenga, señora. Muy apacible. Se llama Lorita.*" Lane, relieved not to be offered either horse of the Apocalypse, nodded and thanked the groom with a smile. She'd been outfitted in a pair of brown jodhpurs and a cotton shirt and been given a hat suitable for fending off the sun. On the advice of Leonora, she had wrapped a scarf around her head, obscuring most of her hair.

"It's a good thing you aren't a blonde," Leonora had said. "That would really have drawn the attention."

A fourth horse was ridden by a man who worked for Fine and knew the local countryside, Arturo Cruz. He appeared almost too serious for someone his age—what was he, twenty-five at the most?—Lane thought, and then realized it was because he was armed. She glanced toward the hills. Did he always travel armed, or was he expecting he would have to use that gun? At that moment he seemed to notice her. He watched her out of dark eyes, shaded by his large hat, and then nodded at her, turning back to attend to the mule. The remaining three horses were for the returning hostages.

"It's a long day's ride to the prospecting site," Fine said to Darling. "It's a good stopping point. There's a village about three miles down the valley from the site. San something. Maybe Cruz can find something out there, though the police chief said they couldn't get a word out of them." He shrugged. "Par for the course, I suppose. I don't think people much like talking to the police anywhere." He dropped his voice. "You're out of your mind taking your wife. I wouldn't allow it."

Darling momentarily contemplated not allowing Lane to do something and gave what he hoped was a convincingly rueful nod. "I doubt I could have kept her from coming. She's an experienced horsewoman and very observant. And she might be able to help Cruz gather information."

"Listen, Darling," Fine said, his voice dropping. "You'd better have this." He slipped Darling a revolver.

Darling held it for a moment, thinking to reject it as overdramatic, and then slid it into the back of his belt under his jacket and gave a quick nod.

"Señor," said a voice behind him. A groom offered to hold El Diablo's reins while he mounted, but Darling shook his head. He put his foot into the stirrup and swung his leg over the saddle. El Diablo immediately began to illustrate his diablerie and flung his head up and down, whipping in circles and whinnying in protest. Darling, taken unaware, nearly lost his seat but folded forward and managed to take control of the reins. After some moments the mount gave way. "Ironic name, my aunt Nora!" Darling muttered.

Fine waited for the introduction to die down and then slipped a box into one of Darling's panniers. "Ammo," he mouthed and then stepped back.

A small crowd had gathered on the street outside the hacienda. The old gatekeeper had positioned himself in the doorway and had been joined by several people from the cafeteria that was adjacent to the gates inside the compound. They knew the expedition was to find that geologist, but murmured their speculation about why the gringos were bringing a woman. Scott swung himself unaided onto El Demonio and seemed to relish the burst of turning and protest. He was clearly an experienced horseman. He grinned happily.

Lane was seated with much less drama, and Leonora came to stand beside her, resting her hand on Lorita's neck. "Good luck, my dear," she said quietly to Lane. "I almost envy you."

"You won't by the end of the day. I expect I'll feel as if I've been hit by a bus. I haven't ridden since I was a girl."

They made their way up and over the low hill north of the town and headed downward off the plateau into open country. Scott rode ahead, talking to Cruz, who pointed to the northeast. Lane and Darling rode side by side.

"I shall pay for this," Lane remarked ruefully. "But look at the vastness of this countryside!" The desert seemed to go on forever, still golden with morning light, the sky a limitless, pale blue dome.

"It won't be so charming at high noon, I expect. There's a touch of *The Treasure of the Sierra Madre* about this expedition that is not encouraging." They'd seen the film just before they'd left Canada.

"Ah," said Lane. "Your usual optimism." She looked thoughtfully ahead at their guides. "I'm worried about the young man who was found dead. The one supposedly bringing the ransom demand."

"A bit late, I'd have said," Darling observed.

"Imagine that he'd just got involved with Salinas, and it was his first errand. Maybe he'd got roped in because of money, or the lure of adventure, and he ended up dead right out of the gate."

"You heard Fine. He said people are shot here every day of the week. What is it that specifically worries you besides his admittedly awful fate?"

"Who shot him? Why *him*? To prevent him from coming with the ransom demand? In whose interest would that be?"

Darling nodded. "I suppose in these gangs there are wheels within wheels. Jealousy from another gang, or maybe nothing to do with it. Someone angry that he dared to look at his wife or daughter. But I see your point. And it's apparently caused Salinas to move, no doubt taking my brother with him."

As Darling had predicted, by noon the sun was beating down, flattening the scenery, rendering the horizon a watery blur.

Cruz said something to Scott, and Scott turned to them. "He says there is a little river down there, maybe a mile, and we can rest and water the horses."

From the top of a low hill, they looked down on a scene in complete contrast to the desert they'd been travelling through. A narrow valley shaded by trees wound through the hills, and the slight babble of water was the most beautiful

169

sound in the world to Lane. They clattered down a long, sloping trail to the creek and dismounted.

Lane could feel every muscle protesting as she slid off the saddle. It would be murder to get back on. She took her canteen out of her saddlebag and then released the reins so the beast could join the rest at the creek.

Finding rocks to sit on under the blessed shade of the oaks that grew along the banks of the creek, the party munched quietly for some moments on the sandwiches Cruz took from one of the packs on the mule.

"We have another five hours just to get to the prospecting site. We can spend the night there. There is the nearby village of San Jacinto where I can get food," Cruz said.

"Gorblimey. Five hours," Lane said quietly to Darling. "How's your bottom?"

"Gentlemen don't discuss their bottoms," he replied, shifting uncomfortably on his rock.

"You said you weren't a gentleman."

"In that case, I'm not looking forward to leaping back onto Diablo. And I dare say he's not looking forward to me either, though he has been reasonable enough on the trail."

Stretching her legs out, Lane said, "At this moment, this cool, watery place is the most beautiful I've ever seen in my life. I never want to leave."

"I will see what information I can get in San Jacinto," Cruz said. "Someone might know where Salinas has gone if he is not at his usual outpost. I would advise that you use your water sparingly. There is no more until we get to the well in the village."

"*¡Caray!* We had horses at my grandfather's estate, and I rode the whole time I was there, but I have not been on a horse for a very long time," Scott said, getting up slowly. "I'm too soft from working at the embassy."

"You ride beautifully," Lane said, a little enviously. She'd ridden as often as her sister had when they were children, but she'd never developed Diana's skill and grace.

Scott shrugged, smiling. "I was even a champion at the local steeplechase for several years. Look at me now! I'm like an old man."

There's a story, Lane thought. Perhaps on the long drive back to Mexico City, with Bob, she added, optimistically. Now, they climbed back out of the arroyo, and were on the trail again.

CHAPTER FOURTEEN

"**MRS. RADCLIFFE, IT IS REALLY** important that you tell us everything. Because the man who kidnapped your son is dead, we can't find out who paid him, or why he did it in the first place. You say you didn't know him . . ."

"I didn't! Never seen him in my life before. Why are you badgering me? Why can't you just drop it? Rocky's home, that man is dead. It's over." She turned away, as if she could make the two policemen disappear by so doing.

Ames and Terrell were sitting in Mrs. Radcliffe's dining room around the table. She had let them in with ill grace and had sat sullenly pulling the edges of the cardigan she had wrapped tightly around her body.

"Where is Rocky now?" Terrell asked.

"He's over at Bonny's. I sent him over there when I knew you were coming. No need for him to have to face this all over again. Anyway, why are you talking to me? You should be talking to my husband. He's behind it. You mark my words."

"We're looking at every possibility, Mrs. Radcliffe. He does say he's not behind it."

"He says." She turned to stare out the window, her mouth clamped shut.

"Why did you and your husband separate?" Terrell asked quietly.

The silence went on for so long that Ames wondered if he should pose another question. Finally, she shrugged. "We just didn't get along. I don't like him, he doesn't like me. He said . . ." She clamped her mouth shut again.

"He said what, Mrs. Radcliffe?" Terrell prodded gently.

"He said that I changed after Rocky was born. I don't even know what that's supposed to mean! Of course I changed. Having a baby changes you. He just didn't like not being the centre of attention anymore, and he went off in a huff. There. Satisfied? That's the kind of father he is."

"What concerns us is that Jim Tanney kidnaps your son, and shortly after that, he's killed. It's important that we find out who killed him and why. Until then, Rocky might still be in danger," Ames said.

"Are you saying I killed him? Are you out of your mind? I haven't left this house since Rocky was taken."

"No, Mrs. Radcliffe, we don't think you killed him. But if the person who put him up to this did, we need to find out who that is and what interest he has in Rocky. Because we don't know if he will make another attempt."

"That's my ex-husband for you! Well, I don't know anything, so you can leave now. Haven't I been through enough?"

Ames, feeling that perhaps she had, stood. "Thank you, Mrs. Radcliffe. If you think of anything, anything at all, please call us. Also, can I ask you to keep an extra eye on your son? Make sure the doors and windows are locked for the time being, until we are certain that the danger has passed."

"My God. You think you have to tell me that? You guys don't have kids, do you? Please don't bother me again."

"WHEW. THAT WOMAN is a fortress," Ames said on their way back to the station.

"She doth protest too much, to be sure," Terrell said. "She is definitely keeping something back, and I'm afraid Rocky is in danger unless we find out what it is. This kidnapper was a small-time crook. He lost his nerve and ditched the child. Rocky might not be so lucky next time. I'm actually astonished at how little she sees the danger."

"How'd it go?" April asked when they came into the station. "Oh. Not too well, I see."

"We think she's hiding something," Ames said, taking his hat off and running his arm over his brow.

April snorted. "Everybody is hiding *something*," she said.

"Not everybody," Ames said. "I'm not. He's not." He pointed at Terrell, who was putting his cap on the peg by the door.

"See, that's just not true. You both are. I can't believe you don't see that. Even I am. Several things, probably."

"Is this women's intuition or something?" Ames asked.

"It's common sense, sir."

Ames turned to Terrell, who'd been backing away toward his desk. "Quit trying to hide. What do you think? Are you full of secrets?"

Terrell shrugged. "I think she's right, sir."

"I knew it!" Ames said with triumph, winking at Terrell, and giving a not-quite-subtle-enough tip of the head toward April.

"I think, sir," Terrell said, stolidly ignoring his boss, "that it's possible that if she does have a secret, Mrs. Radcliffe I mean, she'd likely tell her best friend." He looked at April. "What do you think?"

April nodded, considering. "I think that's probably right. There's a high likelihood. Who is her best friend?"

Ames said, "I'm assuming it's Bonny Sunderland, her neighbour and chief babysitter, by the sound of it. They have children the same age and seem to be in and out of each other's homes."

"Bonny Sunderland. That's interesting. I know her husband," April said.

"You do?" asked Terrell, approaching the front desk.

She shrugged. "Mr. Sunderland runs that Top Hat eatery down the street. My dad and I go there sometimes. That's how I know."

Ames nodded. "Well, if you have any more brilliant insights, pass 'em on. I'm going upstairs to telephone Cooper. He's looking into things at his end. Maybe he has something, because we sure don't. And then I think we should tackle Bonny Sunderland."

"Let me know how I can help," April called after him and then smiled at Terrell. "Are we still going to the pictures tonight?"

"Yes, of course," Terrell said nervously. "Shall I pick you up?"

"We're walking. Is 'picking up' the right term?"

"Well, that's as opposed to 'meeting there.' What would you prefer?"

"Why don't we go have a pre-movie supper at the Top Hat? My treat."

"No. I mean, yes, let's eat there, but my treat."

"Don't be so hidebound! You can pay for the film. We could leave from here. Do you have a change of clothes here?"

Terrell felt himself flush, and flush again because he was embarrassed about the first one. "Yeah, I do. But what about your father?"

"What about him? You think he should come along and supervise?" She smiled engagingly.

"No, I didn't mean that. What about his dinner? Don't you usually do that?"

"He managed fine without me for months. Anyway, he's going to the Legion tonight. It's his usual night. Good grief. You *are* hidebound if you think a man needs a woman to make his dinner."

THE SITE WHERE Bob Darling was supposed to have taken samples was almost indistinguishable from the countryside around it except for a simple ramada of thin branches comprising a roof and four supports that had been built to shade the geologists. It had evidently been prepared in anticipation of his arrival. An empty packet of cigarettes and the remains of a campfire were nearby, an enamelled pot knocked over with the drying residue of some sort of food in it, swarming with ants. A small wooden box full of canvas sample bags sat under the structure, ready to be filled.

"We'll camp down there," Cruz said, pointing. A short distance south they could hear the sound of a creek. "It is part of the same stream system as the place we had lunch."

Cruz rode a circuit that took him in a circumference of about thirty feet from where they stood.

"What's he looking for?" Lane asked. She was aching to dismount and did not look forward to having to ride on if Cruz was not happy with what he found.

"To see who has been here recently," Scott suggested.

"All right," Cruz said upon his return. He threw his leg over the pommel of his saddle and slid to the ground. "We'll camp here." He took the bridle off his horse and released it to go to the creek.

"Thank heavens," Lane said, dismounting, acutely aware of new aches and pains, and stood with her hands on her hips looking down the length of the shallow creek valley. A light breeze had blown up, and she closed her eyes for a moment in bliss. There was a village perhaps half a mile away, a collection of adobe houses and two large trees that seemed to loom over the place.

"That's San Jacinto," Cruz said. "I'll go there when my horse is watered and see what I can find out. You should pick a place where you will sleep."

IT WAS ONLY six o'clock, but Darling felt he could go to sleep that very minute, if not for a gnawing sensation of hunger. "It's funny, one does nothing at all but sit on the back of that beast while it does all the work, and I'm tired and ravenous," Darling said, coming to stand next to Lane.

"The minute Cruz turns up in that village, it's bound to get back to Salinas. If we aren't already being watched," she said.

Scott had already placed his saddle on a flat piece of ground just above the creek. He said something quietly to Cruz, who had come back for his bridle in preparation for his ride down to the village. Cruz shook his head and sighed. They watched him put the bridle back on his evidently reluctant animal. He turned in the saddle to give them a wave and set off down the narrow valley.

"He thinks everyone knows we are here," Scott said, pulling out a packet of Charros cigarettes. "These are the real thing. Pure tobacco and nothing else." He held it toward Darling and Lane, who both declined, and then took one himself, lit it, and inhaled deeply. "I don't know why I smoke these. I think the smell reminds me of my childhood. They're pretty rough."

"It's beautiful here," Lane said, beginning to undo the cinch of her saddle where the horses stood at the edge of the creek.

"Whoa, whoa, whoa," Darling exclaimed. The Devil apparently took a dim view of being disturbed during his drinking time and clattered sideways, bumping the Demon, who aimed a nip at his neck. "This is how everyone got anywhere not so long ago," he said. "I don't get nearly this sort of back chat from the company car."

As Lane was lifting the saddle off her horse, Scott approached and offered to help. "Ma'am," he said, holding out his hands.

"Thank you, that's very kind. I think I can manage. Oh, wait, I brought a camera I just want to fish out of my saddlebag." She took out her camera, and then Scott, ignoring her protestations, took the saddle, looked around the site, and found a place that satisfied him about fifteen feet from where he'd put his own saddle.

"I think this will be comfortable enough. It's not the Gran Hotel, but the air is pretty fresh." He said all this with his cigarette in the corner of his mouth. "I think, if you want to take pictures of a typical Mexican town, you will get a good view on the rise over there." Having said this, he watched her for some moments. "You were in London during the war?"

Lane turned to him. "Yes."

"It seems everyone there was doing war work."

She nodded. "Probably not too different from the US or Canada."

"What sort of thing did you do?"

She smiled and looked at him. "Typing, in an office. Very dull, I'm afraid." Was he going to ask her something else?

He nodded and took another pull on his cigarette and then tossed it on the ground. "They taste pretty vile, actually."

Darling, having negotiated a peace treaty with the Devil, dropped his saddle next to Lane's and turned to tackle the bridle, something, it turned out, Diablo was delighted to be free of.

LANE AND DARLING stood side by side, on the hill Cruz had shown them, looking down at San Jacinto. The sun was low and cast an orange glow across the scene. They could just see small figures moving about at the edge of the village.

"No one would believe these colours," Darling said. "I flew over North Africa once, and it was this sort of colour." Darling held out his hand for the camera and flipped open the lens. He snapped a picture of the village and wound the film forward, turning to Lane. "May I? You really are at your most glamorous."

"To be sure. I've just come from the salon. By all means. Let me be pointing with dramatic emphasis toward the village." She suited her action to her words.

"I'd like to capture our little camping spot. They'll get a rare old treat at the Rexall in Nelson when we take these in. I'm used to a much smaller camera, I must say. Or rather, I mustn't. It feels rather sneaky taking pictures of the village from way up here. Sneaking up on it unawares." They walked along the crest of the hill.

"He's coming back," Darling said suddenly. He aimed his camera at Cruz, riding slowly toward them. "Do you think he's found something out? Espionage during the war had nothing on this!"

"Nothing, of course," agreed Lane, beginning her descent to the camp, where Scott was standing perfectly still, watching Cruz return.

"I BROUGHT SOME tortillas and a bottle of mezcal," Cruz said when he had rubbed down his mount and begun the lighting of a small fire. "And we have some cans of American pork and beans."

"What did you learn?" Darling asked. "And how much did it cost? I will of course reimburse you."

"They normally would be afraid, but they told me quite

180

willingly. I made this same trip when your brother first went missing, and I could see they knew something but wouldn't tell me. Now someone has turned on the tap. They have moved their two captives to a location in the mountains over there." Cruz prepared and served the food as he spoke.

"Two?" Darling exclaimed. "There were three in the party."

"They said one, the Mexican, was shot trying to get away."

This threw them into a worried silence. "What does this mean?" Darling asked after a few moments.

"It means he means business," Cruz said. "It means we must make no false moves."

"That poor man! What in God's name would Salinas consider a false move?" Lane frowned into the darkness.

"That," said Scott, "is a very good question."

After some moments, she got up and took their bowls.

"I'll do the washing up," she said. She was oppressed by the death of the man who had not been named. By now the fire was the only illumination, and Lane moved out of the circle of light to the creek edge. She knelt by the creek and rinsed the bowls, pulling up handfuls of sand and pebbles from the bottom to rub over the tin surfaces, and then rinsed them again. She placed them upside down on a low, flat rock and then looked down the valley toward the village.

The darkness was velvety and for a moment seemed absolute, and then she saw that there were several dim yellow points of light coming from a few of the houses. Of course, she thought. No electricity. It was a darkness that seemed from another time. Above her, a gasp-inducing dome of stars swept across the sky. She had slept out many

181

a night in France, and in the more remote parts of the country the night had been deep enough to reveal the universe shimmering above her, but this was something else. A great band of light swept across the southern sky. The Milky Way as she had never seen it. She could hear the three men talking quietly behind her, but was reluctant to let go, just yet, of this transcendent moment.

CHAPTER FIFTEEN

"**H**I, MR. SUNDERLAND," APRIL SAID with a wave of the hand as she and Terrell came through the door at the Top Hat. "Anywhere okay?" It was early and there was only one other couple, sitting by the window, who both stopped eating to stare at them.

Tim Sunderland, a tired-looking man in his mid-thirties, looked up from the glass he was polishing and smiled. "Miss McAvity. You slumming from the café this evening?"

"I'm not at the café right now. I'm holding the fort for Sergeant O'Brien at the police station. He had some sort of heart attack. This is Constable Terrell."

Sunderland shook his head. "Oh, I'm sorry to hear that. He and his missus come in once in a while. I've seen you around," he said to Terrell in a friendly enough voice. "You can sit anywhere. I'll get the menus."

"How's your little boy?" April asked, slipping off her cardigan and hooking it on the back of her chair.

"Oh, you know. A going concern. We've started to be a lot more careful since Rocky got snatched. I guess you were something to do with him getting home." Here a nod to Terrell.

Terrell shrugged, smiling. "The kidnapper did that. He gave up on the project for some reason."

"It's the damnedest thing," Sunderland continued. "What d'you think happened there?"

"We're still investigating that," Terrell said, looking at the menu.

"We have a ladder in our backyard, and I moved the thing into the garage, I can tell you, when I heard that's how the kidnapper got in next door." He leaned forward and spoke in a hushed tone. "In fact, I think he actually tried to get into our Johnny's room. I found the ladder knocked over in the yard when I went to move it."

Terrell looked up at this. "How's that, sir?"

"Just like I said. I had the thing up against my apple tree because I was pruning it back in the spring, and when I went out to move it the day after, when Rocky was taken, I found it lying on the ground. I figure the guy thought he could get a hold of our boy. Good thing the guy was caught. Good thing he's dead, if you want my opinion. Oh, I know, you can't talk about the case." He winked. "What'll it be?"

"I'll have the beef stew, I think," Terrell said, wondering if Sunderland would be quite so chipper if he'd seen the remains of the kidnapper caught in the paddlewheel of the *Moyie*.

"Yeah. Same for me," April said.

184

"WELL?" SHE SAID as they walked toward the Civic Centre later. "What do you think now? Maybe that guy was trying to kidnap Sunderland's kid and not the Rockford kid at all. Was I right to pick the Top Hat?"

Terrell nodded thoughtfully. "I guess you were. It might change how we have to view the kidnapping."

April beamed with satisfaction and slipped her arm through his. "I love working for the police department."

"Really? After two days?" Terrell tried to sound natural, though he was acutely conscious of her arm.

"I loved it after one day."

He loved having her there after one minute. But of course, he couldn't say so.

"SO," AMES SAID, swirling the sugar off the bottom of his half-drunk cup of tea. "You're suggesting it was random. He just wanted any old kid?"

"I'm not sure I'm saying that, sir. But it is something we have to take into consideration. I stopped by there this morning and Mr. Sunderland showed me where the ladder had been and where he found it. He had it jammed pretty well between two branches of the tree. It couldn't have fallen over. He believes someone tried to take it. I went next door to look at the ground directly under the Radcliffes' window. We probably should have done that right away the first day, but we were so anxious to just find the child. The grass grows right up to the edge of the house there and hasn't been mowed recently, but I did see that it looked like a ladder had been put up there. I wondered for a second if the kidnapper tried the Sunderland house first. If that is the case, it could suggest the kidnapping might not have anything to do with something going on in the Radcliffe family."

"So, someone out there paid Tanney to kidnap any old child? I don't see the point. Let's see if we can trace his money. He was probably paid in cash, but it's all we've got right now."

"And I wonder if Cooper would mind if we went back across the lake to look over that place he found Tanney camping in the forest," Terrell said.

A few phone calls later, Terrell announced that Cooper was happy to have them come across and have a look, and Ames had reached someone at the small savings bank in Castlegar who told him Tanney did have an account at one time, and he couldn't discuss it over the phone.

"I'll take the car to Castlegar. You might as well give that bike a run." Ames turned to April. "Can you hold the fort? I'll be back in a couple of hours and Constable Terrell's gone most of the day. Call Thompson if there's a real emergency." He stopped on his way upstairs to get his hat. "What'd you guys go see last night?"

"*Dead Reckoning*. All about a murder!" April said happily.

"I don't think you're such a well-brought-up girl. You have an unhealthy appetite for death."

"You can talk, sir!" she called after him. "Be careful, sir," she said to Terrell, and then settled with a sigh at the front desk.

"THEY THINK HE might have tried to take Johnny before getting Rocky. You'd have to be an idiot to believe that," Bonny said. She and Linda Radcliffe were sitting on the grass near the lakeshore, watching the boys play in the sandbox.

Linda listlessly smoothed the blanket they were on. "I told you, don't throw sand at Johnny!" she called out to her son.

"So much for them pinning the blame on your ex-husband."

Linda chewed her lip. "I'm still married to him, you know. Anyway, I don't care. The guy is dead. He was a creep. Good riddance to bad rubbish."

"Yeah," Bonny said, nodding. "You're right. Good riddance, eh?" But she was glaring at the grass they sat on.

Linda looked over at her. "What's the matter with you? You look like you haven't slept in days. I don't know why you're so bothered. He was horrible. I'm glad to see the end of him."

Bonny sniffed and ran the back of her hand under her nose. "Yeah. He was, okay?"

AS HE LEANED out to look at the lake, Terrell's mind was in a whirl. He couldn't get his mind off April and his own boldness in reaching for her hand in the theatre. She'd glanced quickly at him and then back at the movie, but she hadn't removed it. Paradoxically what troubled him the most was how comfortable they were together. The whole thing was moving forward quickly. Maybe too quickly. He remembered several people looking at them as they took their seats, and the momentary silence that fell, and then the whispers. Had she noticed it? He hadn't the nerve to ask her. It wouldn't be fair to her. None of it was fair to her.

The water churned beneath the ferry, and he sighed and tried to take momentary comfort in the beauty of the mountains rising and receding in endless graceful blue rows away from the lake.

"Hey, aren't you the officer who was over the other day?"

Terrell turned and saw one of the crew, a young man in his early twenties, dressed in coveralls and holding a thick coil of rope. He nodded. "Yes, I am. Constable Terrell, Nelson Police."

"Well, good. I heard the Mounties got your man and then lost him right off this ferry. But I found something after they were here trying to figure out what happened. I meant to call them about it, but seeing as you're here, I'll go get it."

"Thanks. I'm on my way to the Creston detachment right now."

The crewman disappeared through a metal doorway and came back a short time later. "I had it in the drawer in there." He held out his hand and dropped a bullet into Terrell's palm. "I'd say that could fit in a little number two Enfield. I signed up just near the end. Never got overseas, but we did learn to shoot one of those. And I already asked. No member of this crew even owns a pistol, so it wasn't from any of us."

Terrell looked at the bullet in his hand. He also recognized it. It hadn't been shot. "I suppose it could have been from anyone riding the ferry just about any time. Where did you find it?"

"As a matter of fact, it was only a couple of days ago. Over here." He led Terrell to a mooring post on one side of the pulled-up ramp. "It was right behind this. The rope was used that morning, so when it was moved, there was the bullet. I don't know where it rolled from though."

Terrell leaned over to look between the mooring post and the wall. "Do most people stay in their cars on the ride over?"

"It's about a forty-minute ride, so if the weather's nice like today, lots get out of their cars. On a bad day, no. Quite a few go upstairs, and the rest sit in their vehicles. I just thought it might be important, because I don't guess most people have handguns on them, let alone a pocketful of loose bullets."

"Thanks. I appreciate this." Terrell shook the young man's hand and returned to his bike. The Kootenay Bay terminal was in sight.

THE SHOT CRASHED into the silence, stirring panic in the horses. The Demon was the first to bolt, causing Cruz, who had made a return trip that morning to San Jacinto and was still mounted, to duck forward, clinging for dear life. His horse raced blindly across the desert in the direction of the low hill where the geological crew had been exploring. The other six horses thundered after him.

A second shot twanged off the dry rocky ground, causing the mule to skitter anxiously and trot off in the opposite direction, while the three people who were sitting by the creek dove for cover. Cruz had his pistol out and shot several times in the direction the gunfire had come from.

The third shot didn't come at once. Lane, Darling, and Scott scrambled up out of the creek to stand behind the hill and look out across the desert, where it appeared Cruz had finally brought his horse and its followers to a halt. "Where did it come from?" Darling asked. He had his hand at his back, feeling for his own gun.

There was a sound of rock falling, and the third shot came binging off a rock very near Lane. She and Scott threw themselves to the ground, but Darling had his gun out and was on his feet, scanning the top of the hill. Lane looked to where Cruz and the horses had been, only to see they weren't there. They must have gone down into the creek farther along. He fired two shots.

The sound of hoofs receding in the direction Cruz had gone brought Darling out into the open. A lone rider was racing away, holding a rifle.

"There goes the bastard now. Maybe he didn't expect anyone was armed. Stay here. I'm going to check around the back."

"I didn't hear him at all. He must have been lying in wait. We didn't see anyone the whole morning." Scott sounded perplexed and worried. "Maybe they've been keeping us in their sights all along. Maybe a shot to warn us?"

"About what, exactly?" Lane asked irritably. "If it's the bandits, you'd think they'd be trying not to draw attention to themselves. Is this how they usually operate?"

Darling was back. "It's clear. He was alone. And Cruz is on his way back down the creek with the horses. What the hell was that in aid of?"

When Cruz returned he was grim. "The mule is gone."

Lane saw Scott reach unconsciously to his saddlebag. He must have the ransom money there.

"When we went out to look for Señor Darling when he first went missing, nobody shot at us," Cruz said. "We knew that if his party had been kidnapped, we'd probably have to wait for a demand. This"—he nodded toward the source of the shots—"I don't understand. And I also do not understand why we never got that demand."

"There was the young man who was found dead back in Fresnillo. Someone suggested he was the courier, but he was shot before he could deliver the ransom demand. Could it be a rival gang?" Lane asked.

Shaking his head, Cruz said, "Then the rival would have taken the hostages and made a demand of their own. According to the people in the village yesterday, Salinas has them. They didn't know why a ransom demand hasn't been made. Salinas always makes a demand." He walked out and scanned the horizon toward the village far below them. "I don't understand this. Maybe they wanted to see if we would return fire. Now they know we are armed. I should perhaps have been more careful." He looked at Darling. "You fired a weapon." It was somewhere between a statement and a question.

Darling nodded. "I couldn't see where to aim. By the time I saw him riding away he was out of range."

"I'm going back to the village for supplies," Cruz said. "They probably heard the shots. We can tell them we were surprised because we are not armed. If they are communicating with any of Salinas's men, they can pass that on. But if that was one of his men, he will tell them we are. He won't allow anyone to approach their compound armed."

"I'm going with you," Darling said. "They can see that I am a mild-mannered Canadian and pass that on to Salinas as well."

"They'll be fine," Scott said as he and Lane watched the two men head down the valley at a quick trot, the sound of hoofs echoing and receding off the hard ground.

Lane could feel her heart pounding high in her chest, but she believed that Cruz was likely right. These were warning shots. Maybe. Or very bad marksmen. Who would they have been wanting to shoot?

"If it was this man Salinas, who would he want dead in our party?" she asked.

Scott shook his head. "I don't know. Certainly not you or your husband. Excuse me for saying so, but you are worth money. If he did want someone dead, maybe Cruz? If they could shoot our guide, we would be lost. They could finish me and take the two of you for their collection. I really don't understand it."

"You're from the British embassy. You're worth money also."

"Yes, you could be right. But they might not know that. Lives are expendable to this type of man. We have seen that already."

She turned back to the desert, where the two riders had slowed and were walking along the edge of the gulley from which the shots had come. "Something doesn't add up," she said.

Scott nodded but looked at her curiously. "Why do you say that?"

Lane thought for a moment. "There's some over-egging going on."

"But who is over-egging this particular pudding?"

"Good question. All I can say is that there's too much extra going on. If you're a bandido, and you make your money kidnapping people for ransom, it should be straight-forward. Kidnap, demand, collect, release. Anything more and you're asking for trouble. Here a young man possibly associated with our bandido is shot, and now someone comes to shoot up the party bringing the money. It's almost as if someone is trying to interfere with the usual practice."

"You've thought about this," he observed.

"You're bound to, I should think, when someone tries to kill you."

"You're a remarkable woman. I don't believe you spent the war being the little typist." He smiled and threw a pebble at the creek. If he expected an answer, he was to be disappointed.

LANE WAS WATCHING, unable to move, looking into the dark. She wondered how she could see so well when it was dark. The man lifted his hand and shot. Lane turned her head away, but when she turned back the victim was still falling, falling, as if he would never reach the ground.

She woke with a gasp, her heart pounding. She'd had the dream before, or something like it. She was lying on her back, her head on her saddle, the khaki sleeping bag twisted in a way that constricted her movements and made her feel momentarily trapped.

She glanced over at Darling, who was still asleep, and exhaled a relieved breath. The sky above was still an infinity of stars, but now she felt small under it, lost almost. Why dream this again now? She shook her head at her own stupidity. The gunshots. They'd brought it all back. The day she'd been wrenched from her own youth, into a sadder, darker world. Watching their man die at their drop in France because there'd been a leak and they'd been betrayed.

She turned on her side and was looking into the darkness, when suddenly the whole world became a symphony of yipping and sharp cries and barks. A pack of coyotes somewhere nearby, crowing over a kill.

CHAPTER SIXTEEN

ALMA'S EMERALD-GREEN DRESSING GOWN. LANE held it, clutched the spilling silk to her chest, and felt an overwhelming fear come over her. She looked ahead, trying to see through the dark, and then had the idea that she had looked behind her, but had not moved her head. There was someone ahead in the darkness, and she was moving forward, walking toward a grey light. She must stop. Turn back. But she kept moving, convinced now that she would find not just Alma, but the man, too. She knew Alma was tied up, and if she could just untie her, she could save her. But the silk rustled in her hands and flew up like a bird escaping.

Lane's eyes opened suddenly. She was lying on her side, her hands crossed under her throat, her hip hurting where she must have lain on a rock. It was near dawn. The fear from her dream rested like a stone under her folded hands, and she shifted to where the ground felt smoother. It was another nightmare. Turning to lie on her back, Lane looked up at the greying sky. It was the morning of their third day. Why Alma again? They'd found her dead in the barn. A smart girl from a dirt-poor family. That was what that silk dressing gown had done for her. It had killed her. It was still hard for her to take in how they'd found her: dead, tied to a chair, her face bleeding, one hand crushed.

Why was she dreaming about her now? She closed her eyes and willed herself back into that dark tunnel in her dream. What awaited her at the end? What had she feared? With an intake of breath, she knew. The real traitor. The one that had surprised everyone. The man who had manipulated Alma into funnelling money to the Breton underground. And Alma hadn't been able to resist. She'd taken some of that money and bought herself a green silk dressing gown, one little luxury in her sorrowful life.

She saw herself again, crouching behind the low hill with her contact, watching Charlie fall, hearing the scream and then the second gunshot. Watching the two men take the radio and run into the forest. She realized something about that memory suddenly stood out. Something she couldn't put her finger on.

"You all right?" Darling whispered. He'd turned in her direction, his sleeping bag twisting.

Startled out of her thoughts, she looked at Darling lying beside her on the ground, his head on his rolled-up jacket.

"A pebble under my hip."

"Princess!" he accused her, snuggling farther into his sleeping bag and closing his eyes.

She smiled, and then got back to trying to remember. It was funny how quickly you could forget a face when you wanted

196

to conjure it up, and then it would pop up out of nowhere when you least expected it. At the moment, Harrison's face eluded her. She felt this urgency to capture the memory of it. It was the second dream about the same thing. Her endeavours were interrupted by the sounds of stirring in their camp.

The morning was beautiful, fragrant with the water from the creek and a green smell from the trees that stood along the winding edge of the water. Coffee was boiling in an enamelled blue pot, black with soot from the campfire. It smelled wonderful, but the mood was sombre. The visit to San Jacinto the night before had provided food in the form of tortillas, fresh tomatoes, and beans cooked in a clay pot. Darling had carried half a dozen eggs back gingerly. The villagers, according to Cruz, had no idea about the gunfire, and did not know if or when Salinas would approach them. Perhaps they were silenced by the presence of Darling, whom they stared at unabashedly.

After breakfast, Lane and Darling climbed up to the hill where Bob had last been working.

"Cruz doesn't look happy about this waiting. I think he senses something is amiss," Lane said, looking at the ground as she walked.

"I'm not happy either if it comes to that, and I'm almost certain Scott isn't. What are you looking for?"

"I don't know. Clues, I suppose. I wonder how long they were here."

"I have no idea. But I do feel the longer we have to wait for this bloody bandit to announce himself, the more complicated it could become. Why have they not come, demanded their money?"

197

Lane nodded. "And for that matter, why is Scott with us? Cruz is bilingual, so we don't need Scott along to translate. He could have stayed in Fresnillo, waited for us to come back so he could drive us back to the city. His obligation certainly doesn't include putting his own life in danger."

Darling nodded. "Perhaps he was told to stick with us by the embassy. No one expected to get shot at. Until yesterday we didn't even know for sure that Salinas has Bob."

"AFTERNOON, CONSTABLE," COOPER said, looking up from the desk upon which he had slung his long legs, as Terrell came through the door. He dropped his booted feet onto the floor and stood up. "It's a long way to come. I hope it's worth your while."

"I like getting the bike out for a run, especially on a nice day like this."

"Why don't you follow me? It's a bit south of here." The site was some eight miles down the road away from Kootenay Bay. The stolen car had bumped off the main road, cutting a swath that was barely discernible after so many days. Cooper turned the cruiser off the road and drove onto the wide margin.

Cooper pointed toward the thick pine forest. "We have to walk in. Tanney had that last car he stole dumped just over there. That's how we found the place. There was evidence he'd gone on into the forest on foot. Sniffed him out the rest of the way. He had a campfire going, if you can believe it, in this heat. He looked pretty rough after a couple of days of hiding."

Following Cooper into the darkness of the wood, Terrell tried to imagine what might have been going on in the kidnapper's mind. He'd deposited the child on the side of the road where anyone could see him and found a way to make that anonymous phone call, and luckily the child was seen almost right away, before he'd taken it into his head to wander into the road. Then Tanney had headed into the forest to hide out. Terrell shrugged. Perhaps Tanney just wasn't too bright. Maybe he couldn't make up his mind about what to do, or where to go. Perhaps he wanted to be caught. The whole thing was strange.

"There's where he had the fire," Cooper said, stopping suddenly, pointing at something that wouldn't even have qualified as a clearing—just a little space between trees. The fire had been built inside a small circle of rocks that looked hastily gathered. "We stamped out the fire and took him in. He didn't have anything with him except a blanket. Was glad to hear the child was picked up, the nerve of the guy! Said he hid in the woods to make sure he'd be picked up by someone. And then wouldn't tell us anything except someone was going to pay him to kidnap the boy, but he didn't feel right about it, and he was coming into some money anyway."

Terrell stopped and considered. "Did he sound like he was after that particular boy, Rocky Radcliffe? Or was it just any old kid the guy paying was after?"

Cooper looked surprised. "What are you saying? He could have kidnapped anyone?"

"We only think it must have been Radcliffe because that's the boy who was taken," Terrell said. Against this, he asked himself, why hadn't Rocky made a fuss when he was kidnapped? Had he known the kidnapper? If so, the kidnapper had been after Rocky. It didn't hurt to think about the alternative, though.

"Hadn't thought of that. Why, exactly?"

"I visited the house next door to the Radcliffes' this morning, and a ladder had been moved. The neighbours think the kidnapper might have been after their child initially. He's a friend of Rocky's and they spend a lot of time in each other's houses. It opened up the possibility that Rocky wasn't necessarily the target."

"Hmm." Cooper began to walk concentric circles away from where Tanney's fire had been, scanning the ground. Terrell imitated him, only going in the other direction, to make sure nothing was missed.

When they'd passed each other at about the fifteen-foot mark, Cooper suddenly said, "Hey!" and squatted down to collect something out of the thick layer of dried undergrowth. He stood up, holding an Enfield No. 2 by the nose in a handkerchief.

"So, Tanney was armed," Cooper said. He broke the pistol. "Two bullets in the chamber. He wasn't expecting a sustained assault. Here. You take it. Kidnapping happened in your jurisdiction." Cooper thrust the handkerchief and pistol at Terrell as if he couldn't wait to get rid of it.

"Was it fired?" Terrell looked down at the gun in his hand.

Cooper turned his mouth down and shook his head. "Tanney didn't fire it at anyone during the kidnapping. We would have heard about it. I suppose he had it along in case there was trouble."

"Having the Mounted Police arrest him might be considered 'trouble,'" Terrell remarked. "Why didn't he use it to resist arrest?"

"See, that's why I said I think he wanted to be picked up. He came out like a lamb. Like he was tired of roughing it."

Terrell nodded. They continued their circling.

"Not much more to see here, except his rubbish," Cooper said. He waved his hand and then started back toward the vehicles.

"Did he have a sleeping bag of any kind?"

"Just a nasty-looking army blanket. We burned that thing, I can tell you! I know, you'll ask why we didn't keep it as evidence, but the child was all right and it really was disgusting."

"When you arrested him, he told you his name, but not the name of the person who wanted the child kidnapped, is that right?"

"Yup. I guess whoever it was scared him, and he didn't want to give up his name in case it got back to him."

Terrell nodded and pursed his lips. "So that person might have killed Tanney to keep him from revealing who he was."

"That seems about right. Someone else could have wanted him dead. He was a petty criminal, after all. Bound to have cheated someone out of something."

"That's the question, sir. And whoever killed Tanney would have to have been following you, and then gotten on the ferry at the same time. I suppose it's pretty normal for people to get out of their cars on the trip over, so he could reasonably count on Tanney being available to shoot. Can you describe the scene again?"

"I wish I could say more than I did, Constable. It was just like I said: he was being compliant, and I had no fear he'd escape off the ferry; besides, I'm armed if he did give any trouble, so I let him just wander around, hang over the edge watching the scenery. It was pretty hot that day, so no one wanted to stay in cars."

"Then you lost sight of him? Had most other people got out of their cars?"

"I see what you mean," Cooper said. "He could have got lost among the others. Like I said, I wasn't too worried. I had my eye on him, and then someone dropped one of those giant chains. It was painfully loud, and I turned to see what had happened. When I turned back, I didn't see him where he'd been, leaning against the side. I went over there and saw he was gone, and thought he'd gone to the bathroom. We were nearing Balfour and that's when it got hard. First, we had to prevent people getting off so we could check all the cars, which made people pretty mad, and when we'd done that, because I was about four cars from the front, everyone had to drive around me to get off. By then I knew he wasn't on the boat at all. I honestly thought he'd either fallen or deliberately gone overboard to get away. Pretty strange, because he seemed eager to get the whole thing behind him."

"He could have been shot without anyone noticing and been tipped overboard."

"With that damn chain racket, I figure that must have been it. I guess you don't know what he was shot with?" Cooper asked, his head cocked slightly.

"According to our medical man, the bullet exited the wound, so it's at the bottom of the lake now, I guess. Small calibre, though," Terrell said. He was following Cooper out of the wood. "Something like this, I guess." He held up the gun. He thought about the bullet in his pocket. It might have fit this gun.

"Well, I patted him down when I arrested him. Nothing on him; obviously he thought he'd be able to come back and get it. He wouldn't have risked me confiscating it."

As they stood by the vehicles, Terrell said, "And he said he was coming into some money. Did he say from where?"

"I figured you guys would sort that out. It's a damn sight harder when the guy is dead. You've got a real case on your hands! I'm glad it's not ours. We have illegal drugs and guns coming over the border just now, so we're pretty busy." He opened his cruiser door. "I'm not too worried about that one being smuggled in, by the way. It's a British gun. I think a lot were issued to Canadians in the war. Those aren't the ones coming over the border. We finished here?"

Terrell paused a moment. He'd been about to mention the bullet he'd been given, but Cooper seemed anxious to get back. Instead, he shook hands and thanked him, and watched him turn fast in the road and head back toward his detachment, gravel flying up from his back tires.

He put the gun in his pannier still wrapped in Cooper's handkerchief, strapped on his helmet and goggles, and climbed on.

"YOU DID WHAT?" Ames asked. He was genuinely puzzled by this. It suggested a lack of responsibility in Terrell that he could not have imagined. "I don't think you should have done that."

203

"Yes, sir." Terrell stood at attention, Ames pacing a few steps either way before him. They were in Ames's office because Terrell had requested a private interview the minute he got back to the station.

"And I don't see how you can fix it without us looking like idiots."

"Yes, sir. I am prepared to look like an idiot if you think we should tell them."

Ames ran his hand through his hair. "Just tell me what you had in mind."

"Sir. When I was given the bullet, my first thought was that we could ask Dr. Gillingham if the wound could have been caused by this type of bullet. If we hadn't found the gun, I might not have told Cooper about the bullet anyway."

"But then you found the gun. It seems logical you would have said, 'Oh, looky here, I have a bullet from this very type of weapon!'"

"I see that, sir. I think I initially didn't say anything because I wasn't at all sure the bullet was relevant to the case. Anyone could have dropped it there at any time. Then when Cooper found the gun at the kidnapper's campsite, I was trying to understand why Tanney would have had the gun in the first place. It was clear to me that this bullet did not come from this particular gun, because Tanney didn't bring it out with him when he was arrested, so it was still lying in the forest as he was being killed and dumped in the lake. That being the case, and, as Cooper said when he handed me the gun immediately, the case being ours, I don't know, I just didn't say anything. And besides, I was more interested in having him describe to me exactly what happened on the ferry."

"And? Sit down." Ames had tired of pacing and sat on his side of the desk.

Terrell, sitting on the edge of his seat, still at attention, told Ames exactly what Cooper had said.

"So, if there were a lot of people out of their cars, we could put something in the paper asking anyone who rode the ferry on that sailing to come forward. Maybe one of them who was closer to Tanney saw what happened."

"I'll do that right away, sir."

Ames considered. "Get Miss McAvity to do it. Find out what you can from Gilly."

"Yes, sir. Thank you, sir." Terrell rose and prepared to leave.

"Constable," Ames began, then paused. "Let me know what Gilly says."

LATER THAT EVENING Ames sat on the old picnic table with Tina at the Van Eyck garage up the lake. "I don't think I could be the chief," he said, tossing a rock toward the water.

"And why not?" Tina asked. "It sounds like you did what you were supposed to."

"It's natural for Darling to do that sort of thing. He's the commanding type. We expect to get bawled out every now and then. He's almost always right, too."

"Do you think you were wrong?"

"No, not at the time. It wasn't a bawling out really; I was just surprised, because Terrell is a very good officer. Well trained, for sure, but also in himself. He's level-headed. He always seems to know what the right thing to do is. I just can't understand why he kept the bullet a secret."

"Well," Tina said with a sniff. "It's not like the Mounties share everything with you guys!"

"I know. *I* might keep information back, but it wouldn't be like Terrell to be small-minded like that."

"Do you feel bad about what you said because it's possible he had a good reason?"

"Maybe. He didn't seem too sure about why, I'll say that. I guess that's why he asked to see me the minute he got back. Even that felt funny. I think he was feeling unsure about his decision by the time he got back to the station. It just feels unnatural to be in charge, I guess, when being in charge means you have to have words with people. I don't think I have the personality. I hate any sort of discord."

"Rubbish! Anyone can do it when they know the job well enough to know how it should be done. And you know the job pretty darn well." She kissed him on the cheek and rested her head on his shoulder.

"Thank you. I just feel I have so much to learn from the chief still, I guess. I always think, 'What would Darling do?' For some reason I didn't this time."

"See, that to me is a sure sign that you *do* have the personality. You acted out of your own surprise about it. You knew there was something odd about it, and you wanted to try and find out. You didn't need Darling to guide you. You have your own sense about what's right."

He put his arm around her, pleased to see it in this light. "How about we stop talking about me and talk about having a wedding? Or would you like to just have a secret engagement forever?"

Tina lifted her hand to look at her ring. "It's funny. My dad knows I have this, but he's too polite to ask, and obviously I don't wear it at work, so no one else sees it."

"Mom's acting funny. She looks at me and sighs, in a way that makes me feel guilty. Should we put them out of their misery?" Ames asked.

"I guess we better. Who are you going to ask to be your best man?"

"I'd like to ask Terrell, if he ever speaks to me again."

"Don't be an idiot. He's a professional. He wouldn't take that sort of thing personally. But I am surprised . . . not the inspector?"

"I don't know. He seems too fancy. He's my boss. Terrell is my friend, as I see it. How long do you need to plan a wedding, I wonder?"

"A licence, some sort of vicar, a church, and a dinner. It's not that difficult, I don't think."

"We wouldn't get a honeymoon right away," he cautioned.

Tina suddenly became serious and pulled away from him. There was a reason they'd not planned the wedding yet. "Daniel, where are we going to live?"

CHAPTER SEVENTEEN

L ANE WAS STRUGGLING FOR BREATH. She tried to turn or move but she couldn't. The darkness was complete. For a moment she thought it was another nightmare, that she would wake, but then she became aware of the smell. Some sort of sacking covered her face and it was full of dust, choking her with every breath. This was too real. Then the pain. The front of her body felt as if she'd been hit repeatedly with a cricket bat, and when she tried to move, a rib screamed at her.

She coughed violently, causing more pain, desperate to move her hand up to her face to pull away whatever was covering it, but her arms were bound against her body.

As another round of coughing convulsed her, she felt someone pulling her to a seated position and then the sack being dragged off her head.

"Ah, señorita, you are awake. I'm sorry about this. I thought it necessary. Here, let me get these off." He unknotted the rope that bound her arms to her body. Blinded by the sudden light, Lane could make out nothing more than a shadowy form with a bright light behind him. Someone tall, with a hat. He spoke with a slight accent and had a soft, resonant voice.

She closed her eyes against the light and tried to speak but managed only a cough. The man reached to the table for a canteen and pulled up a wooden chair to sit next to her. He unscrewed the cap and tilted the canteen to her mouth. She coughed again, then drank gratefully. "I have something stronger if you like." She drank more and he nodded approvingly. "I'm sure you want to ask the usual questions, no? 'Where am I?' 'Who are you?' 'Why am I here?' I would like to answer these, but let us first get you out of all this. My men were a little overzealous. Then you will want to wash up. One of the women will take care of you, and then we can talk, yes?"

Glad to find herself alive, Lane looked at her captor through squinting eyes. He was no more than thirty-five, with a thick black moustache, and a scar across the lower part of his chin. Dark eyes. Matinee-idol handsome. There was a worried look on his face. She thought about the one question he had missed: How had she got here? Now that feeling was beginning to return to her hands and body, she took a breath and then immediately regretted it, as it caused her to squeak in pain.

"Again, I am sorry, señorita. Let us make you more comfortable." The door opened and someone hovered. "*Ah, Graciela. Ayúdale a la señorita, por favor.*"

A woman approached and gently undid the rope binding Lane's ankles and pulled her feet off the cot she'd been placed on, rubbing her ankles gently. She offered a hand to help Lane stand up.

"There. Let the blood return to your feet. It is always the trouble with tying of the legs. Oops! There, that's it. Try some steps. *Órale*. There you go," the man said. He had stood up and was holding an arm out at the ready.

Lane sat back down with a thump, feeling suddenly nauseated. She nodded at the woman. "*Gracias*."

"I am Héctor Salinas de Castillo, at your service," the man said, removing his hat and bowing his head in her direction.

"Lane Winslow," Lane managed to croak, trying to put all the irritation she was feeling into it, and none of the fear. "I'm going to be sick."

The woman pushed a bucket in front of her and said something to the man that caused him to get up and disappear. Lane heard a door close and was violently sick.

The woman offered her a cotton cloth, and Lane wiped her mouth and took the canteen that was offered. Her head was pounding. She saw that the woman was in her forties. Her dark hair, flecked with white, was pulled back into braids. She could smell some sort of brilliantine. Something familiar. She tried to snatch at it. The woman was square, practical, the same sort of flowered apron María had worn to the market. She winced. How long ago had that been?

"Where am I?" Her voice sounded sandy. Yardley! That was it. Yardley lavender brilliantine.

The woman shook her head and shrugged, and then removed the bucket and went out the door, raising her palm to indicate she'd be back in a moment. Lane used the time to look around. It was a simple room with an earthen floor, a small table with two wooden chairs, the cot she was on, army issue, and a chest of drawers with a bowl and a jug, full, she hoped, of water. Two curtained windows let in soft diffused light. Above the cot, a picture of the Virgin Mary. She had noticed this version in Mexico City. Dark face and a blue star-filled mantle. Should she be hopeful at this sign of someone's faith? On the far wall were two posters for films, she guessed, both featuring a beautiful raven-haired woman. She tried to read the names of the films, but her eyes still felt dusty and unfocused.

It was daytime, certainly. What time? With a shake of her head at her own stupidity, and then a wince at the pain that shot through her temple, she looked at her watch: 10:25. She remembered nothing after the moment she had put her head on the saddle and fallen into a deep sleep. With a cry of alarm, she thought of Darling. God, what had happened to him and the rest? She desperately wished she could remember being taken. She tried to remember if she'd heard gunshots, but couldn't. It still didn't relieve her terror that Darling might have been shot as part of her kidnapping. Trying to still her growing panic, she pushed herself off the bed and stood tentatively, causing her rib to hurt. The blood flow had returned to her legs, so she took some tentative steps toward the door.

At that moment the woman returned. Lane dredged up her name from the confusion of her first moments of waking into this nightmare. "Graciela," she said.

Graciela smiled and nodded. "*A lavar, señora.*" She pointed toward the dresser and brought the bowl and jug to the

211

table, along with another folded cotton towel. She poured water from the jug and dipped the towel into it, wrung it out, and began to gently wipe Lane's face.

So unused was Lane to being cared for in this way that she had an urge to take the cloth from Graciela and carry on herself, but she submitted patiently to the administration of the cool cloth to her aching forehead. Then the woman produced a comb and pulled it through Lane's hair, working gently through the tangles. When Graciela was satisfied, she stood up and indicated with her hand that Lane should follow. Outside, the sun nearly blinded her, and she could feel the whump of heat after the relative cool of the room she'd been kept in. She was shown to an outdoor privy. She could feel the eyes of a dozen people on her. Men with guns standing on a scaffold along the perimeter of a tall adobe wall turned to stare, women kneeling at fires looked up, their hands suddenly motionless, and even some children stopped whatever game they'd been playing to stare shyly at her.

Back again and seated at a table with a bottle of orange squash and a plate of beans and tortillas that Graciela had laid out for her, she began to feel a little more like herself, and able to consider her situation. Her fear for Darling superceded any other feeling, but the sight of the meal made her realize she was hungry. The nausea had mostly gone. The plate of hot beans had some sort of herb and garlic and she wasn't sure what else, and a good sprinkling of what looked like crumbled cheese. She had seen the women cooking on open fires, and she took in the slightly smoky smell of the food. She told herself sternly that Darling would be fine, perhaps even now frantic and looking for her. The aroma of the food was penetrating. She'd be no use to Darling if she starved to death. There were no utensils, so she took a soft tortilla out of the towel they were wrapped in and folded it to scoop up the beans. As good as they smelled. After a moment she began to give some thought to where she was. A compound, walled, perhaps a much smaller version of the hacienda mining camp in Fresnillo. Armed guards. And, of course, his name, Castillo. But then she remembered about how Mexicans organize their names. He was Salinas de Castillo. That meant that this was Salinas himself! The man who was reported to have captured Bob and his two companions. She shuddered. And shot one of them.

It was ridiculous how perfectly a fizzy orange drink went with the beans and tortillas, and she drank with something approaching pleasure as the sweet liquid went down her throat, even as she wondered if it was to be her last. She imagined producing it at a King's Cove dinner party and gave a wry smile. She would serve it colder, she thought, if she ever got the chance to serve anyone dinner again. She could see that there was no electricity here. A storm lamp sat ready for use on a shelf in the corner of the room. She imagined never seeing King's Cove again and sat, her hand around the bottle, one question uppermost in her mind: Why had *she* been kidnapped?

There was a light knock on the door, and it was pushed open and Salinas himself came in and made a small bow. "I hope you are feeling much better, Señorita Winslow. May I sit? But of course, I must say Señora Winslow, must I not?"

This exaggerated formality seemed laughable under the circumstances, but she remembered her training instructions during the war. What to do if you are captured. *Your only job is to survive. Keep calm, don't become angry, be co-operative without being servile, never plead, do not make threats.* She gestured to the second chair. "Please." It was, she thought, ironic that she had gone through the whole war without ever requiring these instructions, and now, here she was.

"You are enjoying the food. Good. You mustn't worry about your husband. Neither he nor the guides have joined us. They are still in pursuit of me and my . . . I was going to say 'guests,' but of course, in the interest of honesty I will say 'my prisoners.'"

Relief about Darling flooded her. So, he has Bob and his colleauges, she thought. She stilled an urge to glance around the room, as if that might reveal them suddenly. "Was it you who shot at us yesterday?"

His eyebrows gathered and he shook his head and put one hand on his chest. "Not me, obviously, or I would not have missed." He clamped his lips together and shook his head. "No. I should not make such jokes. I do not know who that was, señora, and it alarms me. My informant tells me there was one man, armed with a rifle. I like to be in control of things, and I have been unable to find out who shot at your party, or, in fact, who shot a man sent with a message last week."

"The young man in Fresnillo?" Lane asked. The food and soft drink had gone some way to removing her grogginess. "Was it a rival gang?" She immediately wished she had not used so pejorative a word for whatever he thought he was.

Salinas smiled briefly and shook his head. "'Gang' is an overstatement, señora, but no. I have control over considerable territory. An enemy would not dare. But you are here, and you are safe with me."

"If you did not send him to fire warning shots, why have you kidnapped me?"

Salinas shrugged pleasantly. "My agent told me you were very beautiful. I had to see for myself. They were not wrong." He smiled with another slight bow and pointed at the movie posters. "They told me you look like María Félix. They are right. She is an actress. My favourite."

But Lane wasn't having it. "I can't believe you kidnapped me to look at me. Someone in your position would do it for its strategic value. Believe me, I am nobody."

"*Brava!* It is evident to me in our short acquaintance that you are very much somebody. You are my guest because I merely wanted to assure myself that no one would be tempted to bring the police or the army. I don't like violence unless it is unavoidable. This situation with your husband's brother is already settled. The money is here with me. When your husband and his guide arrive, there will be nothing left but the formalities. I must think, as the Americans say, of my bottom line. An expression I learned in my time at Harvard. Further deaths would be uneconomical."

Lane fell silent and continued eating. Harvard? she thought. "So, my husband and his guide—I presume you mean Scott and Cruz? Are they on their way now?"

"Two of them, at any rate, have enjoyed the same good night's rest you have. It was really just Tuinal put into a bottle

215

of tequila. No doubt they are themselves just recovering. Are you familiar with this drug?"

"No."

"It is an American sleeping drug. It can make you feel sick and give a headache."

Suddenly Lane had a flash of memory. Being lifted, lying face down, jolted, feeling a sharp pain before she lost all consciousness. She put her hand to her rib. "I think I have a bruised or broken rib."

"*Ah, sí.* I am very sorry about this. It was a long ride from where you were camped. But"—here he smiled—"the good thing about ribs is there is little that can be done. They will heal on their own."

Biting off a retort of "Was that a medical degree you got from Harvard?" Lane sighed heavily and then regretted that as well. "Is my husband's brother here?" She waved her hand to encompass the compound.

"He is safe and in good health."

An answer that raised more questions than it answered. "How long, then, for those men to be released?"

Here Salinas sighed and turned his hat this way and that where it lay before him on the table. "You get right down to business." He nodded several times in grudging approval. "This whole arrangement was simplicity itself, but one or two problems have presented themselves. As soon as I had the men, I sent a bill for payment to the mine manager, which did not reach its destination. I learned that the messenger had been shot. I too thought at first that it was a rival, and I moved my guests to another location. I was quite angry because we have reached an agreement of sorts about territory, but I discovered it was not my usual rival. Who it was, I do not know. Perhaps that young messenger had annoyed someone all on his own." Salinas sighed and leaned back, pulling a pack of cigarettes out of his breast pocket and holding it out to her.

For a moment she was tempted—isn't a cigarette what every prisoner wants? "No, thank you." She frowned. She could not be in a situation she felt less able to understand or do anything about. She took a scoop of the beans and chewed it thoughtfully. Should she play for time? Would time, the great healer—ha!—be of any use here? "Can I ask what herb is in these beans? They are very good."

He smiled broadly. "Ah! You have discriminating taste. It is oregano, but not the one you have in North America. You taste the difference, yes? Also *comino* and *chile*, not too much. I was not sure of your tolerance." He lit his cigarette and dropped the match into a much-used clay ashtray.

Lane listened to the hiss of the match flaring and then said, "You like to cook?"

"No, of course, the women do the cooking, but I take an interest." He pulled in a draught of smoke and blew it into the air above him. "I will leave you now. I am most anxious to discover who attacked your party." Salinas got up and parked his cigarette in the corner of his mouth. With a pang, Lane suddenly thought of Robin Harris, with his everlasting cigarette in the corner of his mouth.

Lane nodded. "Am I confined to this room?"

"My dear lady! You are completely free to go about the compound. My men are armed, and though I would regret

217

it should it come to this, they have orders to shoot if you should attempt to leave."

Mexico City, 1939

IT WAS A small gathering. Not more than twenty women standing on the edge of the zócalo with placards. "Votes for Women!" "A vote for Múgica is a vote for the rights of women!" Lucía was disappointed with the turnout. People passed by as if these sorts of little street protests were par for the course. Few even looked up to see what this one was about. She'd been a child during the revolution, protected in the family hacienda, surrounded by pecan trees and peach trees, playing with her brother Héctor. Never with her oldest brother, Gilberto, who was serious and stuck-up.

Lately, as she had become involved with the movement, he tried to scold her as if he were their father. Only today he had grabbed her arm, yanking her away from the door as she went out the gate onto the street. She'd pulled away, yelling at him that he wasn't her father, and walked rapidly down the street, knowing he wouldn't come after her. He was too afraid of public scenes. Her arm still hurt. If only Héctor were here! He'd be proud, he'd want to come and march with her, and she'd have had to tell him that it was women only, and they would have laughed at the idea of him in a wig and a dress. "Women must free themselves," she'd told him once. Anyway. He was at Harvard, studying law. That counted. He would come back and help the movement.

Women had been granted the right to vote two years before, but the government had not ratified it. It was ridiculous in this day and age! And after a revolution that was supposed to liberate women from their oppression as second-class citizens. But if Múgica won the election, they would win the day.

"Votes for women! MÚ-GI-CA!" she chanted. The other women took up the call, raising their signs up and down.

Suddenly she heard a commotion at the other end of the line they'd formed. Marta was screaming angrily at someone. Now people passing slowed to see what the trouble was. Their line dissolved, as the other women pressed toward Marta to see what was happening, to stop it.

A city policeman had Marta by the arm, and more police were approaching. They waded into the group and began to push and shove. Lucía rushed toward Marta, her sign up, as if to hit the man who was dragging Marta.

"Stop it!" she screamed. "We have a right!" She aimed her sign, with its thin wooden handle, at the head of the policeman and managed to knock his hat off. Around her she could hear the scuffles and shouting increasing, as if all the women had joined the battle with the police.

She heard a loud male shout. "Stop at once. You are all under arrest!" Then a shot, and a second. This stopped everyone; Lucía turned and was surprised to see everyone frozen, mid-battle, as if they had become a Diego Rivera mural on a government wall. It could be called *The Revolution of Women*, she thought. A mist was gathering over it, and she tried to clear her eyes, blinking hard. It was beautiful. A painting full of action and colour. She wanted to hear what someone was saying. A woman—was it Eva?—was looking at her, reaching out, but the sound

219

was muffled, as if unseen hands were pressing into her head, covering her ears, wanting to stop her from hearing. Was that her name being called? She felt herself smile, could feel her own hand moving toward Eva's. And then the darkness.

Harvard University, 1939

HÉCTOR PRESSED THE black earpiece to his ear. "*¿Qué? ¿Mamá? ¿Qué dices?*"

"It is your sister, *mi vida*." Then she stopped.

"Are you crying? What's happened?" Héctor looked up and saw the dean whose office he'd been called to standing, looking helpless, his eyes on the carpet, his hands dangling at his sides as if they'd lost the power of movement.

"*Lucía, mi vida.* She's dead. A . . . a protest. Your father won't . . . you must come home!"

LUCÍA, HE THOUGHT, looking out the window as the train pulled out. Light. She was all light, his sister. Light and joy and passion. She burned like a flame. His father hadn't had time to talk to him. His guts burned at this. His secretary had said he had an important meeting.

Did his father know, he'd asked the secretary—what was his stupid name?—that his daughter was dead? Had been shot in the street? "I will have him call you when he is free." Alonso. That was his name. Alonso, the running dog for his father.

"Are you coming home?" His mother must have given the phone to Gilberto. Gilberto at least would talk. He was sounding more and more like their father. "Don't bother our mother. She has enough to cope with, with the burial."

"Burial? That sounds like something for a criminal! Why not 'funeral'? Why is she coping alone? What is our father doing? He is the head of the family."

"Father, quite rightly, has stepped away. She will be buried in a public cemetery."

"I don't understand." Rage was beginning somewhere near his heart. "We have a mausoleum at the Panteón de Dolores. Why—"

Gilberto had cut him off. "She brought shame on us with her public antics. She is no longer part of the family." And then he'd rung off.

ONLY HIS MOTHER and a few of Lucía's friends had come to the funeral. There had been no gathering afterward, they had all faded away from the small gravestone with her name and dates, the meagre wreath, all their father had provided money for, and now he and his mother were in the back of the car. She was folded in sorrow, her black clothes making her nearly invisible in the quiet dark at the back of the Bentley. Héctor had held her gloved hand. He tried to imagine how he would ever talk to his father. He envisioned shouting at the old man. But even as he thought of what he might say, what he could no longer hold inside, he knew it would do no good.

CHAPTER EIGHTEEN

"I DON'T KNOW, CONSTABLE. THE THING is screwy." Terrell and Ames were at lunch in the café, where they'd managed to wrest a couple of sandwiches from Marge. She served them up with a demand to know what they were doing about the kidnapping, and an observation that with them at the helm, it was no wonder no one was safe.

When she'd disappeared into the kitchen, Ames leaned in. "You think there's any chance someone would kidnap *her*?"

"What are you thinking, sir? About the kidnapping, not about Marge."

"Let's start with Tanney. I drove all the way out to Castlegar to that little bank he used. According to the bank manager, he would put his pay in regularly, like everyone else, and take money out to give his mother for housekeeping. Then suddenly the pay envelopes stopped, and he started bringing in larger amounts of cash. He did that two or three times at irregular intervals, but not on the usual Friday paydays, and then a couple weeks ago he took all of it out. Everything."

"That sounds like someone who's planning to move away in a hurry. How much money are we talking about here?"

"Nearly fifteen hundred dollars. I went back to see his mother and she didn't know anything about that money. He gave her money regularly and that's all she knew about. She's in a bad way now, because what she has is running out. She does own the house, though, so maybe she'll be all right. Anyway, she gave me a photo of him. We ought to see if anyone recognizes him around Nelson."

"Whew! So if you're Tanney, planning to do a bunk, why stop on your way and kidnap a kid?" Terrell asked. "And why is he planning to run away?"

"And that kidnapping. Let's imagine you're going to kidnap someone. Would you put a ladder up against a house in the middle of the night and yard a squirming, possibly yelling kid down it?"

"No, sir. I'd be more likely to try to snatch him outside, when his adult isn't paying attention." He took a bite of his grilled cheese sandwich and then put the sandwich down. "We found the front door unlocked."

Ames nodded. "Lots of people leave their doors unlocked. It's a small town."

"Yes, but she said she'd locked it."

"So, someone opened it and took the kid that way. Then why all the fuss with the ladder?"

Terrell sat back, turning his coffee mug. "I don't know. But what if it was someone he knew? They put up the

223

ladder, wake the kid, and say, 'We're going to play a trick on Mommy. Go and unlock the front door and we'll hide.'"

Ames sat up. "We need to go look again. For one thing, there is that ladder in the next-door neighbour's yard. We were caught up in trying to find the kid right away, so we didn't take a good look at the scene."

"WHAT DO YOU want?" Mrs. Radcliffe stood in the doorway, with Rocky looking up at the two policemen from where he sat playing with some wooden blocks.

Ames explained. "We're still concerned about the kidnapping, ma'am. We just want to go over the scene more closely."

"Go to your room, Rocky." She pushed the child toward the hall, and after one more look at them, he went off in the direction of his room. "Why? The guy who did it is dead. We just want to be left alone and try to forget it."

"Ma'am, that individual is dead, yes, but the person who paid him to do it is still out there. The more we can learn, the more easily we'll be able to thwart another attempt," Terrell said.

Mrs. Radcliffe took a deep breath. "Fine. Don't be all day about it." She stepped aside just far enough to let them through and closed the door behind them.

Rocky, who'd settled in to play with his cars, didn't see why he had to leave his room after he'd just gotten there. He put up a protest as his mother pulled him out. Waiting till they were gone, Ames pushed up the sash on the window. "Yeah, see?"

224

Coming behind him, Terrell looked at what Ames was pointing at. Scuff marks on the sill, removing the white paint and exposing the fresh wood underneath.

"The ladder definitely was used. But was the kid taken down it? I agree with you. I don't think so. It's risky for one, and even if you knew the kid, would you be able to keep him quiet?"

"Let's ask Rocky. He wasn't talking too much before, but maybe now he will remember."

They went back into the sitting room and Ames squatted down next to Rocky. "Do you remember anyone coming to the window when you went away?" Rocky ran to hide behind his mother.

She sighed. "It's no good. He won't tell me anything either. I'm not even sure he remembers. He must have been completely mixed up, getting taken out of the house at that time of day. Like I said, it doesn't matter anymore, does it? Can we just leave him alone?" She picked him up and he hid his face in her shoulder. "Are you finished here?"

Ames nodded. "Almost. We just have to check a couple more things."

She turned and walked into the kitchen with her son, asking if he'd like something to eat.

"Sir, I wonder if we should see if that ladder next door fits these marks?"

Back in the boy's room, Ames looked out the window that gave onto the backyard. "The fence between these two properties is low. It would be easy to get the ladder over and then back again. I'll ask her about the unlocked front door again and look around the front yard for anything we might have missed. You go get the ladder."

Terrell knocked on Bonny Sunderland's front door and explained that the Radcliffes had no ladder, and could he look again at the one they had in their backyard?

"Oh," she exclaimed and then looked behind her. She was chewing gum vigorously, which gave her an air of being a teenager. Terrell wondered if she'd been drinking. "You think he used our ladder?"

"We want to check, just to make sure."

"Okay. I guess so. Go on through." She gestured through the living room toward the kitchen. Nelson residences were mostly built along the hills that rose steeply from the lakeshore. The height difference between the front of the houses and the back was marked, so the stairs from the kitchen down to the backyard were much longer than the three steps up to the front door. "Do you want any help?" she said to him as he descended.

"No, ma'am. Thanks."

The ladder was still where he'd seen it the day before. He looked closely at the top of the ladder for white paint chips from the windowsill next door, and then at the bottom for residues of mud. He found both, but noted that the Sunderland house also was white, so it could have been used by the Sunderlands for their own purposes. He lifted it over the fence and dropped it carefully on the other side, and then went out the back gate and in through the Radcliffes' back gate.

It was the work of a moment to see that this ladder had indeed made the marks on the sill, and that tiny slivers

226

of white paint that adorned the top of the ladder showed exactly where it had leaned against the windowsill.

"You know what I think?" Ames said, as they started back to the station. "I think if Tanney did this, he knew the kid."

Ames stopped mid-stride. "Mrs. Radcliffe says she didn't know Tanney. Let's show her the picture. Maybe she knew him as someone else. It stands to reason that if she knew him, the kid might have known him before he was kidnapped as well." They turned back up the hill.

"No," Mrs. Radcliffe said, looking briefly at the photo and then handing it back impatiently. "I don't know him." She looked past the two policemen where they were standing in the door and waved. Bonny Sunderland was coming from next door with her son. "Now if you don't mind, I'm busy. We're taking the boys to the beach."

Terrell touched the brim of his cap as he passed Mrs. Sunderland, and then said, "Oh, actually, excuse me, ma'am. Have you ever seen this man before?" He showed her the picture.

Bonny Sunderland frowned at it, whooshed at her child to go inside, and then took the picture. Then she shook her head. "No." She sounded petulant, and Terrell wondered at it. "Who is he?"

"The kidnapper," Terrell said, taking the photo back.

DARLING STOOD UP awkwardly and clutched his head, groaning. He'd been sick, and Scott, who'd gone looking for traces of Cruz and Lane, looked like he would be sick at any moment.

"I can't see any sign of them along here. All the horses are gone except ours." Scott drew in a deep breath and seemed to fight off the moment of illness. He walked back toward Darling.

The sun had begun to throw heat, and Darling, in the grip of a pounding headache, a turning stomach, and outright fear, looked toward where those two horses now pawed restively at the ground. El Diablo and El Demonio. They'd be there at the last trump, he thought grimly. But they knew something was wrong.

"I see they left those two," Darling said. "Have they been kidnapped? I don't understand how we didn't hear anything at all."

"We were drugged," Scott said flatly. "Something in the tequila. Or the food."

"Then it *was* Cruz," Darling said angrily. "He probably works for Salinas!"

"Or some rival. Someone in the village might know. This is not what I expected . . ." Scott trailed off.

"What do you mean by that? You expected something?" Darling turned on him.

Scott held his hand palm outward and shook his head. "No, I only meant I expected we would get a representative from Salinas, who would come and negotiate." He took his horse's reins. "We better hurry, if we are to find where they have gone."

Darling's mind still felt addled, as if he couldn't order his thoughts. One thing had been clear: he feared for Lane, but now he added to this a suspicion that he could trust no one. "If she's been killed . . ."

"No, Inspector. Please don't think that. They won't do anything drastic, I feel sure. If they meant to kill anyone, they would have done it." He held the reins of the Devil toward Darling. "When you think of men like Salinas, you must always think in terms of money. It is unlikely he would hurt a valuable asset."

Darling took the reins and hoisted himself painfully onto his saddle. Diablo seemed to sense his suffering and did not, for once, execute his dance of rebellion, but waited passively to be told where to go.

They'd been shot at the day before. By whom? Darling was not at all convinced that Lane was safe wherever she was. His nausea began to ease up on the ride to the village, and he was left with only the headache and the grinding fear. Cruz. If he worked for Salinas, or another gang, the mine manager certainly did not know it. Cruz had been keeping Salinas informed through someone in San Jacinto, no doubt. Perhaps he was behind this staged shooting attempt. Was the idea that he would deliver Lane, and Salinas could then demand twice as much for all his captives?

"Do you still have the ransom money?"

Scott, riding alongside Darling, glanced behind him and reached for his saddlebag. The ties were hanging loose. He reached into the pouch. He didn't have to say. Darling pounded his fist on the pommel of his saddle.

"Someone in this town had better know something!"

"Yes, Inspector, they probably do. I am not so sure they will tell us."

As they approached the village, Darling noticed what he had not before. There was not a single electrical pole

229

or wire. There would be no telephone. He felt a surge of desperation. "Ask them where the nearest telephone is."

The villagers who were outside, tending fires, washing clothes, busy about their day, stopped and watched silently, as if Scott and Darling were a funeral cortège.

Scott leaned over and asked an adolescent boy leading a donkey burdened with wood and brush, "*¿Dónde está el cacique?*"

The boy pointed down the street with his chin, not taking his eyes off Darling.

At the end of the dusty street, past a row of whitewashed adobe houses, there was a small marketplace. The vendors, almost all women or children, sat on the ground under canvas awnings, waving flies off their produce. The red tomatoes and rusty-orange squash provided some splashes of colour in this dust-hued scene. A laugh rose up at a table behind the vendors, where several men sat. They looked up at the sight of the newcomers.

Scott dismounted and touched the rim of his hat. After a few words, they were summoned to the table, and chairs were brought out.

"I don't want to visit, I want to find my wife," Darling whispered furiously, leading the Devil around to the rail beside an adobe building with a blue door.

"Yes, Inspector. I understand. Please, leave this to me."

One of the men, whom Darling assumed to be some sort of village elder, said something to his companions, and all but two got up and went to inspect the Devil and the Demon where they were tethered and then leaned against the wall, smoking.

Scott indicated Darling should sit, and then removed his hat and began to talk. As he spoke, the two men turned to look at Darling and nodded sympathetically. Scott asked them something, and they both shrugged. He talked some more. Darling had never felt more helpless or enraged, and it took all his willpower to watch this theatre play out. He turned to say something, but Scott put up his hand.

"A moment, Inspector." He turned to continue with the two men, pointing at Darling. The two men looked at him with more interest. One of them shrugged and tilted his head, a pantomime that suggested he might know something, but not much.

The man spoke and pointed northeast and then shrugged again. There was a moment's silence.

"A telephone," Darling prompted.

"*Ah, sí*," Scott said, and turned to ask.

The second man made a flicking motion away from himself toward the south and said something.

"Not close," Scott said. "Farther than where Salinas is and in the wrong direction."

"Well, what does that mean? Do they know anything about my wife?" He glared at the man he assumed to be the headman, because he'd been doing most of the talking.

Scott put up a mollifying hand. "Please, Inspector. Remain diplomatic. What they know, they will tell us. I told him you are Canadian and will ensure they will be paid. We are discussing how that might happen."

A woman approached the table with a bottle of amber liquid and four glasses, and the elder poured out four slugs and pushed one toward Darling, with a smile and an encouraging nod. "*Canadiense*," he said as if it were an invitation.

Darling shook his head.

"Please, Inspector, take the drink," Scott said quietly out of the corner of his mouth.

"And get drugged again? Not on your life," he said back, smiling and nodding at the headman.

"They are drinking too; we are safe, I think. It will be an insult not to."

Darling tamped down his protest and took up the glass, raising it. "Cheers," he said.

The two men laughed, and with a "*¡Salud!*" tossed the drinks down. Darling felt the smoky liquid burn down his throat and land with a searing thud somewhere inside him.

There was more talking and more shrugging and more laughing, and then Scott rose and offered his hand to each of the men. Darling followed suit, finding his hand enfolded and vigorously shaken, his arm patted, the word *canadiense* repeated several times approvingly.

"One of the men from San Jacinto will ride with us a short way, just until we are near the compound."

"And then what? We ride in and demand the return of my wife and brother? Then we'll become hostages!" Darling snapped.

"The man says he heard that Salinas is just doing this to show you how much power he has, and that having your wife as a guest will guarantee that we do not bring police or the army. He has asked that we come alone." Scott gave a slight shake of his head. "He will probably stick by the original bargain. And he is famous for liking beautiful women."

Darling reined the Devil sharply, a move the Devil did not like and said so. "What bargain? There has been no bargaining yet, I thought. I thought the guy with the demand for ransom was killed. Is this Cruz again? He's been behind this, making deals?" Did Fine actually know this was how it would go all along? Did Scott? Darling felt himself in quicksand, unable to find any solid ground.

Scott shrugged, motioning Darling to continue. Their guide, riding up ahead, was paying them no mind. "You might be right. Perhaps Cruz knew all along. Maybe he has taken the money to Salinas, and that is why they say he is prepared to honour the original bargain."

Beginning to feel that he was but a minor actor in some vast unknowable drama, Darling rode on, fixated on something Scott had said, his heart ramping up anxiously. "What did you mean, Salinas likes beautiful women?"

Scott shook his head encouragingly. "It is nothing, Inspector. She is perfectly safe now. Salinas is a gentleman."

"A 'gentleman'?" Darling asked with unalloyed disbelief. "Safe 'now'? Was she not safe before? And how do you know he's a gentleman?"

"I am sure it is nothing to worry about. She is very self-reliant, and he will admire that, as I do. According to the cacique, he is a man of his word. Please, Inspector. If we continue to talk, this gentleman with us may become suspicious. Let's get there and see what's what, okay?"

"DO YOU HAVE my brother-in-law and the other geologist?"

"But I have told you I do, Miss Winslow. Perhaps if you see them, you will be convinced?" Salinas sighed, seeming disappointed at her lack of trust. "Alas, I do not have them here. They are at my other hacienda. Do not worry yourself. They are safe, and when your husband comes, we will conclude the whole business."

They were sitting in the shade of the compound wall at a table, drinking lukewarm Coca-Cola.

"Yes, actually. I would love to see them. Perhaps they could sit with us and drink Coke." She tried to keep the annoyance out of her voice.

"I can see you are still worked up, señora. I promise—"

"Of course I'm 'worked up'! I've been kidnapped, I don't know if my husband is alive or dead, or Cruz or Scott for that matter, and I don't know what's happened to Bob . . ." She forced herself to calm down, remembering the instructions for capture: *Do not become angry or make demands*. Right. She took a deep breath. "What I mean to say, Mr. Salinas, is that I am worried about the fate of the men. I apologize for my abruptness. I'm feeling a little powerless."

Salinas shook his head admiringly. "You are a remarkable woman. Not many would behave as you are under these admittedly difficult and unpredictable circumstances. And you have extraordinary power." He waved at the film posters. "She does it acting, but you are the real thing. My man was right. He is a great admirer of yours."

She inclined her head graciously. No need to tell him she'd been trained for this sort of thing. Seeking to move the spotlight off herself, she said, "It seems a long way from Harvard to here."

"Yes. I see how you must wonder. My family is very influential, and my father has vast business interests. I had a sister, younger than me by two years. She was at the university in Mexico City. They sent her to university only so that she would be a suitable wife to the son of another man like my father. But she was devoted to truth, like you, and brilliant. Much smarter than me. She became angry, as so many women did, that the government passed a law to enfranchise women in 1937 and then did absolutely nothing about it. They still can't vote, more than ten years later!"

"Goodness, I had no idea," Lane said.

"She wrote pamphlets, took to the streets from time to time with like-minded colleagues. My parents were furious. After all, they are in the pocket of the government. My father is, anyway. My mother was always guided in her fury by him. They told her she was bringing shame on the family with these public protests and she must stop, but she refused. One day there was a scuffle with the police at one of the demonstrations, and she was shot." He paused here, as if he might not go on.

"How very dreadful for you! A beloved sister is a great loss."

Salinas nodded and cleared his throat with a shrug. "Our parents were so ashamed of how she'd died that they buried her secretly and said her name was never to be mentioned. She was buried among strangers. Of course, I dropped out of university and came home at once, my heart filled with anger at them and the police. The rest, I think, you can imagine. If my parents refused her, then I must refuse my parents, and here I am, using what business acumen I learned at my father's feet for my own purposes."

Lane sighed. "I'm sorry. It sounds like she was a wonderful person." If she was surprised that his tenderness did not extend to any of his victims, she did not say. After another lapse of time, she said, "Are my husband and Mr. Scott safe, Señor Salinas? I would feel less worried if I knew."

Frowning, Salinas said, "This Señor Scott. He is from the embassy. An undersecretary. This is another thing I don't understand. Why send someone so high up on this trip? They have others who would do as well."

Lane shrugged. "He speaks Spanish. Perhaps it was to show how seriously the embassy takes this." She wanted to add that no one likes foreign nationals being kidnapped.

He shrugged. "Maybe you are right. It is just unusual." He smiled suddenly. "Come. You will soon see for yourself your friends. I sent Cruz for them, but they found someone in the village to bring them." As if he'd planned it, there was a shout from one of the sentinels along the wall. "There. Your party is arriving. You may reassure yourself."

He invited her to climb the stairs that ran along the wall leading to a lookout platform. The wooden platform creaked with the added weight of Salinas and Lane, and the lookout pointed southwest, where Lane saw three riders approaching about three hundred yards away. As she watched, one of the riders stopped and detached himself from the group and began to retrace his steps.

"I don't understand," Lane said, her hand shielding her eyes from the westerly afternoon sun. "There should be three. Is that Scott leaving them now?"

"No. It is one of the men from San Jacinto. They had instructions to bring your husband and Scott here to me."

"Then where is Cruz?" Lane anxiously watched the approaching riders, waiting for one of them to be clearly visible as Darling. Had he met the same fate as Bob Darling's Mexican guide?

"His job is done. He brought you here. Once he saw that they would get here on their own, he went home."

As this sank in, Lane turned on him, aghast. "Cruz is your man?"

He smiled at her. "Exactly, señora, he is my man, very trusted. How astute you are! Though he is a staff member at the mine. He has what you might call a double role."

She tried to understand the enormity of having been in the hands of Salinas the entire time. Thomas Fine, who trusted Cruz implicitly, couldn't have known. She turned to him. "What is your intention, Señor Salinas? Will you be holding all of us hostage?"

He shook his head, smiling indulgently as if to a child. "I like you, Señora Winslow, and I am not completely mercenary. If we can conclude the business of your husband's brother satisfactorily, and I have a certain guarantee that I will not be visited by the police or the army, I will be happy to return you and your husband to your own lives. He is a lucky man, and I am a romantic at heart."

CHAPTER NINETEEN

"IS THIS THE PICTURE OF** the guy who died on the *Moyie*?" April asked. She held up the photo that Tanney's mother had given Ames.

"That's right," Terrell said from where he sat at his desk in the back of the room.

"I've seen him around," she said thoughtfully, gazing at the photo. "What a way to die!"

Getting up, Terrell went over to the desk and took the picture. "You've seen him around? Where?"

"You know, around town, like at the movies, or at the Chinese one time. Usually evenings."

"You sure it's him?"

"I'm pretty good with faces. I don't know the woman he was with, but if I saw her again, I bet I'd know her right away."

So, Terrell thought. Tanney had a girlfriend and a bit of a social life here in town. "By the way, he wasn't killed by the *Moyie* paddlewheel. He was shot and fell off the *Anscomb*

238

and somehow got tangled in the wheel as the *Moyie* went by. He died instantly. Wouldn't have felt a thing."

April nodded and took the picture back. "That's a relief! I can ask around if you want."

"Why don't you mention that to the sergeant? I'll stay here with the phone."

Smiling, April went up the stairs with the photo and knocked on Ames's door jamb. "Excuse me, sir. I was just talking with Constable Terrell about this picture." She held up Tanney's photo. "I've seen him around town a couple of times, and he was with a woman. I was going to offer to ask around for you, like at the places I saw him."

Ames flipped over the writing pad on which, if the truth be known, he was doodling, and put down his pencil. He wanted to say, "April, do you really have to call me 'sir' like that? We used to date, after all," but instead he said, "That's a good idea, Miss McAvity. The constable suggested that it's possible Tanney actually knew Rocky, and that's why it was so easy to get him away."

April was about to respond when Ames frowned. "The only problem is, Mrs. Radcliffe said she didn't know him, so that means it's unlikely the kid did."

"I'm going out after work to run some errands. I can ask around. I know for certain I've seen him here in town, and not that long ago."

April's initial inquiries yielded nothing. The gas jockey at the Esso station down the road said he could have been one of fifty different guys. The girl at the Civic Theatre ticket booth, just readying for the first show, turned her mouth down and shook her head.

"He mighta been a guy who came here with a girl once, but I never look very hard."

Then on a whim April stopped by Sunderland's restaurant.

"Boy, you never come in here from one month to the next and now twice in a week," Sunderland said. "Where's the fella you were with?"

"He's working. I am too, as a matter of fact." She said this with a measure of pride. Here she was, actually making inquiries! She pulled the photo out of her purse. "I've seen this guy around town, not too long ago, but I can't remember where. You see a lot of people in here. Does he look familiar to you?"

Sunderland took the picture and looked at it closely. "Wow. This must have been taken a while back! He's a friend of Bonny's from high school." He didn't sound too pleased about it.

"THANK GOD!" DARLING exclaimed, hugging Lane hard, causing her to squeak at the pain in her rib. "You can't imagine what I've been thinking!" He held her away from him with his hands on her arms. "Are you all right?"

"A slight bruise on a rib or two; otherwise, perfectly," Lane said. "You?"

"I am now. But are you sure nothing's broken?" He looked at her with concern.

"It's a little painful, but otherwise not grave. Don't fuss."

"What the blazes happened?" He looked around the compound, the gates of which had been thrown open when they dismounted. Darling had had eyes for nothing but Lane. Now he could see that there were plenty of people around them, all of whom had stopped what they were doing to watch, and a disconcerting number were armed with rifles.

"Darling, let me introduce Señor Salinas, our host."

Salinas, who'd been standing behind Lane, removed his hat and nodded in a genial manner. "Welcome, Inspector Darling. You are a lucky man. Miss Winslow is most agreeable."

Darling nodded curtly. "Yes, thank you. May I ask if you have been finding my brother, Robert Darling, most agreeable as well?"

Salinas laughed, throwing back his head, causing the men with rifles leaning against the compound wall to nod and smile, glancing at one another. Lane noticed Graciela standing next to some other women in the doorway of an adobe dwelling built against the wall. She did not smile but watched her boss with a steady gaze, her mouth set in an expression Lane could not entirely decipher. *Skepticism* was as close as she could get.

"You are what I used to hear described as a 'card' in my Harvard days, Inspector Darling. Please. Come in. I have refreshments and we can talk." He stood aside to point the way through the door into the room in which Lane had woken up addled in pain, though when, she could not rightly remember.

Salinas snapped his fingers at Graciela, who went inside with the women.

"And this is Mr. Scott, from the British embassy," Lane said. Scott came forward and offered his hand.

"Ah, yes. Mr. Scott," Salinas said in a voice no one would have called warm. He shook Scott's hand, looking closely at him, and then said, "Well, come in. Make yourself at home."

When they were sitting around the table, Salinas leaned back in his chair. A bottle of mezcal stood on the table, along with a bottle of milk-coloured liquid and some soft drinks with a small metal bottle opener and some glasses. "Food will be here in a minute. I can see the anxiety you have, Inspector, but as you can see from your wife, I am a perfectly harmless person. No one has anything to fear from me. We will talk when we have eaten. It has always been surprising to me how quickly North Americans want to jump into the business of the day, eh, Señor Scott? Mezcal? It is the best. I have it made at one of my farms in the south. Or perhaps you will try a local drink, pulque. Also mine. It has great spiritual value. But no. We will start with the mezcal. It is less . . . startling than the pulque." He poured out four small glasses and pushed them over. "*Salud*, and welcome," he said, shooting back his drink.

With some misgivings, Darling followed suit, earning a nod of approval from their host.

Salinas seemed to be waiting till all the glasses were empty. Lane, feeling a bit in for a penny, in for a pound, swallowed hers and winced, but thought in the end that it was a smooth enough drink. Only Scott held his, looking sullenly into the liquid. Finally, in a silence Lane felt was increasingly menacing, Scott drank his down with a great show of reluctance.

Salinas smiled and nodded, deflating the tension in the room, and leaned back with one arm slung over the back of his chair. "Tell me, Señor Scott, how you came to be involved."

Darling sighed. He felt he'd barely recovered from the drink in San Jacinto. "Mr. Scott," said Darling, just as Scott had been about to respond, "has been a big help to me, to us."

"Of course. And he is most welcome." Salinas bowed his head, giving Scott another keen glance. "Undersecretary, I think?"

"Yes." After a moment Scott asked, "How did you know?"

Salinas tapped his temple with a forefinger and winked. He turned to Darling. "There, Inspector, are you happy? Your wife is safe, your brother is safe. Soon it will be all over." Darling heard the glittering edge of a knife in that tone, but was it meant for him, or Scott? He glowered at his host.

"Mr. Salinas went to Harvard," Lane said to break the tension. "Tell us about that. How did you find it?"

Salinas relaxed and smiled, waving his hand in a modest rejection of any intended compliment. "My father is a wealthy businessman, and I am his youngest son. The legal profession, for which I studied, did not agree with me. I wanted to be rich like him and my brother, who is his right-hand man." He shrugged. "Now I have my own business." Lane could see that he was not going to repeat the story about his sister, and she had not expected him to. This was to be a contest of male will, she thought, and his attendance at Harvard gave Salinas a high card. He had snapped it up, to her relief. She did not want him feeling one-upped.

"Your business is . . ." Darling began and felt a sharp rap on the top of his foot. "Is diversified, I see."

Beaming, Salinas said, "Exactly! Everything from agave to livestock to, well, you know, this and that. And here is our food."

Graciela and two other women came in carrying bowls and utensils, and a large, round-bottomed clay pot, which they balanced in the middle of the table on a kind of crown woven of rushes. They placed a spoon by it and set the bowls out.

"*Birria*," Salinas said. "Goat stew. I believe you will enjoy it very much. I raise the goats myself."

"It is delicious," Darling said after a few moments, in spite of himself. He'd had about enough of the man's towering ego, and he was anxious about the almost electric feel of underlying threat. This was a man who had killed the Mexican guide sent by the mine without a thought, and no doubt many others in pursuit of his "business" interests. He tried to keep in mind what Scott had said to him: that he needed to think of Salinas purely in terms of money.

He looked up at Scott now. He was eating quietly, looking down at his food. Indeed, he'd said barely a word since he'd been brought in, apart from a quick exchange in Spanish with the man who took their horses, and his question to Salinas. Had he been pointedly looking at Lane a moment ago? Why? It was as if he were sizing her up in this ridiculous setting they found themselves in. He wondered if Salinas's obvious distrust of Scott was rubbing off on him. Darling glanced across the table at Lane and tried to see if he could knit together any of the disparate things that had happened to them since they'd left Mexico City.

"Thank you, Mr. Salinas." Darling leaned back, his bowl empty. "Tell me, how *did* you enjoy your experience at Harvard?"

"Very much. It helped my English, I made business connections there. I disappointed my father. I believe he

244

hoped to bring me into the legal arm of his business. 'You will be one wing of our business, and your brother will be the other,' he used to say. But me, I am a whole bird. I like to fly on my own."

Darling smiled and gave a little tilt of his head in acknowledgement.

"That is good, no?" Salinas said.

"Very," Darling said. He waited.

"You will ask how I keep on the good side of the law, because it is true that some of my practices are unorthodox." Here he smiled modestly. "Some of my crops might be considered illegal, even. I can say I have an arrangement. Our police are not well paid, and I can offer a bit of help. It works for everyone, no?" He waved his hand in the direction of Graciela and the other women who stood against the wall, waiting. Like the butler and footmen at a country house, standing at the ready to serve, Lane thought. The marks of power and wealth do not change whatever the setting.

The dishes were cleared, and coffee brought in mugs, hot and very milky and sweet with perhaps a touch of some sort of spice?

"I know you are anxious to know of your brother, Señor Darling, but really, the business is already over. I have my payment; in truth it is slightly more than I asked for in the beginning. My messenger, unfortunately, was shot, so you will not know what I asked for, but what I have will do. The only thing to arrange now is the rendezvous."

Darling sat silent, stilling his rising anger at being part of these theatrics. Finally, he said, controlling his sarcasm as he might, "Oh, good. Then you have the money."

"Certainly. Cruz was kind enough to bring it when he escorted your wife here."

"May I ask, by the way, what was the point of bringing her here? I'm assuming in a drugged state, as I can't imagine she would not have kicked up a fuss at being dragged out of a deep sleep and taken somewhere against her will."

Salinas smiled broadly, looking at Lane, as if imagining her spirited response to being kidnapped. "I see you are upset. There is no need. As you can see, she is in the best of health. Cruz told me she was remarkable, and I wanted to see for myself." He smiled and then shrugged. "If I am honest, I also wanted to ensure you would come on your own. Others in the past have been tempted to involve the *Ejército Nacional*, the army. I have learned over the years that this is best avoided. Though I do have many friends there as well." Here, a modest smile.

Lane had watched these interactions, and, like Darling, tiring of Salinas's continual flow of self-aggrandizement, she wondered if it would be best for her to leave them to it. She could make the excuse of trying to find out how birria was made. She stood. "I wonder if you gentlemen will excuse me. I need a little air, and perhaps I can help the women and learn how that lovely meal was made."

Salinas leaped up, followed by Darling and Scott, who shot a look at her. "Please, madam, avail yourself of anything you like. As you know, the women do not speak English, but I am sure they will find a way to explain, perhaps even show you which herbs are picked for it. Señor Scott and Inspector Darling and I can finish up these trivial last few details."

As she was leaving, she heard Salinas. "Tell me about the horses you came on, Señor Darling. They are animals of great spirit. Normally these are horses for Mexicans, but . . ."

It was still hot outside, but a slight breeze came from somewhere. There was a kind of lethargy in the centre of the compound. The guards were leaning over the wall on the scaffolding, smoking and talking, though they all turned to look as she came out. Children, some anxious at the appearance of a stranger approaching, some smiling shyly at her, sat on the ground, or with the women on the benches in the shade of the wall.

It looked as though everything had been cleaned up from the lunch and they were now chatting and fanning themselves. Graciela stood up and nodded and then called Lane over with a forward scoop of her hand.

"*Delicioso*," Lane said, patting her tummy.

"*¡Ah, sí! Gracias. Cabra.*" She put her hands to her head, forming little horns, and made a bleating noise.

"*Cabra*," Lane imitated with a laugh. "'Goat' in English." She too made the little horns and repeated, "Goat."

Lane considered how to mime, "How do you make the stew?" She made a stirring motion with her hand and then shrugged, with her hands out in a question.

"*¡Ah! Cómo hacerlo. Sí. Venga, señora.*" Graciela led Lane to the kitchen, which was located in one of the adobe structures. A fire burned low within a surround of adobe bricks in the centre of the earthen floor. There were clay containers with what looked like corn kernels in a liquid, and several large black grinding stones. Graciela picked up

247

a round-bottomed ceramic pot, blackened on the bottom with use, and placed it on top of the bricks, to demonstrate how the stew had been cooked. She pointed inside and began to list ingredients very slowly on her fingers. Lane understood *goat* and thought something like tomato and then heard the word *oregano*.

"Oregano?"

"*¡Sí, orégano!*" Graciela said enthusiastically. "*Mucho tiempo,*" she added, miming the pot on the makeshift stove, and then sleeping and waking up. "*Orégano mexicano.*" She reached to where a bundle of dried herbs hung from the low rafter and took a pinch in her fingers and put it into Lane's hand.

It smelled pungent like oregano she'd smelled in Europe, but different. It had an overtone of . . . she tried to find words, and it came to her that it was an overtone of the very desert they'd ridden across.

Lane smiled. "A long time." She pointed at the fire and then her watch and ran her finger around the dial.

"*Sí. ¡Así es!* 'Lon time'!"

"*Gracias,*" Lane said, taking Graciela's hand. Graciela responded by putting her hand up to Lane's cheek and nodding. Then she put a hand gently on Lane's rib, nodding again.

Surprised, Lane had the momentary feeling that Graciela was trying to heal her with her touch. She smiled and said again, "*Gracias.*"

The door to the house where Salinas had been hosting the negotiations opened and the three men came out, blinking in the bright sun. Salinas pulled a pair of dark glasses out of a pocket and put them on, surveying the courtyard.

"There is still a great deal of day left, Inspector. I will have your horses brought, and one of my men will take you to where you may find your brother and his colleague. You will have enough time to ride back to the camp near the prospecting site."

Lane joined them while Salinas shouted something at a couple of his men, who trotted off toward the stables.

"All done?" Lane asked.

Darling shrugged. "I will be happy when I've laid eyes on Bob."

Salinas turned at this. "You will find him in the best of health, Inspector. Both of them. You have my guarantee."

"You must thank Graciela for me, Señor Salinas. She has shown me how to make that wonderful stew. And I am grateful for the way she cared for me."

"She is a good woman. She is a *curandera*. A healer. She has great power. She is the widow of one of my men. A very loyal man who died a year ago."

How might he have died? Lane wondered. Was she a willing servant of this man? She felt again Graciela's gentle touch on her rib and wondered at it.

A man in a large straw hat and the loose white trousers and shirt that seemed the universal costume among Salinas's men approached on horseback, leading the Devil and the Demon.

Salinas nodded in appreciation. "Very fine horses. What are their names?"

"Devil and Demon," Darling said. "Where is my wife's horse?"

"Devil and Demon," Salinas said, laughing. "*Diablo y Demonio*. You are honoured, Inspector, that they allow you to ride them."

"Where is my wife's horse?"

Salinas shook his head with a smile, as if Darling's impatience were that of a child. "She is there. Do not worry. I will send Miss Winslow with someone to Fresnillo in a day or two. It cannot be longer, I'm afraid, as we are moving everyone to my other home. It is a security precaution. And I have business in the city."

Darling looked thunderously at Salinas. "Absolutely not! I insist she come with us now."

Salinas raised an eyebrow at Darling with the merest scraping of a smile. "With what, Inspector, will you insist? I have your weapon. It will be returned to you by my man in good time."

"You cannot keep her prisoner here. It is completely outrageous!"

"'Prisoner,' Inspector. It is an outrageous word. I have no intention of imprisoning your lovely wife. She is my guest until I am certain that you have not involved the *federales*. Besides, I am not convinced you can keep her safe. I am not happy that someone shot at your party. She will be safe here."

Darling dropped the reins decisively. "Well, I'm not going without her." His voice had modulated to steely decision.

"Look here, Salinas," Scott said suddenly. "I'm going to have to insist that she be allowed to come with us."

"Ah. You too are insisting, Señor Scott. The hand of your embassy does not have reach here. In fact, I am scarcely able to understand your presence here. Please do not insist. It will only erode our friendship further."

Lane watched. Salinas was outright threatening embassy staff. Did he have this sort of power, or did he just think he did? And why his obvious hostility to Scott? She glanced at the undersecretary, who had an expression of studied impassivity. With a wave of surprise, Lane too found herself suddenly wondering about Scott. Was Salinas right? Scott certainly was high up for this sort of assignment.

"I'm not going without her," Darling said again.

"Darling," Lane turned to him. She had listened to this conversation with growing unease.

"Nope. Can't be done. I stay."

"Señor Salinas, may my husband and I speak privately somewhere?"

Salinas waved his hand toward the house where they'd eaten. "Please. Don't be all day. Time is passing."

"We need to think about this carefully," Lane said when they had closed the door.

"I don't think we do. Scott can go get Bob and take him to Fresnillo, and then you and I can follow with that madman's 'guide.' And what the blazes does he think he's protecting you from? He's the real danger. He'll just hold you for more money."

"I don't think he will. And, for what it's worth, I think he is genuinely interested in my safety."

Darling barked a mirthless laugh. "And I am not? What does he think he is protecting you from? My incompetence?"

Lane reached out a placating hand. "Don't be silly. I don't think we should object to Salinas's plans, lest he become impatient."

"*He's* impatient? I'm sorry. I'm not going without you and that's that."

"He's holding all the cards. I don't see that he will change his mind, and I'm not afraid to stay." Lane paused. "What if I were a man?"

"I don't follow. You're palpably not," Darling said, staring at her.

"Would we be having this discussion if I were a man? You would see it entirely differently. You would be pragmatic and see that you hadn't any other option. You might flip a coin to see which one of us would go, but there wouldn't be all this fuss about not going without me."

"Don't be . . ." He was going to say "silly" but changed it to "too sure." "If you were one of my men, I wouldn't leave you here, just the same."

"This is what I think: Salinas is worried about who shot at us. We have no idea who the target was. It would be far safer if I stayed, and you got Bob and his colleague to safety."

He harrumphed. She was probably right. On the other hand, he very much did not want to leave her in Salinas's care for another two days, for all he might be a gentleman.

CHAPTER TWENTY

"DON'T LIKE IT," DARLING SAID. Every fibre of his being rebelled at the idea of leaving her behind.

"We came here to get your brother, and we are this close to it. Are you going to stand on some masculine pedestal declaring you can't leave the little woman? That's my point. If I were a man, you'd be halfway there by now."

"Shows what you know. It's women who are usually on pedestals, though you've fallen off yours, I can tell you that for nothing!" At this Darling turned to go out the door.

"Where are you going?"

"To have a chat with your buddy, Salinas."

Lane longed to follow him, but she thought better of it. She used the time to survey the shadowy room. There was a window at the far end, built into the outer wall of the hacienda, and she went there now and pulled it open, letting in a gust of warm, dry air.

The desert sloped away to the west, dotted with nopal cacti and slightly fragrant with some aromatic plant. Perhaps the oregano, which must grow out there. It occurred to her that she could, if left alone, escape through this window, and in the next instant she saw movement and perceived that Salinas kept armed men in the heights around the compound. She sighed and wondered what it would be like to spend another couple of days here. She could help Graciela and the women with cooking, thus increasing her range. She was just imagining a dinner party in King's Cove with everyone sitting down to bowls of goat stew and bottles of lukewarm soft drinks, when the door opened and Salinas and Darling came in, followed by Scott.

"Ah, Señora Winslow. The inspector and I have been talking. He is not willing to leave you in my care. I must say this is completely understandable to me. He is a man. A man, well, is a man. And, he has certain responsibilities." Salinas shrugged, smiling ruefully, helpless before the imperatives of this life.

Lane looked at Darling, who had his hands behind his back and was gazing innocently at one of the movie posters, very nearly aping Salinas with a little shrug. "What are you saying?"

"Just this, Señora Winslow. If you do not mind terribly, could you ride out with one of my men to collect your brother-in-law? My man will ride with you all the way to Fresnillo. I will send the inspector along in a day or two with Scott. Inspector, if you would step outside, I must have a word with your wife."

"Just a minute," said Scott, his face flushing angrily. "That's not what we agreed. We agreed I would stay here with Mrs. Darling, and Darling could go ahead as planned."

254

"You too, Señor Scott," said Salinas coldly, indicating the door.

Hesitating, Darling looked at Salinas and then Lane, and catching a tiny movement of her head, he nodded and went out, not without a nearly audible sigh, followed by a clearly resistant Scott.

"Señora, you do not mind? I'm afraid he does not trust me. Of course, he is right in some ways, but I respect him." He tilted his palm from side to side in a gesture that suggested he more or less respected Darling. Going over to a table he opened a drawer, pulled something out, and returned to her. He opened his hand and revealed a small pistol. "The one I don't trust at all is Scott. I want you to take this. It is a derringer. It was my grandfather's, and I have kept it in good condition."

Lane stepped back in surprise. "I can't take a family heirloom from you, Señor Salinas, especially as I won't need such a thing."

"Please, do not hurt my feelings. I want you to have it. My gift to you." He smiled and pointed at his poster of María Félix. "For her sake if not for yours. And"—he shrugged—"I do not know that you won't need it. Have you fired a weapon before?"

"I have, yes, but . . ."

"Of course you have." Admiration in the smile and shake of the head. "This is very ordinary and not complicated. Keep it in a pocket. As you see, there are five extra bullets in the chamber built into the handle." He demonstrated on the weapon. "Do this for me. Please. I will feel better."

Reluctantly Lane took it. "I will send it back with your man when we reach Fresnillo."

He shook his head and folded her hands and the gun between his own two large palms. "No. You will not. Thank you for taking it."

OUTSIDE, LANE, HOLDING the bridle of her horse, looked at Darling. "How did you do this?"

"I took your advice. There, you are a man now, and you will go get my brother, and Scott and I will stay here. Salinas and I understand one another. We men do, don't you know." He grimaced slightly. "And don't worry about the fellow he's sending along with you. It's our old friend, Cruz. Safe as houses." He turned so that his back was to Salinas, who was issuing instructions to that man, and whispered, "Salinas has his family. Charming man, all around, don't you agree? Great admirer of yours, I understand."

"Well then," Lane said. She didn't want to leave him any more than he wanted to leave her, as it turned out. But Darling's solution had been artful. "You can spend some of your time learning how to make that nice bean dish I had yesterday, since our roles are reversed. And get to know poor Scott. I feel as if our host has taken against him because he represents the government in some way."

"I will borrow an apron from that nice woman."

"Graciela," Lane supplied.

"Darling, please be careful." He had lowered his voice again. "I mean it."

"So do I. Please try not to aggravate him." She felt a kind of wild desperation at leaving him, and took his hand.

256

"It's all very well all of you being manly, but the first rule of being captured is not to swagger about when you've been captured."

"Me? Swagger? Why, thank you. So, you admit we've been captured. For a moment I thought you believed yourself to be at a weekend house party."

"SEE THIS?" AMES said, holding up the photo of Tanney. Bonny Sunderland glanced at it and looked away with a supreme lack of interest. "This is apparently your very good friend, since you were young. Jim Tanney."

"Who told you that?"

Terrell watched her face curiously. It was remarkable to him how many people were prepared to believe that if they just denied things energetically enough, they would be believed.

"Your husband, actually. I didn't get the impression he thinks much of the friendship. Are you the woman Tanney's been seen around town with?"

Mrs. Sunderland clamped her lips more tightly together.

"I'm afraid this changes everything, Mrs. Sunderland. Between the business of your ladder and Tanney's taking Rocky, you are on our radar for this." He stood up. "If you're not prepared to talk to us, I'll have to ask you to come down to the station. Constable, could you go next door to Mrs. Radcliffe and ask if she can keep Mrs. Sunderland's little boy for a bit longer?"

"Sir," Terrell said, making for the door.

"I won't go. You can't make me. I haven't done anything wrong!"

257

"I'm asking for you to come voluntarily, Mrs. Sunderland, to assist in our inquiries. I could ask Constable Terrell to get an arrest warrant, but I wonder if that is necessary."

"Don't I get a lawyer or something?"

Ames nodded to Terrell, who had paused by the door, to go ahead. "And Constable, could you get in touch with Mr. Sunderland, and let him know we will be talking to his wife, and see if he can get a lawyer?" He turned back to his obdurate witness. "Now, I could cuff you but I'm sure it's not what you'd like the neighbours to see. How about you come along quietly?"

APRIL LOOKED UP as the door opened and Ames came in with Bonny Sunderland.

"Could you get some water for Mrs. Sunderland, Miss McAvity? We'll be in the interview room."

"Yes, sir. Could I have a moment, sir?" She led him over to the counter and pulled over her notebook, quickly scribbling, *That's the woman I saw him with.*

Ames nodded. "I'll make her comfortable downstairs. You bring the water. I'm expecting the constable any minute, maybe with a lawyer."

Terrell came back shortly with a very nervous-looking young man in a suit. "This is Thomas Edwin, sir. He'll be Mrs. Sunderland's legal counsel."

Edwin offered a slightly clammy hand to Ames. "Sergeant. I . . . I don't know the client and I've never done this sort of thing before. I just started up with Padgett. He said it would be good experience. Er . . . is my client under arrest?"

"No, Mr. Edwin, she is not. I have asked her to come down here in order to answer some questions she refused to answer when we visited her home."

"What . . ." Edwin hesitated as if trying to determine if this might be the right question. "What is the charge?"

"There is no charge as yet. Her neighbour's child was kidnapped, safe home now, thank God, and it turns out she knew the kidnapper. She did not reveal this prior. It has been complicated by the fact that said kidnapper is now dead, shot by someone while in the custody of the RCMP."

"Dead?" Edwin glanced anxiously at the door as if the whole thing was more than he had bargained for.

"Correct. What I want to know is what her friendship with this man entailed, and what she might know about the kidnapping that she has not told us."

In the interview room, which felt crowded with four people in it, Ames and Terrell faced Mrs. Sunderland and the worried-looking young lawyer.

Terrell looked at his watch and wrote down the time of the interview next to where he'd written the names of those present.

"All I really want to know, Mrs. Sunderland, is why you didn't tell us you knew Tanney, and how much you know about the kidnapping. So. How long have you known Tanney?"

She turned to the lawyer. "Can he ask me that?"

"I think so, yes," he stammered uncertainly.

After a moment's sullen resistance, she said, "We went to school together. With Linda too."

Terrell raised his eyebrows. "Excuse me, do you mean Linda Radcliffe?"

"Yes, she was Linda Bolen then."

Terrell made a note and underlined it. Linda had categorically denied knowing him.

"And you kept up your friendship?" Ames asked.

"What do you think?"

"I don't know. That's why I'm asking you."

The lawyer moved nervously and looked about to say something.

"Yes, we 'kept up the friendship.' After all, Linda . . ." Then she clamped her mouth shut again.

"Linda what?"

Looking sulky, Mrs. Sunderland seemed to be struggling with what to say. "Linda moved here from Penticton when she got married, and I married a Nelson boy pretty soon after and moved here too."

That's not what she was going to say, Terrell thought.

"And how did Tanney fit in? He lived in Castlegar."

She shrugged. "His mom moved there from Penticton after his dad died. You know, he'd come into town for this or that."

"You and Linda Radcliffe both kept up this friendship with Tanney?"

"No. Not her so much 'cause, well, you know. They didn't get along that much."

Ames felt his heart take a leap. "Why didn't they get along?" Here surely might be the cause of the kidnapping. Some sort of childhood vengeance.

"I don't know, they just didn't."

"I find it hard to believe that as her best friend you wouldn't know."

"Do you tell your best friend everything?" Mrs. Sunderland crossed her arms and stared straight ahead.

"Was this a plan you and Tanney hatched together?"

"What do you mean 'hatched'? Are you saying *I* had something to do with this?" She glared at Edwin, who shrugged nervously.

Terrell spoke suddenly. "I wonder if what happened is that you went up the ladder and woke Rocky and told him you were going to play a little game, and then sent him out to the front door, where Tanney could collect him."

Mrs. Sunderland's face grew beet red, and she jerked her head to the side, looking away from all of them at the blank wall.

"Why? I wonder. Why would Tanney want to kidnap Linda's child?" Ames took up the next question.

There was a long silence.

"Because it was *his* child, you moron!"

September 1942

THIS TIME, LANE sought out the field officer, Morris, first thing. She hadn't wanted to see Harrison. She didn't like how he could not seem to trust her. In any case, it had been Morris, not Harrison, who'd sent her out on that last disastrous mission. She sat outside Captain Morris's office, bobbing her crossed leg nervously. She wondered how long Alma was meant to have been gone on this mission. She remembered her shock when she'd found the money taped to the underside of Alma's bedside table. She hadn't told Alma what she'd seen. Her shock when she realized Alma was the reason Charles had died. She had to tell them. She knew they wouldn't answer her question, but she had to take the risk. "Sir." She stood and saluted as he came in.

"What is it, Winslow?" He bristled with impatience.

"It's Alma, sir. Alma Ryan, my flatmate."

"I know who she bloody was. What of it?"

"What was her mission?"

"You know I can't tell you that." He made to go past her into his office.

"No, sir, I mean, it's Alma. The leak."

The officer pulled her into his office and shut the door. "What are you saying?"

"She had ninety pounds hidden in her bedside table, but then needed to borrow ten from me. That means it's someone else's money. She couldn't resist taking some of it for herself, so she bought herself a silk dressing gown. The dressing gown is gone and so is the rest of the money. You've sent her in, but she was never planning to come back, and neither is whoever went with her. She was going to deliver the money to some Breton nationalists. I don't know what she thought would happen, or if she knew Charlie would be shot. I don't know what went wrong, or why she was shot. But she was the leak. But I think someone else here is as well, maybe had been manipulating her, or maybe they were working together."

The field officer sat down hard, his hand to his mouth. "Bloody hell," he said. "I didn't hear what was said, they were in his office, but she had a blazing row with Harrison."

ANTOINE HAD BEEN shocked to see Lane and had looked anxiously behind her into the night to see if she'd been followed. He'd pulled her down to the ground hard. Lane's mission had been to drop in to evaluate things on the ground, find out what more was needed. She'd had a rough landing, her parachute had become tangled, and she was cross and tired. She didn't appreciate being pulled about.

"First Alma, now you. Is this a new offensive?"

Lane ignored the question and asked in surprise, "Alma is here? Who is with her?"

"No one. She was alone. She's buggered off into the house with those Breton nationalists. I was about to leave my cover to meet her when she met them, as chummy as you please. Imagine my amazement when I saw they seemed to expect her. Well, one of them, anyway. Alma gave them something, and then suddenly one of them hauled her away into that barn. I don't think it's what she expected. She had a bag, like she was going to stay. She wasn't planning to go back to England. She was shouting at him." He looked away. "He tortured her. I could hear her. She is a traitor, but . . ." He spat.

Horrified, Lane looked back toward the safe house. Alma, the money, the silk dressing gown all crowded into her mind. In the next moment they watched Charlie walk into the clearing from the woods to their left of the safe house, looking for them. Lane wanted to jump up, to wave and warn him the house had been taken over, but before she could move, a shot rang out, and he fell forward.

Feeling a wave of horror, Lane clutched at Antoine's wrist. "We have to get her! They've killed him, and they are going to kill her! She had their money and she thought she'd be safe."

"They'll have to get in line behind me! All right, let's wait until dark. We can decide if there is a way."

They would never get the chance. In the next moment they heard a woman's scream, and then the shot.

CHAPTER TWENTY-ONE

"I THINK YOU KNOW MR. CRUZ," Salinas said, with hardly a blush of shame.

"I do, yes," Lane responded, attempting a courteous smile and failing. Her rib still hurt abysmally from her initial voyage to this compound. She was checking the cinch on Lorita and contemplating another long period on horseback.

Scott, who had been watching the preparations, came forward and spoke urgently in Spanish to Salinas, waving an arm in Cruz's direction. He received what even the non-Spanish speakers could see was a sound rebuff.

Darling watched the proceedings in silence, his mouth set in a grim line.

Lane approached him, leading Lorita. "It will be fine. Oddly I feel quite safe with Cruz. And though I suggested you could keep busy trying to learn how they make those corn tortillas, I suppose you will be kept busy playing games of chess or something with our host."

"Just because we've designated you the man, that has not made me woman enough to be allowed into the kitchen, alas. I'm afraid I'll have to content myself with two days of manly verbal jousting with *mein* host. Perhaps there actually is a chess set somewhere here."

She dropped her voice, pretending to have a last intimate farewell. "I should warn you that he keeps armed men in the hills around here, so don't do anything rash should you tire of the jousting."

"Of course he does. Apparently, I'll see you in a couple of days. Good luck with Cruz. I can't think how he'll explain himself to his bosses at the mine. I should think his life as a double agent is finished."

"We must go now, Mrs. Darling," Cruz called from near the gate. He was already mounted and was leading two horses.

"Off you go," Darling said, trying to sound chipper. He linked his hands to give her a step up.

"You will be sleeping in a soft bed by tomorrow night, Miss Winslow," Salinas said, looking up at her. He took her hand and kissed it. "It has been a pleasure. And please, I will take care of him and send him back in excellent condition."

"Equally, Señor Salinas. Can you thank Graciela for me especially? She has been so kind."

"Consider it done."

Scott watched the proceedings with growing fury. "This is outrageous. I must be allowed to accompany her!" He moved toward Salinas, and immediately two men came from nowhere and took his arms to hold him back.

"If I do not send her husband with her, do you think I would trust you?" Salinas said. A word from him and the gate opened.

They clattered out and into the desert, Lane riding next to Cruz, wondering what on earth they would find to say to each other. But then she remembered that Salinas had his family and wondered what that entailed. Salinas, charming though he was, was ruthless. How many people did he command through sheer fear? His own entourage, plus all the people in villages all around who were not active members of his brigade. They must, she conjectured, pass information, and support the bandits with food and who knew what else.

Cruz broke through her thoughts. "I am sorry, Mrs. Darling." He didn't stipulate for what, but Lane thought she knew. "I did not mean to hurt you. I learned you have a painful rib."

"I don't think it's broken, just rather bruised. I will survive." She wanted to ask him about his family, where he lived, how he had become entangled with Salinas. She wondered if he was happy with his situation. Instead, she asked, "How far away are the men?"

"It is about five hours. We have left late, and we will arrive close to dark. We will stay there, and then we will cut across a short way and up onto the plateau to Fresnillo tomorrow. We will be there by early afternoon."

"How will Senor Salinas know that we have been delivered with no involvement from the police or army?" She hoped she would not have to try to persuade Thomas Fine not to contact either authority.

Cruz spoke without looking at her. "I leave you when we near the town and will ride back immediately to bring your husband and Mr. Scott."

They rode along in silence but for the sound of hoofs on the dry ground. Because of their late departure, the sun was already directly overhead, and the air seemed to have stilled completely so that the heat pressed in from all sides.

After what seemed like hours, Cruz suddenly spoke again. "I will not ask you to keep my role a secret from Mr. Fine."

"What will you do?"

"I will work only with El Jefe now. I hope that with my skills I may find other ways to be of use. I speak English, I understand the American mentality. There are other mines and North American enterprises all over the country. I am loyal. That alone has value."

He meant of course that he was loyal to Salinas, not to his recent employer at the mine. "Do you not live in Fresnillo with your family?"

Cruz shrugged. "We did, yes. El Jefe has already relocated them."

They stopped to rest under the shade of a solitary mesquite that spread its thorny branches in a wide arc. The horses drank from a tiny rivulet of water snaking through a shallow arroyo. Lane sat on the ground and drank from her canteen, worrying about having to get back up on her horse. The contrast of the bare landscape they were riding over and the densely forested green surround of her home in King's Cove struck her forcefully. Life seemed uncomplicated here in this grove, and for a moment she relished it. Over there, all around, was sun and heat; here was shade, cool, rest for the eyes. She took off her hat and let the slight uptick of a breeze cool the sweat on her forehead, her needs pared down to this one sensation.

She fanned herself, wondering how Darling was getting along with Salinas. "I wonder what my husband and Salinas are doing," she mused. In these circumstances, with the close-lipped Cruz, she knew this question to be rhetorical, even whimsical on her part to expect him to answer. She could feel her voice shake slightly, a sign of her anxiety.

There was a momentary silence, and then Cruz surprised her. "He will be charming your husband. It is a great skill of his."

Wondering what form this charming exercise might take, Lane nodded. "He will have his work cut out for him with my husband. He is as immune to charm as any man I know. Maybe Mr. Scott will be charmed."

For the first time since she had met him, Cruz uttered a brief laugh. "Then I hope your husband knows how to at least act charmed. Salinas becomes impatient when he thinks his efforts are going to waste. As for Scott, he has gotten off on the wrong foot, as you say, with Salinas."

Not wanting to think about what an impatient Salinas would be like, Lane got up. "Ought we to move on?"

Back in the saddle, they fell again into silence, as if this were what this desert required of them. Lane was trying not to worry. Darling did not suffer fools gladly, and Salinas was a very special kind of fool. Appealing, clever, narcissistic, ruthless. And, she thought, surprisingly sentimental; perhaps the death of his sister had something to do with this. She worked herself into a state of calmness with the knowledge that if Darling found a way to annoy Salinas, he would still be worth more money alive than dead. But Darling himself was no fool. And he had a kind of honest charm of his own. Perhaps they would keep each other amused. Scott, she realized, was a separate sort of problem. No, not a problem, she conceded. He'd been offered as a generous impulse by Herridge at the embassy. He had been useful in getting them this far, and as a translator. What surprised her a little was that he seemed to have so few diplomatic skills. Salinas had become suspicious of him almost right away, and Scott had made no effort to mollify him.

LANE FOUND THAT the monotony of the steady ride across the bleak countryside had sent her mind tumbling down the crevasse that was that day Charlie and Alma were shot. What she thought next almost made her pull back her reins. When Charlie and Alma had been shot, the nationalists hadn't waited. They'd collected the radio equipment and disappeared. That meant they hadn't known that she and Antoine were expected . . . but Alma *had* known!

SEVERAL MORE HOURS passed, and Lane was finding both her jumbling thoughts about Alma and the ride gruelling. The day was dying, and while the ball of sun poised above the western horizon was an impossible shade of luminescent gold, the dropping temperature reminded her they might still have some distance to go. It looked as if there was nothing all around them for miles but desert and low hills, but then Lane suddenly saw, as if it materialized out of the very ground, the distinctive black shape of an hacienda in the distance.

"Is that it?" she asked, not daring to hope.

Cruz nodded.

The horses picked up their pace as if they too sensed the end of the day's journey. Two armed men watched them from the wall and shouted something to people inside. When they arrived, the wooden gate was pulled open, creaking and grinding, and they rode through. The first person Lane saw was Bob Darling, standing among the crowd of men, women and children, his hand up, shading his face. When he saw her, his hand clutched his forehead and then he threw it up, waving.

"Lane!" He pushed forward and was there to embrace her as she dismounted. "What in all the heavens . . . Where's Fred?"

Lane smiled in relief. He had grown a beard and his hair was past his collar, but he looked well fed. Was this captivity, or had he been growing this beard from the moment he left Vancouver? "He's fine. Señor Salinas is holding him back as insurance. He'll be along, I hope, in a day or two. You look pretty well. They've been feeding you properly by the look of it."

"I'm afraid if I see another bean or nopal cactus I'll lose the will to live. My Spanish has improved, though." He shook his head and looked at Cruz and frowned, turning back to Lane. "I just don't understand how you are here. I can understand Fred haring down here to rescue me, but what madness induced him to bring you?"

"I induced him to bring me. I will explain about Cruz later. Where is your colleague?"

"Arnie's in bed over there." Bob Darling, looking worried, waved at an adobe house behind him. "He's picked up some sort of bug. I hope he's over the worst, but he's lost weight and is feeling pretty awful."

"Will he be able to ride out tomorrow morning?"

"I think he'd ride away from here even if he was at death's door."

Cruz was leading the horses to an enclosure where two boys took charge of them. He issued instructions in Spanish and then returned to where Lane and Bob were talking.

"Bob," he said by way of greeting.

"Arturo, good to see you. Thanks for bringing Lane and my brother to help. I was wondering if we'd been forgotten."

Cruz nodded. "I will accompany you most of the way tomorrow, and then I must go back for your brother."

"Good, thank you."

"Señor Salinas has asked that the authorities not become involved." More a statement than a request.

Bob gave an easygoing wave. "Not on my account. I'll just be happy to get out of here. I'm not so sure about the mine owners though. They don't want this sort of thing to keep happening."

"Has it happened before?" Lane asked.

"A couple of years ago, apparently." He smiled suddenly. "Let's go have something to eat and drink. You must be famished! There is a lovely sunset to be had, and the stars at night are out of this world."

Lane smiled at his little joke. She'd always liked Bob. He was affable and cheerful, where Frederick could be serious and impatient. Nothing seemed to faze him. She thought suddenly of his fiancée in Vancouver, Isabel. How very unlike they were when she saw Bob in this context. He almost appeared to have enjoyed his time in captivity. Isabel, she was certain, would approve of none of it. She had a wild thought that the minute he got home and had a shave and a haircut, he'd be off to another dangerous place to work. Was this difference what was behind their embarrassingly long engagement?

When Bob had shown Lane to where she would be sleeping, once they were alone, he became serious. "They killed our guide, Pablo Ramírez. He put up a fight when they surprised us in the middle of the night. He was ridiculously brave. I don't think he's been properly buried, and his family may not even know yet. I will have to go tell them myself when we get back. He was really heroic. It's a bloody shame."

AMES AND TERRELL sat dumbfounded, and Edwin was gaping at his client. Only the sound of Bonny's vigorous work with her gum was audible for a few moments until Terrell cleared his throat, though not with a view to saying anything.

"Are you saying that Rocky is Jim Tanney's child?" Ames managed.

"Yeah, but you didn't get it from me."

"Mr. Radcliffe doesn't know? He believes he is Rocky's father?"

"That's right." She looked at her watch.

It was going to be like pulling teeth, Terrell could see. "So Tanney wasn't kidnapping him for money." It was not a question so much as a realization.

"I don't know about any money. He got into a kind of mood lately about Rocky being his and he wanted to have him. He was going to take him away. He said he was coming into money and could look after him. Move to Alberta or someplace."

Terrell leaned forward. "Mrs. Sunderland, why did you help him? I had understood that Mrs. Radcliffe was a close friend."

She shrugged and looked accusingly at her lawyer, who she began to realize was going to offer nothing in the way of assistance. "Who said I helped him? Anyway, it wasn't fair, was it, little Rocky not knowing who his real father was? Now he never will know him," she finished glumly.

"Did you talk to Mrs. Radcliffe about this? About why you thought it was important for Rocky to know his real father?"

"She wouldn't listen to me. She didn't want him to know anything about Jim. They fell out the minute she got pregnant, and she married Radcliffe right away to cover it up. She met him in a bar, as if that's a good place to meet anyone. Poor sap! I don't blame him for running off."

Hardly the thing to say about a best friend, Ames thought. "Why do you say that?" he asked.

"Oh, don't get me wrong. She's a great mother and everything, but she's kind of bossy, and she doesn't like anyone else to be the main person in Rocky's life."

"And when she was frantic about where he was, did you do anything to relieve her fear?" Ames was finding much to dislike in this woman.

Mrs. Sunderland was sullen and fidgety, and said nothing. She looked over at Edwin again.

"Well?" Ames said.

"I knew the kid was going to be all right."

"But she didn't. Can you imagine how she was feeling?" This was a genuine question. Ames wasn't sure she could imagine how anyone outside herself was feeling. "I want to know when you decided to help Mr. Tanney. You've been seen around town with him. Perhaps you met and decided on a plan."

"Who's seen us around town? That's a lie!"

"I'm afraid it's not."

She shrugged, giving up the pretence. "He's a friend. He was unhappy. I knew he wouldn't do anything bad to Rocky. He loved him."

"He loved him?" Terrell asked, surprised. "He had a relationship with the child?"

Sullen again, Bonny crossed her arms. "No, but . . ."

"So how is it he loved him if he had no contact with him? And he left the child on the side of the road on his own, by the way."

"Look, she wouldn't even talk to Jim. We used to all be friends, you know. Now she's too stuck up to even see him or let him see little Rocky. Poor kid never even met him. His own father!"

"And it didn't bother you that you were plotting against your best friend?" Ames asked. "I'm very curious. Why would you do that?"

"She had it coming," she said peevishly.

Suddenly Edwin did speak. "Will you be charging Mrs. Sunderland with anything? I believe she has answered your questions."

"You mean besides aiding and abetting in a kidnapping?" Ames asked irritably.

"Until you can prove that Mrs. Sunderland indeed had anything to do with the kidnapping, I don't believe you have grounds." He seemed unsure about this.

Ames sighed. The child was back, and they had the bigger problem of who killed his father.

"I have sufficient grounds, Mr. Edwin. The ladder was hers, and she told us outright that she knew the boy would be safe, which means she knew who had taken him. And she collaborated with him. Kidnapping or aiding in a kidnapping is an extremely serious offence with considerable jail time attached to it."

"Anyone could have taken that damn ladder!" she snapped. Edwin put his hand up, as if to stop his client from saying any more.

"So, you *are* arresting her?" he asked.

Ames glanced surreptitiously at Terrell, who studiously held his pencil above his notes. He thought about her child at home. "For the moment you are free to leave, Mrs. Sunderland. I'll type up your statement and will ask you to come in tomorrow afternoon to sign it. Please don't leave town. It is very likely that charges will be brought."

"I will be coming in with her to verify the statement is accurate," Edwin said, apparently relieved that there was a clear road ahead for some sort of action on his part.

"By all means," Ames said, getting up. It was, he thought, like dealing with a group of surly high school kids.

CHAPTER TWENTY-TWO

"**Y**OU KNOW THAT BULLET YOU gave me?" Gilly said.

Terrell nodded at his telephone receiver and then said, "Yes."

"It's the right size. It definitely is the right size for the wound. As I said, he was shot at point-blank range at the temple. Shooter would have been standing right by him. It did not penetrate the central mass of the cerebrum, which likely would have stopped the bullet of a small-calibre weapon. That's why it didn't lodge in his brain."

"Thanks, Dr. Gillingham," Terrell said. He hung up and opened the drawer, taking out the pistol Cooper had found where Tanney had been camping. So Tanney had been shot by a gun like this, at point-blank range. Who would have followed them onto the ferry? What if it was someone who knew he had money? After all, he apparently had fifteen hundred dollars. Whom had he told? The gum-chewing Bonny came to mind. She probably knew, if she had collaborated with him to take the child. He'd have to find out where she'd been the day Cooper and Tanney were coming back.

If she had shot him, could she have heaved him over the side of the ferry on her own? She wasn't a big woman. It seemed unlikely.

He picked up the phone and asked to be put through to the Creston detachment to speak to Cooper. He was out. Terrell asked the Mountie on the line, "When Sergeant Cooper picked up Jim Tanney from that campsite, did you book him and collect what he had in his pockets?"

The man on the other end of the line said, "We did book him. Cooper asked me to do it, in fact. Tanney had an inexpensive watch and a wallet. A few dollars. We returned them both when he left with Cooper."

"No large sum of money? Did he say anything about why he gave up on the kidnapping?"

"Maybe six dollars. One minute. I'll check." There was a rustling of papers, and he came back on the line. "Six dollars and thirty-two cents. I remember, he had the change wrapped up in the bills and it was in his pocket. Nothin' in his wallet but an expired driving licence. As to why he dropped the kid, I did ask. I think I said something like the man who was paying him to take the kid must be pretty mad about now, and he said he probably wouldn't have gotten his money anyway. So I said, 'A big waste of time, then.' And he said he wouldn't know what to do with a kid, anyway."

"Did he mean the man who was paying him, or himself?"

"Himself. I think his exact words were 'What am I going to do with a kid, anyway?'"

"It's a real puzzle, sir," Terrell said to Ames after his conversation with the Mountie. "There's no sign of the money. According to Creston, he had a little over six bucks in his pocket. We'll have to check where Mrs. Sunderland was on the day of his death, of course, but did he hide the money somewhere?"

"And there's still the question of where he was getting it in the first place. He said he was 'coming into' some money from somewhere. Obviously not from anyone who paid him to kidnap Rocky; it seems like he was kidnapping him on his own account, and then maybe just thought better of it. So, he gets rid of the kid and is now waiting for more money. From where?"

"Blackmail?" suggested Terrell.

Ames snapped his fingers. "Mrs. Radcliffe! Let's go!"

"HOW DID YOU find out?" Linda Radcliffe said, sitting stiffly at the kitchen table. They could hear Rocky playing with his cars in his bedroom.

"So, it's true," Ames said. Terrell wrote. "Can you tell us about it?" Terrell noted the kindness in Ames's voice.

"It's the same old story. I got in the family way just at the end of high school, and I left home because I wasn't going to give my parents the satisfaction of saying 'I told you so.' I met Rocky in a bar. Too much to drink, if you must know. You'd have thought I would learn."

"Did you keep it from your husband?"

"Of course I kept it from my husband! I despised Jim. I think I almost persuaded myself the baby was my husband's. He loves that kid. He might as well be his father."

279

"Mrs. Radcliffe, was Jim Tanney blackmailing you?"

Her face dissolved into astonishment. "Was he what? What would I have to give him? I live on the scraps Rockford sends me, and there's sure not any left over. I can barely go to the pictures once in a while."

Terrell's pencil scratched across his notepad, and before Ames could formulate his next question, she spoke again.

"But I'll tell you this: I wouldn't put blackmail past him. He was always a conniving little snake. Never liked to earn a dollar if he could get it some other way. He used to steal money from his own mother when we were kids. Shoplifted too. When I got knocked up, I cut him off completely. I didn't ever want my little Rocky to be stuck with a dad like that. I'm not sorry he's dead. I couldn't believe it when you told me it was him."

"That's why you pretended not to know him?"

"Does this have to get out? I can't afford for Rockford to stop sending me money."

The next question was awkward. It had the potential to destroy a friendship. "Mrs. Radcliffe, have you and Mrs. Sunderland ever had a falling-out?"

She looked up at this, surprised by the question. "What's that supposed to mean?" When Ames didn't answer, she bit her lip. "Are you suggesting she had something to do with this?"

"You were all friends at school. I wondered if there might have been something, some old grudge?"

"Who doesn't have some old grudge, for God's sake? The two of them were always thick as thieves. Jim was always more her friend than mine. They even dated in grade 12.

I never did understand her taste in men. Sunderland's a boring stick-in-the-mud. But I guess he's better than a two-bit chiseller like Jim."

Ames nodded, and Terrell looked up. "Mrs. Radcliffe, was Bonny upset about your affair with Mr. Tanney?" he asked.

"Affair? Don't make me laugh! It was a one-time thing. She was upset at the time, but by then she wasn't with him anymore."

They did have good reason to believe Bonny Sunderland was involved in helping Tanney kidnap the boy, but Ames was reluctant to say it. Let sleeping dogs lie, his mother would have said. The thing was over, Rocky was safe, Tanney was dead. He gave an internal shake of the head. What they had to do now was find Tanney's killer. "Mrs. Radcliffe, where were you on the afternoon of August 11?"

"What day was that?"

"The day Rocky was back."

"Oh, Bonny and I and the kids were down at the beach, trying to put things back to normal for the kids. Ask anyone."

LEONORA FINE ENVELOPED Lane in an embrace. The gate-keeper at the mine had sent a boy scurrying to the Fines' house to tell them that Bob, Arnie, and Lane had returned, and she'd been hurrying down the walk toward the gate to meet them.

"Thomas will be over the moon! I've sent word to him at the office. Bob, look at you! You look like you've been vacationing on a desert island! That beard! Hello, Arnie. So good to have you back!"

Bob nodded and helped Arnie slide off his horse. "Arnie is awfully ill. Can we get him inside and get a doctor? The ride here has been gruelling for him."

"My word! Of course." She rushed forward to help walk the sick man into the house.

"GLAD TO BE back. I'm sorry we didn't make it to the site and get some samples," Bob said when Arnie had been put to bed and the doctor sent for.

"Don't be silly! No one cares about that! Let's get you something to eat and drink and then you can go to your quarters and sort yourself out. We'll have a big dinner here tonight. Lane, you brave thing! But where is your husband?" She looked past Lane at where the gate was closing.

Lane explained that he'd be along the next day or the day after with Scott, and why. "I'd love to have a bath before anything else."

"I would too," Bob said. "I'll head home and come up when I'm more presentable. We can tell you the whole story then. I'm just glad Arnie's in good hands. I'll stop by and tell his wife."

Equipped with bath salts and a silk robe for after, with instructions to take all the time she needed, Lane went gratefully up the stairs to the beautiful room that she felt she'd not seen for months, though it had been only four nights. She luxuriated in the bath and then lay down on the bed in the silk robe and closed her eyes.

And then she opened them. The silk robe. Alma's bloody emerald-green silk robe! She sat up, puzzled to yet again be revisiting this episode. It lay practically in the dark ages

282

compared with where she sat now. She remembered when they'd gone to arrest Harrison, the man who'd betrayed them. He must have sensed he was done for because he'd disappeared. He'd cleared out his flat and vanished. She remembered her anger at his having been her commanding officer, grilling her, doubting her, dismissing her ideas, when all along he'd been playing his own double game in the middle of a war. It came to her now forcefully. He had told them about Charlie, maybe even instructed them to kill him. And Alma. Harrison had been using Alma to deliver the money to the Breton nationalists, playing on her weakness for money and the nice things she'd never had. She'd been expendable to him. Lane sat up, plumping the pillows behind her, frowning at the window, where the evening was beginning to descend.

All along she'd believed Alma had been in it with Harrison, that she had betrayed them, caused the nationalists to be there when Charlie arrived and had him shot. She shook her head. They must have tortured her to find out if there was another drop. Alma must have known there was, that she herself was coming with Antoine. She must have! Why did she not tell them? What did Alma say that made them satisfied it was only Charlie who would be coming?

Had she been upset they'd killed Charlie? But that would have made her more likely to talk. She would have seen they meant business, that her own life was in danger. But she hadn't. There hadn't been time. She'd been tortured, then shot, without ever revealing anything about Lane and Antoine.

"Why?" Lane said quietly to herself. Had Alma had second thoughts? If she'd been working with Harrison, had she thought better of it and decided just to run away? But it had been too late to pull back. Harrison would have had her shot just to cover his own tracks. And *he* hadn't known about Lane and Antoine because she had got her orders from Morris. If he had known, he would have waited and had them shot as well. For the first time she felt gratitude for the service's ethic that the right hand should never know what the left is doing. But she thought of poor, gullible, wasted Alma with a great well of sadness.

And when it had all been over, her new commander had delivered a terse "Well done." Never another word about it, or Harrison, or where he might have gone. Had he been caught finally? He'd have been executed if he had been. He was a traitor. Perhaps it was just as well she hadn't known.

Maybe it was meeting Salinas that had dredged up these memories. He had that same sort of ability to casually use people for his own ends. He, at least, was charming. Harrison had not been. He'd been British to the core. Short, slender, wiry, full of repressed angry energy. A small man with big ambition. An imposter, as it turned out. A soldier's soldier, always in a temper, snapping at underlings, commanding through fear. No one would have suspected him, if it hadn't been for the damn green silk robe Alma couldn't resist buying for herself with some of the money she was supposed to be delivering to the Breton underground.

Lane dressed, pulling herself away from those memories, sorted what she could do with her damp hair, and went downstairs to be greeted by a very relieved Thomas Fine.

"I don't know how you did it, my dear, but I've never been so glad to see anyone! Arnie's wife is with him upstairs with Dr. Alcaraz. I think they'll arrange to get him back down the hill to his own bed when the doctor is finished. Bob will be over soon, and I want to hear everything. I can't understand how you were allowed to come on your own without your husband. It's shocking. Now, a drink!"

Lane shrugged and accepted a gin and tonic. "Salinas wanted to be sure no one would call out the army. I was in very good hands, really."

Fine shook his head. "Well, it's no job for a woman, that's all." He took an irritated drink and then sighed. "I understand Cruz has gone back to fetch your husband. He's been invaluable, I must say. Is that thing strong enough?" He waved his glass at hers and stood over his drinks trolley looking like he needed the drink more than his guests did.

Was it her office to tell him Cruz was not what he'd seemed? Yes, she decided.

Lane approached Fine and said quietly, "There is actually a problem with Cruz."

Thomas frowned and stood uncertainly, a hand still resting on the trolley. "He's all right, isn't he? He's not been hurt or anything?"

Lane shook her head. "He's fine. It's not that. I'm afraid Cruz works for Salinas and has for some time. I don't know if he did it willingly at first, but Salinas has moved his family away from Fresnillo, and though he may not have been keeping them actually captive, he certainly has them within his own sphere. When Cruz comes back with Frederick and Scott, he will drop them off on the outskirts of town as he did us and then return to Salinas."

This revelation caused Thomas Fine to go white and put the drink down, as if he were afraid he'd spill it. He staggered backward to a wingback chair and sat heavily. His wife looked up from where she sat by the fire, waiting for Lane to join her. When she saw his face, she jumped up and hurried to his side.

"Are you all right, darling? Lane, could you get María up here? She has some knowledge of first aid."

"No!" Fine put up his hand and sat up straight. "There's nothing whatever wrong with me! I've just had a shock, that's all. Give me my drink!"

Lane took the drink off the trolley and handed it to him.

"I'm sorry, Mr. Fine. It is a shock, I know. I was pretty shocked myself."

Leonora looked a question at Lane.

"It's bloody Cruz!" Fine said, anger bringing colour back to his face. "He's a bloody turncoat! Works for Salinas now . . . no . . . has for some time."

"Lane, is this true?" Leonora said, blanching.

Lane nodded. "Cruz knew where we were the whole time. I think Cruz was keeping them advised through villagers near the prospecting site where Bob was headed. Someone shot at us, and Cruz scared them off. Salinas swears it wasn't him, but I'm not sure it wasn't just a ploy to warn us not to try any funny business."

"This is horrendous! You poor thing! You could have been killed!" Leonora exclaimed.

"And I'm afraid that it was Cruz who drugged us all with some new drug from America . . . something with a T. Salinas told me himself. It was in a bottle of tequila he brought back from the village where he'd gone to get food. I woke up with a badly bruised rib inside Salinas's compound." Lane took a large gulp of her gin and tonic. "This he did confess to, Salinas, I mean. All he wanted, he said, was a guarantee that the authorities would not be involved. He could not have been more hospitable. He's keeping Frederick for the same reason."

To a rapt audience Lane told the rest of the story of her time in Salinas's hacienda. "But the Mexican that you sent with Bob was shot by his men."

"Oh, God! Pablo Ramírez. How will I tell his family?" Fine put his hand over his face and emitted a great sigh.

There was a knock on the door and Bob was shown in, newly shaved, his shaggy hair slicked back, and dressed in clean slacks and a white shirt. "What's happened?" he asked, surveying the scene.

"Bob, tell me about Ramírez," Fine said, indicating a chair and mixing him a drink.

Sitting down next to his host, Bob shook his head. "It all happened so fast. We were sitting by the fire, and Cruz suddenly got up and took out his gun, telling us to get down. Pablo went for his sidearm as well, and next thing I knew he was down."

"Did Cruz . . . ?"

"No. I don't think so. He was shot by someone behind him, more or less. The next thing I knew, two other men came out of the darkness, also armed to the teeth. One even had a bandolier. It was like some bloody comic opera! We were told to mount, our hands were tied, we were blindfolded, and our horses were led I don't know where. It was then I noticed Cruz had disappeared. Poor Pablo tried to defend us." He looked at Fine and shook his head. "He was a good man. I liked him. You know, none of those men tried to take a potshot at me or Arnie. We're worth money, I suppose," he added grimly. "Where is Arnie, by the way?"

"He's going back to his own house as soon as Alcaraz is finished with him. His wife has been frantic. It sounds like he gets sick easily, and this mess made it worse."

Bob nodded. "I'm glad. He was in a bad way. Listen, Tom," he said urgently, "I'd like to be the one to tell Mrs. Ramírez. I was there."

Fine nodded dumbly.

"Salinas is only interested in money," Lane said. "Kidnapping is business, as he sees it." She sighed and took another swallow of her drink. "He did very well out of us. We brought some money with us, and we added it to the kitty. I suppose there is a kind of honour there. When I was hijacked, I found out his men also took the money from where Scott was keeping it. When I say 'his men,' I guess I mean Cruz. Anyway, Salinas said he would honour the bargain and release Bob and Mr. Grant, declaring he got even more money than what he initially asked for."

Fine growled, "Bloody scoundrel! I'll have the law after him. He's no better than a thug!"

"A Harvard-educated thug," Lane pointed out. "But I'm hoping we don't involve anyone else until Cruz brings back my husband and Mr. Scott. In any case, the way Salinas tells it, he has a number of allies in the army and the police."

"GOODBYE, INSPECTOR. PLEASE, look after your own María Félix. You are very lucky. And"—here Salinas nodded—"she also is lucky." Salinas patted the neck of the impatiently prancing Diablo and nodded at the man to open the hacienda gate.

Darling struggled for a moment. What to say? He'd been this man's prisoner, charming as he was. He could see, however, that he genuinely seemed to believe this was a good basis for a cordial relationship. Feeling duplicitous in every way, he offered his hand. "Thank you, Señor Salinas. And thank you for providing your man to get us back."

"Think nothing of it," his host said, smiling, and stood back to watch the three men ride through the gate and out into the desert.

CHAPTER TWENTY-THREE

"**H**ERE'S WHAT WE HAVE." AMES waved his hand at the objects arrayed on his desk. "A photo of the dead man taken while he was still entangled with the *Moyie* paddle, a bullet of the same calibre as this gun Cooper found. It's not bloody much. Had any ideas about why you didn't mention the bullet, by the way?" He looked up at Terrell with interest.

"No, sir. Not as yet." He had given it a good deal of thought, though. The closest he could come was that he had a feeling he needn't mention it to Cooper. This was so palpably nonsense that he did not feel he could discuss it. He cleared his throat. "The gun has only a few very smudged fingerprints, as though it had had a half-hearted wiping," he said.

"That's strange, though, isn't it? Why wouldn't it have Tanney's prints on it? He's out there roasting weenies by the fire, his firearm handy in case of bears or Mounties. He'd have no reason to wipe the thing clean. And Cooper's?"

"No, sir. He picked it up with his hanky. The question I have is, who wants Tanney dead?"

Ames grunted. "Who wouldn't want him dead? He sounds like a real winner. But okay, let's take the question seriously. Let's start with Mrs. Radcliffe. She has a brief, ill-considered hitch with Tanney and gets pregnant. She never liked him, and apparently shunned him ever after. What if he started pestering her to see Rocky? He's a big mistake in her past that could ruin everything. She has a good reason to want him dead."

At this point April, who'd been listening for a few seconds, knocked on the door. "I don't see a woman with a child sneaking onto a ferry to shoot her embarrassing mistake, I'm sorry. That's pretty cold-blooded."

"Oh?" Ames asked.

"I'm just offering my opinion. I'm not saying a woman couldn't have done it. I just don't think it was her. She has a child, after all. But I guess that's no guarantee of anything."

"The person being blackmailed is the more obvious candidate," Terrell said. "And I do believe Mrs. Radcliffe that she was not the victim. Who then?"

Ames turned to April. "Did you have a message?"

"Oh, yes. Sorry." She handed Ames a piece of paper. "This man called and said he understood from his shift head that we were looking for information about what happened on the ferry the other day. He said he couldn't talk now because he was due at work, but you could call him tomorrow morning before he goes out again. Name's Zack Graham."

"That's all he said?" Ames asked, taking the paper.

"Yup. I'd better get back down. That phone won't answer itself!" With that April turned and ran back down the stairs.

"That's something, sir," Terrell said. "This might help. I still don't know how anyone could heave a dead body off the ferry without being seen by someone."

"YES, DAD, I'M perfectly fine. Listen, this is costing a fortune. Just let Isabel know everything's all right, will you?" Bob was on the telephone to Vancouver. "No, I'm not sure. There are things I have to finish up here. Yes, I promise to let you know."

He hung up the receiver and sighed. He had a whisky to hand and picked this up and drank deeply. It did not assuage the guilt he felt. He stood up and left Thomas Fine's plush office. "All done," he said to the others gathered around the fire in the sitting room, trying for cheer. "I didn't tell Dad we don't quite have Fred back yet. He'd only worry."

Lane, who'd been staving off her own worry, stood. "I think I'm for bed now. I'm beginning to feel as if I've been on horseback for a month."

"I really think we should see the wonderful Dr. Alcaraz for that rib, my dear," Leonora said, standing also.

Lane shook her head. "There's nothing anyone can really do with ribs. And anyway, it's already feeling a bit better. I'm sure it is only a bruise. I'll be as right as rain tomorrow."

"If you're completely sure. I'll show you around the hacienda tomorrow, and perhaps we can go back into town to the market when María goes. You said you enjoyed it."

"I would love that," Lane said. "Good night, and thank you again for your kindness."

Upstairs, Lane prepared for bed, worried that she might not sleep because of her anxiety about Darling. And, in truth, her rib still ached. She thought with sadness about Bob's mission the next day to talk to Mrs. Ramírez about her husband. And then her mind turned to what she was beginning to think of as the "new Bob." When she'd first met him, he'd brought Isabel to their wedding. He'd seemed mild and a bit buttoned-down. Now he was . . . she searched for a word. Looser, freer. More, she thought, himself. Wondering what that would mean for Isabel, who might prefer the other version, she said a few words in her heart to Darling and felt herself drifting off to sleep.

She woke with a gasp, heaving air into her lungs as if she had stopped breathing for a moment. She was relieved to see a grey light coming into the room through the crack in the curtains, grateful that she was alone and far from the Fines, their bedroom being at the other end of the hall. She waited for her heart to slow down and then got up, pulled the curtains open, and looked at her watch: 6:20. Her window looked out on the main gate of the hacienda. She could just see over the wall at the desert stretching away to the east, a faint golden line of sun beginning on the horizon. Below her there was already activity. Someone was working in the garden, and men were heading toward the miners' cafeteria next to the gate. She pushed the window open and relished the cool rush of morning air, filled, wonderfully, with the smell of bread baking in the large kitchens.

Still filled with the residue of anxiety these episodes left her with, she went back to bed and tried to remember if she'd been dreaming. The inability to breathe had wiped away any remnants of dream, but an image stayed in her mind from a dream she'd had before, about Charlie in France, falling right before her eyes. Executed on Harrison's orders. Alma too. And where had Harrison gone? He'd disappeared before he could be arrested. He must have travelled to France and joined the Breton underground. Of course, if he'd been caught and executed, she never would have found out, but if not, he could never return to England. It was his mother who had been from Brittany.

They'd got little joy of their alliance with invading Nazi forces and had, she recalled reading after the war, quarrelled among themselves.

She did some deep breathing exercises and then allowed herself to drift back to sleep as calmness came over her again.

LANE AND LEONORA sat in the lovely enclosed back garden of the house, having a light lunch. Bob and Thomas had gone off to the main office to discuss getting the samples back, and what the future might hold for the new mine site. Everyone had been reasonably cheery in the morning, but there was the underlying anxiety that Darling and Scott were not yet back.

"It was very brave of you," Leonora said. "I don't think I could have done it." There was something wistful in her voice.

Lane regarded her for a moment and smiled. "I'm absolutely convinced you would do anything you had to do to protect someone you love. And it's not particularly brave to go riding under the protection of armed men. The only brave thing was doing it in spite of knowing what my behind would feel like at the end!"

"But you knew by the end that Cruz was one of them. Weren't you afraid? He could have done anything! Killed you both on the way back!"

Lane shook her head. "I don't think so. Salinas wouldn't have wanted me dead, for a start. He's almost entirely motivated by money. And he's a bit of a dreamer. Salinas, I mean, not Cruz. I remind him of his favourite movie star, María Félix. Do you know her?"

"I don't go to the local films, of course, but you can't miss all the posters." She turned to look closely at Lane. "I can see what he means. She's considered one of the most beautiful women in a country full of beautiful women." She took a forkful of salad. "I don't know what earthly good beauty is, really. I think it can fool women into thinking they are in an advantageous position in life, but we all end up the same way in the end, don't we? On a lower rung below some man." She coloured. "Oh, please don't take me seriously. I love Thomas. He's wonderful. He's given everything to me, even provided me a life of some adventure and travel. I'd probably never have moved here on my own."

Lane nodded, regarding Leonora with interest. She was at once so brave and independent, and yet very much the traditional wife, living to support her husband's work and ambitions. "I suppose," she said finally, "all our lives turn out a little differently from what we expected. I expected to study history, perhaps write scholarly papers and teach at a women's college at Oxford until I retired to a cottage somewhere with a cat. But then the war came." She shrugged.

"The war." Leonora shook her head. "We hardly felt it here, really, except for the increase in the mine production to supply the American war effort. I had hoped to pursue my studies too. Thomas really doesn't believe in women working. I came from a rather aristocratic family as American families go, and girls like me are sent to college to polish us up, so a suitable man can say, 'This is my wife. She studied law. She's given it all up for me.'"

At that moment María came through the door onto the stone patio. "Señora, they are here. Señor Darling and Señor Scott."

"Not Mr. Cruz?" Leonora asked.

María clamped her lips tight and then said, "No, señora," and withdrew into the kitchen.

"DO YOU HAVE everything you need?" Lane asked Darling. They were in their room and Darling was preparing to take a long, welcome soak.

"I have you, in one piece. I need nothing else. Don't worry. I won't hug you till after my bath. I can see you recoiling."

"I'm doing no such thing. Well, not entirely." She smiled. "But how was Cruz when he left you? Thomas was fit to be tied when he heard the news."

"I bet. Funnily enough, he was a bit talkative. I think he's the kind of man who doesn't like loose ends, and a loose end here is who shot at us that day."

"It really was nothing to do with Salinas?"

296

"No. The bandido sends his love, by the way, the blighter!"

"Bath!" Lane said, handing him a large fluffy towel.

MARÍA HAD CLEARED away the lunch things, and when she'd put the dishes into the sink for the day girl to wash, she went upstairs. She'd not yet cleared the coffee things from the study, where Señor Fine and Bob Darling had had a hasty meal before going to the mine offices.

The door was ajar, and she was just about to push it open when she heard a voice.

"Yes, sir." A long pause. "I see, sir. Yes. I'm just not sure, sir. It was surprising . . . yes, I see. It wasn't my impression . . ." Another pause. María almost fancied she heard a raised voice coming down the line. "All right. Yes, I see. I'm sorry, sir. If you think this best. Where do I go?" Scott had a pencil poised over a small notebook. He nodded. "I didn't know there was a road there. Yes, sir. The army will hold him."

María waited, but heard only the receiver being dropped onto the cradle. No goodbye. The man was making no move to leave. She took a risk and pushed the door a little wider so that she could see who it was. Scott had his back to her and stood leaning forward with both hands on the desk, his head slumped as if he'd heard bad news. Finally, after a long wait, he slowly began to move. He threw his pencil on the table and took up the notebook.

María retreated quickly and hid in the recessed doorway into the library. Scott, walking slowly, went into the dark hall, looked toward the library and then back the other way, as if trying to find his bearings, and then walked at a snail's pace back toward the sitting room, as if he were reluctant to return to the others.

"THANKS FOR COMING down here, Officer. I've got a few minutes before the turnaround to go back up the lake."

"You said you saw something unusual, Mr. Graham?" Terrell said. They were standing at the side of the ramp, where one or two cars still waited to board.

"You know, thinking about it, I don't really know. But I noticed that guy who went overboard, because he was with the RCMP officer in the cruiser when they boarded. I remember wondering if he was a prisoner or something. But then the officer got out and the other guy did too, and he wasn't cuffed or anything, so I assumed they were friends or something. The guy went to stand at the railing, and when I was winding the rope onto the cleat near him, I saw him take a wallet out of his pocket and open it, and it was full of bills, like, I mean, really full. He just sort of opened it and looked at it like he wanted to make sure it was all there, and then shoved it back in his pocket. He didn't seem to notice that I was pretty close to him."

"I guess you couldn't tell how much he might have had?" Terrell frowned. Cooper had said Tanney's wallet was empty.

"No, but it looked like hundreds, honestly. I was surprised anyone would walk around with that much, let alone bring it out for anyone to see. Asking for trouble."

Nodding, Terrell made a note. Could Tanney's death be just a simple robbery? "Did you see anyone else around him?"

Graham considered. "The officer was getting something out of the car, because I remember looking that way. I wondered if he knew how much money the guy had on him. Anyway. I didn't think it was any of my business. Then something happened with the chain we put across the ramp during the crossing, so I had to go. All hell broke loose because it had come unlatched. It fell on the metal deck and made a hell of a racket. Everyone was looking at where the noise came from, and I ran over to take care of it."

"Where was Tanney, the guy who went overboard, in relation to the chain?"

"Oh, now, let me see. He was closer to the prow, on the right, looking into the wind. The latch for the gate was at the prow as well, but right on the opposite side. On the port side, or the left. It was meant to be right across the opening, and the latch is on the right, so the whole thing fell toward the left, if you see what I mean."

Terrell wrote. Graham had unwittingly revealed the thing Terrell thought almost more important than the fact that Tanney was carrying a lot of money. "So, when you reattached the chain, you would have dragged it to the right side, near where the man was standing?"

"Yeah, but there were cars parked there so I couldn't see him very well."

"Did you see him still there when you latched the chain?"

"I honestly couldn't say. I wasn't paying too much attention to the people. I was working on the gate and mad at Arch, because he did a bad job of latching it in the first place."

"How long after you reattached the chain did Officer Cooper raise the alarm about his passenger being missing?"

"Um . . . maybe fifteen minutes? He went to the skip, I guess, and told him he'd been looking for the guy, well, his prisoner, everywhere, and wondered if there was some closet or something he could be hiding in. He told the skip he'd have to check every car and asked for us to help."

"You did that when the ferry landed?"

"Yes. We'd searched the boat while we were still underway, then held everyone up and made them open the trunk of their car. They were mighty upset at the delay. Luckily it wasn't a full sailing. I think there were about twenty cars. Anyway, there was no sign of the guy."

"Are you the one who found the bullet?"

"No, that was Archie Evans. We all heard about it though! Did the guy ever turn up?" He looked behind him. "Oops, I gotta go. Anything else?"

Happy not to have to answer his question about the dead man, Terrell waved him on. "Thanks very much, Mr. Graham."

CHAPTER TWENTY-FOUR

MARÍA SAT AT THE KITCHEN table, her lips tight, looking out the back door toward the garden. Over and over in her head she heard Scott saying, "The army will hold him." What did this mean? Who would the army hold? Cruz? Or had Scott decided, now that he and everyone else were safe, to involve the army after all, to try to go after Salinas? She shook her head. Good luck to him! The army wasn't reliable, and Salinas had men everywhere.

She shook her head, as the truth came to her about why she was worried. She didn't like the way Scott was on the phone, almost whispering like he didn't want anyone to hear. He was hiding something.

"IT'S BEEN LOVELY having you here, even under such awful circumstances," Leonora said, holding Lane's hands in hers. They were standing in front of the embassy car early the following day. Fine was holding a pipe in one hand, talking to Darling and Scott, and Bob Darling stood listening to them, his hands in his pockets. When Darling was free, he offered his brother his hand.

"See you come home soon. Dad's relieved you're not dead or imprisoned, but he'd like to see you. No doubt Isabel would as well."

Bob nodded, retrieved his hand, and put it back into his pocket, and then he rocked back and forth on his feet for a minute, as if considering what to say next. "I'm not sure when I can be back up there, if you want the truth. Can you tell Isabel—"

"No, I cannot," interrupted his brother firmly. "Any telling had better come from you. You're off her, I gather from all this hemming and hawing. She deserves to know so she can get on with her life."

Bob coloured and turned to look at the men climbing into the bus heading for the mine. "I don't really know how to say anything to her."

"Well, I'm not doing it. Good luck. I don't envy you."

"You're a cold bastard, you know that?" Bob said with some affection.

"Yup. Well, don't do anything stupid. I'm not coming down here to rescue you again!"

Bob saluted with an enormous smile. "Righty-ho!"

"Anyway, we better get going," Darling said. He was finding this farewell more affecting than he'd expected. He cleared his throat. "It's a ten-hour drive." Darling patted his brother on the shoulder and was making for the open passenger door, when he saw that Lane had turned and was disappearing into the house with Leonora. "Typical. Now what?"

"Leonora just remembered something she wanted to give Lane," Fine said. "One thing you can count on, the ladies are always going to be late."

Not having found this to be generally true, Darling nevertheless nodded. "You think it's going to be all right with Salinas? He won't be raiding you for more ransom?"

"The way I hear it, he doesn't go to the same well twice. There are other companies. Fruit companies, oil companies. The place is rich with North American interests."

"Some comfort, I guess," Darling said, looking at his watch.

LEONORA HAD HER hand on Lane's arm. They were standing in the hallway, out of earshot of the gathering outside. "I don't know if this means anything, but María was very worried about something she overheard on the phone yesterday. Scott was talking to somebody. I didn't even know if I should pass it on, but she was so insistent. She doesn't trust him, she says. She thought he was being furtive."

Lane asked, "What was it she heard that worried her?"

Leonora told Lane what María had said. "But you know, I think it's just that the embassy is tired of foreign nationals being held and they've made plans to try to stop it. I can hardly blame them. I mean, it's their job to look after the Brits."

Lane smiled. "And Canadians. Of course, you're right. That will be it. If they are planning some sort of campaign against Salinas, I'm not surprised he didn't want to be overheard. You told me yourself, you can't really know who he owns, even here in this town."

"I'm sure you're right. Just . . . you know . . . be careful. I kept this back so we could talk for a moment. It is a little something for you to remember us by." She handed Lane a parcel wrapped in brown paper and tied with string. "It's only a little embroidered tablecloth, but they are so typical of the region. I have scores of them myself!"

LANE SETTLED IN the back of the car and waved as they pulled away toward the hacienda gate. Once on the cobbled road outside the gate, Darling turned to look at her. "What was all that in aid of?"

She held up her parcel. "She wanted to give me this embroidered tablecloth. It's really very kind of her. I should pick some of these up as gifts for everyone at home."

Darling raised his eyebrows slightly. It was more than that, and he knew it, but she only gave him a quick penetrating glance and turned to look out the window.

"It's a lovely town. I wish you had come to the market with me. You'd have loved it. I learned so much."

This caused Scott to look at her in the rear-view mirror. "It's a real slice of local life, that market. I'm glad you got to experience it."

Lane paused for a moment, tilting her head unconsciously in a question, her mind on what she hadn't learned. "There are still so many things I don't understand about this whole business. Why did that young man have to die? The one who brought the ransom demand? The odd thing was, Salinas didn't know."

"Listen, ma'am, it doesn't do to go trying to understand all that. People get shot in this country all the time. There's

304

stuff going on politically that we at the embassy just try to work around and stay out of."

Lane sighed. "I suppose you're right. I just don't like not knowing, I suppose. I feel like we are driving away leaving more questions than answers."

"And money," Scott said ruefully. "Like I said. It all boils down to money for people like that. Hell, maybe it all boils down to money for most people."

"Do you believe that?" Lane asked from the back seat. "What about love? Or patriotism. You can't look at the war we've just been through without seeing how many people acted out of a sense of duty and love of country, at least where I was."

Scott regarded her for a moment again in the mirror. "You have a generous view of human nature. But I guess you're right on that one. Not too many people were getting any money for doing their bit. What do you think, Inspector Darling?"

Taking a moment, Darling watched the road ahead. They had left the town and were driving across the high plain. A wind had whipped up farther out on the desert, sending little swirls of dust into the air. "I think you don't have a dirty great war like that without someone making a lot of money. But you're right. Not us, the poor sods who had to fight it."

"I'm a little surprised your brother didn't come back with us, after all that," Scott observed, pivoting.

"He doesn't like to leave things half done. He wants to finish the job he started. And"—he shrugged—"I think he likes it here."

Lane glanced across the seat back at Darling's profile. Or he doesn't want to go home to his fiancée, she thought. She settled back to watch the passing expanse of desert. Poor Isabel.

"Well, more power to him. He seemed to almost enjoy being kidnapped," Scott said. He had his window open in an effort to keep cool, his elbow leaning on the frame.

"He's always loved adventure. It's why he went into geology, because it meant he could spend his life out in remote places. But I know he feels very keenly the loss of Mr. Ramírez, their guide. I don't think he could ever forgive Salinas for that. He told me that Salinas's charming 'I've been to Harvard, aren't I clever' manner made him sick," Darling said.

"It's a terrible thing to lose someone on an expedition," Lane remarked from the back seat.

Scott's eyes in the rear-view mirror again, watching her. "You speak as if you've experienced such a thing yourself." His voice was friendly, charming, curious.

Lane felt something inside go immediately on the alert. She shook her head. "No, thank heaven. I've never been in a position to have that sort of thing happen. But it is terrible, really, when someone dies for no fault of their own. Poor Mr. Ramírez. Leonora told me he left a wife and family. He was betrayed by circumstances." Like Alma. Like Charlie, who had been so much on her mind lately. He too had left a wife and family. He too had been betrayed, but not by circumstance, by a man who'd been playing his own game all along.

She could feel Scott glancing again at her in the mirror, and then look back to the road. She felt a growing sense of unease.

"I look forward to my soft drink," she said with sudden cheerfulness. "I rarely drink them at home, but they are quite addicting, all sugar and fizz."

Scott laughed. "I know what you mean. I drink a lot of the stuff here because the water isn't that safe some of the time. That and beer!"

"I'm afraid I drink a Coca-Cola nearly every day at lunch." Darling turned to smile innocently at Lane. "I know you imagine I drink coffee, but it's not much better for you."

The car had begun to slow down, and Lane and Darling looked at the road ahead. Coming into view was another army checkpoint.

"THERE CERTAINLY WASN'T a penny on him when we found him," Ames observed after hearing Terrell's report from his visit to the ferry terminal. "And his wallet was still in his back pocket, completely empty."

"Yes, sir. Exactly. And according to Cooper, when he was picked up, he had six dollars and some change in his pocket. It made me wonder if robbery was the actual motive for his killing. Either someone knew he had money and followed him, or someone saw him looking at it and seized on the opportunity," Terrell said. "And that doesn't answer the question of how he got that money when he was supposedly in custody with only six dollars, according to Cooper."

Ames shook his head. "Maybe someone on the ferry followed them to give him the money, and then either someone else saw the exchange and took advantage of the moment to rob him, or the person gave him the money and planned to kill him to get it back before the trip was over."

"You mean the person he was blackmailing."

Ames looked excited. "Yes, why not? He's being black-mailed, he's mad about it and wants his money back. And wants to get rid of Tanney once and for all. Once he's made the handover, he sees he has a chance. Tanney's been arrested, and it's handed to him on a platter because Cooper hasn't even cuffed Tanney. He just lets him get out of the car unsecured and wander around at will. The minute Cooper has his back turned, he makes his move."

"Helped by the very convenient distraction provided by the chain coming unlatched and falling noisily?"

Ames shrugged. "It *is* unlikely he'd have his gun handy just at the right moment. Maybe, but what if he's the one that makes that distraction happen? Unlatches the chain and then shoots him and dumps him."

"I wonder if we should talk to Cooper again. Maybe he saw more than he is aware of. Do you want me to get in touch with him?"

"Yes. Give him a call. See what you can get."

Terrell grimaced slightly. "I was thinking it might be best to do it in person."

Ames looked up at this, peering closely at Terrell. "Your instinct again?"

Terrell felt his face warm. "I'd just like another wild ride on my bike, I guess, sir." He did like going on the open road with the Triumph, to be sure. "I was thinking that it would be possible for him to map out on paper the way things were on the ferry. Both of us might see something we missed."

"Of course, you're right. I wish I could go with you. Not on that contraption of yours, obviously, in a car like

308

civilized people, as O'Brien would say. In fact, I've plans to go up and see O'Brien. I can do that without leaving April alone in the station for too long."

A telephone call established that Cooper would be back at the detachment at nine the following morning and Terrell was welcome to come across to see him. He apologized that he could not come back to meet them on their patch, but he was in the middle of his investigation of the drugs and firearms coming across the border. He could give him an hour.

CHAPTER TWENTY-FIVE

"**G**OOD. YOU'RE HERE IN TIME to get me out of here," O'Brien said. He was standing beside his bed, buttoning up his shirt. "I told the wife you were coming so not to bother coming to get me."

"You're allowed out already?" Ames asked, but at the sound of raised voices and commotion in the hall, he turned to look through the door. "What's going on?"

"I dunno. They brought some woman in in the middle of the night. I think she'd taken something. It sounds like it was touch and go. Maybe she's had a relapse."

A nursing sister appeared at the door. "You all ready, Sergeant O'Brien?" And then she walked to his bedside table, her eyebrows raised. "You were planning to leave this behind?" She held up an envelope with his name written on it in bold print.

O'Brien snorted. "It's all nonsense. I don't need all that. I've lived this long perfectly well without following some nursery school list!"

The nurse handed the envelope to Ames. "Could you see that Mrs. O'Brien gets this? I've spoken with her. She's expecting it." She turned back to O'Brien. "If you'd been following this food and exercise guide all along, Sergeant, you wouldn't have been in this pickle in the first place."

"God, you're worse than my wife!" O'Brien grumbled, closing his suitcase.

"We'll miss you too, Sergeant!" She smiled, perhaps a trifle too cheerfully. "Sergeant Ames, the doctor would like a quick word before you go."

Ames nodded. "I'll meet you at the elevator," he said to his colleague. "And leave the suitcase. I'll get it." He followed the nurse into the hall.

"Ah. Sergeant Ames, I understand. I'm Dr. Watford."

"Yes, how do you do?" Ames said, shaking hands. "What can I do for you? I hope it's not secret instructions for Sergeant O'Brien. I'm already in trouble with him for aiding and abetting the enemy."

Watford smiled and shook his head. "No, but it's something I think the police ought to know about. Normally there's confidentiality to consider, but we're seeing a disturbing trend. Last night, we admitted a young woman who was having a severe reaction to drugs combined with alcohol. Amphetamines and, I suspect, cocaine. We nearly lost her, and she's not the first one. There have been four other admissions in the last couple of weeks. We've been lucky, but one day we won't be. Usually it's young people, but this woman has a little child at home. Her neighbour brought her in. I don't know who was looking after the child." He stopped and clamped his lips shut as if he didn't want to say what he thought. "I wouldn't normally do this, but I think there's a problem in town. Some sort of influx of illicit drugs. I . . . I think if I tell you the patient's name, perhaps you can use it to begin to trace the source. I just wouldn't want her arrested or charged."

Ames frowned. The manual was pretty clear on the penalty for possessing drugs. If he got this woman's name, he couldn't see any way out of arresting her. On the other hand, the doctor made sense. She could be the lead to tracking down where the drugs were coming from.

"Sergeant?" Watford asked. "I'll tell you nothing if your plan is to arrest her. She was very, very ill. I don't think she knew what she was taking. I see her more as a victim here, and she does have a child at home."

With one last mental grab at "What would Darling do?" Ames made his decision. "Okay, Doctor. I won't arrest her. This time."

Watford looked relieved. "I understand. No second chance. That's fair. Her name is Mrs. Bonita Sunderland."

THE OFFICER TOOK the passports and, as had happened on their trip up, walked away with them to consult with other men who were lounging by a small broken-down hut. After some moments he returned, handing two of them back to Scott, and then went around to the passenger side and opened the door.

"*Usted bájese*," he said to Darling.

Darling turned an inquiring face to Scott.

"He wants you to get out," Scott said.

"Why?" Darling didn't budge.

Lane by this time was leaning forward, watching the soldier.

"*¿Por qué?*" Scott asked, leaning over Darling to look up at the officer.

The soldier answered, speaking quickly, and indicated with his hand that Darling should get out.

"It's all right. They just want to check your papers with you there. They might ask you to empty your pockets. It's a nuisance, but not out of the ordinary. Unfortunately."

Darling sighed, glanced back at Lane, and stepped out of the car.

It all seemed to happen at once. First, Darling saw Lane's hand come up toward him, and then he registered a look of both warning and panic on her face. With a wave of alarm, he made to get back into the car. Then he felt himself pulled forward so roughly by one arm that he nearly tripped. Trying to right himself, he reached out to the only thing around, the man pulling at him, and he clutched at the man's jacket. He heard a loud slam at the same moment and whirled around to see the car pulling away at speed, sending up a spray of gravel and dust.

Horrified, he yanked his arm out of the grasp of the man who held him and began to run after the car, knowing already it was hopeless. After fifty yards he stopped, gasping for air, leaning forward and resting with his hands on his knees. He could feel dust coating his throat and coughed, trying to spit it out. The car, carrying his wife and Scott, apparently in his new role of kidnapper, was a mere blip on the horizon.

The soldier who had pulled him out of the car approached, and Darling turned and recoiled at the outreach of a hand. "Where's my wife being taken?"

The soldier made a pacifying motion with his hand, palm down, moving it up and down, as if he were trying to slow a speeding car. "*Está bien, señor. No se preocupe.*"

"No, it's not bloody *bien*!" Darling shouted. He stormed toward the other men, who stood by their own car. He banged on the roof of the car and pointed toward the cloud of dust that was the only trace of his wife. "We go after her, now!"

The men all shrugged but didn't move. Then the man handed him his passport. "*Su pasaporte, señor.*" He seemed to be aiming for maximum cordiality.

Darling grabbed it. "I don't want my bloody passport, I want my wife!"

LANE WAS FLUNG back in the seat because Scott accelerated so precipitously. She struggled up to look out the back window with dismay. She lurched forward, pulling at Scott's shoulder.

"What the hell are you doing? What's going on? Please, go back. You can't leave him there!"

Scott's response was to clutch the steering wheel with both hands and speed up.

"Stop! Just stop!" Lane was assailed by a combination of fear and rage. What was going to happen to Darling? Why had Scott abandoned him?

She reined in her terror and swallowed hard to control her rage. He was driving at a dangerous speed on a gravel road. She'd be no use to Darling if they skidded out and rolled. Leaning forward over the seat, she tried for calm. "Mr. Scott. Please stop the car for a moment and tell me what's going on. Please."

The car slowed but did not stop. Lane's fear that they would skid dangerously on the gravel road abated slightly. "I'm sorry, Mrs. Darling. I'm under orders." Much to her amazement he sounded genuinely regretful. "But you needn't worry about Inspector Darling. He's not in any danger."

She remembered now what Leonora said that María had heard: "The army will hold him." She struggled to understand why on earth the Mexican Army would want Darling. Had his brother done something illegal? Had he gone missing the moment they'd left the hacienda in Fresnillo, and now the only way they felt they could get at him was to keep Darling? Hold him hostage till Bob turned himself in? Only then did she question why they were speeding away from the scene in this reckless manner. The soldiers could have hustled Darling into their vehicle and driven him off. But if that were the case, they would have held Scott and her at gunpoint till they were gone.

"What do you mean he's not in danger? He doesn't speak Spanish, and from what I hear the army is unreliable. Is someone paying them to kidnap him now, for ransom? Is it Salinas again?" She could feel her anger rising again at the thought. Salinas with his smarmy, disingenuous charm.

Scott sighed and settled into a steady forty-five miles an hour. "It's nothing like that. I assure you they will take him to a place of safety and eventually he'll be allowed to return."

Lane frowned and looked out at the bleakness of the empty desert. It held no pleasure for her now. If it wasn't Darling who was in danger . . . "It's me? Why on God's green earth would you want me? Or whoever you actually work for." Again, Salinas came to mind. Did he own this man as well? She tried to imagine a British embassy official falling in with a criminal. There was always money. Lord knows, everyone had made such a fuss about how it was all about money.

"Do *you* work for Salinas?"

Scott laughed. "No, ma'am. I work for the British government. I'm not an idiot. Anyone who gets into his clutches never gets out!"

"You appear to be kidnapping me, if what you say about my husband's being safe is true. What does the British government want with me?"

His eyes appeared in the rear-view mirror again, watching her. Then they were gone, and the car was slowing. Lane turned to look out the window. What now? Scott slowed enough to make a sharp left turn onto a small side road. She looked out the back window and saw the main road to Mexico City disappearing behind them.

"Now where are we going?" she asked, her heart pounding out a renewed blast of fear.

He did not answer for some time, and then he said, "I believe we are taking you in, ma'am." It sounded for a moment as if he had something to add. But he only clamped his mouth shut and drove on in silence.

DARLING BANGED HIS fist on the roof of the army vehicle again, and then regretted it. His hand was already aching from the first time, and he was feeling completely impotent. He spoke slowly and loudly, realizing he sounded like a cartoon English speaker who thinks he can make foreigners understand by shouting at them. "You take me to my wife. Do you understand?" He pointed down the road, which now lay quiet, and innocent of all traffic either coming or going.

The man in charge of the group shrugged and tilted his head apologetically. "*No, no se puede, señor. Disculpe.*"

What Darling heard for what felt like the tenth time was "no." He stilled an urge to hit the car yet again and turned to look at the road.

Like Lane, he had at first thought this had something to do with him. In some way *he* had transgressed some unknown law, perhaps in the process of securing his brother's release, but when they didn't take him anywhere or do anything but continue to look apologetic, he began to wonder if it were Lane who was the object of the exercise. Scott was taking Lane somewhere.

He swallowed, suddenly terrified. He imagined Scott taking Lane to a remote location . . . and then he stopped himself. Whatever else might be wrong with the undersecretary, he really did not seem like a rapist, and it would in any case do no good to work himself up.

"*¡Ah, señor, mire!*" The commander was patting his arm and pointing down the road where a cloud of dust announced the approach of a vehicle. "*¡El autobús!*"

For one wild moment Darling hoped it would be Scott returning with Lane, but he saw quickly that this was a bus, and a very antique one at that. Two of the soldiers ran into the road, flapping their arms to get the bus to stop.

The thing would have been new in 1931, Darling thought, looking at it. There was a rack along the top that held baggage of all sorts tied on with ropes, and the bus seemed to be full of people who were all now looking anxiously out the windows. Darling remembered the story about a bus being stopped by the army and understood why.

The driver opened the door with the lever, looked out at the soldiers, and lifted his head in inquiry. Words were exchanged, and then the driver looked at Darling and nodded.

The soldiers gave Darling a push toward the bus, the commander saying something that ended with a reassuring volley of nods and "*¡Está bien!*"

Knowing he wasn't going to get anywhere with his military companions, Darling shrugged and got onto the bus. Though it was headed in the wrong direction, it might be going to a large enough place that he could get to a telephone. Maybe even Fresnillo. The only person he felt he could trust just now was Thomas Fine. With some faint hope he stood in the aisle looking for an empty seat.

Now that it had become clear that the army was not interested in anyone on the bus, the passengers had relaxed back into their seats and now watched Darling with interest. Halfway along, a woman waved a friendly hand at him. "*¡Aquí, señor!*" She moved into the window seat, and Darling moved up the aisle and sat down next to her, nodding.

"*Gracias*," he said. The one bit of Spanish he felt he could really command.

She laughed delightedly. "*¡Americano!*" Immediately a hubbub rose up as everyone seemed to talk at once.

He heard the door being closed, and the bus pulled away from the stop with a loud grinding of gears.

Darling shook his head and said, "No, Canada."

This elicited more exclamations of delight, and a barrage of questions to which he could only shrug. It was clearly some sort of second-class conveyance. The passengers appeared to be rural, farmers perhaps, the men wearing the white trousers he'd seen on the vendors in the city, and shawls and aprons on the women. They carried bundles wrapped in cloth, or baskets, and in the racks above the seats, all manner of cases and cloth-wrapped parcels were stuffed. He heard the clucking of a chicken somewhere behind him.

The woman next to him pulled the cloth off a small basket and took out something that looked like it was wrapped in corn husks. She offered it to him with a smile. "*Tenga, señor. Un tamal.*"

He sighed. He was on a bus going the wrong way, and he had no idea what was happening to Lane. Only his hope that the bus would fetch up in a large town reduced his fear somewhat.

Completely unsure about what he was in for, he decided that it might be considered rude to refuse an offering of this kind, so he nodded and took the item, looking at it in perplexity. The woman laughed, said something that caused everyone around her to laugh, and then showed him how to unwrap the corn husks by demonstrating on her own. "*Un momento,*" she said suddenly and reached into the basket for a little bottle of something red. She took back the tamal, jammed her thumb into it and poured some chili sauce into the hole she'd made. With an enormous smile she offered it back, and then watched happily to see him eat.

It was not bad, he decided. He remembered eating something that tasted like this in that Mexican restaurant in Tucson on his honeymoon. He smiled and nodded, chewing on the strange texture, trying not to think about that thumb, and was plunged into misery at the thought of the honeymoon. He chided himself for wondering melodramatically if he would ever see her again.

CHAPTER TWENTY-SIX

"**W**HERE'S THE CONSTABLE?" AMES ASKED, taking his hat off and wiping his forehead wearily.

"Gone off to see that Sergeant Cooper, like you said," April replied. She was surprised at Ames's appearance of frustration. "Was Sergeant O'Brien being difficult?"

"Of course he was," Ames replied. "But it's not that. There seems to be a growing drug problem in town. A . . . a woman was brought into the hospital last night all doped up and nearly didn't make it, and apparently, she's not the first."

April's hand flew to her mouth. "Oh, no! Did they say who? No, of course they didn't. They can't. But that's awful. Gosh, I wonder if it's someone I know."

Ames sighed. "It is, sorta." He hesitated. The doctor had shared it with him so that the police would have a leg up in tracing the source of the drugs. April was the police now. "If you must know, it was Bonny Sunderland." He saw April about to speak. "And not a word! It was given in confidence so we can try to trace the drugs."

"As if I would betray a police confidence! I was only going to say, her poor little boy and husband! What are you going to do?"

"The doctor is going to telephone when we can go up and talk to her."

April nodded and straightened some papers on her bench. "Do you think she'll even talk to you? She didn't think much of you two last time you had her in. I imagine if she thought she might be arrested, she'd shut right up like a clam."

"I promised not to arrest her, though I'm not sure about that. Our police officer manual of 1944 is pretty clear on the subject."

"So, you have a heart! Surprise, surprise! I wonder if I ought to tell Tina. She'd be mighty surprised as well. Sir."

"Very funny." With that Ames trudged upstairs to his office and flung himself into his chair. This did not give satisfaction, so he followed it up by swinging his feet onto his desk. Better, though the sight of his two-toned wingtips did not soothe as much as it usually did. April was right, he thought glumly. Why would Bonny Sunderland, already hostile as all get-out, tell them a thing? Maybe by the time the doctor phoned, Terrell would be back. He had a better bedside manner.

Then he thought of April and how kind she had been to Mrs. Tanney. Now *there* was some bedside manner! He picked up his phone.

"Yes, sir?"·

"Do you have to call me that?"

"Yes, sir. What do you need?"

"When the doctor calls, I want you to go up there. We can talk about what you should ask."

ASIDE FROM WISHING April had been with him, Terrell had a glorious ride. The day was perfect, sunny, and almost hot. It was hard to beat that flow of warm air on his face. He'd felt a bit impatient on the ferry ride to Kootenay Bay, but he had finally settled in to the swirl of water and the view of the mountains that formed a perfect blue-green rim around the lake. Now he was sitting opposite Sergeant Cooper at a desk, a bottle of Coke to hand.

"You don't worry about skidding on that thing?" Cooper asked, leaning back on his chair.

"Not too much. They trained us pretty well in the army. Of course someone could plow into me. Then I wouldn't have much of a chance. I have to be a good defensive driver." He took a drink of his soda. "Thanks for seeing me. I had a talk with one of the guys on the ferry. You know, we put out a request for information. I guess we just want to put together as complete a picture as we can about what happened there. I just thought it might be, and no offence intended, sir, that there's something you might have observed that you didn't remember or think important at the time."

"None taken, Constable. Well, good, then. What did the ferry guy tell you?"

Terrell leaned forward and related what he'd been told about the money, and then the sequence with the falling chain. "Two things, of course. One is he had a wallet all right when we fished him off the *Moyie*, but it was empty, so whoever shot him most likely took the cash, and of course it opens up the possibility that it was a crime of opportunity. But also, you reported that he had very little money on him when he was picked up."

Cooper frowned thoughtfully. "That is very strange. His wallet was definitely all but bare. I wonder if someone was keeping an eye on him all along and followed us onto the ferry. Perhaps handed him the cash and then waited for an opportunity to take it back. Maybe when he saw me, he got scared Tanney would give him away, so he killed him. I certainly didn't have him in my sight the whole time. I didn't think there was any need to on the ferry. More fool me." He shook his head and sighed.

"Or, I suppose, someone who has nothing to do with the kidnapping and all the rest of it saw the cash, had a weapon, and took it and shot him," Terrell suggested. Did Tanney suddenly having cash prove the existence of this third party? Unless the ferry witness only thought he saw cash, but simply witnessed Tanney opening his wallet to see what he had. "I guess there's a possibility the ferry guy actually didn't see cash, just the wallet. The next thing is the chain. I'm not sure the ferry guy understood how significant that was, because it was most likely the chain falling that covered up the sound of the shot, though it is hard to believe someone was ready with the gun. Do you have paper and pencil?"

Cooper nodded and fished a sheet of paper out of a side drawer on his desk, offered Terrell a pencil, and then leaned forward on the desk. He clasped his hands to watch the constable at work.

"So, the ferry is roughly this shape." Terrell drew a sort of elongated egg shape. "If we look down on it from above, without the whole second passenger deck, we can maybe place the cars. Now, the ferry guy said there were no more than about twenty cars on board. Can you recall? I assume they were all driven toward the front, and there would be space left at the back?"

"Yes, that's right."

"Okay, can you recall how many rows there were going right to left?" Terrell surprised himself by asking this. There'd been three rows on his way over just now.

Cooper nodded. "There were three, I think."

"Okay, good. Let's sort of sketch them in. Anything big? A bus or large transport truck?"

Cooper thought, and then shook his head. "No. A couple of pickup trucks and a small van. Plumber, I think." He leaned over. "There was definitely a pickup truck here, and maybe the van was halfway back."

"And the rest were passenger cars. Can you show me roughly where your cruiser was?"

Cooper smiled and gave his head a little shake. "You're being pretty thorough, here, Constable. You think it's going to help?"

"I'm just trying to get a picture, sir. It might help us figure out where the guy came from and how he could act so quickly, especially in dropping the victim overboard with no one noticing."

"All right. Well, here's my cruiser here. In the middle, but closer to the front." He took the pencil and drew a little oval.

"Now. The last time you actually saw Tanney with your own eyes, where was he?"

"Right here, looking out at the scenery." He pointed to the right-hand side of the ferry quite near the front.

Terrell drew a stick figure. "And then where were you when the chain fell?"

Cooper thought for a moment. "I was back here, I think. I had Tanney yapping in my ear the whole way, so I didn't want to talk to him on the ride over. And I like watching the wake. When the chain fell like that, so near, I swung around to look at it, like everyone else who was standing on the deck."

"It was so loud it sounded close? I have the chain falling over here, according to the man I talked to." Terrell pointed to the left side of the front, a whole boat length away.

Cooper's eyebrows constricted a little and then his face cleared. "Yes, I guess that's right. I thought it was right next to me because of the noise."

"Did you look to see where Tanney was then?"

"Not right then. I was looking toward the noise. When the commotion was over, people stopped staring and got back to talking or looking out at the water, and that's when I saw he wasn't where I'd seen him. I just assumed he'd gone off to the john, you know. I wasn't worried. There's nowhere you can really go on a ferry. After a cigarette I began to wonder and went off to find him. The rest you know."

Terrell sat back, looking at his sketch. Had he advanced his understanding any with this exercise?

"Did you see anyone near him? I mean, before the chain fell."

"To be honest, I wasn't paying that much attention. There were maybe ten or so people on the lower deck, counting two ferry workers. The rest were either in their cars or had gone up to the upper deck, I guess." He shook his head and looked up at the ceiling and then back at Terrell. "Now I think of it, there was at least one man leaning out near him. That could be something."

"You *did* see someone near him?" Terrell's eyebrows came together. "Could you describe him?"

"Not really. He wasn't extraordinary in any way. Youngish guy, under forty probably, brown trousers, tan shirt, and a peaked cap, smoking a cigarette."

"You didn't notice where he went when the chain fell?"

"Nope. And I unfortunately couldn't spot him in a lineup. He had his back mostly turned. Now if you don't mind, Constable, I have to mosey. I'm the only one defending the border." Cooper stood and stretched, and Terrell stood as well.

"Mind if I take this, sir?" He held up his drawing.

"You go right ahead, Constable, fat lot of good it will do you."

Terrell smiled. "I had to try, sir."

IT WAS AFTER noon as Terrell boarded the ferry back across the lake. He got off his bike and looked up and down the length of the boat. As the ferry got underway, he walked to where he thought Tanney must have been standing. The first thing he realized was that there were very few people standing on the vehicle deck. Most were upstairs, where there was some inside seating. Second, he confirmed that if Tanney had been standing just to one side of the vehicle exit, he could have been largely hidden by a car. But his third realization seemed so obvious he put his hand to his forehead because he hadn't thought of it before, though it was all around him. The noise on the ferry. He stopped to listen. There was the roar of the engine, people on the car deck almost shouting at each other over the sound of the wind and the engine. Metal doors opening and closing, workers moving car blocks, and who knew what all. You could, he realized, especially if you were right at the side of the ferry where the wind was strongest and the sound of the water churning loudest, shoot someone at close range with a small revolver without anyone thinking it was anything more than the other noises on the ferry.

He turned to look at the car parked right behind him at that moment, and he saw that anyone looking at him would be able to see only his head above the car. It would, under these circumstances, have been very easy to rob Tanney, shoot him, and throw him overboard. He walked to where he thought Tanney must have spent his last moments and looked down at the churning water and sighed. He looked up at the second level and saw the few people standing outside, looking out at the lake. There were perhaps ten, spread out across this front railing, only three of whom would be able to spot him, and one of them was looking out, and the other two were talking. It was, he thought, amazingly possible that no one standing there would have seen anything unless they were looking right at Tanney and whoever it was right at that moment. In fact, they too might all have directed their attention to the noise of the chain falling.

DARLING WISHED SOMEONE would open a window. It was stifling inside the bus. His seat was near the back, and every bump in the road registered on his back. The driver had the radio on as loud as possible, no doubt with a view to entertaining the passengers, some of whom were singing along. The music sounded to him like some species of polka.

He turned to his companion, who had given up the effort of trying to communicate, though she did flash him a cheerful smile, nodding encouragingly, from time to time.

He pointed down the road and said, "Fresnillo?"

"*¿Mande?*"

"Bus . . . going to Fresnillo?" He moved his hands in what he fondly imagined was the facsimile of a moving bus.

"*¡Ah! No. Saltillo.*" She made a driving motion with her hands. "*Vamos a Saltillo. No Fresnillo. ¿Entiende?*"

Darling nodded. Now what?

"*¿Quiere ir a Fresnillo, señor?*"

This he was sure he understood. "*Sí.*" He nodded.

Several people had now become interested in the conversation, and an older woman in front of him who was travelling with two small children turned around.

"*Mire, bájese en San Jacinto. De allí se puede. ¿San Jacinto, sí?*"

San Jacinto. It must be the same place he had gone with Scott. "*Sí,*" he said again. "*Gracias.*"

Several people nodded and smiled at him encouragingly. Help had been offered, communication established. Very satisfactory.

In what seemed like less than ten minutes, he felt the bus slow and saw that they were turning east. A row of spindly

329

trees at the side of the road led to a village, where the bus lumbered to a stop. The radio was turned off and the driver stood up and pushed open the door. "San Jacinto!"

Darling was given a gentle push. "*Aquí, señor. San Jacinto. De aquí, otro autobús pa' Fresnillo. ¿Entiende?*"

Darling jumped up. "*¡Sí, sí! Gracias.*" He made his way down the aisle to a chorus of goodbyes, and turned to give everyone a wave before he stepped down. He thanked the driver and put his hand in his pocket to pay his fare.

"*¡No, señor, está bien! No se preocupe,*" the driver said, smiling broadly. He waved his hands against any payment. "*¡Buena suerte!*"

San Jacinto, in the silence that fell when the bus had lumbered back up to the main road, was barely recognizable to Darling. A child urging some goats out of the village stopped to look at him, and Darling smiled at him. Of course, he and Scott had ridden in from behind the town somewhere, not on this road. He walked toward the centre of town and then recognized the little square, where the market had been and he and Scott had been given mezcal, and then he stood, nonplussed. He had been given to understand, he thought, that a Fresnillo-bound bus would come through, but he had no way of knowing when. Perhaps, he thought suddenly, there was someone here with a car who could drive him there. He looked at his watch. It was barely one thirty. He could scarcely believe the sequence of events that he'd endured had taken so little time. He'd heard about the famous Mexican siesta. Had he arrived just in the middle of that?

"*¡Señor canadiense!*" a voice called.

He turned to the building outside which the hitching post stood and saw the man he had been introduced to as the headman waving enthusiastically at him. He hurried up to Darling and seized his hand, shaking it vigorously.

"*¡Bienvenido, señor! ¿Dónde está su compañero?*"

"*No compañero*," said Darling, shaking his head. "A bus, to Fresnillo. I need a bus." He pointed back toward the place where the bus had stopped.

The headman shook his head and then made a hand motion indicating Darling should wait. "*Espérese, señor.*"

The man disappeared inside the building and came out with a young man who was wearing glasses, his shirt sleeves held up with sleeve garters. The older man was talking rapidly to him, and then the younger man came forward, offering a hand.

"Good afternoon, mister. I am Francisco Pérez de Aguilar at your service. You are lost?" He spoke with a deep accent but had clearly learned English in school and spoke it with precision.

Darling felt a flood of relief at the possibility of being understood. "How do you do? I am Inspector Frederick Darling." The full title felt indicated by the young man's formality. "I am not lost . . ." How to explain in a way that could possibly make sense? "I need to get the bus to Fresnillo. I was travelling with my wife, and I believe she has been kidnapped. I don't know where she has been taken and I must get help."

"Kidnapped! But by who?" the young man exclaimed.

"Someone from the British embassy. I think." It sounded ridiculous to him.

Francisco shook his head. "That is unusual. But possible." He shrugged. "There is, I am sorry, no bus to Fresnillo today, or tomorrow. It comes two times a week."

"But does anyone have a car?" Darling asked urgently, despair beginning to take hold. "I must get to a telephone to call the authorities!"

Shaking his head, Francisco said, "What authorities, mister? If someone from the British embassy is the kidnapper, what authorities? My uncle has a *camión*, a truck, of course he will be happy to help you. But I think you should see someone else. I don't think anyone in Fresnillo can help. The foreigners there? It is a foreigner who did this." He gave a little tilt of his chin to emphasize his logic.

Darling shook his head. "Thank you, I appreciate your thinking, but I must get to Fresnillo. My brother is there, and there is an American there I can trust."

Francisco shrugged. "Please. Wait here. I will see that you have something to drink. Then I will go for my uncle."

Darling sat down nervously on one of the wooden chairs in the shade of the ramada at the edge of the square. He had occupied the same chair, it now seemed, weeks ago. How long would this take? Planting his elbows on the table, he held his head in his hands and closed his eyes. He could not remember feeling more powerless in his life. Having to place himself and the safety of his wife in the hands of complete strangers terrified him.

"*¿Señor? Un refresco.*" A young girl carried a round tray with a bottle of orange soda and a glass and placed them before him. She flipped the lid off expertly with a bottle opener and nodded at him. "*¿Algo más?*"

Darling thanked her and shook his head. She paused a moment and then went back into the building that Darling assumed was a bar. He put his hand around the bottle—not cold, exactly, but cool enough, and before he poured it, he looked down the nearly deserted street. Where had Francisco gone? Then, feeling slightly guilty, because he was very thirsty and he'd come to rather enjoy orange soda, and who knew if Lane was getting anything, he poured it into the glass.

The thought of Lane, the magnitude of his fear at not knowing what had become of her, suddenly overwhelmed him, and he sat staring at the glass and the half-empty bottle. At that moment the glass looked just as half-empty.

CHAPTER TWENTY-SEVEN

THE CAR SLOWED AND THEN stopped in what was most evidently the middle of nowhere. Lane looked around in all directions. There was nothing but desert as far as she could see.

"Why are we stopping?"

"I'm sorry, Mrs. Darling. Please don't get out of the car unless I say so, and please do not attempt to run. I'm armed, and as you can see"—Scott showed the inside of his jacket and then waved his hand to indicate the countryside—"there is nowhere for you to go, and in any case I'm quite sure I'm faster than you. I was the gold medallist in the hundred-yard dash in my day."

"Does that mean you slow down after a hundred yards? I may still be in with a chance." She stopped. This was no time for jokes, and she could feel the acceleration of her heart. "Are you planning to kill me? Could I ask you to inform my husband if so. I don't want him left in limbo." She remembered then the little derringer in her pocket.

It would be no match for what he had shown her, and she couldn't see herself shooting him in any case.

Scott shook his head, smiling. "Really, Mrs. Darling. You're being overdramatic. Do I look like a killer to you?"

"I spent the war seeing a lot of people who look like they'd help grannies across the road, who had no trouble killing. Why are we here, wherever here is?"

"I'll have to put a blindfold on you, Mrs. Darling, for the next half hour or so."

"Oh, right. So I can't see all the landmarks we're passing and make my way back from wherever you're taking me."

He smiled. "Now I'm getting out, and if you'll shift so you're near the door behind me, I'll put on the blindfold."

"Oh, for God's sake! Give me the damn thing. I'm quite capable of doing it myself," Lane said crossly, refusing to move.

He made no reply, leaned forward to take something from the glovebox, and then got out of the car and opened the driver's-side rear door. "Ma'am." He shrugged apologetically, indicating with his hand she was to get out of the car. "Turn around and put your hands behind your back."

She obliged, thinking any stalling would just extend this nightmare even longer, and then said, "What is this about? As you have pointed out, I can't escape, and now I can't see. You might as well tell me what's going on. What did you mean, you're 'taking me in'? In to what, or whom?" She'd like to have asked if this was something to do with her war work, but that would reveal she was something more than the housewife she was posing as. She slid back into the car at his orders. She could feel the car beginning to move again.

"I really don't know the specifics. I have orders and I follow them. My understanding is that it has to do with war crimes."

Lane sat back in the seat with a thud. War crimes? What fresh hell was this? She moved so that she sat forward. "War crimes? What war crimes would those be? Whose war crimes?" Her mind raced. She tried to remember what action she had taken during the many dangerous and yet somehow dreary assignments she'd had that could be interpreted as a war crime. She'd never had to kill anyone, though she'd been trained to do it if need dictated it. She'd hit a German over the head pretty hard with a heavy torch, when he'd accidentally come across her hiding just after she'd struggled out of her parachute. Luckily, he'd been alone. She shook away her thoughts about anyone who might have died because of her failures. The man from the safe house . . . Charlie, Alma. No, she mentally shook her head. That had not been her failure, though she could never shake the idea that if she'd paid attention, she would have seen it coming, seen the treachery right in front of her. Was this about Alma? No. Impossible. That had all been investigated, someone charged. "Well?"

Scott was silent for a long while, his right elbow perched on the window, thoughtfully chewing the nail on his index finger. "If you want the truth, Miss Winslow, I find what I know a little hard to believe, now that I've spent some time with you. You're plucky, brave even. You handled all that stuff with Salinas well. But I could see that you were used to being in tough situations. You don't lose your head; you make sure things turn out the way you want them. That only served to convince me it might be true, that you were some sort of spy. Even so, I have a hard time believing you'd kill someone to cover up your own treachery, but as you say, you also look like someone who'd help a granny across a street, so . . ." He shrugged.

Lane felt like she'd been sandbagged. Killed someone to cover up her own treachery? After some moments she said, "I can assure you I have never killed anyone, and certainly not to cover anything I've done. You will appreciate I can tell you no more. I am bound, I'm afraid, by an act I agreed to adhere to in Britain." She shouldn't have said even this much, but the situation demanded it.

"The Official Secrets Act."

"Whom are you acting for? Surely not the Americans, or some enemy of Salinas? The British?" Were they using this ridiculous ploy to get her back into harness? It wouldn't be the first time they'd tried. She tried to think who would be behind such an absurd approach. Certainly not Major Hogarth at the War Office, who had been so helpful the last couple of times she'd visited England. Hogarth was a straight shooter if ever there was one. And who even knew she was in Mexico? She didn't know anymore who might be in charge of this sort of thing.

Her musings were interrupted by the car suddenly coming to a halt. Her head wheeled in the direction of the side window. "Why are we stopping?"

"Just do as you're told, ma'am, everything will be fine."

She heard the door open, and she felt herself being pulled out with a strong hand. When she was on her feet, a gust of hot air stroked her arms and legs. She had this desperate fantasy that she might never feel fresh air again.

"Wait, my bag." She turned her head back toward the car, but Scott held her firmly.

"You won't need it just now, ma'am. I'll . . . I'll get it for you, make sure it goes where you are going."

Lane turned toward the sound of his voice. There was doubt there, she realized. Hesitation. His voice had gone softer and lost its sure edge. Why? He was pulling her gently but firmly away from the car.

She stopped, resisted his pull. "Mr. Scott, what aren't you telling me? This is rubbish. If I'm being detained by British authorities for a crime I most certainly did not commit, then I must know what is behind it."

He tried to coax her along. "Ma'am, please . . ."

She resisted again. "Is it the British? Or is this someone, something, else?" But why would they come after her on trumped-up charges? "Is this just a ploy to get me back to Britain? Have they persuaded you that it would be all right to kidnap a British subject if there were some sort of treason charges attached? Is that what's happened here?"

Not answering her, Scott pulled her along more forcefully, and then they stopped.

Footsteps told her someone else was present, but no one spoke. She heard vehicle doors opening and sensed the presence of something larger than a car. Scott was back. "I'm going to lift you up and put you in the back of this van. You can feel your way to a seat along the side there."

She felt herself lifted, as if she were a bride being carried across a threshold, and placed on a metal floor. Doors were slammed shut, and a latch was thrown. In the dark silence that followed she lifted her head and took in a big gulp of air, and then another, exhaling slowly to quell her growing panic. And that's when she smelled it, lifting past the rust and the mildew and the dust: the distinctive scent of tuberose.

"**THIS WAS NOT** my idea," Darling said angrily. "There's no earthly help you can offer, and believe me, no one is going to put up a penny if you're planning to add me to your collection. In fact, I think my boss would think himself well rid of me!"

Darling was addressing this speech not to Thomas Fine, whom he had been hoping to find, but to his recent adversary, Salinas, who had met them at the bottom of the hill where his compound sat.

"I understand your anger, Inspector. But you underestimate me. I can do a good deal more than Mr. Fine at this moment." Salinas nodded at the truck driver who had been waiting for an indication that he could drive off down the road back to San Jacinto.

"Now how am I going to get to Fresnillo, and a telephone, and the police? On one of your beastly horses, I suppose!"

"Come, Inspector. More faith! I am pledged to rescue your beautiful wife. I have resources that others may not have."

"I shudder to think," Darling said ungraciously, watching the truck he'd come in bumping down the road in a cloud of dust. Could this man really help? He seemed to have his figurative thumb in every official and unofficial pie. "Yes, all right then, what resources would those be?"

"There, you are coming around to my way of thinking. Come with me." He jerked his head toward a squat, corrugated-iron building and led the way. Two men were standing by it, armed with what Darling was sure were Winchester Model 1894 rifles. He remembered seeing somewhere that they'd been in use on the west coast by Canadians preparing for a Japanese invasion.

Salinas lifted his head toward the wooden doors across the building, and the two men pulled them open.

"There, Inspector! Not just horses, horse*power*!" He waved his hand toward a very shiny Rolls-Royce Phantom Saloon. "It is a decade old, Inspector, but an absolute classic and runs like the wind, even on our roads."

APRIL SAT BY Bonny Sunderland's bed, having been given just five minutes by the nursing sister. She was in a room by herself, which surprised April. The wards typically had four or five beds. Had she been obstreperous when she'd been brought in? Or was there an element of her being in isolation because it was drugs, and other patients should not be exposed to this criminal behaviour?

"How are you feeling, Mrs. Sunderland?" she asked kindly.

Bonny opened her eyes and looked at April. "What's it got to do with you?"

She looked, April thought, actually green. She'd read about sick people looking this colour but never imagined it could be true. "I'm with the Nelson Police."

"Oh, great!" Bonny turned her head away, closing her eyes.

"You're not in trouble. We just want to know about where you got . . . what you took."

"I don't know what you mean. I ate something, that's all. Leave me alone."

April sighed, unsure about how to proceed. She didn't want to have to be heavy-handed, as if she even knew how. "The doctor filled us in. We know what you took."

"Bully for you. Go away!"

Worried that if Bonny made a fuss she'd be made to leave, April said, "The thing is, Mrs. Sunderland, those drugs are illegal. Well, not the alcohol, obviously, but all we want to do is find out where you got them. You could have died, and we want to stop that from happening to anyone else."

"Good for you." Bonny pulled her covers up to her neck and turned away from April, her eyes closed, as if she were going to sleep.

"Because of the drugs, Mrs. Sunderland, you are liable to arrest. We don't want to do that, but there have been a couple of people brought in, and we want to stop it."

"Why don't you ask them, then?"

"Please. We just want to help." April felt her chance of getting any useful information slipping away. Bonny seemed bitter and unrepentant, and certainly not swayed by the idea she could be arrested.

Bonny turned back toward April angrily. "Oh, for God's sake! I had them left over, okay? Are you happy? I got them from . . ." She clamped her mouth shut.

"From?"

"Oh, it doesn't matter now. He's dead. Tanney, okay?"

April sat back. Is that where Tanney was getting his money? "Do you know who he got them from? Was he working for someone?"

"How the hell do I know? He just always had stuff when I needed it."

April nodded. "How long has he been . . . supplying . . ." Was that the right word? "Supplying you with these drugs?"

"*Drugs*. You make it sound like I'm a drug fiend or something. It was just reefers, mostly. You could always buy a deck off him. He just had some powder and pills last time."

"Since when, though?"

"I don't know. Half a year? He told me these were the last of it. He'd come into some money and he was leaving, so I bought what he had."

"He never told you where he got them?"

"Would you? It was probably more than his life was worth."

"Miss McAvity, I think it's enough now. She needs her rest."

April nodded at the nursing sister who had stepped into the room, and then turned back to Bonny. "Get well, Mrs. Sunderland. When you're better I'd love to talk to you some more."

"I sure wouldn't love to talk to you."

APRIL TOLD AMES and Terrell what Bonny had said. They were gathered around what they all thought of as O'Brien's counter.

"Tanney, eh?" Ames said. "So that was his game. He was telling his mom he was a shop floor supervisor, and he was out pushing drugs. I guess Bonny actually doesn't know where he was getting them."

"It accounts for all the money, too," Terrell said. "And it could be behind his killing. He could have been killed by whoever was supplying him."

"Yeah, but why?" Ames asked. "I imagine it's not that easy to find people to do that kind of work for you."

"Maybe he threatened to expose his supplier," April said. "Maybe he saw the chance to get more money all at once by blackmailing him. If he wanted to go away with his son . . ."

"Boy, with his death and now this drug thing, I'd almost forgotten he'd tried to kidnap his son. But what you say makes sense."

April smiled, her face going slightly pink. She glanced at Terrell, who gave her a brief, encouraging smile.

"I wonder if Cooper knows Tanney was handling drugs?" Terrell said. "He's dealing with drugs and guns coming over the border. Maybe I'll call him."

"Good work, April," Ames said. "Yeah, find out what he knows, Constable."

"I THINK WE might have to change our habits. Sometimes I just don't have it in me to pit myself against her," Ames complained after they'd ordered coffee and sandwiches from an especially disobliging Marge. "I feel like she might put poison in our coffee one day."

"That wouldn't be good for business, sir. Anyway, I talked to Cooper. He thanked me."

"And?" Ames asked, turning his gaze away from Marge, who'd placed their order and was now standing by the counter, smoking.

"And nothing. I got the feeling he didn't want us coming any closer to his investigation."

"Yeah, but we're dealing with Tanney's murder. You'd

think there'd be an overlap. No, that won't wash. You think Cooper will try to take over our case?"

"He might. What's our next step, sir?" Terrell thought the Mountie might very well want to take over the case, just when they'd like a few questions answered.

"Our next step is to search every place Tanney might have kept supplies. He had a gun, we know that; he might have had others, and he might have put his stock of drugs somewhere as well. Let's get a warrant to search his house, and, a long shot, maybe he had a locker at the power plant that still hasn't been reassigned."

"Yes, sir. I'll go to the judge right after lunch. I'm wondering if we should go back to where he was camped after he got rid of the child. It looked to me like he'd been there longer than a few days; maybe he cached some stuff around there."

"Wouldn't Cooper and his boys have looked at that already? It's near them. On their patch, in fact."

"Not necessarily, sir. Not if he only just found out today Tanney was involved in selling drugs. When he and I went there, it was still to do with the kidnapping."

"You're right. You get the warrant, and we can go across and check his campsite first, then go to his house and the power plant."

"Should we inform Cooper, sir?"

Ames considered this as Marge came into view with their coffee. "Not just yet. If he's not going to play, I don't know why we have to fall over ourselves to include him. If we find anything relevant to his investigation, we can tell him then. Thank you, Marge."

If Marge appreciated this nicety, she didn't say.

"HOW ARE YOUR wedding plans coming along, sir?" Terrell asked as they drove to the ferry.

"Well, you know."

"No, sir."

Ames looked out the window, the warm air blowing his blond hair away from his forehead. The truth is he hadn't thought much about the wedding in the last couple of days. With Darling gone, and the case getting more complicated every minute, he felt a surge of guilt about Tina being stuck with the planning, such as it was. "It's just going to be a small wedding." He gulped. He was supposed to have asked Lorenzo about using the restaurant for a lunch. He'd promised Tina he would. She loved Lorenzo's Italian restaurant as being much the fanciest place in town, and since it had been rebuilt after a fire earlier in the year, it was even more beautiful. And then he remembered something else he hadn't done.

"Say, I don't know if you'd, you know, be willing to stand up for me? Be my best man, like?"

Terrell turned to look at his boss. "Me, sir? Are you sure? What about the inspector? Weren't you his best man?"

Ames nodded. "Yes, but I guess I thought it should be more like a friend. I mean, he's my boss. I'm sure he doesn't expect it. It'd be like asking my father or something. I might ask him to make the speech, though, because I don't have my father."

Terrell felt a sizzle of happiness. "If you're sure, sir, I'd be honoured. Does this mean I can hound you about your planning?"

345

"Watch it!" Ames said good-naturedly.

"This might be a quixotic trip, sir. Maybe Cooper already knew about Tanney's involvement in the trade and will have cleaned everything up already," Terrell said, changing tack.

"Yes, perhaps. In fact, I wonder now if Cooper has been keeping back information. Fair enough, I suppose, if they've got a big investigation going on and they don't want any of the hoodlums tipped off."

They sat in silence until they'd been loaded onto the ferry. "Upstairs?" Ames asked.

"I prefer it down here, sir. We can go stand where Tanney made his last stand."

"You have a twisted sense of humour, Constable," Ames said, following Terrell to lean along the rail.

CHAPTER TWENTY-EIGHT

"**I WAS PUZZLED, INSPECTOR, ABOUT YOU** being shot at on your way to find your brother. As I told you before, I had nothing to do with it. It would not have been in my interest to kill the goose, eh?" Salinas smiled and nodded.

They were sitting in the back seat of the Phantom, and one of his men was driving at unnervingly high speed along a barely discernible dirt road.

"I had my men look into it, because I obviously cannot have this sort of thing going on in my territory. I spoke with friends in the police and the army, and I found out something very curious. If you hadn't come along just now, I would have dropped it. I assumed the business with your brother was concluded and you and your lovely wife were on your way home. Now it is of interest."

"You couldn't cut to the chase, as they say in the movies?" Darling said impatiently. "What did you learn that is in any way related to what has happened to my wife?"

"I am getting to that, Inspector. Capitán . . . well, I won't say his name, but he is an associate in the army. He confided to me that his men had been directed to stop your car on the way out of Mexico City. He could not at once tell me who had ordered this, but then I learned that it originated high up, from a foreign power, at the level of a diplomat."

"We were targeted deliberately? I thought it was a regular sort of thing. That's what Scott said."

"Ah, yes. Scott. I knew I didn't trust him, and I was right. It was simple. They wanted to check your wife's passport. Apparently, the information they sought was confirmed by the army. He told me that there would be a second stop on the way back to the city. I assume this happened, or you would not be here."

Reeling from the idea that they had wanted to look at Lane's passport, Darling took hold of one thing. "What do you mean you didn't trust Scott? Did you know something you didn't tell me?"

"Believe me, Inspector, if I had any knowledge that he would kidnap your wife, I would have done everything to prevent it! I only meant that something did not smell right about him. Can I use this expression? And I was right. He was acting on behalf of someone else, whether at the embassy or somewhere else, I don't know. I do not completely understand what his game is. They had planned to have a Mexican driver who speaks excellent English, but at the last minute, they assigned this Scott. I believe, for reasons I cannot fully understand, that while they were helping with your brother, the object of their involvement was to get hold of your wife. It might be best at this point to think about why your wife would be so important to someone."

Darling sat back, thinking about Lane's passport. She still did not have a Canadian passport. She was still travelling as Lane Winslow. He sighed. She often used her maiden name still. Had she not bothered with a new passport because she wanted to continue being "Lane Winslow" officially? That was silly. It wasn't official at all. They were married. She was, before the law, Lane Darling, née Winslow, pure and simple. He looked out the window and then, unnerved by the speed with which the desert was passing, turned to look at Salinas.

"I don't know," he admitted.

"Ah!" said Salinas with a broad smile. "A woman with a mystery that even her husband does not know! It raises her even more in my estimation. Of course, such a beautiful woman should be a woman with secrets!"

Wanting to say, "Oh, do shut up," Darling took a breath and said, "Where are we going now?"

"Ah, of course. My associate, the *capitán*, said that the plan was to stop your car, remove you, and Scott was to take your wife. They were to meet another vehicle where she was to be transferred and taken—" The car was ascending a low hill and at that moment hit a bump that sent them both slamming to the left. "*¡Ey! ¡Cuidado!*" Salinas shouted through the sliding window into the front.

"Taken where?" Darling asked, righting himself. "Back to the embassy? Why go through all this rigmarole? Why not just detain her at the hotel in Mexico City?"

"Yes. That is the strange thing. And he is not taking her to the embassy. To a borough of the city called Coyoacán. This aroused my suspicion. I had at first thought that perhaps Mrs. Darling was wanted 'officially,' if you will, but now I do not think so. In the world in which I live, Inspector, this has more the flavour of a private vendetta."

LANE LAY BACK on the floor of the van and closed her eyes. She contemplated trying to hoist herself onto the seat Scott had assured her was there, but with her hands tied it seemed too much trouble. There was some sort of argument going on somewhere away from the vehicle. She could hear Scott's raised voice but couldn't distinguish what he was saying. The second man . . . her eyes flew open only to stare at the blackness of the blindfold. But like the light she began to perceive along the bottom of the blindfold, a light was growing in her memory. The silk dressing gown, Charlie folding over, dying a hundred feet away where they could not reach him from where they were hiding . . . Harrison!

She turned her head toward the sound of the voices. That *was* Harrison! The clipped, arrogant way he bit off his words. The tone of dismissal. He was dismissing Scott now. She took a deep breath. It wasn't Harrison, of course it wasn't; she'd recognized that smell of tuberose that Captain Herridge had been wearing in his lapel. But his voice bit into her memory. Harrison had escaped before they'd got off their duffs and arrested him. Everyone assumed he'd gone to France, to the Breton nationalists he'd betrayed them all for. No one had ever mounted a real search for him, or for many of the other war criminals who had taken advantage of the chaos of war to get rich. Somehow, he'd fetched up here, name changed, different-coloured hair, glasses, about five stone heavier, now a respected member of the British delegation in Mexico. She tried to imagine the dapper, slim, and quite short Harrison as this bloated man she'd met at the embassy. But it was impossible. He would have to have created a whole new persona, new name, new history, new rank, forged education and military history documents. The problem was that voice. Now that she recognized it as Harrison, she could not shake the idea. If it was, had he come straight to Mexico after the war, and then set about remaking himself? How would he have got entry into the staff at the embassy?

The argument had stopped, and someone got into the passenger side of the van. There was an order, and the engine started up, sluggish at first, and then it caught, and the van began to move. Lane felt herself rocked as they lurched forward. There was a shout, and someone banged on the side of the van twice, hard. "Stop! For God's sake . . ."

Lane turned her head in the direction of the desperate voice. Scott! Being left behind. Why? But Scott's voice receded as the van she was in moved.

He'd been her captor, yes, but she felt that she knew him somehow. Now he was gone, and she was left alone in the hands—yes, she had to face it—of the man she'd exposed as a traitor. Fear swamped her. She hadn't recognized the escaped Deniel Harrison on that afternoon in Mexico City, but he had recognized her.

SCOTT STOOD ON the road paralyzed as if he'd lost all power of movement. He could scarcely take in the events of the last few moments. He couldn't believe that Captain Herridge had told him his job was done. He'd just driven off, leaving him behind, in the middle of nowhere, and some man Herridge had brought with him had swiped his diplomatic car and driven off.

With an enormous sigh that managed to suck in the lingering dust from the receding vehicles, leaving him choking and coughing, he turned in a circle to look around. He was absolutely alone in the middle of the state of Zacatecas. The silence echoed in his ears. The sun was high and tending westward, hot and unrelenting, and the sky was huge, bigger than the earth he stood on.

He felt suddenly small and fought back, drawing himself up. It was what? Ten miles back to the main highway to Mexico City? He could get a lift back to the city there. He patted his back pocket. He still had a wallet and some money.

His thoughts turned to Mrs. Darling and Herridge. Where was he going with her? And why hadn't the van she was in travelled back toward the Mexico City highway? Was it some sort of shortcut back to the city? And what was Herridge doing? He began to trudge back along the dirt road to the highway, his mind in turmoil. He could hear Mrs. Darling's voice saying, "I can assure you I've never killed anyone . . ."

DARLING AND HIS host had fallen into silence. They'd driven past the army checkpoint; it was gone, leaving only the small hut, abandoned and crumbling. Darling had given his mind over to endless contemplation of what might be happening to Lane, his imagination failing in the end. Why would Captain Herridge have a vendetta against his wife? Of course! Something from the war, no doubt. Something big that she had never told him about, and likely never would. His heart sank at the sudden fear that she would not be given the chance. He looked up as Salinas banged suddenly on the window, saying something urgently to the driver, who slowed down and then stopped. He was about to ask what was happening, when the driver began to back up, again at a speed that seemed highly inadvisable to Darling.

"Look at this! We have found a desert rat!" Salinas said almost gleefully, rolling down his window. Darling looked across through the window, and there, looking dusty and very much the worse for wear, was Scott. He'd been sitting on the ground and was now scrambling to his feet.

"Lost, Señor Scott?" Salinas asked.

"Thank God," Scott said. "We have to find them!"

"COOPER AND I should have looked farther. We just sort of looked around the perimeter of the fire," Terrell said. "I can't believe we missed this!" They were standing in front of a low moss-covered shed that looked like it had been an outbuilding for some long-gone homestead. It was set well back in the trees, and ancient though it appeared to be, it had a stout low door with a brand new brass lock on it. A Deco 79.

"You got the key?"

"Very funny, sir. Would you like me to break it off?"

"It would be quicker to shoot it off," Ames said, "if only one of us had brought a firearm. Anyway"—he shrugged—"this is in Cooper's domain. We'd better stop by the detachment and tell him."

Terrell nodded. "I'd like to come back out with him to see what's here. It might help us understand what Tanney was up to. If there are drugs in there, or firearms, then he might have had direct contact with Cooper's smugglers. I mean, when he went to ground, this is the place he picked. I don't think it was an accident."

"Off we go then."

COOPER HAD HIS feet propped up on a chair and was leaning sideways against his desk, looking relaxed. "You have been busy," he commented, as Ames described the shed and Tanney's involvement with drugs. He slid his booted feet back onto the floor, swivelled around, and opened the central drawer in his desk, taking out a pad and a pencil, and began to write. "Where was the shed, again?"

Terrell explained where it was in relation to where Tanney had been camping.

"Well, thanks, gentlemen. As you can see, I'm on my own here, so I can't get out there just now, but it'll keep." He stood up, causing Terrell and Ames to stand up. "I'll give you a ring to tell you what I find." He flashed them a smile. "You've saved me a bit of work here. I wouldn't have thought to look out there."

Ames, feeling dismissed and annoyed about it, stood in the doorway holding his hat. "If Tanney has something to do with your case, shouldn't we be working it together? If we're going to find out who killed him, then it's bound to be something to do with the fact that he was pushing drugs."

Holding his hand out to indicate the outside door, Cooper said, "That's a good point, Sergeant Ames. The trouble is, as I see it, we're going to have to take over the Tanney case, since you've pointed out he was likely involved with our smugglers." Another apologetic smile. "But let's not worry about that now. I'll call you to let you know what's in there, as soon as I can."

Ames sat fuming in the passenger seat as they cruised out of Creston on the long drive to the ferry terminal.

"Sorry, sir," Terrell said.

"It's not your fault. We were right to go check; there is definitely something going on with that shed in the middle of nowhere. What aggravates me is that he might be right about having to take over the case. I just don't like his lack of collegiality. If you know what I mean."

"Yes, sir. Do you think talking to our bunch in Nelson might help?"

"We'll come across as crybabies then, won't we? Mommy, Daddy's being mean!"

"I don't know why we don't go on investigating at our end. After all, the doctor said at least four people had been brought in from overdoses, and that doesn't count all the people who didn't get sick but were taking something. And we still have Tanney's house and work locker to look at. Sunderland said she bought everything he had, but he might have been lying to her about that. We have our search warrant, after all."

"Yes. Good point."

"Now, sir, would you like me to book the restaurant? And by the way, what day are we thinking of getting married?"

LANE TRIED TO sleep on one side and then the other, the only comfortable option with her hands tied behind her back, but the pain from her still very sore ribs did not allow for any real comfort. The trip had been interminable. She remembered the trip up to Fresnillo had taken ten hours, and their return trip had been interrupted not an hour in. No one spoke to her, and she felt herself bruised by the bumps and turnings of the van. She was certain that they were not on the highway by the roughness of the ride.

Dust seeped in from the undercarriage, making her feel as if she could not get a whole breath. When she'd been training, she'd been subjected to practice interrogations and long periods of isolation in dark rooms. She struggled to muster whatever skills she'd used to endure those experiences. She tried breathing more slowly, closing her eyes, and calming herself, trying to focus on something else, but she was out of practice and unsettled by the unpredictable lurching of the vehicle. Eventually she began to focus on the noise of the engine, finding that it made her feel grounded, as if the outer noise somehow induced a spurious kind of inner peace.

She felt the van stopping for gas twice, could hear the gas cap being unscrewed and the nozzle inserted, heard pleasant exchanges between the gas jockey and the driver. Never in all that time did she hear the other man speak, the one she was sure was Deniel Harrison.

They finally arrived somewhere. The back of the van opened. Two men pulled her out, and she was barely able to stand. She coughed violently, inducing a sharp pain in her ribs, and tried to speak, but a man told her angrily to be quiet in accented English. She had the idea it was nighttime because she heard no other traffic.

The room she was put into was such a relief after the sheer purgatory of being in the van for all those hours that she almost relished the feel of the scratchy blanket on the bed she was pushed onto.

After what seemed like hours, she heard the door open. Footsteps approached and the blindfold was pulled off roughly. Dust had built up along her eyelids, so she blinked several times in the vain hope of clearing the irritation off.

She found she was in a meagrely furnished room with a table and two chairs, the bed she'd been on, and very little else. On the table was a long-necked clay jar—like the ones she'd seen at the market, her addled brain offered—and next to it a glass, which she earnestly hoped would mean she might get water at last. She felt so bruised internally that she could not imagine eating anything. This lot was unlikely to give her food anyway, she thought grimly.

The man who had taken off her blindfold now busied himself with the handcuffs, which seemed to give him trouble. It became clear he didn't have the right key. He banged on the door to be let out and shouted something irritated to someone outside the room. In five minutes, he was back and held up the key in an almost friendly manner. It was the right key.

With relief she tried to bring her arms around to the front, and then cried out at the pain. She moved more slowly, and finally, her hands in her lap, she began to rub her wrists.

The man was Mexican, and she was not sure if he spoke English. He had said nothing to her and now stood by the door as if he were waiting for someone else.

"Wh . . ." she began, and found herself almost unable to speak. She coughed and cleared her throat again. "Why am I . . ." Another attack of coughing that caused her to double over, her ribs protesting.

The ridiculousness of her predicament impressed itself upon her. It was the second time in a very few days she'd found herself lying on a strange bed in a strange room. There really ought to be a limit to this sort of thing! "Where is my husband?" she finally managed.

The man standing by the door only shrugged and gave his head a shake. Scott had assured her that he was fine, that the object of this had been to capture her. She tried to take comfort in this and then thought about Scott. He had most assuredly been working for Harrison. And yet she had the distinct impression he'd been left behind. Had he begun to come around to her way of thinking? Or had Herridge/Harrison told him it was official business?

The thing that settled in her mind with a crystalline clarity was that Harrison had recognized her, and thought she'd recognized him. And that he had not brought her to the embassy. He was afraid he'd been discovered. What would he do to eliminate the threat she posed?

CHAPTER TWENTY-NINE

"**H**ONESTLY, I HAD NO IDEA this would happen." Scott, sitting in the back of the car with Salinas and Darling, was in a rebellious mood. His boss had deceived him by pretending that bringing Mrs. Darling in was an official endeavour, and now, after he'd jogged ten miles in the searing heat, Salinas was treating him like something he'd found on the bottom of his shoe.

Darling, who had been falsely accused of murder once himself, knew how convincing and how slippery a trail of lies could be. Why should Scott not have believed his boss? Yet he didn't find himself convinced by this apparently co-operative Scott.

"Who did Captain Herridge say she was meant to have killed?" he asked.

"He didn't tell me much, just that she was a traitor and had killed one of their best agents and disappeared."

"Disappeared from where? Did he say they'd arrested her and she'd got away?"

"I don't know!" Scott said. "He never said."

"You accepted what he said without question?" Darling persisted.

"Of course I did! Herridge is my boss, and the third secretary of the embassy. I had no reason to disbelieve him."

Salinas, who had no patience for this methodical interrogation, said, "And nothing about her convinced you it was a lie?"

Scott bridled. He did not want to answer questions put to him by a criminal. But he thought about Mrs. Darling. The truth was, nearly everything about her made him doubt what Herridge said.

"You're quiet now, eh? So, you did know something was wrong! And you did nothing. Just let that *imbécil* cart her off! I should open the door and throw you onto the road. I would like to. But maybe I can think of something worse." Salinas turned disgustedly to look out the window.

"Did he say anything at all about what he was planning to do once he had her?" Darling asked.

Scott nodded. "Yes. When he alerted me to the problem, you know, when he asked me to drive you, he told me I was to bring her in, and that he would contact his people in England, and she'd be sent there for trial. I thought I was just to bring her back to the embassy, and the military police or someone would take charge of her. I didn't expect . . ."

"No, well. How could you?" Darling said.

"Do you know what, you stupid gringo, you are lucky I am here," Salinas said. "I at least know from my contacts that she is being taken to Coyoacán. I have a little place there. We will find out where he has taken her and get her back. It is a desirable town, and many people with means have houses there. I bet your boss has means way beyond his embassy salary, because he is acting like a criminal."

Darling felt some hope. If Herridge was lining his own nest, and he clearly was comfortable acting outside the law, then perhaps some contact of Salinas's would likely know. In fact, he was a bit surprised that Salinas, with his vast network, had not already crossed paths with him.

Echoing Darling's thoughts, Salinas said, "I'm surprised I haven't already heard of this *pinche* English crook."

At last, the car was making its way through a treed and sunny town, interspersed with fields and high leafy hedges. They drove around a square and then past a church with a plaza in front of it. Well-dressed people passed along the streets and sat on the benches, talking or reading. A flower seller sat on the stairs of the church, with buckets filled with great bundles of white flowers.

"I live just past Santa Catarina here," Salinas said, pointing at the colonial church.

The car stopped on a narrow street, and the driver got out and went to open an ornate cast-iron gate. They bumped slowly along the cobbled driveway and parked next to a large pink adobe and stone building.

Salinas waited while his driver opened his door and then stepped out, dusting his shoulders as if proximity to Scott had soiled him. "Here we are. Let us get to work."

A man opened the large wooden front door from inside and inclined his head deferentially to Salinas, who greeted him and then delivered a volley of instructions.

"Please, there are two bathrooms upstairs and one downstairs. Scott, you can go downstairs. My cook will prepare some food and drink, and in the meantime, I will call people and find out where Mrs. Darling has been taken."

"Should we not contact the police?" Darling asked.

Salinas gave a short laugh. "Please, Inspector. You are not in Canada now. Please allow me to take care of these matters. Enjoy my home. It is yours."

Restored by a wash and some food, Darling and Scott sat in a vast sitting room full of leather furniture. They gazed at the many paintings and a combination of expensive antique silver, framed portraits, vases, and folkloric figures. The floor was rust-coloured tile spread with various woven rugs. They were seated in front of a fireplace with a high arched mantel. Salinas had not yet returned from wherever he'd disappeared to.

"'Little place,' the hell! Nice life if you can get it," Scott commented. "I have an actual small apartment in the Pedregal, very modern, very nice, but this, whew!"

"Perhaps you could stop gawking and put your mind to the problem," Darling suggested. "I want you to tell me everything, right from the first moment you met us. What did he say, what did he do, what did he say afterward to you? Anything. Everything."

Scott, whose brash self-confidence had been severely undermined by the indignity of being left behind in the middle of the desert, and his own growing doubts about Herridge's behaviour, nodded. "All right. Well, let's see. After you contacted the embassy, he came to get me, so that we could hear from you together and come up with a plan to help you. I mean, it was all pretty much as expected."

"When you came into the room to see us, did you notice anything about his behaviour?"

"No." Scott shook his head. "Yes. He was going in ahead of me and he suddenly stopped, and then I think he said I should go in first. And then you were there for the rest of it."

"Good. Do you think he recognized her then?"

Scott thought. "I'm not sure. I thought it was . . . well, he kind of likes to make a grand entrance. Like I should go in and announce him sort of thing. Maybe he recognized her when we were talking. It was only after you left he told me we have a problem, that she, Mrs. Darling, worked for the Special Operations Executive and had killed one of their people, and by the time they found out she'd slipped out of the country."

Darling sat back, stunned. "Special Operations? That's what he said?" He knew by now she'd done something clandestine, but the SOE? And how had Herridge known that? If he did, *he* certainly didn't seem to feel bound by any Official Secrets Act.

"Yes. Does it mean something?"

To say more would expose Lane even further. "What else did he say?"

"He just told me he needed to think. About an hour later he called me to his office and said he was cancelling the driver, I was to take over, and then he said he had to be sure, and that he would arrange for the army at one of the checkpoints to get your passports. When the passports were returned, he wanted me to take a quick look before I gave them back to you, and to call him when I got to Fresnillo. I did call him, but he said the man at the checkpoint had already told him what name was on her passport. I asked him what I was supposed to do, and he said he needed time to alert the British authorities, so I should carry on with the mission. But I should never let her out of my sight."

"And what do you know about the people who fired on us?"

"Nothing at all! I swear! I thought it was him, or some other bandit." He made a movement with his head to indicate Salinas upstairs. "I was terrified!"

"Then you telephoned him from Fine's house at the mine."

"Yes. He told me to phone when we had your brother back."

"And?"

"Well, I was a little bit . . . I don't know. Reluctant. I mean, I'd spent time with her by then and I had a hard time believing what he said was true. Anyway, he told me what to do, and I asked him if it wouldn't be easier if I just drove you back to the city, and he told me to do as I was told. And then he dumped me in the middle of nowhere like some left baggage! Do you think it's true, what he says?"

Stilling a desire to urge him not to be a complete moron, Darling said, "Of course it's not true! But something is very wrong with Herridge. Let me think." Darling got up and paced. Someone must know what the truth was. Lane had said she thought she recognized him. That could only mean from her time in the . . . God almighty! SOE. Hogarth! Major Hogarth must know something. He looked at his watch, and then realized it was getting dark outside. Seven

364

thirty. It would be what, in England? Blast! Three in the morning. Or maybe earlier. Mexico City must be well east of British Columbia.

At that moment Salinas came downstairs. He'd changed into grey slacks and a golf shirt. "*Bueno*, I have found out about our friend, the Capitán Herridge. Have you had enough to eat and drink, Inspector?" He seemed to be studiously ignoring Scott.

"Thank you, yes," Darling said, though in truth he had hardly touched his food. "If I wanted to make a call to England—"

Salinas didn't let him finish. "But of course, my friend! You don't need to ask. Is there someone there who can help?"

"There might be, but she won't be at work for some hours." Then he smote his forehead and reached into his back pocket for his wallet. "I'm an idiot!" He pulled out bills of various currencies and dumped them on the coffee table and reached into a small inner pocket. Hogarth, making him swear never to tell Lane, had given him a number where she could always be reached in case of an emergency. And this was an emergency. "Can you put this call through for me?"

"Inspector, it is the middle of the night in England, you will not reach anybody."

Darling thrust the paper at him. "I will reach this person. She is a major in the armed forces over there. She knows my wife, and I think she was involved with the SOE."

"The what?" asked Salinas, taking the paper and hurrying back upstairs, indicating Darling should follow him.

"Some sort of special branch during the war. I think my wife . . . well, I don't know."

365

"Yes, of course! I am not surprised." He led Darling into a spacious office, with books lining the mahogany shelves, and a view onto the dark street below. He pulled the drapes and then went to the telephone on the desk and began an urgent communication in Spanish with someone. In a few minutes he put the phone down. "It is arranged. They will alert us when the call is put through."

Darling looked around the plush office, with its paintings and thick rugs. "My wife is not the only one who is a person of mystery. You live out in the desert but keep this beautiful house here."

Salinas waited a beat. "I must be many places, Inspector, to keep an eye on my business interests."

Darling cleared his throat. "You will forgive me, Señor Salinas, but in Canada what you do would largely be considered illegal. I mean no offence."

Salinas, sitting on the corner of his desk, smiled broadly, "None taken, Inspector. But you wished to ask something?"

"Yes, I suppose my question is, how do you get away with it? You seem to have the police and the army on your side, as it were."

"There was much to do, Inspector, to bring our country into the twentieth century. Land for the peasants, industrial production, modernization, the war effort. Business that could aid in this development has been encouraged and supported by the government, even foreign investment if it helps the cause of modernization. Businessmen like myself are largely tolerated by the authorities, provided we are—ah, your call!" He reached over and picked up the receiver. "*Sí, un momento.*" He handed it to Darling.

"What bloody time is it?" he heard. "Sorry. Who is this?"

"Major Hogarth. I'm sorry to call you at this hour. It's Frederick Darling. You said I might call if need be."

Major Hogarth's voice immediately lost its gritty sleepiness. "Inspector Darling. What's happened?"

Darling explained as succinctly as possible about Lane being accused of murder and being kidnapped by a Captain Herridge, third secretary at the British embassy, and his suspicion that it might be connected to her work with the SOE.

"Great. Wonderful. You know about that then, do you?" Her voice suggested it was not at all wonderful.

"It was not she who told me, I promise you. What we need to know is, who is Herridge? Why would he accuse her of this, pretend to his staff that he was delivering her to British authorities, and then kidnap her?"

"Just a minute. Let me think. What does he look like?" Darling could hear a bedside lamp being snapped on, and then another woman's voice asking what the hell was going on.

"I don't know. Middle height. Five nine, maybe. Black hair, moustache, glasses. Very overweight. I'd give him two hundred pounds. Fifties?" There was a long pause, during which Salinas looked at Darling with a questioning expression.

"Look, Darling, I can't tell you anything—"

"That's enormously helpful," Darling snapped.

"Just wait. I can't tell you anything, but you've got to find her. Do you have any pull with the authorities over there?"

Darling glanced at Salinas. "Plenty, apparently."

"Good. Find her, have him arrested on, well, kidnapping charges, and I'll contact the British embassy first thing in"—pause—"well, it will have to be now I suppose. They can take it from there."

"But who is he? Is he something to do with you?"

"Need to know, I'm afraid, Inspector. Suffice it to say I suspect I know who he might be. Someone who's been off our radar since . . . well, for a while. Can you just take care of your end?"

"Certainly. Find a kidnapped woman in a city of three million in a foreign country. Give me a couple of hours."

"Look, I know how you feel. I wish I could help, but I'm in my pyjamas five thousand miles away. Where can you be reached? I'll see who we have out there. Do not under any circumstances look for help from the embassy for now. We'll have to do some things at our end."

Useless, thought Darling with irritation. He put his hand over the speaker and said, "She wants to know where I can be reached."

Salinas wrote his number on the back of an envelope and pushed it over. Darling conveyed this to Hogarth. "There's someone here who will answer at any time of day."

"Look, I won't tell you not to worry. You should worry. If this is what I think it is, she is in grave danger."

Darling felt his stomach turn over. "There's a man here who seems to know people. He might know where he's gone to ground."

"Good. It sounds like Lane is not the only resourceful one in your family. Get there at once and do whatever you can to hold Herridge. I'll be in touch."

Darling looked at Salinas and nodded.

"Good," said Salinas. "I have some men waiting outside. We will go."

CHAPTER THIRTY

"**Y**OU'VE PUT ON WEIGHT," LANE said.

"Shut up. I do the talking here."

Lane sighed.

"You managed to get away from me. I knew I'd find you somehow, one day."

"I think you'll find that you managed to get away from all of us," Lane said. "Can I have some more water, please?"

"You ruined my career. I don't lightly forget that sort of thing. Bloody women! I warned them from the beginning it was a mistake having the female element in the SOE," Herridge said, ignoring her request.

So, he's nursing a grievance, Lane thought. One of those who hated women in intelligence. He wants to have his say now. That is why he has not killed me outright. "Was our being shot at the other day something to do with you?"

"The man I sent was a bloody incompetent! There will be no mistake this time. It did, however, provide the information that you were armed. That was useful."

370

So, he has people. He has a lot more to lose now than just his career. She thought about her little derringer. It had been taken sometime during the initial kidnapping.

"You know, I didn't for a minute recognize you. You've managed to change nearly everything about yourself. Except, apparently, your desire to risk your career. Instead of leaving well enough alone, you've gone to all this trouble, and you'll be found out. It's not the first time. You went to all that trouble to have Charlie killed and then tried to cover it up by having Alma shot as well. It's classic—please forgive the pleasantry—overkill. That's how I realized it was you who betrayed us."

Herridge's fist came down on the table, making Lane jump. "I said, shut up! I'm in charge here. God, I hated you right from the beginning. You thought you were smarter than everyone."

Lane stifled an impulse to point out that she'd been smarter than him in that one instance and sat silently. They were in a small room, below the main floor, she guessed. There was a narrow window to her left through which she could see stairs ascending to street level, illuminated by a streetlight. Alas, the window, like so many she'd seen in Mexico, was behind a fancy cast-iron set of bars. On the table was the pitcher of water. It was dotted with beads of moisture, and she became acutely aware of her thirst. The glass next to it beckoned. She reached across the table for the pitcher and began to pour herself some water. His arm flew out and he struck her hand hard, sweeping the pitcher and the glass to the floor with a loud shattering and a flood of water.

The door opened, and an alarmed-looking man put his head in.

"Get out!" Herridge shouted, and the door closed hurriedly. He pulled his hand back and locked his fingers tightly together on the table, his face red, in a seeming attempt to take control of himself. "I said, I am in charge now." He gave his head a convulsive little twist as if releasing a knot in his neck. After a moment he spoke again. "I had a career. A proper, rising military career. I had a wife and a son. Because of your interference I lost it all. I had to leave my wife and child behind. I don't even know what's happened to them. He'd be fifteen now, my boy. For all I know he's been told his father is dead. Dead! What does that do to a child?"

They're well out of it, Lane thought, but did not speak. Her hand where he'd hit it still hurt, and she held it cradled in her lap.

Finally, she spoke. "What about Charlie's child? His father really *is* dead."

Herridge sat rigidly, his fingers turning white from the effort of holding himself in place. He began to nod his head, as if saying "yes" over and over. "I dreamed of finding you. I mean actually dreamed it. I dreamed of telling you what you've done to me. I'd wake up sweating and furious because it wasn't real."

"Really, Captain Herridge—"

He finally released his hands to hold up one finger. "No." He shook his finger at her. "I talk, you listen. And when I am finished, I will shoot you, and your body will never be found." He reached into his jacket pocket, pulled out a revolver, and placed it on the table under his hands.

"**WE'RE SORRY TO** bother you, Mrs. Tanney. It's been a difficult time for you. Would it be all right if we looked through Jim's room and so on? Maybe your basement?"

Tanney's mother sat in her wheelchair watching them closely. She looked exhausted and, if anything, thinner than when they'd last seen her. "How is that going to find my son's killer? He's not in this house, is he? So why should you be looking around here?"

Terrell spoke up. "It may help us, ma'am. Your son might have been killed by someone he knew or did business with. Maybe he fell out with someone. There might be letters or something that would help. Why don't we let Sergeant Ames get started and I'll make you a cup of tea or coffee?"

"I can make my own damn tea, thanks very much. You just go help the sergeant and then you can both leave."

In the small, messy bedroom at the back of the house, Ames shook his head. "She's pretty bitter. I'll start with the closet and all his pockets, and you take the drawers, under the bed, and mattress."

They had stopped at the power plant with their warrant to search Tanney's locker, but the foreman told them they'd already emptied it and given the locker to a new worker. He said they'd bagged whatever was in there—some coveralls and a pair of boots, he thought, and maybe a lunch box. Someone was supposed to take it to Tanney's mother, but he wasn't sure if anyone had.

They'd found the bag in the manager's office, pushed behind a desk. Ames had opened it on the way to Mrs. Tanney's house, but aside from a very mouldy sandwich in the lunch box, it contained exactly what the foreman had said. Overalls and some boots.

"It would be useful if we actually found a letter or some notes or something, now that I think of it. I was just thinking we'd be looking for some sort of stash of drugs," Ames said, as he felt through the few jackets and one suit that he was sure had belonged to Tanney's father. There was a suitcase in the back of the tiny closet, and he pulled this out and opened it on the bed. Empty. He shone his flashlight into the corners of the closet to reveal only dust balls.

"Sir," Terrell said suddenly, holding up a blue school notebook.

Ames came out of the closet and coughed, brushing dust off the sleeves of his jacket. He took the notebook and began to turn the pages. It was filled with columns of letters and numbers. The figures were written in a schoolboy hand, the pencil pressed hard into the paper. Dollar signs very likely indicated money transactions.

"'C,' 'R.' Drugs?" asked Terrell. "Cocaine, reefers. He takes them in, sells them, collects, and writes down the amounts. Then he has to give most of it to someone else, I'm guessing. His supplier."

Ames continued leafing, but after five pages, the entries stopped. He was closing it when he saw something on the last page: "28 m E 110 S. It looks like some sort of coordinates," he said. "Good. It's something. We can figure it out later. Let's finish up in here."

Terrell turned his attention back to the three-drawer dresser. There was little enough in it. Two flannel shirts, some socks, which he turned inside out, and several pairs of underwear in the top drawer, all looking like they'd been part of his wardrobe for several years. He emptied all of these onto the bed and felt around in the corners to no avail. The middle drawer contained only a boiler suit and a belt. In the bottom drawer he found a sweater, moth-eaten and decades old. Had it been his father's as well? Some magazines of an unwholesome subject, two ties, and several undershirts. He lifted these all as a bunch and heard a clink. Throwing the items on the bed, he looked in the drawer and found a small brass key. "Sir. I wonder if that would fit in that Deco 79 lock on the shed?"

Having turned the drawers over and checked in the basement, they were satisfied that the key and the notebook were as much as they would find.

LINDA RADCLIFFE CLOSED the book she was reading to Rocky and leaned over to kiss him good night.

"It's still light out, Mommy."

"I know, sweetie pie, but it is long past your bedtime."

She stroked the hair away from his forehead. He had seemed perfectly fine when the police had brought him back, but he had gradually become more clingy, less happy about going to bed at night. She had tried once to talk to him about what happened, but he'd become tearful and said he couldn't remember, except about the man telling him to just wait and not to get up when he'd left him beside the road.

Once it became clear that that complete moron Tanney had been behind it, she thought the best thing was to put it all behind them. After all, he could never bother them again, though she'd shrunk from telling Rocky that the man who'd taken him was dead. Best to move on.

She kissed his forehead again and stood up. "Sleep tight!"

"Don't let the bed bugs bite!" he answered.

Just as she was closing the door, he spoke again. "Mommy, will Auntie Bonny come to the window again?"

"YOU'RE SAYING THAT Mrs. Sunderland came to the window on the ladder the night Rocky was kidnapped?" Ames was writing in his notebook. "That's what he remembers?"

Linda Radcliffe sighed and shifted in her chair. "That's what he told me. That she came to his window and said he should go open the front door because his daddy was there, waiting to come in. Of course, the minute I got him back to sleep I was over there banging on the door. I was seeing red, I can tell you. Her husband was furious and told me Bonny was in hospital and wasn't I ashamed of myself. I told him I had no idea what he was talking about, but that I'd found out she was behind the kidnapping all along. I might have said I'd 'get' her for it. He slammed the door in my face."

"I wish you'd come to us right away." Ames sighed. He'd have to talk to Bonny Sunderland about more than the drugs. And how far was Mr. Sunderland involved? Maybe talk to him first.

"How was little Rocky today?"

She shrugged. "He seems all right. I sat with him till he went to sleep, though he did seem a little less scared than usual. He said he got scared when he opened the door and instead of his father there was this strange man who picked him up and carried him to a van."

"I guess being able to talk about it helps a bit. I'd like to be able to talk to him myself. Could I come by after school?"

"I've told you everything he said. Just leave him alone. Shouldn't you be talking to that bi . . . to Bonny? He said she's in hospital, so she won't be hard to find! She belongs in a loony bin, if you want my opinion."

"Thanks, Mrs. Radcliffe. Listen, if he says anything else, Rocky, I mean, or you think it's okay for us to talk to him, let me know. Thanks for coming in. This is very important information."

Ames stood thoughtfully at the top of the stairs, after escorting Linda Radcliffe out of his office. He didn't entirely disagree that Bonny Sunderland ought to be in a loony bin. Or maybe someplace that housed wacky teenagers, because that's how she behaved.

"I still think the most important thing now is to track down the drug connection," he observed to Terrell later. "I mean, I guess we'll have to charge her with aiding and abetting a kidnapping eventually. Never mind the drug charges we could throw at her."

"Where's her husband in all this?" asked Terrell.

"Well, yes. Where indeed? We're going to have to bring him in . . . no, ask him to come in. After all, we don't know he's involved. Maybe his wife is just crazy because of the drugs she's been taking."

The phone trilled on Ames's desk. "Yes?"

"Sorry, sir, I forgot to tell you in all the excitement that Sergeant Cooper telephoned just to let you know that the shed was empty and didn't look like it had been used for some time. I hope that means something to you."

"Thanks, Miss McAvity." Ames put down the receiver. "I still feel ridiculous calling her that. Anyway, Cooper called, and the shed was empty and hadn't been used for some time." Then he looked closely at Terrell. "You don't trust him, do you?"

Terrell sat in silence for some time, his mouth clamped thoughtfully as if he was contemplating how to put it. "I think he's just throwing sand in our eyes. He doesn't want us involved in his case."

"You don't believe him?"

"I'm not sure. That padlock was brand new."

"Well, yes. But we have no real reason to doubt Cooper. He's just doing the usual 'This is our case, butt out of it' we get from the Mounties. It may have been brand new, but it's perfectly possible that if that was where Tanney stashed his drugs, he sold them all and took the money. There was all that money he had in his wallet the day he died."

IT WAS HOPELESS. Lane could see that. Herridge was a massive presence across the table from her, made larger by what was beginning to feel like a rant. She determined to keep quiet and looked at the table. She wanted to look around the room again, though she knew she would see nothing new. There was at least one man standing guard behind the door, probably armed. Even if she could fight her way out, she would not likely make it past him.

"Look at me when I'm talking to you!" His voice had risen in pitch, and his near hysteria caused a spike of alarm in her. Her only hope was to keep him talking. Why, she wasn't sure. The outcome was inevitable. No one would find her here.

"Yes, I'm sorry. You were angry that women were recruited. I understand. You didn't think it was right."

He seemed surprised by her sudden passivity. "Exactly. Too stupid, you see. I mean, most women can't even put a decent meal on the table for their husbands, let alone do intelligence work. Not built for it. Look at you. I don't know who told you you were clever. Some indulgent nanny, no doubt." He stabbed at his head. "Thick. Thick as a pile of bricks."

Class warfare as well, thought Lane, with that nanny comment. Her heart sank. Not only was escape impossible, but it was clear to her he had some sort of persecution mania and seemed prepared to bore her into submission. She tried to fight her growing despair. *Your only job is to survive*, she recited to herself. She could not risk looking at him again, searching for any, any possible weakness. *Do not appear to study your captor's mannerisms or appearance.* But she thought of Darling, of his kindness, his love, his charcoal eyes, all that she would never know again.

CHAPTER THIRTY-ONE

——————

"**I**T'S A LOVELY DAY FOR a picnic. Where are you taking me? Up the lake somewhere?" April buckled her leather helmet and pushed some stray hair underneath it. Terrell had taken the picnic from her and secured it in the panniers.

"Way up the lake. We get a ferry ride and everything."

"You're up to something!" April said, climbing on behind him. "We're going back to the scene of the crime!"

"Not exactly. But there is something I want to check. Two birds, one ride."

"Oh, goody!"

It was a sparkling day and April, forgetting police protocol for the moment, wrapped her arms around Terrell's waist and rested her chin on his shoulder as they travelled toward the ferry terminal in Balfour. She marvelled at how warm he was, how right it felt.

As he kicked the bike stand in place on deck, Terrell recognized Zack Graham, the ferry worker he'd talked to earlier, and gave him a nod. The ferry was well under way, and Terrell and April stood looking out across the lake, when Graham approached them.

"You sure are making a habit of this," he commented, tilting his peaked cap back and wiping his forehead. "Nice day for it, though." He looked with interest at April.

"This is Miss McAvity. She works with us at the Nelson Police Department. Zack Graham."

"A girl cop? That's a new one! Couldn't get any men?"

April sighed and was about to say something back, when Terrell spoke.

"Miss McAvity has been a vital part of the investigation."

"Hey, no offence meant, it's just a surprise is all." Graham put his hands up and smiled. "I mean, the Nelson Police seems to be full of surprises. You caught that guy yet?"

"Not yet."

Graham looked at them and shook his head doubtfully. "Well, good luck."

"Seems to me," Terrell said blandly to April, "Mr. Graham left just in time. He was digging a hole for himself one way and another."

"You can't pay attention to that sort of nonsense," April said. "I put up with all sorts of stupid stuff in Vancouver. It got pretty offensive at times, I can tell you."

He looked at her, concern registering on his face. "I'm sorry, you didn't say . . ."

"Please, if I complained every time someone said something rude about women, I'd have nothing else to talk about! I just ignore it, unless people start getting gropey. Then I let them have it."

"What? Did they go that far?"

"No, they wouldn't dare with the sergeant there. I don't think he thought much of women in the force either, but at least he stood up for the rules."

Terrell sighed. "Well, I guess that's something we have in common. What spheres other people think we ought to stick to."

April nodded. Whatever she endured would have been much worse for him, she suspected. "Well. Not everybody, thank heaven."

Terrell pulled the bike to the side of the road at the terminal in Kootenay Bay, his goggles perched on the forehead of his leather helmet. He looked at his speedometer. "Remember this number: 5028."

"5028. Got it. Why?"

"I'll tell you later."

They rode for about half an hour until they got to the slight bend in the road near the place Tanney had camped. Terrell turned onto the grassy verge and stopped, lifting his goggles to check the speedometer. "5056. Ha! Yes!"

"Twenty-eight miles?" asked April.

"Exactly." He got off the bike and held it for April to slide off, and then walked it across the grassy meadow, counting his steps. When they arrived at the edge of the forest, he propped the bike behind a tree and continued counting.

"Where are we?" April asked, swatting at a cobweb as they walked through the dense underbrush.

"Shh! 102, 103, 104, 105. Twenty-eight miles, 110 *steps* south. Gotcha!" He stopped and pointed. "That," he said, "is the shed we found the day before yesterday, and it is exactly at the coordinates in Tanney's notebook."

April walked toward it. "The one Cooper called about. But he said they broke the lock. That lock's not broken."

Terrell hurried forward. "You're right. It looks exactly like it did when we were here." He felt around in his jacket pocket and pulled out a key. "I'm glad I brought this. You're sure he said he broke the lock off?"

"Yup. Completely sure."

"Maybe this is a new one then. It's a Deco 79 like the other one. The key might not work, but it's worth a try." He bent over and put the key into the lock and turned. The shackle released with a satisfying "clack," and Terrell pulled the lock down and twisted it off, pulling at the door.

"Oh, my aunt Betty!" April exclaimed. "Did you know this was here?"

The entire back of the shed was piled with wooden crates, about the size of apple boxes. Terrell counted quickly. At least eighteen.

"What's in them?"

"I can guess," said Terrell. "Stay out here. I'm going to see what's what." He ducked inside and looked at one of the boxes on the top row. Nailed shut. He looked around for anything he could use to pry open the lid. That's when he saw a hammer hanging on a single spike on the wall. Whatever was in here, they must open these crates and take things out and seal up the boxes again. Whoever "they" were.

Fitting the claw under the edge of the lid, he heaved, and the lid gave with a loud squealing of nail scraping on wood. He pulled away the lid and pushed aside the packing straw. Revolvers! He took out his handkerchief and pulled several out to have a look. Webleys, Colts, God knew what else. He replaced the weapons, pushed the packing material back in, and quickly hammered the lid back on, and then tried another box.

"What's in there?" April called in the door, seeing Terrell sit back on his feet, looking puzzled.

"The first box was guns. This looks like some sort of cans of tomato purée or something."

"Are you sure?" April ducked into the shed and crouched next to Terrell.

"At a guess," Terrell said, holding one with his handkerchief and trying to read the label, "they are from Mexico, and since importing tomatoes is not illegal as far as I know, it's possible there is something else in here."

"Should we take one and check?"

Terrell thought. "I don't want to leave any trace of our having been here. On the other hand, this must be a storage place before the stuff is sold on. If we don't take one, it could all be gone, and we'll have no proof."

With sudden decision, Terrell slipped the can, wrapped in the handkerchief, into his pocket, and then nailed the box shut. "Now we gotta get out of here," he said, taking April's arm.

"The lock?" April said, pointing at the door they'd left ajar in their hurry.

"Oh, yes. Damn!" Terrell latched the lock and then checked his pocket for the key. "Let's go!"

"Are we going to tell Cooper?" April asked as they trotted back toward the bike.

384

"Not on your life," Terrell said. "Not this time."

"I'm supposed to be mowing the lawn and then I'm going out to Tina's," Ames said crossly when he picked up the call from Terrell. "What's up?"

Terrell glanced at his watch. "You're just starting your day now, sir?"

"I slept in. Now what's so important you're calling on the one Saturday we agreed to take off? I thought you were going on a picnic with Miss . . . April."

"I did, sir. I cheated a little bit and went over the lake to where Tanney camped out, and we took another look at the shed."

"Busman's picnic? And?"

"April told me that Cooper had said that he'd broken the lock off and there was nothing inside. That wasn't quite true, sir."

"Wow!" Ames said when he'd heard the whole story. "No wonder Cooper was trying to get us to butt out. He knew stuff was there. But it is part of his investigation. And he's trying to keep us out of it."

"Yes . . ." Terrell hesitated.

"What?"

"It struck me that he could be lying, sir."

"Yeah, to get us to drop the thing."

"No, sir. I wasn't thinking that."

HERRIDGE SPOKE LOUDLY in English to the man he'd summoned. "Get this cleaned up." He waved at the broken jug and glass. The man hurried out and came back with a

385

broom, a dustpan, and a metal garbage tin and, glancing nervously at the gun sitting near Herridge's hand, began to sweep the mess into a pile. Some of the shards were under the table, so he bobbed at Lane and said, "*Dispense, señorita*," as he reached under with his broom. Lane moved her legs to one side so he could get at the pieces under the table. He leaned over and checked the floor by her feet, and then nodded, scooping everything up and dumping it in the tin.

"And bring another one," Herridge ordered.

"How did you end up working at the embassy?" Lane asked. She would keep him talking, play into his inflated sense of his own brilliance. Though in the next minute she wondered for what purpose. She was just staving off the inevitable end. But she'd been right in her question. He was smiling.

"Ah. I don't mind telling you. We've got time." The water pitcher and glasses had been replaced. She nodded and he poured water as if he were pouring a claret from Bordeaux at a posh dinner party. "I was able to get away right under everyone's noses! Eh? One of our fishing friends who got our agents out took me across and I made my way to Vannes, where my mother's family had a farm. When the war was over, they began to round up liberators like me as if we were collaborators, if you can imagine such a thing, so I left. I emigrated to Mexico, started a new life, and took advantage of my diplomatic skills to get into the international relations game. I created a past for myself, keeping an eye on German activity in Mexico, and the embassy was delighted to have someone with some knowledge of the country on its staff. Third secretary. Not bad, if I do say so myself. It wasn't hard. These public school boys that populate our embassies see someone aping their manners, pretending they've been to Rugby or Eton, and they trust them automatically. It's a terrible weakness." He smiled and leaned back, regarding her. "But I like this country. I'm glad I chose it. It is full of opportunity for those who aren't afraid to work for it. *Voila.*"

"You certainly had everyone fooled." She tried to feign admiration but found it heavy going. She stopped herself from asking what skills he could possibly have parlayed into a diplomatic job. Enough to forge a fake curriculum vitae, she supposed. "You do not think of yourself as a collaborator? You helped the Nazi occupation. Isn't that what you did, really?"

He leaned back and tented his hands under his chin. "I was working for a free and independent Brittany. It is certainly not the same. Not at all the same. Alas, my cause has been washed away in the tides of history. I now look to myself. My position at the embassy, my connections here . . . these offer opportunities to secure my future." He put his hands on the table, palms up. "It is too bad you will not be able to see all of this spectacular country. The coast is beautiful. I have a wonderful house on a hill overlooking the Pacific Ocean near Acapulco. I go there for my holidays. I should have loved to have you as my guest." He waved his hand upward. "In fact, this house is lovely. Too bad you've not seen my best rooms during your stay, which, unfortunately, will be short. As interesting as this has been, I'm afraid we'll have to end our conversation. I have a dinner engagement. One of my men will take you away when I am finished here." He was holding the gun, moving it from hand to hand. "I've dreamed of this," he said, almost to himself.

Time was running out. Lane put her hands in her lap, clasping them tightly, searching for any way out. It was then she realized there was a slip of paper on her lap.

"You will shoot me yourself, then?" Lane asked, and then nodded as if she saw all. How could she manoeuvre a chance to look at it? "You don't normally mess about with the rough stuff, do you? You had someone else take care of Charlie and Alma when they got too close to that cell you were running. How many other people would have died if I hadn't stopped you?"

He sighed heavily. "You would have, for a start. You would not be such a pain in the neck now. I regret that. But no matter. Once I knew you were . . ."

But Lane stopped hearing because she had been looking hard at the water jug. The man who brought it had left the door unlocked. The jug was almost full and had that lovely long neck that could be swung. She imagined grabbing the pitcher, upending the table onto his lap, striking his head. He'd put on all that weight and would be slow to respond to the table toppling. Could she do it before he got a proper grip on that damn gun? She suspected he had only one man outside the door. She would have the element of surprise. She prayed that whatever combat skills she'd learned but rarely used would still be intact. Risking everything, she pulled the paper to where she could see it under the edge of the table and glanced down. She swung her eyes back to Herridge, but he was engrossed with his own plans.

". . . obviously not here. A nice drive up into the mountains. No one will ever find you, but it will be a lovely resting place."

Lane, her heart beating with some combination of abject fear and exhilaration, said, "Tell me, do you know El Jefe? A man called Salinas? You might run in the same circles."

"Ah, yes. The kidnapper. It's funny you should mention him. I don't know him personally, but he has quite an empire. His drug business with his exports up north must be worth tens of thousands just on its own. You should have befriended him. He has contacts everywhere, as I understand it. Very lucrative contacts in the export of heroin. He exports as far north as Canada. In fact, he grows the stuff. He is my dinner engagement. We are going to talk business. It will be very advantageous to both of us, I think."

But it wasn't so very funny that Lane had mentioned him. The scrap of paper, miraculously dropped there by the cleaner, contained two words only: "Help near." In her surprise, she glanced toward the window

"WELL, IT'S NOT tomato purée," Ames declared. The three of them were seated around Ames's desk with the remains of the picnic that Terrell had brought in, a can opener, and the open can.

"At a guess, some form of heroin. It is obviously meant to be processed somewhere up here," Terrell said, looking at the dark syrupy liquid.

"So now what, sir?" asked April.

Ames shook his head. "I wish the boss was here. So let me think. It stands to reason that this is being brought across the border, as Cooper said, so it does have to involve the RCMP, and he is a Mountie. But he's been lying to us, but maybe for good reason. It's a highly confidential investigation, he can't afford to blow their cover." He sighed. "We've kind of put our size nines in it. I don't know how we can go back to him and say, 'Oops, we took one of your cans of heroin.'"

"But that's it, sir. What if it *is* one of *his* cans of heroin?"

"Meaning?"

"Well, look at this. I've been all over the death of Tanney every which way but Sunday. We keep thinking there's another person involved. But what if it is only Cooper and Tanney?" He moved forward animatedly. "When I was drawing the picture of the ferry deck to get the lie of the land, as it were, he first told me he'd been standing aft, and then corrected himself when I pointed out that the falling chain had been on the foredeck."

"What are you saying, exactly? Or rather, are you saying what I think you are?" Ames asked, and then sat back. "Jeepers!"

"Wow," April said.

"Tanney's selling drugs, and has a lot of money suddenly, so if, and it's a big if, he's actually working *for* Cooper, maybe Cooper had to get rid of him when he drew attention to himself by kidnapping little Rocky."

"Exactly, sir. After, when Tanney goes to hide out after the kidnapping, where does he go? Right to where the shed is, because he's already used to going there. I even wonder if, when Tanney decides he wants to get his son back and run away with him, he actually blackmails Cooper, and that's what put the nail in his coffin. You remember Cooper didn't say anything about searching Tanney—he already knew Tanney had the fifteen hundred. If he'd 'found' it in a search, he'd have to check it in at his detachment. This way he can steal it before he dumps him in the water. One thing that became clear to me the other day is that the ferry deck is really noisy when it's travelling. He could have shot him without anyone hearing him. That chain was a stroke of good luck, because Tanney would have been into the water before anyone saw."

"That means Cooper is as bent as a streamer hook!" April exclaimed.

They both turned to stare at her.

"My dad's a fisherman."

Ames shook his head. "We are running away with ourselves here. We have absolutely no proof that there's anything wrong with Sergeant Cooper except that he's got a tricky undercover operation going and he doesn't want it messed up by small-town police plods like ourselves."

"Then let's plod out and get some!" April said. "This is a lot more fun than the café!"

"You, Miss McAvity, are plodding nowhere but down to answer the phones. This has become much more dangerous than anyone expected," Ames said firmly.

CHAPTER THIRTY-TWO

"WHERE ARE WE?" DARLING ASKED. "And why did you leave Scott behind?"

"He is an idiot."

"You're not going to have him killed or anything, are you? He knows an awful lot about you." That could easily apply to me, Darling thought glumly.

"I am not an idiot. He knows nothing more than every government minister knows. Businessmen like myself are a big help to this country, as long as we don't get too crazy. No, he'll go back to being under-whatever-he-is at the embassy. His only crime is that he is gullible, like so many English, don't you agree? They always think they know more than anyone else, yet they are as easily deceived as children by people with manners."

"Where are we again?"

"Ah. I've looked into this man. He has built up a little paradise for himself using his diplomatic cover. His activities include drugs and prostitution. He thinks he is meeting me for dinner. But his henchmen don't like him very much."

"Are you so sure he has her here?"

"Oh, very. Now we must think of how to let her know we are here, and to sit tight until we get her out. We must be careful because if he is armed, he could still shoot her. His plan is probably to have her taken away and disposed of. He does not like getting dirty himself." He tilted his head and turned his mouth down in thought. "But . . . if it is a vendetta, as I think it is, he may be crazy enough to do it himself."

It had never been Lane's way to sit tight. Fear constricted Darling's breathing. They were in Salinas's car, parked a few houses away from the one he said she was held in.

"I have told the men to wait for us, and act normal, and, if possible, give her a sign. I'll try to look in the window, so she knows we are here." Salinas smiled happily. "This is better than a María Félix film!"

"And then?" Darling asked repressively. It was not a comfort to know that Herridge was armed.

"We wait. There will be a moment when he gets up to leave, or he tells one of his men to take her. I don't want to risk surprising him if he has a gun pointed at her."

"Are his men armed?" Darling looked out the window of the car. How many of Salinas's men were armed?

Salinas looked at Darling. "Inspector, this is Mexico. Now stay here. I'm going to look."

"Not on your life!" Darling said, getting out of the car.

Salinas walked along the dark street and descended a set of stairs in the front of house. There was a low barred window from which a faint light was visible. He poked his head around the corner of the deep frame and then pulled back and joined Darling, his face troubled.

"We have a problem. He is holding a gun. We will have to be careful how we do this." If they mistimed what they were doing, Lane would be shot. He carefully pushed open the door so they were standing in an unlit hall, and whispered something to the man posted outside the door of the room Lane was being held in. They hovered in the darkness of the hall. The guard in turn whispered to Salinas.

"He says the Englishman is talking a lot. He doesn't understand what he is saying."

That's Lane, Darling thought, she's kept him talking, buying time. What he didn't know was that Herridge's mood had changed.

"WHAT THE HECK is going on here?" O'Brien demanded.

"Sergeant! What are you doing here?" April asked, rattled by his noisy entrance. "I mean, how are you feeling?"

"I feel just fine, thank you. Couldn't stand being cooped up in the house with the wife flapping over me. Thought I'd come down and see what's what, and what do I find?"

"Me?" suggested April.

"What's going on? Is anyone else here?"

"Sergeant Ames and Constable Terrell are upstairs, sir. There has been a . . . a turn of events, I guess you'd say, in our case."

"*Our* case?" O'Brien went to the bottom of the stairs and bellowed, "Sergeant! Get down here!"

April's heart sank. This would spell the end of her very short career with the Nelson Police, and just when it was getting good.

Ames came down the stairs three at a time. "Sergeant O'Brien? Are you allowed out? Didn't the doctor say six weeks?"

"Sure, if the goal is to kill me, six weeks of being molly-coddled at home should just about do it. So, I come here, and what do I find?" He waved a hand at April.

Ames gave a little lift of the chin to April, and she took the hint and went outside. She stood on the street, undecided, and then turned and headed for Sunderland's eatery. Might as well keep working.

"Now, look, Sarge. The doctor said you were to take six weeks, and we asked April to step in and man the phone. She's had training, after all." He was about to say she'd been quite useful with various parts of the case, and then he thought that would only wave a red cloth at him.

"She's a woman!"

"Yes, that she is," agreed Ames. "And she's fit in quite well. She knows police protocol, and that's been handy."

"Is this Terrell's doing? He's always mooning after her."

"No, it's my doing. We have a murder on our hands, and now drugs and guns imported across the border. We needed someone to hold the fort, that's all."

"Murder? Guns and drugs? What happened to kidnapping?"

"It's a long story," Ames began. He didn't feel he had time to tell it, really.

O'Brien settled on his stool. "I've got all day," he declared. The door to the station opened just at that moment.

"No, you don't," Mrs. O'Brien said firmly. She was short and plump with white hair in a short frizzy bob, but she had the look of a sergeant major. "What do you think you're doing? You're coming right home this minute." She took O'Brien firmly by the arm. "I'm sorry, Sergeant Ames. I just stepped out to buy some groceries."

O'Brien's transformation was complete. He got up meekly and submitted to being led away. At the door he turned and said, to Ames's surprise, "Is she any good?"

"She's very good, Sarge. Not you by any means, but she's holding her own."

"Well, that's something."

Ames stood outside and watched the O'Briens walking up the street. The missus had slipped her arm through his, and Ames heard him say, "Anything decent for dinner, then?"

SUNDERLAND WAS PREPARING for the evening. There were no customers. People who wanted a mid-afternoon break were inclined to go to the café instead, though it surprised April that more customers weren't driven away by Marge.

"Hi, Mr. Sunderland. How's it going?"

"Oh, hi, Miss McAvity." Sunderland sat down heavily in front of the table he was setting, letting the utensils clatter onto it. He shook his head. "I don't know. I can't understand any of it. I mean, I know Bonny can be a little, I don't know, immature sometimes, I guess. But I never suspected anything like this. It's like I don't know her at all anymore. I mean, drugs! And actually helping that good-for-nothing kidnap Rocky! And now the guy's dead. For all I know, she did that too! I wouldn't be at all surprised!"

April nodded. Sunderland's bewilderment was understandable. "How's your son?"

"Oh, I got my mother to come take him. I don't know who to trust. I sure don't trust her so-called best friend, Linda."

"You never saw anything unusual in Mrs. Sunderland's behaviour? Or money, maybe, going missing?"

"Like I said, she could be pretty immature. She was like a teenager, her moods going all over the place and that. But now you mention money, I did go to the bank to put in my takings about three weeks ago and I was surprised that there was something like fifty dollars missing. I asked her about it, and she said she had to take our boy to the dentist. I accepted that, like the fool I am, but I never knew there was anything wrong with his teeth. Turns out there wasn't."

"That was the first time?"

"Well, I mean, I think there were a few dollars here and a few there. Out of the housekeeping. When I'd ask about why the coffee had run out, she'd say the price of everything is going up. Turns out she was feeding it to that bastard Tanney the whole time! Sorry, miss."

"Oh, I know how you feel. Did he come around the house?"

He nodded miserably. "Once or twice when I was there, like for dinner one time. 'Old friend from school,' she called him. I guess he was over there a lot more when I was here working. I couldn't understand it. He was a horrible person. Put his feet up on the furniture, called me 'buddy,' like he owned the place. I asked her one time why she was friends with him. I told her I wanted it to stop. Of course, she lost her temper and told me I couldn't tell her what to do." He was looking down at his hands folded on the table, but then he looked up suddenly. "But you know what, I remember now, she didn't look mad as much as afraid. And I don't think she was afraid of me. She knows I'd never lay a hand on her." He slapped his palm on the table. "That's it! She was afraid of *him*! I bet he was blackmailing her in a way. Maybe he told her he'd tell me about the drugs or something."

"I wouldn't have put it past him. You know, Mr. Sunderland, I don't think you need to worry that she killed him." She hoped. She crossed the fingers of her right hand where it was sitting in her lap. She was pretty sure that wasn't something she was supposed to say.

"If she did, I wouldn't blame her. I'm only sorry I didn't. I don't know what's going to happen to us when she gets out of hospital." He sighed deeply and moved the utensils around into their proper place settings.

"When is that?"

"They said a couple of days. The combination of stuff she was taking was pretty strong. She kind of took too much."

Maybe she was being blackmailed, thought April. Maybe that's why she helped Tanney kidnap Rocky, and maybe she was trying to kill herself.

"YOU KNOW, YOU ruined my life once, and here you are, back to do it again. I won't let you do it this time. You think I won't do the dirty work myself? I do it often. I like it." He held the gun up now, pointing it at her. "I'll like it when I do it to you. It's like tidying up a room and getting rid of the garbage. You feel a kind of satisfaction."

Lane held her breath. He would kill her outright from this distance, even with that small thing. And then she exhaled sharply, as she focused on the gun. It was the pistol Salinas had given her.

"Ah, you recognize it! We found it on you when we picked you up. Such poetic justice." He lifted it again and took aim, squinting with one eye shut. She heard the snap of him cocking it. She remembered the old saying about not carrying a weapon because it might end up killing you.

With one move, Lane grabbed the neck of the ceramic jug and threw the table up and over. The gun went off with a deafening report as it flew out of his hand, and the table crashed awkwardly onto his lap. He half stood and was knocked back against his chair by the impact. The chair slid back, and he began to scramble backward, trying to gain a footing. She brought the heavy jug of water down on his head just as he lost the battle and fell backward with the toppling chair. The jug smashed and water flew in all directions.

The door burst open and Darling, Salinas, and several other men rushed in. Lane was standing by the overturned table, holding the neck of the jug still in her hands, breathing heavily. "Gentlemen," she said, before Darling smothered her in an embrace.

"Just like in the movies!" Salinas cried.

"WELL, HE'S GONE home. Now where the hell is April? Has she gone home too?" Ames asked.

"Doesn't sound like her, sir. What are you thinking we should do? I mean about Cooper?"

"I think," Ames said, "that we should keep an eye on him. Catch him in the act. Then we should go to Inspector Guilfoil, here in town at the local detachment."

At that moment the door opened and April came back. "All clear?" she asked, looking around.

"Yup," Ames said. "Where've you been?"

"Well, sir, I didn't want to waste time, so I just thought I'd pop over to see Mr. Sunderland at his restaurant. You'll never guess what I learned!" She looked past Ames at where Terrell was standing and was rewarded by seeing him smile and then cover it with his hand.

"Yes?" Ames asked.

"Bonny Sunderland was definitely hooked on drugs, and she even began to use the household money, and then take larger amounts out of the bank and find excuses for it. She was afraid of Tanney. Sunderland thinks he was blackmailing her as well. And I wonder, sir, if she took too much because she wanted to, you know . . ." She let this thought trail off.

"Boy, if we didn't know where he died, she could definitely be in the frame. She must have wanted him gone very badly. But you're saying she was trying to kill herself?"

"I'm not exactly saying that, but I wonder. She still has to be in hospital another couple of days. I don't think he knows what's going to happen when she does come out."

"Sir," Terrell said. "I don't think any of us could do the surveillance you're suggesting. Cooper knows all of us. I think, maybe, we should go to Guilfoil now. If it's what we think, he's involved in international smuggling and even murder. It's really for them to deal with."

Not for the first time, Ames wished that Darling were there. What would he do?

April glanced over at Terrell and gave a little nod.

"Yeah. Of course. You're right. Let's sit down and organize everything we've got. Including that damn bullet, Constable." Ames narrowed his eyes, looking at Terrell. "You've suspected something wasn't right with him all along, haven't you?" It was more a declaration than a question.

Terrell just said, "Sir."

"WE CAN'T GET married till your boss comes back," Tina said. They were outside at the picnic table. Her father had put some hamburgers on the barbecue, and the three of them sat, enjoying the mild breeze off the lake in the late afternoon. The sun would not go down for another hour and a half.

"Trouble is, I haven't heard from him. I've left a million messages at his hotel. But Terrell is being pretty helpful. He's going to organize Lorenzo's and talk to the vicar."

"I'm worried this is going to all get too big. I just want a quiet wedding."

Her father shook his head. "Come on, honey. It's a once-in-a-lifetime thing. You don't want it too quiet. Your mother and I had to hurry up and marry because I was shipping out, but even then, she got a nice wedding dress, and we had a little party. We didn't have a honeymoon till '19, when I got back. We went out to Vancouver for a few days. What are you two thinking of for a honeymoon?"

"Oh, come on, Dad. No one needs anything like that. Daniel is busy at the station, he can't take time off, and what are you supposed to do here while I'm gone?"

"No siree, you aren't using me as an excuse! I'll manage just fine on my own." He looked thoughtful. "Hmm, though I guess I'm going to have to hire someone once you're hitched."

Tina looked outraged. "Give someone my job? I don't think so! I'm not quitting work just 'cause I'm married!"

Her father frowned and glanced at Ames. "I mean, I assumed that when you're married, you'd want, you know, to look after your husband. Your mother worked at the feed store before we married, but then she stayed home. What do you think, Daniel?"

He didn't get a chance to answer.

"Daniel is a big boy. He's looked after himself all these years. He sure as hell doesn't need me sitting at home polishing my nails! And anyway, look at us. We've lived here together since Mom died, and I work at the garage and look after you, don't I?"

"Daniel?" Mr. Van Eyck said.

Ames considered. What did he believe about this sort of thing? Sure, his mother stayed home, but she had to because the post office where she'd worked let her go when she got married. That's what they did then. And then his dad went to the war in France. The truth was, he really didn't mind if Tina kept working. Why shouldn't she? She liked it and she was good at it.

"It's not really true I've looked after myself, sir. My mother has looked after me. But I'm prepared to give it a go. I don't think I'm in a position to tell Tina what to do about that sort of thing, and I wouldn't want to. I mean, she's good at what she does. And anyway, Constable

Terrell would hate it. She knows exactly what to do with his darn Triumph."

"It's not like I want to lose the best mechanic I've had," Mr. Van Eyck said. "But what happens when—"

Tina interrupted him. She saw that Ames had gone pink. "Oh, for Pete's sake, Dad. How about we cross that bridge when we come to it? Now, did Mom keep her wedding dress? Might as well not spend extra moolah if we don't have to."

Van Eyck looked at Ames and winked. "I warn you, she's very tight with money!"

CHAPTER THIRTY-THREE

———

"**A**RE YOU SURE YOU WILL not join me for dinner tomorrow? There is a restaurant nearby that has been here since the last century." Salinas had had the Rolls-Royce pull up in front of the Gran Hotel, and he was standing on the sidewalk talking to Lane and Darling.

"It is very good of you; however, I must get back to my job," Darling said. He did not want to be indebted further to a man whose morals scandalized him. "I don't know whether to thank you or not. You put me to a lot of trouble by kidnapping my brother; on the other hand, you helped rescue my wife."

Salinas had the decency to look sheepish. "Ah, yes, Inspector. I nearly forgot. This is the least I can do." He reached into the inner pocket of his Savile Row jacket and pulled out a very full envelope and handed it across. "It is all there. Such debts should not exist between friends."

Darling took the envelope and nodded. Lane offered her hand to Salinas. "Goodbye, Señor Salinas. Thank you."

He seized her hand in both of his and then raised it to his lips. "Dear, dear lady. Miss Félix is only an actress, but you are the real thing! It is for me to thank you!" He held her hand a moment longer. "More than anything, you remind me of my beloved sister Lucía, brave like her, full of goodness like her." He kissed her hand again.

They stood for some moments on the sidewalk, watching his car swallowed by the traffic, a stream of red tail lights flowing past the zócalo.

"He's a real prize," Darling said. "The most charming murderer I've ever met, and the most aggravating, because he will never face punishment for any of his many crimes. Lady Justice is looking the other way in this country. A bath and a drink?"

"But a man of feeling." She turned to him, smiling. "A bath and a sleep, I think." She sighed. The adventures of the last hours had induced a profound sense of exhaustion. "I wonder what will happen to Herridge? He's someone else who has escaped justice all this time." They had delivered Herridge to the police, and thence to the military attaché at the embassy. Word was that they had been expecting him.

"That, I suspect, will depend on your Major Hogarth. She told me she'd be in touch with the embassy, so with any luck they ship him back to England and let justice take its course."

"I may have to go and testify, if it comes to that."

They walked up the steps and into the lobby.

"¡Ah, Señor y Señora Darling! Did you enjoy your trip to Zacatecas?" The desk clerk smiled and reached for their key. "You have had a number of telephone calls while you

405

were away." He handed Darling a pile of folded papers. If he noticed Lane's dishevelled condition, her clothing still damp and dirty, he did not even hint. "It is late, and perhaps you have not eaten. May I have sandwiches sent to your room?"

"Oh, yes!" Lane sighed. "That would be perfect!"

"NO. I'VE CHANGED my mind. I've had an idea. We want to see what he's up to. He lied about the contents of the shed, and I think he'll have to move it sometime. I'm thinking you could telephone and say our photos haven't turned out, would he mind if we make just one more visit to his patch to retake them. Tell him you want to go at, say, eleven tomorrow morning. Then I'll go well before that. Is there a place I can hide the car where he won't see it?" Ames had come in both excited and worried. On reflection, as he'd dropped off to sleep, he decided that turning the whole thing over to Guilfoil would be a risk. Cooper would no doubt convince Guilfoil that everything was part of the investigation, and that he had had nothing to do with the death of Tanney. They would close ranks. Ames's many calls to Darling's hotel had yielded nothing, and he was beginning to worry. The hotel had said he had gone on a trip with his wife, had been expected home several days before, and had not yet returned.

"You're thinking he'll want to hurry up and get rid of what's in the shed before we get there? It's worth a try, sir."

"Yes, but it's tricky because it's the middle of nowhere. Also, we have no idea if that is where the drops are made, or when. But I think the problem Cooper is having is that

406

we know about the shed, and this might pressure him to act right away. He's killed a guy, and he knows we're getting close to something. I'd bet anything if he has an associate, he will contact him so he can get the shed cleared out and get rid of the evidence before eleven."

"I'll go make the call now," Terrell said.

"WE'D HAVE TO hide the car somewhere where he can't see it," Terrell said when he'd made the call. Cooper had sighed and sounded slightly impatient but had not blocked the plan to go retake the photos.

"What's on the other side of the road?"

"I can't completely recall, but I'm pretty sure it's low brush sort of thing. If we go early, we'll have time to figure it out."

In the morning, the station had an air of tense anticipation. April, who had come in at six, was watching the two men as they armed themselves and got extra ammunition. They rarely took firearms, and April could feel her own rising anxiety. She reached for Ames's camera case. "Don't forget this. And be careful," she said. She had heard the police in Vancouver say this. It was a reminder to be alert, to act judiciously. She wondered how often the police had to go into this kind of danger, in the open, far from help, possibly exposed.

"WHAT IF THEY came here last night? It would be safer," Terrell said. "That damn shed might already be empty. Or maybe we'll be lying here all day and no one comes." They were across the road from the turnoff where the shed was. They'd found some thick underbrush to hide the car behind, with no little difficulty, causing Ames to wince with every scratch of twig and bump on the undercarriage, including a severe jolt when Terrell drove over a large rock hidden in the tall grass. They were now face down on the side of the road, hidden among the deep growth of bracken fern.

"That would be a nuisance. I'm already damp from lying here. It's in the middle of nowhere, so maybe they risk it. Shh!"

A vehicle was approaching from the south. It was a false alarm. The truck, a late-model Ford, sped past, kicking up gravel.

Then their luck improved. It took another half hour, but finally a vehicle actually slowed. Ames and Terrell flattened themselves and Terrell took out his field glasses. Ames, who had already prepared the camera, glanced at his watch. Ten after nine.

"It's got Washington plates," Terrell whispered.

They watched as the car turned and bumped over the grassy verge, past the large outcrop of stone where Rocky had sat waiting for someone to pick him up. It stopped and the driver's-side door opened, but nobody got out. The driver finally put one booted foot onto the running board and lit a cigarette, creating a meandering trail of smoke above the open door. Periodically his hand became visible, flicking ash onto the ground.

"He's waiting for someone," Ames said.

Terrell suddenly gripped Ames's arm. "Here, sir."

Ames had heard it at the same time. A green pickup truck pulled off the road and parked beside the first car.

For a moment Ames was worried it was not Cooper after all, and they'd been dead wrong about the whole thing, but it was indeed Cooper who got out and stretched, then looked up and down the road. There was no other traffic. He had his tunic off and the sleeves of his white shirt rolled up, his black suspenders stark against the white.

Ames positioned his camera and clicked. They both winced. It sounded too loud in the silence. But they needn't have worried. Cooper, satisfied that there was no one else on the road, strode over to the other car, just as the other driver got out. They shook hands. They heard Cooper ask if the other man had had a good drive up. He had. Click. Cooper patted the other man on the back. Click. He took the proffered cigarette. Click. After another few moments of inaudible chatting, they started into the forest. Click.

They waited until the men had disappeared and they could no longer hear the murmur of their voices.

"Now!" Ames said.

"Sir, if we go a little south and enter that way, we can come up on the rear of the shed. It will provide some cover."

"Lead the way."

With pounding hearts, Terrell and Ames waited until it was clear Cooper and his companion had disappeared into the trees and were not coming back out. Then they bolted across the road and made for the edge of the wood twenty yards farther south, in a trajectory that would land them behind the shed.

"It's about 120 paces from the verge, due west," Terrell whispered, and then he winced as he trod on a stick that cracked loudly. They both stopped and waited, listening.

There was only silence at first, then Ames put his hand on Terrell's arm and pointed. Voices. They had to try to get closer without being heard. With infinite care they moved five yards and then waited. There was the sound of something being moved. Another five yards, and then the outline of the shed came into view, its wood so aged that it almost disappeared in the shadows of the trees.

Ames readied his camera. The two men had come out of the shed, their heads just visible above its sloping roof.

"Why haven't you moved this? I've got a new shipment with me and now we have to find somewhere else for both this and the new stuff." The man from the Washington car. He sounded annoyed.

"I've had some complications. I had to get rid of someone who decided to bite the hand that fed him. I need to get someone else. We have to shift somewhere else right away. I've got some plods from Nelson sniffing around. I obviously can't move the weapons out of there myself."

Ames glanced at Terrell, his eyebrows raised.

"What about the cans? They need to get to your chemist. Why are they still there?"

"I told you. I lost my staff. I'll take them, all right? I just have to get time off to drive up there."

"Listen, this is a penny-ante operation for the boss. It was an experiment, you understand? Montreal is lucrative, Vancouver is lucrative. This is the middle of nowhere. You told us we could get stuff up to the mining camps and the like. If you're not up to it, we can call it quits now. We can't afford to have stock sitting idle."

Cooper shook his head. "You don't have to worry. I've got this in hand. I've got someone in mind. We'll be up and running in no time."

"I'll leave you what I've got, 'cause I ain't going back across the line with it. But if it doesn't go nowhere, you won't be either, d'you know what I mean?"

"Hey, buddy, you don't need to worry, I told you. When we're finished loading my pickup, I'll shift everything. In fact, I have a place in mind."

"And I'll take that money you owe me."

Cooper sounded shaky for the first time. "It's in the truck. I've got it."

Terrell and Ames watched as the two men moved boxes away from the shed. They could hear the bang as each box was dropped on the truck bed. The whole thing took another twenty minutes. Waiting until they were sure the shed had been cleared, they stood up slowly.

"Damn, I hate surveillance! It's a knee killer," Ames complained in a whisper. "I need to get a snap of the truck. Come on!" He began a low run toward where the vehicles were still parked.

They were less careful about the snapping twigs, pausing from time to time until they heard the two men again.

"I want what you owe, and I want the money for this shipment," the Washington man was saying.

They heard a door open and then close again. Then the Washington man spoke again.

"Whoa there! What the hell do you think you're doing?"

"Throw your piece over there, get that last box out, and leave it on the ground. Then get in the car and don't come back."

Ames wanted to move closer. Things had certainly taken an unexpected turn. Signalling to get Terrell to follow, he crept forward till the two cars came into view. Cooper was standing by his car, holding his weapon with both hands, aiming it at the other man, whose hands were up.

"I mean it," Cooper said. "Make one wrong move and I'll shoot you. Resisting arrest. I'll be a hero. Breaking a drug and gun scheme. Who's going to know?"

"Keep your hat on, buddy. I'm going, but I warn you, anything happens to me and you're a dead man."

"I'll take that risk. Get in your car."

Ames risked it. Click.

The Washington car peeled off the verge and swerved back onto the road going south. Cooper stood, his gun still in his hand, watching the car until not even the dust it raised could be seen. Then he went back to his truck, threw his revolver on the seat, and went to collect something in the grass. The other man's gun. He picked up a box, threw it into the back of the truck, and slammed the gate.

Ames and Terrell barely spoke until they were at the ferry terminal. They had a thirty-minute wait, and they sat numbly in the car.

"I thought for a minute he was actually going to make an arrest," Ames said, finally. "Maybe he'd been doing some sort of undercover thingummy. I mean, maybe he still is."

"Do you really think that, sir? After what we heard? He practically admitted to killing Tanney."

"Yeah, and why not arrest the guy? He let him go."

"I think he's in trouble no matter what," Terrell said. "That American guy certainly has his own boss and cronies who probably would be happy to come up here and get rid of Cooper. They won't put up with him stealing their business. They probably don't want to dry up a source of money, either."

"I think we go to Guilfoil. I still haven't heard back from Darling. What the heck is he doing?" Ames looked at his watch. "We should get back by five. We can still catch Guilfoil at the detachment."

"I agree with you, sir, but Cooper could still paint this as a legitimate operation."

GUILFOIL SAT BACK on his chair and shook his head. "Where the hell is Darling?"

Ames explained.

"He left you two complete amateurs in charge? You're on very dangerous ground here. What you're telling me is preposterous. I want that film. We'll develop it here, thank you very much, and I want a written statement with everything you heard on your so-called 'surveillance' of one of our men. Did you write down the number of the Washington plate?"

"Yes, sir. That is, I memorized it. Green lettering, P 20158," said Terrell. Guilfoil wrote that down.

"I FEEL LIKE a kid who got sent to the principal," Ames said, out on the sidewalk. "He did just what I thought he would do. Darling will come back and learn all about how we botched the investigation and besmirched the reputation of the RCMP, and we'll be looking for jobs as sweepers down at the train station."

They were standing outside the detachment, momentarily unwilling to go back to the station. "And we lost control of our murder investigation," Ames added glumly. "I feel like a drink."

"I do too, sir, but I think we should go let Miss McAvity know we got back all right. She'll be worried."

"She'll be worried about you. She couldn't care less about me."

"THANK HEAVEN!" APRIL cried, jumping off her stool. "I thought something awful had happened. How did your surveillance go?"

"Just peachy," Ames said, taking off his hat and trudging up the stairs to his office.

"Inspector Darling telephoned," she called after him. "I told him everything that's been going on here. I wanted him to know how well you two are doing!"

Ames turned and looked down at her. "Oh, good," he said listlessly, and then he was gone.

April looked at Terrell, puzzled and frowning. He just shrugged. "You can go on home, Miss McAvity. Thanks for looking after things. I've got some notes to write up."

"'Miss McAvity'? Fine, then, 'sir.' I left a note about a drunk and disorderly, and a householder who said some teenagers were drinking all night in the alley behind Ninth Street."

Terrell turned and walked back to her and stood with his hands in his pockets. "I'm sorry, April. We've just had a very bad time with Inspector Guilfoil down at the detachment."

April looked stricken and put her hand on his arm. "Well, why didn't you say so? I'll go home and leave you to it. I'm sure it's not as bad as you think. How could it be? You two are such great policemen! If . . . if you made a mistake, it was made honestly, if you know what I mean. But for the record, I don't think you made a mistake, whatever happened and whatever Guilfoil thinks about it. You'll see!"

In the next moment, Terrell did something that surprised them both. He took his hands out of his pockets, held her hand, and kissed her softly on the mouth.

CHAPTER THIRTY-FOUR

DARLING CAME INTO THE ROOM and threw his hat on the bed. Lane was sitting on the balcony with a cup of coffee between her hands, watching the activity in the street below. The sun cast a glow on her face. She really was beautiful, he thought. María Félix be damned.

"All hell has broken loose in my absence," he said, joining her. "Are you going to eat that?" he asked, indicating her empty plate.

"I was hungry. What sort of hell?"

"The kidnapping has turned into a murder and illegal drugs and weapons investigation, O'Brien had some sort of heart attack, my two men are off surveilling an RCMP officer, and April McAvity seems to be in charge of the Nelson Police now."

"Wow! Is O'Brien all right?"

"He has to stay home for a few weeks."

"It's a good thing April had that policing course, then."

"I really must stop going away. I'm going to wait a couple of hours and try to get Ames. He's supposed to be running the place." He sighed. "In the meantime, what would you like to do? We're leaving tomorrow, so this is your chance."

"How about the Palace of Chapultepec? The waiter tells me it's not to be missed."

"Palace it is, then. Ah, good. That will be one of them now!" The phone was ringing.

"*Un momento, por favor,*" said a voice.

"Darling? Is that you? Guilfoil here. When the blazes are you coming back? All hell has broken out here."

Darling nodded. These were the very words he'd used moments ago. "We'll be back the day after tomorrow."

"It's about your men."

"I see."

"Look, it's too much for a long-distance call. You come see me the minute you get back."

Darling bridled slightly at the peremptory tone of command. But Guilfoil, from what April had told him, might have *casus belli*. "I will. Anything I can do from this end?"

"Listen, there doesn't seem to be anything anyone can do from any end. Just get back here in a hurry!"

TERRELL WAS HAVING trouble sleeping. Kissing April had thrown his whole world into chaos. He felt he'd momentarily lost his mind, as if his psyche had pushed past his own anxious caution.

He got up, thinking a walk would clear his mind, and having dressed and put on his shoes, he crept down the stairs so as not wake Mrs. Fisher, his landlady.

"Is that you, Jerome?" Mrs. Fisher came out of the sitting room in her pale green dressing gown with her hair in a bewildering bristle of tiny curlers. "Can't sleep?"

He nodded, shrugging. "You either?"

"I don't know what it is. Some nights I'm just wide awake. I start thinking about Mr. Fisher, you know . . ."

"I understand." Terrell nodded sympathetically. He knew that her husband had died a decade earlier of a heart attack. He'd been only forty-three.

"Well, it's not your problem, anyway. Why are you awake? Is it that case you're working on?"

What should he say? "Sorta."

She looked quizzically at him. "You know, Jerome, I heard some talk about you taking that nice girl from the café to the cinema. Let those old busybodies talk all they want. They just like to put their oar in where it's not wanted. You know what I learned from being married to Rick? That if you get a chance to love someone, you grab it with everything you've got."

He looked down. She'd come close to the mark, and no doubt whatever the busybodies were saying, it wasn't good. "I appreciate your kindness. I don't want to make life harder for her . . . I . . ."

"Rubbish! If she loves you, she won't care. It would be unusual, I grant you. People here aren't used to that sort of mixing, but everyone would get over it." She gave a nonchalant tilt of the head. "Everyone got over me and Mr. Fisher."

He looked at her in surprise. "What had to be got over?"

"Rick was Jewish. You should have seen the furor that caused. It was 1920, and boy, was this town small, if you

418

know what I mean. My parents, well, my dad, he said to me, 'You love him, my girl, you marry him. It's all that matters.' My mother, she had to endure the endless advice from the neighbours whenever she stepped out the door. I think she'd rather I didn't marry him, but she came around in the end. And so did everyone else who mattered. Some people are born ignorant, and they stay that way. It's not worth living your life to suit them!"

He smiled. He understood now why she had been so quick to give him a room, and why when Akio Sasaki had come from an internment camp, she had offered the extra room in her house. "You're very kind, Mrs. Fisher. You've given me a lot to think about."

"Well, mind you think straight. Now get out there for your walk. Maybe it will clear everything up for you." She gave him a little pat on the arm and disappeared back into the sitting room.

"GOOD MORNING, SIRS," April said, as Terrell and Ames came into the station. She held a note out to Ames, but glanced at Terrell, who could not look away for a moment, but then nodded and made as if to go to his desk. "Inspector Guilfoil telephoned first thing. He'd like to see you both."

"Now?" exclaimed Ames, who had not missed the glance between April and Terrell. "We spent two hours with him yesterday!"

"Maybe he enjoys your company," said April. "I had the feeling when he said he'd like to see you 'right away,' he meant right away."

"What's going on?" Ames asked as he and Terrell walked down toward Front Street.

"I don't know, sir. Maybe he found something out. He was pretty upset with us."

"Not about that, and you know it. That little glance between you and April. What was that all about? She was blushing to beat the band."

"Nothing, sir." Terrell could feel his own face flushing.

He would have liked to tell Ames about his conversation with Mrs. Fisher. He'd been surprised and comforted by it. But he didn't feel it was the sort of thing he could talk about with his superior, as friendly as they had become. And it would reveal his hand where April was concerned. A little grunt escaped him. As if everyone, including the inspector and all the old gossiping busybodies, didn't know how he felt about April. He wished the town was not quite so small.

"What?" Ames demanded.

"What, sir?"

"You grunted."

"Shouldn't we be preparing to see Inspector Guilfoil? After yesterday I guess we're in for another drubbing."

Guilfoil looked pointedly at his watch when they were shown in. "Sit."

They did.

"I sent a couple of my men out to look at that shed you described, and it was empty. Not even a lock on it. However, I have the photographs you took, and I must say there is nothing in either case that suggests to me that this is not a legitimate operation. Furthermore, I have received a complaint from Sergeant Cooper himself since I last saw you. He reports that he was travelling on the ferry from Kootenay Bay and got into conversation with one of the workers, who told him he had delivered to you, Constable Terrell, a bullet found on the deck. Cooper notes that it was a bullet matching the gun he delivered to you, and notes that you failed to inform him of this important piece of evidence." Guilfoil looked expectantly at Terrell.

"Sir," Terrell said after some moments. He cleared his throat. "I had begun to conceive the idea that the only person who could have killed Tanney was Cooper, Sergeant Cooper, I mean, himself. I believe that what Sergeant Ames and I heard from him on our surveillance confirms this. Though I had not fully formed this idea at the time I was given the bullet, I felt a sense of caution from that moment. Since Sergeant Cooper himself had handed me the pisto . . ." Terrell hesitated. He wanted to say that the most ingenious way to get rid of a murder weapon was for the murderer himself to hand it right over to the police, pretending it belonged to the dead man. But sensing that Guilfoil would not welcome that sort of speculation, he continued, "I also wanted to deliver it to Dr. Gillingham to see if it would be a match for the bullet that killed Mr. Tanney, sir. He did confirm that it was."

"Cooper had no business handing that pistol over in the first place. There is nothing about this case that should ever have been picked up by you. I shall be taking over the whole thing, including the murder, and the drug problem in town. You two can go put your feet up until your boss gets back. If anything, *anything* at all comes your way on this, you are to bring it straight to me. Is that clear?"

Ames rubbed his hand over his chin. He was confused and angry. Could the Mounties just horn in on their case like that? Yes, drugs were a federal crime. If the drugs in town came from that racket going on at the border, then it was certainly federal. If Tanney was involved with the selling of those drugs and he was now dead, the murder was probably theirs as well, but . . .

"Yes, sir," he said finally. "I understand. I'll deliver our files right away."

Guilfoil nodded with satisfaction. "That's the stuff, Sergeant. That will be all."

"HE AS NEAR said, 'There's a good boy' as I've ever heard," Ames said, taking a deep breath once they were on the sidewalk. "I'll tell you something for nothing. They're going to close ranks and let him get away with it. It's infuriating!"

"Yes, sir. I guess we'd better get back and get those files for him." Terrell started up the hill.

Ames followed him. "Aren't you mad about it? How can you be so calm?"

"I am, but I'm not sure what being mad is going to do for anyone. Maybe he's right. Maybe Cooper is innocent of any wrongdoing."

Ames stopped. "You've changed your tune! That's ridiculous. He's as guilty as sin, and you know it!"

April looked up as they came into the station. "There's been a telegram from Inspector Darling." She handed Ames a brown envelope. "I hope he won't be delayed coming back!"

422

"Just about right now, I hope he will be!" Ames said, pushing his thumb along the seal and unfolding the missive. *What in hell going on? Stop. Back Wed. Stop.*

"I guess he heard from Inspector Guilfoil. I'll get started on the files, sir," Terrell said with a sigh.

"THAT WAS LOVELY! What a beautiful park, and the view from the palace is wonderful. You could see those two peaks as clear as clear can be! I shall devote my life to learning how to say their names." Lane took the pin out of her straw hat and was about to pull the hat off, but changed her mind and reset the pin.

Darling already had his jacket off and had loosened his tie. Throwing himself on the bed, he said, "I shall devote myself to a siesta. We may be at seven thousand feet or whatever it is, but it's hotter than blazes."

Lane sat next to him, but perched on the edge of the bed, as if she were about to spring up again.

"No siesta for you?" Darling asked.

"No, I don't think so. I think I'll go for a stroll by that beautiful building with all the tiles, and perhaps look a bit more at the old city. There's so much to see here and we've barely scratched the surface."

"How unrestful you are. Fine. I know a covert shopping operation when I see one. Remember we can't carry a lot of stuff back. And please avoid being kidnapped." He was joking, but he felt a little pinch of anxiety about her being out on her own.

"I will, darling." She leaned over and kissed him. She had no intention of dawdling along Avenida Juárez looking at the shops.

The doorman bowed slightly in his livery and asked if she would like a taxi, but she smiled and shook her head. "It's such a lovely day. I'll walk, thank you."

And walk she did, straight back to the British embassy. She climbed the stairs, glancing up at the window from which Herridge had been watching her on her last visit. "I'd like to speak to Mr. Scott, if I might," she said to the receptionist.

She was directed to a chair, where she sat, her face grim, her hands folded over her handbag. The marble foyer was tall, cool compared with the street outside, the noise of which barely penetrated through the thick walls.

She looked up at the sound of hurried footsteps.

"Mrs. Darling! This is excellent. I was about to call you at your hotel." Scott was smiling and holding out his hand. "Please, come in." He spoke for all the world like someone who had never kidnapped her and delivered her to someone intent on killing her. "I . . ." He stopped and fumbled with the doorknob. "I'm sorry, you know, about . . . well . . . everything."

Everything, thought Lane. She sighed and thought of how near she'd come to dying and inclined her head slightly toward him. "The thing, Mr. Scott, is that you weren't to know what kind of man you were working for."

Contrite, he led her up a broad staircase. "I've just been in with the ambassador. They are anxious to talk to you. Do you mind? I was just on the point of sending a car for you. Inspector Darling?" They had reached a landing, and he held his hand out toward a long hallway.

"He is having a siesta after our visit to the palace. I was anxious to discover what has happened to Herridge. I assume he has been bundled back to England to face trial."

Scott nodded and stopped in front of one of the many doors in the hall and knocked. He did not wait for an answer but pushed the door open and stood aside for her to enter.

A trim man of middle years rose at once from a deep armchair at the sight of her. He put down his drink.

"Your Excellency, this is Mrs. Darling."

"That was fast," the ambassador said. He approached her holding out his hand.

Scott did the honours. "Mrs. Darling. May I present Ambassador Benwick of the British delegation?"

"How do you do?" Lane said, shaking Benwick's hand. "Your Excellency."

"And this is Mr. Carter, first secretary," Scott continued.

Lane shook his hand. "How do you do?"

"Sit down, sit down! Drink? How are you after your ordeal?" Benwick said, offering a chair. He nodded at Scott, who took himself off. It would take, Lane thought, watching him leave, some time for him to redeem himself. Carter and Benwick settled into armchairs, and looked expectantly at Lane.

"I'm very well, thank you," Lane said. "No, thank you, I won't," she added to the offer of scotch.

"I feel I must apologize, Mrs. Darling. Scott explained about Captain—should I even call him that?—Herridge. I couldn't have been more shocked. Man led a double life, apparently. I understand you went through a great ordeal at his hands."

"Please, don't give it another thought. I am perfectly

425

well." She wanted to add "no thanks to Scott." She wondered what Benwick knew about Scott's involvement.

"Mrs. Darling. I wonder if you might tell me what you know," Ambassador Benwick said, leaning forward. He wore an expensive striped dark grey suit. Gold-rimmed glasses perched on his nose. His neatly trimmed grey moustache moved as he swallowed a mouthful of scotch.

"All I can say, sir, is that his real name is Deniel Harrison. A major when I knew him. He worked"—she paused—"in the War Office." She was stumped. She could not say she was a member of the SOE, so how was she to explain how she knew so directly of his treason?

Benwick looked at his colleague. "I wonder if we might have the room, Carter?"

Carter got up and sighed. "He is a British subject, you know. If there are any charges, he should be tried in Blighty."

So, he was still in the country. Lane's heart sank as she watched Carter leave. She was about to be pumped for information she could not give to this man, even in private.

"Now then, Mrs. Darling. I'll want the whole story, if you don't mind. I don't need to know details of your work, only of his."

Relieved, Lane began, "What I know, sir, is that he betrayed an operation of the SOE and two people, at least, were killed under his orders. Before he could be arrested, he disappeared. I don't know what happened when the war ended, if he was pursued further. I emigrated to Canada and lost all contact with my former colleagues. You might contact a Major Hogarth at the War Office, Your Excellency. She will know."

"Hogarth, eh?" He nodded, his face thoughtful. Lane could swear he knew her, and well. He looked at her again. "You're sure this is the same man?"

"Quite, Your Excellency. He was . . . he was my commanding officer. I discovered he was working for the independence movement in Brittany when my flatmate was killed." She had already said more than she should, but she was not going to risk Herridge/Harrison escaping a just consequence after all this time by being too parsimonious with information now. "If you speak with Major Hogarth—"

"Yes, that's all right, Mrs. Darling. Thank you for coming in. I'm relieved you've suffered no ill effects from your recent adventure."

"Your Excellency, I believe his activities in this country should be scrutinized. I have reason to believe he has been building up his personal wealth through some local criminal connections. I only hope he is secure even now."

Benwick chuckled. "You have 'reason to believe.' Goodness, Mrs. Darling! You're a dark horse. Between your kidnapping and all the other things that might be laid at his door, we should be able to pin him with something." He stood up and shook her hand, and then escorted her to the door. "By the way, everything in order with your brother-in-law? I am told that is why you are in Mexico."

Lane nodded, smiling. "Very much so, thank you for asking, Your Excellency."

"Don't worry about Herridge." Once in the hallway, he took her hand again. "Thank you, Miss W . . . Mrs. Darling."

Lane wondered, as she walked back along the blissfully shady street, what it was that was niggling her. Something

427

to do with that fateful day. She recalled again how she and Antoine had been on their way to the safe house, how he'd told her to stop. How Charlie had been gunned down and then the sound of the shot that had killed Alma. And then, miraculously, how they had not come in search of them, but had simply taken the radio and left.

How had Harrison persuaded Alma to betray everything? Alma had come from poverty, she knew, so perhaps it was money to start with. She had had contact with someone in the Breton movement for independence. A contact Harrison had set up for her. Alma would take money and information to the contact and bring information back to Harrison. But something happened that Harrison had not bargained for. Alma had fallen in love with the contact and had decided to defect. Alma had been a pretty woman. The contact must have flattered her, persuaded her he loved her, perhaps made love to her.

She could imagine how Alma saw it. Grabbing a chance at happiness by being with the man she loved. Only he hadn't wanted that at all. He wanted her to continue to be a conduit for money, for information about where the SOE agents would be landing next, and what they would be bringing: new weapons, radio equipment. All things they could steal for their own fight against the French. Lane stopped, taking in a breath, and leaned against a low wall, the realization white-hot inside her. The reason that those two men had walked away, not knowing that she and Antoine had been due to arrive to meet Charlie, was because Alma had refused to tell them. Alma had died rather than betray them.

428

Her heart heavy, Lane thought about Alma's last lonely moments, when she would have realized what she'd done, and that she was about to die. She thought about the life she had now, because Alma in the end had refused to betray her. She thought about how she could never tell anyone about Alma's final brave act.

CHAPTER THIRTY-FIVE

"**OH, IT'S LOVELY TO BE** home!" Lane exclaimed, twirling around in the sitting room and then stopping to look at the view of the lake.

Darling had dropped their suitcases in the hall and now came to put his arm around her, that they might gaze together at their view. "More trees than in Mexico," he commented.

She laughed. "You said the same thing when we came back from our honeymoon in Arizona. You're becoming very predictable. Cup of tea?"

He followed her into the kitchen.

"How did they know?" Lane exclaimed. She'd had the cab from town stop at the grocery for some milk and a few essentials to get them by, and she stood now in front of the open fridge looking at a couple of steaks and some vegetables and, of course, a pint of milk. She added her bottle and the eggs and then closed the fridge and looked around. A bowl of eggs and a loaf of bread wrapped in greaseproof paper, no doubt from Gladys.

Darling was already prying a cake tin open and pulling out a brownie, which he held up and waggled at her. "God bless our neighbours!" he said. He put the brownie back in the tin, closed it, and hugged it to himself. "These will be mine," he said. "What are you having?"

"YOU WERE VERY disciplined not calling the station yesterday afternoon," Lane said, buttering their morning toast. "Are you sure you're ready for whatever it is?"

"Ready or not, here I come, to quote my favourite childhood game. What will you do?"

"I shall go thank our blessed neighbours, collect some news, and then I might pop up to town. I'll see. I should restock, and I'd like to get some of that lovely cheddar at the supermarket."

BUT FIRST SHE went to her writing desk and, sitting in the perfect silence after Darling had left, pulled out paper and pencil. She did not allow herself to think but began at once.

High above the desert
there is a river
of stars across the night,
as numerous as
grains of sand, they say.

I close my eyes
on the moving galaxies
to join the shadowed road of sleep

here among those very grains.
When suddenly out of the dark
a crying, yipping din of coyotes.
Their business, like mine,
lies down here.

After fiddling a bit, she sighed and pushed this effort into the drawer with its other poetic companions, hoping as always that it would sort itself out if she wasn't looking, and prepared to go to the post office.

"MY DEAR," SAID Eleanor Armstrong, watching Alexandra wriggling in Lane's arms with sheer delight. Lane had been trying to thank Eleanor and ask how she had known they'd be back the afternoon before, when she'd been assaulted by the Westie.

"Stop that, you silly dog!" Eleanor said. "It was Miss McAvity at the police station I got the lowdown from. I confess, I called to see if they knew when you'd be back. You have heaps of mail. Did you have a good time? Did you find the inspector's poor brother?"

"How much time do you have?" Lane asked, putting Alexandra down and drying her cheek with her sleeve. "Frederick's brother is fine. Though he's being unexpected."

"Go find Kenny among the ashes over there, and I'll get the tea. He'll be delighted to see you!"

"This tops anything! A real live bandit!" Kenny exclaimed. His tea sat in the saucer where he'd poured it to cool, and then he had been so riveted he'd been unable to drink it. "Were you terrified to be in the hands of a man like that?"

"I was protected by his belief that I resembled his favourite Mexican movie star, an actress called María Félix." Lane omitted the real danger, being captured and eliminated by a traitor who was afraid she'd unmask him. She took a bite of her thick, well-buttered slice of Eleanor's raisin bread. She'd not eaten much breakfast and she was ravenous.

"Do tell us about the town and the hacienda, and the market. I've only ever seen pictures, and of course they're all in black and white, but it must have been so colourful," Eleanor said.

"Oh, of course! I'd quite forgotten. I brought a little something." She reached into the basket that she would take up the hill to the Hugheses, when her visit to the Armstrongs was over, and pulled out a small paper-wrapped parcel.

"You shouldn't have!" Eleanor exclaimed. "Thinking of us when all that to-do was going on with the bandit." She tore open the paper and found a small white cotton tablecloth, exactly suited to their kitchen table, with embroidered corners. "Oh, it's hand embroidered with that lovely little typical scene of the Mexican sleeping under a cactus!"

"I must say, I can't think why that is considered a typical Mexican scene," Lane said. "I've never seen a harder-working people in my life."

Eleanor stood with Lane on the grass in front of the cottage door. Kenny had disappeared into the woodshed. She beamed at Lane. "I hope you will stay around for a while now. It's simply not the same without you. Angela has been pining, little Sara keeps asking about you. Even Reggie barked at me the other day about when you might be back."

433

DARLING LISTENED WITH his jaw clenched, while Ames recapped the events that had transpired in his boss's absence. Finally, he spoke.

"And what do you think about Terrell's conclusions?"

"I thought enough of them, sir, to join him on that surveillance. Whatever Guilfoil, pardon, sir, Inspector Guilfoil, says, I believe Cooper is bent and mixed up with the smugglers, and I agree with Terrell. He's the most likely killer of Tanney." Ames sighed. "And I'm afraid he's going to get away with it."

"Were you able to see the photos you took?"

"No, sir. The inspector kept the film as part of the files for the case. Constable took everything else over yesterday. Including the gun, which I have no doubt Cooper used to kill Tanney. Gilly said the bullet, which would certainly fit that Enfield, was the same size as the one that killed him."

Darling picked up the phone. "Ask Terrell to come up, Miss McAvity," he said. "How's she doing?" he asked as he put the receiver back in its cradle.

"Very well, sir. I wish we could keep her, if you want the truth. No offence to Sergeant O'Brien," he added hastily. "She's organized and pretty good with the public, actually. I mean, I thought she could use some experience, so I took her out when we had to tell Tanney's mother the news that he was dead, and she was great."

"You took her out because you didn't want to do it yourself," Darling corrected. "Ah. Constable. Sit." Terrell had appeared at the door. If he had misgivings about the summons, it didn't show on his face.

434

Ames had caught the slight twitch of a smile from Darling at his last remark and relaxed slightly.

"I'm going to meet with Inspector Guilfoil in a few moments, but I have something to say to the two of you before I go. Shut the door."

IN THE CAFÉ, neither Ames nor Terrell was the least bit daunted by Marge. They gave her their biggest smiles and ordered breakfast with extra sausage and told her to keep the coffee coming.

"Don't get used to it," Ames cautioned, but he'd scarcely come down to earth himself. "He'll never say anything nice like that again. In fact, I bet he's already regretting it. No doubt Guilfoil is filling his head with lead pellets even now."

"It was very decent of him, sir."

"I'll say! Did you hear what I heard? Did he actually use the words 'good initiative'?"

"What are you two grinning at?" Marge said, bearing their coffee. "Town's a hotbed of crime, and you two are in here as usual, wasting public money. When's your damn boss coming back?"

They both looked at her, beaming. "He's back!" they said together.

"SIT DOWN, INSPECTOR. Welcome back. I hope your trip was successful. Your brother, I believe, had gone missing?"

"Yes, entirely, sir, though it was a bit more adventure than I'm used to since the war ended."

"That bad, eh? I'm delighted to hear it ended well. We haven't been without adventure in your absence, I'm afraid,"

435

Guilfoil said. He had his pipe in his hand and was filling it from a wooden box on his desk.

In the long interval of watching Guilfoil tamp the tobacco down, light and draw on the pipe, and exhale his first breath of smoke, filling the air with the fragrance of Burley, Kentucky, and Latakia, Darling's misgivings grew. Perhaps Ames would be proven right.

Leaning back and holding his pipe away from his face by the bowl, Guilfoil tilted his head slightly. "Have you spoken to your men?"

"Yes, I have. They described a curious series of events. What are your thoughts?"

"They came to see me. It was the proper thing to do, of course. They thought something might be wrong with a member of the force. They ought to have done it before they set up surveillance on one of our men, of course, but I'll be generous and suppose they were still thinking about the murder they were trying to solve and the proliferation of drugs in town."

Darling felt as though he was in the middle of some sort of slow-motion tumble. Where was this heading?

"What they weren't to know," continued Guilfoil, "is that I already had some misgivings about the detachment out Cooper's way. A year or so ago they arrested someone sneaking across the border, and then the man escaped. In and of itself, not grave. Not tidy, but not grave. But when I saw the photos your men took, I recognized the man from the mugshot they took in the arrest a year ago. I didn't like to see Cooper being so chummy. I had his bank accounts looked into."

"Accounts, plural?" asked Darling.

"Exactly. I can say this much. One containing nothing more than you would expect on a Mountie's pay packet, and the other chock full of cash going in and out. So, you see, we had the whole business well in hand. We didn't need your men larking about."

"You're suggesting my men were right." What he was suggesting was that they were right, and the Mounties had missed it altogether, for all he claimed he'd had "misgivings."

Guilfoil's silence showed him as reluctant to go so far.

"Look, Darling, I'm not prepared to say more than that. You run an unconventional outfit up the road, what with the girl and the coloured fellow, and I'm not saying they didn't make a good effort, but obviously we can't leave this in the hands of a little local force like yours. Drugs are a federal matter. Your corpse was running drugs. Now that it's possible one of our men might have killed him, it is of course way, way above your capacity to deal with. Did your constable tell you how he hid evidence from us? That sort of thing is out of bounds, completely out of bounds. Discipline will be up to you, of course."

His head swimming, Darling thought he'd never heard a compliment so deftly hidden among a cascade of insults. Was he prepared to fight for the jurisdiction of this case? It annoyed him that Guilfoil could easily take it over under his federal mandate, and he, Darling, hadn't a leg to stand on. "I see," he said, finally resolved.

"I'm glad you do. Your constable redeemed himself a bit when he brought over the file. He went over it very

437

succinctly, I'll give him that. He's surprisingly professional, so I think we'll say no more about it, eh?"

"Well then," said Darling, rising, wanting Guilfoil to feel himself dismissed, rather than the other way around. "Nothing more to be done then. I'll look forward to hearing about a successful outcome." He reached out and shook Guilfoil's hand firmly and then put his hat on his head with an air of insouciance. "It's always a trial when one of your own has gone bad, don't you think? One always wonders how one missed it, when all is said and done." He turned and was out the door before Guilfoil could say another word.

On the street, he took a big gulp of the warm, sun-laden Kootenay air, cast a glance up at Elephant Mountain, and murmured, "I think I'll join my excellent, unconventional team at the café."

He stopped by the station and looked in the door at April, sitting attentively by the phone. "Miss McAvity, stick a 'Back in five minutes' sign on the door and come with me."

"But the phones, sir."

"I think we'll be all right for the moment. Come."

In moments they were in the café, sliding into the booth beside Ames and Terrell, who'd demolished most of their breakfast by this time. Darling raised his hand to summon Marge, feeling barely a ripple of concern about the scowl already mounting on her face.

"Pie and coffee all around, Marge, for my excellent team. Thank you so much."

"YOU'VE LET THE case go without a murmur," Lane said. "I admire your self-control." They'd finished their dinner of

438

omelettes and brownies, and sat in front of plates with the very few brownie crumbs that had survived.

"I let it go because it was, after all, a federal case, and my boys, and girl, of course, had solved it with a little good thinking and unconventional leaps of imagination. We handed Guilfoil the thing with a bow on it. I was big about it. I didn't rub it in, though he will take all the credit. I bowed out gracefully and bought my gang a round of pie and coffee, and before you say anything, I was bordering on fulsome with my praise. I'd rather have my team than any of his, any day of the week. Now they can all put their minds to getting Ames married. With a perspicacity I would not have credited him with, he's elected to put Terrell in charge by making him his best man. I'm sure Miss Van Eyck is extremely relieved. She must have begun to think it would never get off the ground."

They both rose and collected their dishes, Lane picking at a brownie crumb that had escaped detection. "That's wonderful. I can tell you're a bit relieved not to have been asked yourself." Lane smiled.

"You can't imagine!" He gazed at her for a moment as she put her dishes by the sink.

"But tell me, what has happened to Sergeant Cooper? Drummed out of the force? Horse and red serge uniform returned?"

"I don't actually know. Guilfoil claimed he has had his eye on him for a while, and what Ames and Terrell found confirmed it for him. It's a good question: Will he be tried? Or will he be merely let go? I suppose he will have a good solicitor who will argue that he was made to do these things by a powerful drug kingpin under threat. Who knows? The Mounties are not ones to air their dirty linen in public. Perhaps he'll be reassigned to the farthest reaches of the realm."

Lane made a skeptical noise. "Having learned nothing. And what about poor Mrs. Sunderland?"

"There again, I don't know. One thing the alert April told me is that Mr. Sunderland has stood by her. He's got his hands full. People who get onto drugs have a hard time getting off."

"Good for him!" Lane exclaimed. "I don't want to sound too much like a bleeding heart, but maybe the love of a good man will actually help. The whole thing must have put paid to her friendship with the kidnapped child's mother. Are you going to charge her with aiding and abetting a kidnapping?"

"We have that in mind; however, first she needs to get better, and maybe her lawyer will make the case that the evil drug pusher compelled her to do this or he'd cut off her supply. I dare say that could even be true. Two crimes with but a single defence. As to the mother of the kidnapped child, apparently her estranged husband came to get her and she moved to the north so her boy could be near his father, and, one presumes, far from her troubled and duplicitous friend."

"I wonder if she told him that the little boy wasn't actually his."

"She did. She had to. With everything out, he'd have found out soon enough."

"How did he take it?"

"Well, therein lies the reason she's been willing to go north to be near him. He told her it didn't matter to him one bit. He loved the boy and would always do anything he could to support him."

"That's rather wonderful. So, what about April? What will you do about her when Sergeant O'Brien is mended?" Lane had her dish mop in hand and was vigorously cleaning the dishes, rinsing them, and handing them to Darling, who was ready with his towel.

"You've put your finger on a sore point. He apparently stopped by the station a few days back. He's going stir-crazy at home. Of course he was ages previous. He's not ready to come back to work for at least a month. He went meekly back home when his wife came roaring after him. He's really in for it now. She's following doctor's orders and taking him off cakes and scones. He's likely to die of a broken heart, which is the only hope for April, I'm afraid. I don't think Dalton is going to let me keep her on, which is too bad. According to Ames, she's a good addition."

"I'm not in the least surprised. I'm dreaming of a day when entire police forces are made up of women who all know what they're doing, and don't make such a fuss about solving a little case," Lane said, handing him the last plate to dry. "Though," she said, turning to him, "I think it's really lovely that you let them know how well they did. I had no idea you were capable of such sentimentality."

"Enjoy it. It will certainly never happen again. I can't think what madness made me lose my normal restraint." He hung the towel on the nail and said, "Scotch?"

Lane opened the fridge and looked thoughtfully at its contents. "I wonder if we should throw a dinner party."

"Whatever for?" he asked, astounded. "Or are you asking the fridge?"

She turned and closed the fridge door. "We used to have fabulous dinner parties when I was a child at my grandparents' house."

Darling, whose family had never had dinner parties of any description, shook his head. "Your grandparents had a fabulous cook and numerous servants to carry it all off, as I recall."

"Are you saying I can't cook my way through a dinner party?" She smiled and held out her hand for a scotch.

Too late, Darling saw his position, and occupied himself with bottle and glass. "Not at all. Why this sudden urge for a party? We've finally arrived at our nice quiet home."

Lane sighed and leaned her behind against the counter, her arms crossed. "To celebrate the goodness of people," she said. She was thinking of Salinas, who had helped her after all, and Alma, who had saved her. What she couldn't say was what she'd realized about Alma. She wondered now how she had not understood at once, when they had seen the men leaving with the radio. When they had seen that she'd been shot. That Alma, misguided, impoverished, ready to betray everything for a man she thought she loved, wanting to buy herself just a little happiness, had never divulged what she knew. Lane lifted her glass, thinking of Alma as that green silk dressing gown, flying up and away from the sorrows of this life.

"We could do something to celebrate Ames's wedding," she said. The thought, anchored in life and celebration, made her smile.

"And where would we put the guests?" They migrated to the sitting room and into their chairs.

"You have a point," she conceded. "I had been thinking of goat stew and bottles of orange soda."

Darling relaxed. The peace of his home sanctuary would remain unruffled. She was not being serious.

"But seriously," she said. "I think a drinks party on the veranda, since we've no place but the kitchen table to seat people. Ames deserves no less."

"Ames deserves no more," he corrected, "but poor Tina might."

ACKNOWLEDGEMENTS

FOR MOST OF MY CHILDHOOD I spent nine months of every year in Mexico. In keeping with my practice of resuscitating the worlds of my childhood, I happily return to yet another haunt of my youth. "A murder can happen anywhere" is my motto. So with gratitude and love I thank Lucy Buchanan Harrison, Pixi Lewis, and Enrique Buchanan for our beautiful childhood in Fresnillo, and for their kind efforts in helping me remember our distant world of sixty-five years ago.

I am indebted to the wonderful people at the SS Moyie National Historical Site and the Kootenay Lake Historical Society. To Sarah Sinclair and Michael Cone, and especially to Robert D. Turner, FRCGS, LL.D, Curator Emeritus, and project historian at the SS Moyie National Historic Site for his generous time and effort in bringing to life for me the treasure that is the SS Moyie and helping me understand its machinery (and a likely place for a corpse!). The SS Moyie steamed up and down Kootenay lake for nearly 60 years from 1898 to 1957 with its graceful paddlewheel, and is fully on view in Kaslo, British Columbia.

A warm and enduring thanks to my dear friend Sasha Bley-Vroman, talented beta reader who truly understands my characters, my use of language and all that I'm trying to do in these stories, and doesn't let me get away with nonsense.

Writing a book can be solitary, but in the background at TouchWood Editions is a wonderful team of people waiting to whip it into shape. Tori Elliott, publisher, whose constant loving support keeps me going; Curtis Samuel, tireless publicist (and great road-trip buddy); Nara Monteiro, editorial coordinator, who has proven to be a warm and supportive new presence. I have the extraordinary good fortune of editors who, book after book, never seem to flag in their enthusiasm: Claire Philipson, Meg Yamamoto, and Kate Kennedy, who among them keep me from being repetitive, changing characters names for no reason, revealing an important plot point too early or too late, and dealing with my often puzzling syntax.

A special thanks to Pat and Rodger, who make it all possible. And when readers reach for the book, it is in no small part because of a magical cover created by the unequalled artist Margaret Hanson. A special warm thanks to Rill Askey, formerly Marilla Wex, whose gorgeous reading for the audiobooks has brought so many people to Lane Winslow.

Thank you to all the indie booksellers who work so hard on behalf of writers, and to the legions of readers who have been wonderfully kind.

I am ridiculously lucky in my family; Biski, Tammy, Teo, and Tyson. They are all creative in their own right, and understand. And, here with me, listening to my whinging, and throwing me a rope when I descend into the dark chasm that is mid-book doubt and despondency, is my dear artist husband Terry. He is never short on a good idea, or a nice place to walk, or a kind word.

IONA WHISHAW is the author of the *Globe and Mail* bestselling series The Lane Winslow Mysteries. She is the winner of a Bony Blithe Light Mystery Award, was a finalist for a BC and Yukon Book Prize, and has twice been nominated for the Left Coast Crime Awards and the Crime Writers of Canada Awards. The heroine of her series, Lane Winslow, was inspired by Iona's mother, who, like her father before her, was a wartime spy. Born in the Kootenays, Iona spent many years in Mexico, Nicaragua, and the US before settling into Vancouver, BC, where she now lives with her husband, Terry. Throughout her life she has worked as a youth worker, social worker, teacher, and award-winning high school principal, eventually completing her master's in creative writing from the University of British Columbia.

WEBSITE: IONAWHISHAW.COM
FACEBOOK & INSTAGRAM: @IONAWHISHAWAUTHOR

THE LANE WINSLOW MYSTERY SERIES

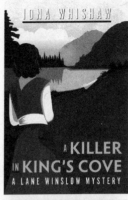

THE LANE WINSLOW MYSTERY SERIES

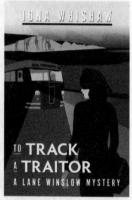